Quiet Freedom

a novel

W.C. Peace

Norlight Press

Copyright © 2016 by W.C. Peace

ISBN-13: 978-0-9962705-0-2
ISBN-10: 0996270507

Beluga and narwhal © Maquiladora / Shutterstock

Greenland Map from Wikimedia Commons user Eric Gaba / username Sting
Creative Commons License: Attribution-ShareAlike 3.0 Unported
http://creativecommons.org/licenses/by-sa/3.0/legalcode
Original image changed by adding more locations and removing unnecessary data

Quiet Freedom may be purchased for educational, business, or promotional use.
Please contact: sales@norlightpress.com

Learn more about the story at – www.quietfreedom.net

Publisher's Cataloging-In-Publication Data
(Prepared by The Donohue Group, Inc.)

Peace, W. C.
  Quiet freedom : a novel / W.C. Peace.

   pages : illustration, map ; cm

   ISBN-13: 978-0-9962705-0-2
   ISBN-10: 0-9962705-0-7

   1. Self-actualization (Psychology)--Fiction. 2. Global warming--Fiction. 3. Polar bear--Fiction. 4. Denmark--Description and travel--Fiction. 5. Greenland--Description and travel--Fiction. 6. Liberty--Fiction. 7. Happiness--Fiction. I. Title.

PS3616.E23 Q54 2016
813/.6   2015914197

Published in the United States by Norlight Press / www.norlightpress.com
First paperback edition
10 9 8 7 6 5 4 3 2 1
First printing: 2016

This is dedicated to all those
who want to know themselves better.

Map of Greenland

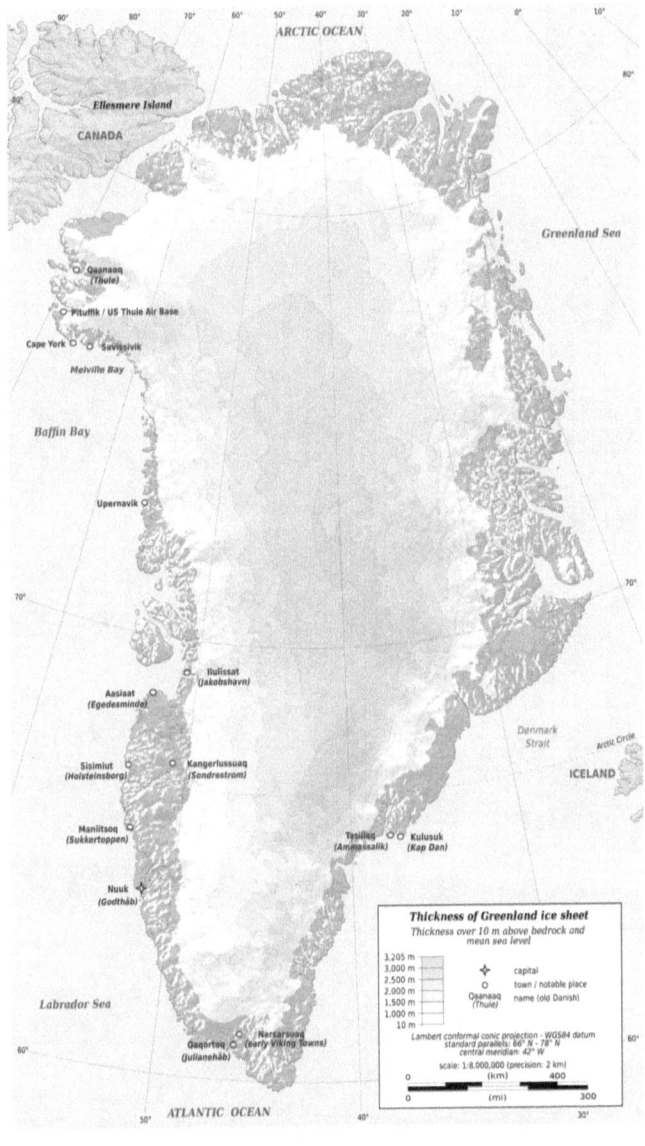

PROLOGUE

The swirls of snow have almost subsided. The helicopter that brought me to this remote place, is a faded memory now. I can still hear the whup – whup sound in my head if I focus on it. I can almost imagine myself flying above where we are right now. Some of the scenery looks like I saw it from the air.

What strange coincidence of events have brought me here? Out here, in the middle of nowhere. Out here, to a place where I think only the foolish must live. A place that few have ever heard about or considered traveling to. A place, that may as well not even exist.

Did I think I could find a sense of who I am out here? The frigid air burns my cheeks. I never thought it could get this cold. They say night-time temperatures in late March reach well below freezing at -25° Celsius. That is -13° Fahrenheit, which sounds a little cozier, until I remember that freezing is still 32° Fahrenheit. I haven't even mentioned the wind chill when it's blowing.

One wrong step and I could die from exposure in the frigid water, I'll be out here for eight days or so. If I screamed for help, would anyone hear me? Why am I here?

At any given moment, I feel a silent desperation of loneliness. I hear only my breath. The dogs are quiet now. The whiteness of ice and snow at times seems like they might be the flattened walls of a place for the slightly crazy. Yet, I feel a sense of freedom here that I've never felt before. It scares me, but I can't run away from it. Having too much freedom can be scary. I must be strong, I must continue.

I can barely pronounce the names of the places I have traveled through to get out here. Kangerlussuaq, Ilulissat, Qaanaaq, Savissivik. At least I can pronounce where I'm at now, Cape York.

The joke is, if you feel like you've been everywhere, there's always Greenland. Except for my one day stopover in Copenhagen a few days ago, I've never been to Europe, Asia, Australia, or anywhere else outside of America, except for a brief trip across the border to Canada. Why didn't I listen to my co-workers? They said, just go to sunny Mexico and relax. Might I be among the dumbest tourists in the world to come here first?

My footprints around me have already been covered by the swirls of snow kicked up from the occasional wind gusts. It's as if the evidence of my existence is being erased before I've even had time to make new ones. Perhaps it doesn't really matter out here, for I feel a sense of timelessness and serenity.

The accident and grief of the recent past seem so inconsequential. What sequence of events in recent memory and in my past have fated me to be standing in the middle of this cold, very cold, barren, white, desert-like place?

Am I here to question the assumptions about my own life and how I live it? Is this the place that will give me the conviction and fortitude to set my own spirit loose from the chains that hold it down? Will I discover a freedom that I have always had, but just never got to know? Or is it a freedom that I once had, and have forgotten?

CHAPTER 1 – RAINY REUNION

There should be some more artwork on the walls, Amanda thought to herself. She had been in this room hundreds of times before and it had just occurred to her how sterile and cold it was. The interior conference room had no windows and bare white walls, a corporate cost cutting move no doubt. Despite this realization, she dismissed the thought as just an echo of her recent visit to an art museum.

She had just given a presentation to her colleagues which didn't quite end up the way she wanted it to. It was just typical office politics for her. Slow and steady breaths she reminded herself. With a check of her wristwatch came the realization that if she dwelled on this meeting any longer, she was going to be late for her lunch date.

Who did she want to become a long time ago? She steadied her frayed nerves from the heated verbal exchanges. Memories of her childhood days of innocence came to mind. Why was she having such thoughts now? Perhaps it was because of her lunch appointment. The office was no place to reminisce.

The lunch hour had just started in Seattle downtown. The dark gray skies and rain clouds that had almost captured the day were parting to reveal patches of blue sky. Down on the waterfront, the piers were home to some of Seattle's famous seafood haunts. The waves which lapped up against the piers and the moored boats, could be heard in the background.

A few tourists made their way outside again from the safety of the area shops, to enjoy the breeze and sunlight, while deciding which restaurant was the best to grab some fish and clam chowder. Across the street, the George Benson streetcar slowed down and stopped.

A voice cried out her name as Amanda jumped out of the streetcar and made her way across the road toward the city aquarium. She turned her head toward the shout. "Stephanie!"

They walked toward each other and embraced in a big hug.

"Some wacky weather we've been having. It's been warm like this the whole day," Stephanie noted.

"I've barely noticed. I've been inside the whole day. Home, garage, to office garage, then up the elevator to my little office."

"I was watching the news and they were talking about whether it might be global warming."

"Yeah, whatever. A few more raindrops, who cares, I'm inside most of the time anyway."

"You need to get outside more often."

"Outside? I'm glued to my computer screen. Deadlines! Hey, I'm hungry!"

The two women walked into a seafood restaurant next to the aquarium. Amanda nudged Stephanie as they approached the counter. "Do you want to share a glass of wine?"

"One of those days again? I can drink a little."

The dining room was filling with the lunchtime crowd as they received their orders and found a table. The pair began to make quick work of their meals. No time to waste on discussion when the belly was aching. It was a comfortable silence that could only come from two long time friends.

Amanda broke the silence by sharing the possibility of receiving a new potential client at work, a client whose business contact just happened to be her old ex-boyfriend from high school who cheated on her.

"How long did you go out with him?"

"I think for six months or so." Amanda paused as she searched her memory banks. "That felt like a long time. I thought he was the one. High school delusions."

"Aren't you the luckiest girl in the world?"

"Rub it in, why don't you," Amanda quipped.

"You know me, how's Chip?"

"There are some rough spots, like any new relationship, but it's going good, otherwise." Amanda's stomach growled.

"Do you ever worry?"

"Worry about what?"

"You know, about finding the right guy," Stephanie added.

"Sister, finding men will never be a problem, neither of us will ever be older than twenty-nine."

"Maybe easier for you to say, sister, try pushing out a little screamer," Stephanie exclaimed.

"How is Haley doing?"

"She seems so mature. You know, they grow up so fast. I'm a little concerned about when she hits puberty."

"Puberty? Isn't it a little early to be wondering about that?"

"I've been reading up on it a bit. The average girl is getting younger and younger when it starts. They seem to be putting so much junk in the food we eat these days. We eat out pretty often, so I'm never quite sure what we are getting."

They both glanced at their meals.

"Are you still thinking of getting a part-time job?"

"My college is having an alumni event, I'm thinking of going next week. Maybe, I'll do some networking. Now that Haley is almost done with kindergarten, I think it's a good idea. I want to have my own identity."

Amanda's designer watch reflected the bursts of sunlight shining through the windows. "It really does sound like a great idea for you to get back in the work scene. Yes, having your own identity is good."

"I can put that degree to good use!"

"I still think of college as an expensive dating service." Amanda frowned.

"It worked for me."

"You get all the luck, Steph. It's too bad we didn't go to the same university. I'm sure some of it would have rubbed off on me."

"You're silly."

"I'm glad to hear you want to get a job and maintain your own identity. I'm tired of some of the mothers at work who live vicariously through their children, especially when the kids are older. They are always telling me about their kids as if I'd known them personally."

"Motherly instinct, perhaps."

"I'm afraid to go out to lunch with some of them sometimes. They ask me when I am going to have one. One woman even told me about an adoption agency. It's good not to forget about your own life."

"Parental pride. What else do they think of your single status?"

"I'm proud of what I've done with my life."

"You should be."

"They give me funny looks sometimes, I can't really explain it. It's kind of condescending at times. Hey, not everyone wants to rush into marriage and procreate." Amanda pointed at herself. "How's Jack?"

"I need to reinvent myself."

"Why?"

"Jack seems a little distant. It's as if he has the seven year itch. I fear that it is true."

"You don't think. . ."

"No, I hope not."

"I heard it was more like a four year itch these days, you must have been doing something right."

Stephanie let out a snicker. "I'm getting my hair done later today, I have a manicure scheduled too. Then I want to head over to the department store to try out some new makeup."

Dark clouds began to win the battle against blue skies as Stephanie and Amanda continued to share their lives.

"I'm sure it's nothing," Amanda added.

"What should I do? You've always been the competitive one. Always another battle to fight and win."

"I'm sure you'll both figure it out."

"I'm afraid to trust my instincts, Amanda."

"I never said anything about trusting instincts, Steph. Think it through. You'll figure it out. Or you could always spy on him." Amanda laughed.

"Whatever, A. It's funny how our lives have taken different paths. I'm a stay at home mom, trying to get into the career world. You're rising fast and going places."

"Don't be so hard on yourself, you've got a wonderful family."

"And a good friend." Stephanie clutched Amanda's open hand lying on the table.

"How long have we been friends now?"

"Twenty-five years," Stephanie responded proudly.

Amanda gulped down the last of the wine.

The clear patch of sky that showed up for lunch had now almost disappeared. The menacing dark skies appeared to be the winner of today's weather war.

"I think we should do a better job of making up for lost time," Stephanie remarked.

"Agreed."

"I'm so glad we finally got together again after two months. We should get together more often. You're working too much," Stephanie added with emphasis as she stood up. "You know, you're supposed to be Haley's godmother too. You're welcome to come around anytime, our home is your home."

A mobile phone rang. Stephanie looked around, but Amanda didn't need to, she knew it was hers. The tender moment between two friends was interrupted by the unceasing demands of a modern technological world.

A few minutes passed as she gabbed.

"Hey, it looks like you need to get going. I've got to get to my hair appointment. I don't want to be late for it, it's so hard to get an appointment with her."

"Sorry, work is crazy."

"We'll meet up again."

"We should have a girl's weekend out, no kids, no boyfriends, no husbands, just the two of us," Amanda declared.

"That's a great idea! Let's plan a trip. . . to the San Juans, Victoria, or the coast! That would be so fun."

"That would be great! I'll call you next week."

As they hugged, Amanda's phone rang again, interrupting their embrace. They headed their own separate ways.

It started to rain. The 'Rainy City' of America held a secret. At nearly 38 inches of rain per year, it rained less than New York City, Miami, Chicago, Houston, and other major US cities. Seattle earned its reputation another way though, cloudy days. With more than 225 cloudy days per year, it ranked in the top five. It was by far, the cloudiest, large US metropolitan city. While in total it didn't rain much, at more than 140 days, it did rank in the top twenty for days per year with measurable rain. Less than 75 days per year were considered cloudless or partially cloudy.

A funny thing had begun to happen though, perhaps only noticed by serious weather watchers or those with better memories. The weather had begun to change from historical norms.

Amanda looked out her office window as the rain started to fall harder. She had a peek-a-boo view of Elliot Bay, but most of her window framed just another office building.

She tried to rub the strain from her eyes and forehead, it didn't work.

She pressed her fingers against the window, the chill felt like cool iron bars, not glass. She made a fist. Her gaze shifted up the walls of the office as she stepped back from the window. On one wall hung her college diploma. A certificate commending her on five years of employment hung next to it. Next to that was a calendar of exotic destinations that appeared to be more fantasy like than any reality she knew.

Without a second thought, she opened a desk drawer and mused at the company newsletters which had mentioned her exploits. Strewn about inside were old business cards that were evidence of her quick climb up the corporate ladder. She was a diligent worker who did her job well.

Her success at work was tempered by the fact that she wasn't yet married. Motherhood was calling sometimes, but the right man had not appeared in her life. In her gut, she didn't think it was Chip, but maybe it would get better. She was around the average age of marriage, but she definitely did not want a 'starter' marriage.

A knock at the door.

It was Billy, her partner in crime at the office of Northwest Marketing Associates. "Amanda, I just got a call from Jason over at Pumpstar. They liked what they saw a couple of weeks ago. He wants us to present the marketing proposal to the executive board on Friday. Don't you love this stuff!?"

"That's great," she responded in a flat tone.

Billy didn't seem to notice her lack of excitement. "He also sent over a list of changes that we should make. . . to uhh. . . better influence the management, if you know what I mean."

"Ok."

"Come on! This is a big account for us. Let's rock!" Billy's eyes lit up. He slid the list of changes on to Amanda's desk.

She reached over and picked up the piece of paper. Her face turned into a mask of disillusionment. "When do they want us to give the presentation again?" Amanda asked the question as if she really didn't know the answer.

"Friday!"

"You mean next Friday, right?"

"No, this Friday!"

"You have got to be kidding me, Billy. It's Tuesday night, I'm ready to go home, and you want me to make all these changes in two days? I'm still working on the Rocket Data account. They want something back by Thursday."

"I'll take the last ten changes, it'll be a cinch. We can merge our changes on Thursday night. We'll be ready for the Friday, 9:30 a.m. meeting." He hesitated for a moment. "We can do this, you just need a good cup of java. I'll go downstairs and get you a cup, ok?"

It didn't bother her before, but Billy's voice seemed to sound more grating than usual.

"Ok. . . but. . ."

Billy had already turned around and run off in the direction of the elevators. She could see him prancing along like a deer amongst the cubicles outside her office. Beyond these cubicles were more offices lined up alongside the opposite wall. It was a pattern that repeated itself around the entire plan of this floor of the skyscraper.

"But. . . I was supposed to have dinner with my boyfriend tonight." Amanda's voice trailed off in the air and through her door into the empty cubicles outside. Everyone else in the office had already gone home it seemed. She didn't hear anyone else. She replayed the vision of Billy prancing through the cubicles in her mind as if there was some hidden meaning to it. Rather than dwell on it further, she picked up her phone and prepared for an ugly phone call.

"Hello," came the voice at the other end.

"Hello, Chip."

"Are you almost ready for me to come pick you up?"

"Chip, I'm not home yet."

"The line sounds really clear, are you in your car?"

"No, I'm still in the office."

"What?!"

"I just found out about an important presentation which needs to be changed for a meeting on Friday."

"Are we still having dinner?"

"Chip, this is an important account for the company, for me. Can you take a rain check?" As she spoke, Amanda wondered what invisible force was putting these words in her mouth. It was as if she had been programmed to respond this way when anything threatened her 'all important' work. Maybe she had learned from her father.

"Amanda, this is crazy. This is becoming way too predictable. How important is our relationship?"

"Of course, it's important."

"It sure doesn't feel like it. If you're just trying to tell me that your screwing someone else, just say it."

"Chip, please don't say things like that."

"When you figure out what is important in your life, call me."

Amanda held the phone in a state of shock, almost speechless.

Chip hung up.

"Bye," Amanda whispered into the disconnected line. She held the phone and just listened to the empty dial tone as if it exuded a calming and predictable effect on her psyche, hurt by the conversation that just took place.

She pulled out a small notebook from her desk drawer. On the front cover it said - Journal. She turned to the first empty page and began writing.

Why do I have trouble with all my boyfriends? Maybe I'm genetically programmed like this. After all, my parents got divorced. Men are pigs. Why do I work so much?

Who am I trying to prove something to? I need to chill out.

The ding of an elevator arriving sounded as soon as she closed her paper notebook. It was the only sound that punctured the absolute silence of the empty office.

Billy walked toward her door.

"Here is your energy drink, are you ready?" He set a cup of coffee on her desk.

Amanda waited for a moment. They played a staring game. He seemed to be staring at her bosom. "Let me have my energy drink."

Billy smiled and walked away.

She stuck her tongue out and made a funny face at him. With that, another night of toil had begun.

10:12. The time on her watch only reminded Amanda of what her life had come to. The parking garage was devoid of cars, the few remaining ones were of the expensive variety. Leaving work at this time of night always made her a bit nervous. Though in truth, she seldom left the office this late. She took her work home. Work was normally a forty hour a week affair, but it sometimes got crazy due to client demands and during certain times of the year. There seemed to be more 'sometimes' she thought.

She looked around, it was silent. Opening her purse, she double checked to see if her pepper spray was ready at hand. Maybe she should buy one of those portable stun guns she wondered. She found her car and clicked the remote. The whistle and flashing of the headlights from the car alarm disarming, comforted her.

As she got settled in, she locked the door, swearing to herself that one day she would take up martial arts. She pulled out and headed back home. A familiar band and song was playing as she turned on the radio.

Amanda wondered why this particular song was still so popular in Seattle after so many years. The song faded out.

"...and now for your fifteen minute news break on KTXY, here's your host, Rick Wilson!"

"Folks, we're having another crazy weather day here in the normally tranquil Pacific Northwest. What looked like a nice day for a little while has turned into a doozy. It is currently sixty degrees. Today's high was sixty-seven degrees, a record. Today's rainfall total is at 4 inches already, and most of that has fallen since just past lunchtime. Tomorrow's forecast looks better. If you can believe it, we should be partly cloudy with moderate rain showers. We might have a record in the making, and it looks like it's causing us some problems. For a traffic update, let's go to Stacy."

"Thanks, Rick. We've had quite a dangerous day out there today. Traffic on the I-90 bridge is clear now following an accident involving five cars earlier. I'm told there have been three fatalities. Five people have been hospitalized - three in serious condition, two critically. Be careful driving out there, it's not worth your life. I've had reports of sink holes and rock slides on numerous roadways. I'm still in the process of getting a complete list. I should have the information on our next news break."

"Stacy, has there been any talk that all this might be related to global warming? I'm no weather expert, but something seems a bit different with our weather these days. What do you think?"

"Are we allowed to talk about this political hot potato on air? Ha ha. It could be, Rick. I don't know. It could be. The one thing I will say from the reports and statistics I've read is that precipitation that would otherwise fall as snow in the mountains is more frequently falling as rain. A quick glance at my rain chart shows that there seems to be a noticeable increase in frequency of heavy rain years."

"A hot potato, no doubt. Stacy, do you have any more interesting Northwest rain facts for us?"

"I sure do. Three of the top five wettest days in Seattle history have all happened in the recent past. Number one is October 20th, 2003, when we received 5.02 inches. On December 3rd, 2007, we received 3.77 inches, and on November 6th, 2006, we received 3.29 inches."

"It's days like this Stacy, when we really live up to our reputation as a rainy city. Maybe this will help keep those Californians away."

"Ha ha. Funny you mention us as the rainy city, Rick. I've got some more interesting weather facts here."

"Let's hear it."

"The US record for rainfall rate is actually in Holt, Missouri. They experienced 12 inches in 42 minutes. Makes today's weather sound pleasant."

"I guess it could be worse."

"The record for US rainfall in 24 hours was in Alvin, Texas. They received 43 inches in July 1979."

"Tough to imagine, Stacy. Just looking outside now, it's coming down in sheets. The rain in those two places must have been like bricks coming down."

"This may come as a surprise to some of our listeners, Rick, but the rainiest place in the entire continental USA is in our own Olympic National Park. The southwest corner of the national park where the Hoh, Quinault, and Queets rain forests are located, average 140 to 200 inches per year depending on elevation."

"Whoa. That will be tomorrow's morning trivia question, Stacy."

"What are we giving away tomorrow?"

"A trip to Hawaii. Some fun in the sun away from the mess outside!"

"I have some bad news for our listeners."

Amanda began to tune out the radio as she concentrated on driving. The casual, almost subtle change in tone from speaking about a bad traffic accident to giving away a trip to Hawaii was disturbing and odd. Let the show go on, always a happy ending.

She lowered the volume as she luxuriated herself in the contoured seat of her mobile cocoon on wheels.

Any worries about conspicuous consumption were dispelled by her desire to reflect her material success. Her salary had increased dramatically after her first college job. She had rewarded herself for this hard work by buying this new car. It was like a second home to her, she felt comfortable in its confines. It had side air bags, anti-lock brakes, traction control, and many other fancy sounding features that she had long since forgotten about.

Many meals were eaten in this car. She never did like eating in a restaurant by herself, she worried about being seen alone. Take out, never eat in, was her rule. Besides, it was a private sanctuary from which she could always call or talk to someone about business. A half eaten chocolate bar lay in one of the mini compartments. Her designer purse sat on the passenger seat.

With the radio turned off now, she concentrated on driving and seeing through her fast moving windshield wipers. She arrived at her condo complex up on the hill near the Space Needle. Parking her car in the garage, she took a few moments to look in the rear view mirror. The bags under her eyes reminded her of some grotesque creature on television. All the luxuries of her car did nothing to help her real complexion.

A sense of relief came over her. At least no one would see her at this hour. Opening the door, she headed toward the elevator as her power suit flashed across the car's tinted glass. Another woman was already waiting.

"Some crazy weather we're having," the woman remarked.

"I'll say."

"It doesn't seem to rain like it used to, we need umbrellas now."

"Huh?"

"Are you from around here?"

"Yes, I grew up in the area."

"I'm just saying, that it seems to rain harder these days, do you think? I remember growing up, we hardly ever needed umbrellas. You could always tell a newbie to the area if they had an umbrella."

Amanda paused as she thought about what the woman said. "Now that you mention it, I think you're right."

"You can't tell anymore, that's no fun."

The elevator arrived and they both walked in.

"Which floor?" the woman asked.

"Eight."

The woman pressed floor buttons four and eight.

"This elevator is so slow," Amanda remarked.

"Isn't life fast enough?"

"You have a good point."

The elevator lurched and stopped at the fourth floor. "Have a good night."

"You too."

The doors closed and went up to the eighth floor, Amanda's floor. The doors opened, but Amanda didn't get out. She was too preoccupied looking at herself in the elevator mirror. The doors closed. Dark bags under her eyes only served as a reminder of her frame of mind. Her mascara was running. "My life sucks." A few more uncomfortable moments passed before she pressed the open door button.

She walked down the hallway toward her condo and wondered about the lives of her neighbors. Were they making love? Watching TV? Or blissfully sleeping? Surely, none of them were still working at this hour she thought to herself. Amanda opened her door.

In the unlit darkness of her home, Amanda noticed the flashing red light of her answering machine. It was the twinkling lights of the city amidst the rain from her balcony view that caught her attention though. The Olympic Mountains stood ominously in the distance from the other side of her wrap around balcony. Only their silhouette remained visible in the night amidst the heavy rain.

She walked over and gazed out, wondering about all the lives being played out in each set of windows where light shone. Were they happy couples? Happy singles? Was somebody looking her way thinking the same thing? The pitter-patter of the rain calmed her.

Changing into something more comfortable, she wandered over to the kitchen and poured herself a glass of wine. She glanced over at the clock on the microwave, the icon of the speedy and efficient lifestyle, it was getting late. She glimpsed her reflection in the microwave door glass, it did not please her, she was tired from a day of hard work. The mighty box of convenience had nothing kind to say. As she set her glass down after taking another drink, the phone rang. Who could be calling at this hour?

"Hello?"

"Amanda?" A frantic, hurried voice, called out over the line.

"Yes, who is this?"

"It's Jack. Did you get my messages?"

"No, what is going on?"

"Something terrible has happened. Stephanie got into a car accident earlier today, she's in critical condition. Haley is here with me. I know that you would be the first person that Steph thinks of and trusts enough to take care of her. Can you take her home? I am going to spend the night here."

"Yes, of course! Where are you?"

"Seattle Skyview Hospital – First Hill, floor five. Do you know where it is?"

"Is that the one off Madison?"

"That's the one. The entrance is on Broadway."

"I'll be right over."

Amanda ran out the door. It was just earlier in the day she and Stephanie had been enjoying a nice lunch and talking about getting away.

Amanda knew where to go, she knew the city well after so many years. It was much better than the suburbs she felt. Her hands clammed up as her mind began to imagine the worst while she navigated the wet streets. She parked her car and dashed to the elevator. She didn't stop to denigrate herself this time. The elevator couldn't move fast enough. The doors opened and Amanda stepped out and speed-walked toward the counter.

"Hi, I'm looking for Stephanie. . ."

"Amanda!"

"Jack!"

They approached one another in a short trot, then embraced.

"How is she?"

"She has a pelvic fracture and major trauma to the head. They said something about her liver and. . ." The strain in his voice was unmistakable, he broke down in tears.

Amanda embraced him again.

"She's in the operating room."

"Where's Haley?"

"She's in the waiting room over there." Jack pointed to a small room down the hallway.

She grabbed his arm to steady him as they walked in the room.

Haley looked up and smiled, she was holding a teddy bear. "Hi, Amanda."

Amanda walked up to Haley, bent down, and gave her a hearty hug. "How are you doing?"

"Is Mommy going to be ok?"

Amanda looked at Haley and turned away for a moment, thinking about what Jack had just told her. She wondered if it was better to tell the truth or err on the side of optimism. She settled for the simple deflection answer. "I don't know. Your mommy is a strong person, she is fighting very hard right now."

"When can I see Mom?"

"The doctors are helping your mom now. Your dad is going to stay here, you can stay with me. We'll come back tomorrow to see your mom." The last few words were difficult to say for Amanda, Jack's description of the situation sounded bleak.

Haley looked up at her dad.

Jack smiled at his daughter, though he could not hold it for very long. "Go with Amanda. When Mommy is better tomorrow, you can see her."

"I'm tired," she cried out.

"I'll go to your house and pick up whatever she needs, then we'll go over to my place."

"You are a lifesaver, Amanda. I don't know what I would do without you. I already called Stephanie's parents, they are flying up here on the first flight in the morning."

"Don't think twice about it," Amanda replied, all the while wondering what she might do without her best friend. Amanda grabbed Haley's hand and began to turnaround when Jack tapped her on the shoulder.

"You have our house key, right?"

"Yes."

She let go of Haley's hand for a moment and hugged Jack. "It will all work out."

"I hope so."

"Call me if you need anything, here is my mobile number." She took out a business card and jotted down her phone number.

Amanda walked down the hallway with Haley in hand toward the elevator. She turned one final time and waved to Jack. Tears welled up in her eyes as she turned around to get in to the elevator again. As the initial sense of shock took its course, she knew the future would never be the same.

"Do I have to go to kindergarten tomorrow?" Haley asked innocently.

"No, of course not," Amanda replied while keeping a firm eye on the road. She glanced at Haley long enough to take a good look at the teddy bear Haley was holding. "Is that a new teddy bear?"

"The nurse gave it to me."

"That's nice of them. Does he have a name? Or is it a she-bear?"

"No, not yet."

It started raining hard again. Amanda refocused her attention and concentrated on getting to their destination. She was relieved as she saw the neighborhood entrance sign amidst the heavy rain. Bear Creek, it read. She had seen it many times before without giving it a second thought. She pulled the car into the driveway of Haley's home.

They both quickly ran to the entrance. The front door swung open.

"Make sure you bring your toothbrush, Haley, and a change of clothes."

Haley ran to her room. She tossed the teddy bear on the living room sofa, it had not yet forged a tighter bond with her.

Amanda's attention focused on a set of family pictures on a table in the living room. There was the group family picture of Jack, Stephanie, and Haley at a park. A picture of Haley smiling while riding a pony, and a picture of Jack and Stephanie on a tropical beach somewhere caught her attention.

Haley's room, down the hallway, beckoned. She glanced at the picture frames mounted on the walls of the hallway. While numerous pictures of Jack and Stephanie's parents and relatives lined the cutouts, it was the cutout with a picture of Stephanie and herself that caught her eye. They were celebrating their twenty-first birthdays during a winter long ago. They had each flown to Florida to meet and celebrate. Best friends forever they were.

She turned away and walked toward the light from the room at the end of the hall.

Haley was just zipping up her small backpack. She looked up at Amanda under the door frame. "I need to go to the bathroom."

"Don't forget to bring your toothbrush too."

Haley squeezed past Amanda in the doorway and went to the bathroom across the hall.

A familiar sight caught Amanda's eye when she turned around to look in Haley's room. "I haven't seen you in quite awhile."

CHAPTER 2 – TWO BEARS

It was Stephanie's old stuffed animal. A large, several feet tall, rotund, panda bear. The sight of Haley's panda transported Amanda back toward a childhood memory nearly twenty-five years ago. It was a memory that stood out above many others.

Her eyes opened wide that morning long ago. It was her birthday present when she turned six years old. She rubbed her eyes over and over and wondered if the creature in front of her was real. It was the largest stuffed animal she had ever seen. The creature was sitting upright in the living room on the love seat sofa, motionless, and imposing in stature. A few moments passed before she mustered up the courage to approach the giant white polar bear that day. It was as if it might come alive at any moment. It was the best present she had ever received.

When it was time to take the new stuffed animal into her own room, lifting her new friend off the couch turned out to be more difficult than she thought it would be. He was so big and heavy.

She was even more excited that day to learn that her best friend, Stephanie, who shared the same birthday, also received a new stuffed animal, a big panda bear.

Haley walked back into the room holding her toothbrush. "Ok, I'm ready." Her soft voice knocked Amanda back into the present.

The momentary recollection was Amanda's first positive thought of the night. Ignoring Haley for a moment, she walked up to the stuffed bear and patted her on its head. She looked around Haley's room to see how the bear was living, not too shabby. Various other stuffed animals sat in different parts of the room. A poster of a tiger was tacked up prominently in the room. There was a lot of competition for attention from other animals. "That's one big panda bear you have."

Haley smiled, a welcome sight at a grim time. "My mom gave her to me."

"Does she have a name?"

"No, my mom said her name is just Panda Bear." She paused. "Is mommy going to be alright?" Haley started to cry softly.

"Did you know that I have a bear like yours too?"

"No."

"When I was younger, whenever I got sad or needed a friend, I gave my polar bear a hug."

"You did?" Haley asked as if surprised, while fighting her tears.

"Do you have a favorite animal?"

Haley picked up a bright white, stuffed tiger.

"Is it a he or a she?"

"A he."

"Bring him along, he can keep you company."

Whole-heartedly embracing Amanda's idea, she grabbed the tiger as they left for Amanda's home.

It was after midnight and Amanda was getting tired. Too many thoughts, emotions, and too much adrenaline were running through her body. Maybe it would all go away soon, like waking up from a bad nightmare. She needed a cup of coffee. Haley slept in the car until they arrived at Amanda's home.

They walked in, Haley and her backpack, and Amanda holding the tiger. Amanda led Haley to the bedroom and then turned around to go hang up her coat. "Don't forget to brush your teeth."

Haley had already closed her eyes and tucked herself under the bed covers when Amanda came back to check on her. It was as if Haley had used up the last of her reserves of energy. She was thankful that Haley hadn't asked about the polar bear she mentioned earlier, for it had been consigned to closet storage for many years.

Gazing at Haley blissfully sleeping, she changed into some pajamas and fell fast asleep next to her.

Amanda woke up to the sound of her phone ringing. Her eyes sprang open as if she had been expecting it. She looked at the clock. 6:04 a.m.

"Hello."

"Amanda?"

"Hi, Jack."

A long pause. "She's gone."

Amanda held the line, motionless, as she sat up and stared out the bedroom window. She turned and looked over at Haley. "What happened?"

"She didn't make it out of surgery."

Another long pause.

"What happened?"

"They said she might have survived had it not been for the swelling in her head."

Amanda's thoughts instinctively turned toward Haley. "Should I tell Haley or do you want to?"

"You're her godmother, go ahead. I'll talk to her after you break the news."

She set the phone down.

Amanda gently shook Haley's shoulder.

She mumbled and pushed away Amanda's hand.

How was she supposed to break this news to Haley? She hadn't exactly taken a course on how to do such a thing. Did children even understand death? "Haley, I need to talk to you about your mother."

The young girl opened her eyes and sat up. It seemed as if she had already sensed something wrong, a child's intuition.

"Your mother tried really hard, but she just suffered too many injuries in the accident. It was time for her to go to a better place."

A few tears streamed down the girl's face, but she said nothing.

"I think your father wants to talk to you." She handed the phone to Haley, who grudgingly grabbed it.

Amanda zoned out in shock for a moment as Haley and her father shared this moment that would define Haley's life forever. As she came to, she realized the phone was lying on the bed and that Haley had pulled the bedcovers over her eyes.

She composed herself to talk to Jack again. The silence of the room was disturbed only by Haley's whimpering. Grasping the phone, Amanda gently stuck the phone up to her ear. "It's me again."

"I'll be by later today to pick Haley up. I need to go home by myself for a little bit. Thanks a lot for your help. Haley's grandparents and Stephanie's brother are flying in later today."

"We'll be here, take your time."

The line went dead.

Amanda sat up and thought for a few minutes about a few of the things that she and Stephanie had experienced and shared together. The thoughts only brought forward more pain. "Haley, Haley."

Haley came out from under the covers and sat up. She had stopped whimpering, but tears were in her eyes.

"Your mother was my best friend. No matter what happens, I'll always be here. . ." Amanda's voice broke down and she started crying uncontrollably. She sobbed hard as she hugged Haley as hard as she could.

To the casual observer, it was obvious who was crying more. Amanda was surprised at how Haley was taking the news so far. She expected a far greater outburst, but she knew better, looks could be deceiving. Amanda tried to hold herself together better, but she couldn't, she cried harder. They held each other tight for several minutes before letting go.

Then, unexpectedly, Haley managed a few words through her now silent tears. "Thanks for taking care of me. But – who will take care of you?"

CHAPTER 3 – THE REAL THING

Three months later and Amanda was still trying to make sense of Stephanie's meaningless and silly death. Any casual visitor to her home would realize that something was amiss. The dishes were piling up in her sink and dust was accumulating. The normally neat and fastidious Amanda was appearing to be anything but. She decided to write in her journal again. There were more important things to think about than appearances. Journal entries were becoming a more frequent and detailed activity since the accident.

> *Whoever said that time heals all wounds must have never been badly wounded. It's been three months and my state of mind only seems to be getting worse. Maybe I should see a therapist? Maybe I should find some support group? How do people get over the death of a loved one? Maybe you're not supposed to. Maybe the living are just condemned to live with their memory. If it is this hard for me, I wonder what it must be like for Haley. But, I think kids are more resilient than we think they are. Probably more so, than us pathetic adults.*

A loose piece of paper dropped out of the notebook on to the floor as she closed her diary in frustration. She picked it up. It was the eulogy she had written for Stephanie's funeral. The memory of giving the eulogy felt fresh as she scanned the words she wrote. One sentence stood out – she was always honest with her feelings, even when others were not.

She stared blankly out her window. This was the second consecutive Friday that she had decided to leave work early just to reflect. A glass of wine and a seat on her favorite rocking chair facing the television did the trick. She had been drinking more and more as the days of miserable grief turned into months. While not yet an alcoholic, if she kept up her current pace, she might very well become one. She was trying to drown her sorrow away in a flood of red wine.

She picked up the remote to turn on the television. Perhaps the drone of the television would further numb out her emotions, but the remote control's batteries were dead. The little handheld wonder of convenience and power was just a useless piece of plastic now.

The blank screen of the television beckoned for its owner to call it to life as Amanda crouched down to hit the power button. Her reflection against the glass immediately made an impression on her as she reached forward to press the button. She looked at herself for a moment, the darkness of the screen hiding her true complexion. Rather than improve her look, it only darkened her image. She gave it no further thought and turned the television on.

The usual stuff appeared as she flipped through the channels. Low brow talk shows, infomercials, old reruns, soap operas, histories of wars around the world, and great battles of the American Civil War. On the sports channels were auto racing, golf, and slick oiled wrestlers putting on a show that always made Amanda wonder whether the action was real, or just an illusion. She flipped through some legal and crime dramas before hitting the news stations. They reported on surfer girl shark attacks, wars and turbulence in distant lands, political shenanigans, stock market gyrations, and the never-ending drama of pretty, young, missing girls of the month.

She stopped channel surfing as she caught a glimpse of a polar bear. It was a special on the polar regions that had just begun. She sat down and was mesmerized by the images as she learned about how the Arctic and Antarctica were distinctly different places.

At first glance they seemed similar, as both were barren, treeless, and cold places. But one had polar bears, the other, penguins. One had been inhabited for thousands of years, the other, only recently discovered and explored. One was mostly a sea area with the edges of countries surrounding it, the other was a continent. One exploded with life on the tundra in the spring and summer, the other remained a land of ice with much colder temperatures.

The episode concluded and she got up to turn off the television set. She saw her reflection again. Her face stared back at her again, but the bags under her eyes had grown darker.

The cool winter air cleared her mind when she walked out to her balcony. The view from here was due northwest. On a relatively clear day she could see the Olympic Mountains to the left, and on a very clear day, in the far off distance to the right, she could imagine Mt. Baker and the Northern Cascade mountains.

There was something calming about being at home while most other people were still busy at work. Today though, she was getting restless. She glanced over at her bookshelf. Her fingers glided over the spines until she reached the last few titles: *Be All You Can Be, The Power Within, A Few Habits of Awesome People.* For all the fancy claims, no amount of positive thinking power would help her now. She wondered if their advice really worked. If it did, why was she so messed up? Even before the accident too.

She was in marketing, how could she have fallen for the claims of such charlatans? Moments of weakness she told herself. She would get stronger.

On the outside she was the model of success, but inside, she was in conflict about her life. These were ideas that she kept repressed as much as possible.

She felt like a scoundrel now over how she could be so desperate for happiness that she needed such help from gurus. These gurus were like short term drugs. The high kept you going for a little while, but then, once it wore off, you were back to square one, maybe even negative one. You might 'move forward' in some areas of your life, but you often took a step back in others. Maybe they worked for some people, but not her.

Despite her reservations about these books, she decided another trip to the bookstore was in order. She could shop the grief away. Maybe a book about death would enlighten her.

The titles didn't shout bestseller. Words like death, final, and loss, seemed to keep repeating among the titles. None of them appealed to her. Maybe she needed to wait a little longer before she was ready to tackle a book on death. She decided to go home empty handed.

A photograph caught her eye though in a discount bin before she could walk out the exit. It was a photograph of two polar bears standing and ready to spar one another on their hind legs, or were they dancing? Amanda picked it up, it was a calendar. Dancing with Polar Bears, $2.99 it said on the red sticker. Immediately, memories of her childhood bond with her stuffed polar bear came to mind. She had put him away in the closet many years ago, grown ups didn't play with stuffed animals. She was a productive, working adult. There was no time for children's toys. Amanda headed for the cash register with calendar in hand.

Retreating back into the warmth of her home, she poured herself another glass of wine. The red liquid disappeared in an instant. The wedding magazines laying around testified to the dreamy reality that she wished about. The dream was even further away now. Maybe she was just extra cautious because of the starter marriage debacle she wanted to avoid. Chip thought she would get closer after Stephanie's death, but she only wanted to push him away even further. His complaints about her looking for Mr.Perfect even before Stephanie's death were only more irritating.

This wasn't the first time she had lost some deep inner part of herself. When her parents divorced, her fantasy of growing up in a happy and photo perfect family disappeared. She had tried hard to overcome the times of despair and lost expectations. Whatever momentum she had from moving in the right direction was gone. A seemingly random set of events had taken from her a lifelong friendship, her best friend. She felt lonely. Yet, while she didn't like this feeling of loneliness, she couldn't trust her feelings with Chip. Perhaps she feared betrayal in any relationship. Maybe it wasn't just a guy problem.

Until recently, the solution was more work, as if it could be a salve for her emotional wounds. Who needed a boyfriend anyway, when the power of the drink was in hand.

"I need to put you up," she announced aloud, referring to the calendar. She flipped to February and walked back out to the living room. "How about here," she remarked as she tacked it to the wall in a conspicuous location. The picture for February was of a polar bear and her cub walking across the ice. It was a surreal and unreal looking photo, Amanda thought to herself. She forced a smile, if only to try and cheer herself up.

Looking around her home, she decided a house cleaning was in order, it was like therapy for her soul. First, the kitchen and all of the dishes that had piled up. She downed another glass of wine to loosen up her inspiration. Then the living room with the various magazines, books, and old photo albums. Then the bathroom with all of its grime and mold. Next up was her bedroom and walk in closet. She grabbed the outfits strewn across the floor and headed for her closet. As she moved outfits around deciding which ones to give away, she moved around some old luggage until she noticed a familiar face in a dark corner.

She let out a gasp.

Looking directly at her was a familiar face from long ago. It was her large stuffed polar bear from childhood. He was decompressing from being squeezed into a corner. She knew he was always there, but she had forgotten about him.

"Where have you been all this time?"

There was no answer.

She stretched her arms and brought him out of the dark closet corner and into the bedroom. The plush fur pressed up against her body. Even as an adult, he was still big. She stared into his black beady eyes then shifted her gaze around its entire length. She rubbed one of his paws, complete with cushy black foot pads. The bear even had the red ribbon that she had tied around its neck to personalize him. His presence reminded Amanda of the feeling and sense of stoic calmness that she always felt around him, whenever she was in trouble as a child.

She gave him a hug as if she would never see him again. At least for Amanda today, stuffed animals weren't just for children anymore.

The wine blissfully put Amanda to sleep, this time on the floor, her polar bear looming over her like a silent guardian. She dreamed about one of the defining moments of her young childhood, the final showdown of her parents' marriage.

It was a day when her father's late nights at the office, or wherever else he really was, finally caused her mother to explode. Amanda had sought shelter in her bedroom bunker amongst an army of stuffed animals.

Hearing a strange noise in the living room late at night, she had decided to investigate. Using Polar Bear as a scout, she had determined that it was safe to go down the hallway. She discovered that her father was sleeping on the couch. A stealth run into the kitchen secured some cookies for herself, and her best friend, apart from Stephanie, Polar Bear.

He was nameless, other than the description of what he was, a big bear. Polar Bear, always in capital letters when she referenced him in her childhood diary, now long lost.

The day she discovered her father sleeping on the couch was the day she gripped her stuffed bear tighter than ever before. It was the day that she first touched her nose against Polar Bear's leathery black nose. And the day that her parents decided to get a divorce.

Amanda emerged from her deep sleep, conscious, but not fully awake. She began to wonder if her behavior when she was younger was a bit odd.

Perhaps it could be explained by Stephanie's insights from reading about how parents in different cultures raised their children. Depending on the way it was done, children matured at different speeds. The field of study was called ethnopediatrics. It was something Stephanie shared with Amanda years ago.

The very concept of childhood was different or even non-existent in various countries, or perhaps more precisely, cultures. In some cultures, childhood was not a carefree time, but rather a time of responsibility and learning. In others, to praise a child for the accomplishment of their tasks was to encourage later disobedience and selfishness.

How one physically raised a child even affected future motor skills, with the age of a child learning to walk perhaps being the first hint. A child kept upright, rather than in a stroller, might walk three months sooner than the average American child, with better hand-eye coordination. In the other direction, some cultures' children first walked up to nine months later.

Loving a stuffed animal as a child and as an adult were two different things, but who cared, whatever worked she thought to herself.

The phone rang and Amanda woke up from the final moments of her extended cat nap. "Hello?"

"Hi, Amanda. Were you sleeping?"

"Hi, Mom. I'm ok."

"How are things?"

Silence.

"Are you still having trouble concentrating? Are you eating and sleeping well?"

"I'm getting by. Sometimes, I feel numb. I feel numb toward everyone and everything, Mother."

"Are you still getting those headaches you were talking to me about?"

"No, but I feel confused. I cry a lot, sometimes. I want to stop being sad."

"Would you like me to come over? It's not good to be alone at these times."

Silence.

"Amanda, do you think you should see a grief counselor?"

Amanda snapped. "Why does everyone in America have to see a therapist anytime there is a problem? Can't they just work through it themselves?"

"Sure, Amanda," Deborah replied, clearly realizing that her daughter was now agitated.

Amanda looked at her new calendar again. "Mom, have you ever seen a real polar bear?"

"Huh?"

"Have you ever seen a real polar bear?"

"What are you talking about?"

Her mom didn't seem to remember the power of her birthday gift from so long ago.

"I think I need to go somewhere."

"A vacation would be good. Where are you thinking of going?"

"Some place different."

"Where?"

"I don't know. It's, it's, not important, Mother," she stuttered. "I'm going back to bed now."

"Let's talk soon. Before I forget, your father called me. He said he's been trying to get a hold of you. Will you call him back?"

"I turned off my ringer earlier."

"He's concerned about you."

"I'm not concerned about him."

"Amanda, it hasn't always been ideal, but he is still your father."

"Mom, I'm going to bed. I'm tired."

The line went cold.

She had gotten more distant from her mother after the divorce. Living with her mother, sometimes she would be the star of her mother's attention, more often, she had felt neglected while her mother sought out other companions or became overly interested in all things work. Visiting with her father and his revolving door of females didn't help either. Or maybe she was just overly needy at times. She hated that feeling.

She remembered how a therapist long ago had said that children from openly high conflict homes had worse outcomes. As scientific as it sounded, it was true for her. While by all outward appearances she was successful, emotionally, she could be a poster child. That's it, it was all her parents' fault that she was messed up.

"Why did she have to die!?" she screamed out.

Her companion, Polar Bear, gave no answers.

Maybe a real one would know better. The stuffed animal was lifeless, despite her imagination.

Her mother's call had stirred her, but she felt the need for more rest. It must have been the wine, alcohol on a near empty stomach worked fast. She let out a yawn.

"I need my privacy tonight."

She walked over to Polar Bear and picked him up. She sat him on her rocking chair, somehow managing to squeeze him in. Rocking the chair back and forth, she amused herself. Then she sprinted into her bedroom and started drifting off to sleep. She dreamed she would go see a real polar bear at the zoo. Maybe Haley would like to come too.

CHAPTER 4 – ZOO LIFE

A large sign stood before Amanda and Haley as they rounded the row of shrubs by the parking lot. Puget Sound Zoo and Aquarium it read.

"We're here!" Amanda shouted.

"We're here!" Haley shouted back.

They bought their tickets and went in. As they passed by a large polar bear sculpture, Amanda noticed several kids standing and sitting on it.

Greeted by tranquil sounds of nature they were not, for a large gathering of young children was massed near the entrance. Chaperones were busy running around doing a head count, it looked out of control. Amanda grabbed Haley's hand and moved quickly to get clear of the group.

First, they decided to visit the aquarium area. Inside were exhibits of sea horses, sharks, salmon, and octopi. The concrete pillars and facades did not help to create an underwater illusion. Before long, whatever sense of tranquility there was, had been broken. They moved on, trying to keep ahead of the mass of children who were now running rampant in the aquarium. They left the crush of children behind inside as they exited out of the dark aquarium into the brighter outdoors.

They arrived at their first outdoor exhibit.

Voices rang out from other visitors. "Penguins! – Over here! – What's in there? – Look at them breakdance. – Can't penguins fly? – Why don't the penguins want to go in the water?"

It was quite clear why the penguins weren't going in the water, at least to Amanda. The water was still, no waves. The video from Antarctica that she had watched on television earlier showed penguins diving into heavy surf off rock or icy cliffs. There was no such challenge here. The still water smelled and looked moldy. It was a cesspool.

Before they even reached the next exhibit, they heard a loud series of 'oohs' and 'aahs.' It wasn't obvious what the fuss was all about as they rounded the corner.

Surrounding a large pool were dozens of children eagerly anticipating something in the water. It was a different group of children.

A stream of water shot up. A bluish colored creature surfaced, it was a beluga whale. Its light blue color turned to gray as it exposed its top to the air. The beluga circled repetitively around the pool edge while delighting the children that were all lined up. Amanda looked on, she felt like she was part of an audience for a freak show. She glanced over at Haley. Putting aside any further such feelings, she tried to be more interested.

As she watched Haley being intrigued by the beluga, she wondered if she was thinking too much. It appeared to have a perpetual smile, perhaps fooling its young voyeurs. Amanda wanted to move on quickly. She spotted the sign for the polar bear exhibit and decided that maybe they could beat this other group of children to it, once they passed the otter exhibit though. They spent a brief minute watching the otters frolic around in their play area. The small little furry creatures could not hold their attention longer as the moment of seeing a live polar bear neared. She grabbed Haley's hand.

Finally, the section that Amanda really wanted to come for, and the attraction that she hoped would put a big smile on Haley's face too, the polar bear exhibit. Amanda couldn't help but over-hear some of the other visitors' conversations as they walked toward the entrance.

"I need to go to the bathroom. – I'm going over here. – No, you stay over here. – I'm tired. – What do we get to see next? – That beluga was way cool!"

They walked under the sign that read: Polar Bears – Un-derwater Viewing. Only a few other children and parents were inside.

The first thing they saw was a large mosaic tiled picture of a standing polar bear. It was inviting visitors to measure themselves up against it. Along another wall were various panels describing polar bear facts. The showpiece, however, was the area set behind a line of thick glass windows. Directly behind the windows was a shallow pool. It was small, bowl shaped, no deeper than fifteen feet, and not very wide at all. Set behind the pool was a small concrete area with a grassy hill rising to the rear of the enclosure. A bright orange ball sat untouched, floating on the water. There was no polar bear.

"I can see him!" Haley shouted. Lying motionless in the far back of the exhibit, was a solitary polar bear. They stared at it amidst the increasing background noise and commotion. A faux stream meandered around some fake rock mounds. Whatever moment of connection between the bear and them was shattered as kids started to stream in.

"Hey, it's over there! – Move! Let me see! – Stop shoving, kids! – We can take a picture with the rest of the class. – I'm hungry!"

While they struggled to maintain their position, Amanda thought she heard what sounded like two women gossiping about their sex lives. They chatted while their children were being entertained as part of a mob. There were no conversations like this on the TV documentary. This was not the Arctic.

Everyone else was looking on, oblivious to the reality of the situation it seemed. A feeling of sadness came over Amanda. She wondered if anyone realized how manufactured the zoo was. She noticed the reflection of the adults and children on the plastic-glass barrier, they were faint when viewed against the pool of water behind it. This is how kids learned their attitudes toward nature. This is how Amanda had learned, at a different zoo, with other animals.

They continued to gaze at the lifeless bear. Amanda noticed a plaque with small photos of each bear. They each had a name, unlike Amanda's stuffed animal. Their names were Snowflake, Icicle, Anatoly, and Simon. All of them came from the wild, only Anatoly was zoo born.

A strange silence soon fell over the exhibit, most of the kids and parents had disappeared. They had seen what they came to the zoo for, another animal. Another animal that they could take off their mental checklist, but one they had scarcely learned anything about. Amanda knew she didn't know too much about polar bears, but she did know one thing, polar bears spent a lot of time on ice. She took another look behind the glass windows, there was no ice at all.

They walked out of the polar bear habitat.

"What did you think of the polar bear, Haley?"

"He looked bored. He didn't look very happy."

Amanda pursed her lips together and looked at Haley. They shared the same sentiments. "Do you want to sit down and get a drink?"

"Ok."

Amanda couldn't help but overhear a conversation between a zoo employee and a visitor.

". . .the sign shows four bears, where are the others?"

"Resting in the back. Sometimes we put two out. We're the only zoo in the world with two males out at the same time."

"So, you rotate among them?"

"Yes, if they are sleeping on the island, then the public gets grumpy, and then I am not happy. When they're swimming in the water, they're popular. When the public is happy, I am happy."

"I guess you better get in there."

"I know."

The polar bear keeper had been conditioned to the whims of the masses, Amanda realized. After all, most people at a zoo aren't content to just watch animals sitting around, we pay to see action.

Amanda walked up to the nearby snack counter and ordered two sodas. As she waited, she noticed a sign advertising a frozen drink treat, available in cherry, blue raspberry, and cola. Amanda remembered drinking these when she was a kid, except this time she noticed something else. The cartoon character promoting the drinks was a polar bear.

It was not enough to have polar bears in a sad looking 'cage.' They were also being used to sell drinks, right across from the exhibit. How many of the visitors - both parents and children - would walk away from this experience with respect for these large, beautiful creatures? Amanda turned her head away in anger and disgust as she paid for the sodas. "Whatever, whatever," she muttered to herself.

"Over here!" Haley shouted.

They sat across from each other at the small table. Again, Amanda noticed the other visitors. A large group of school kids was also in the area. There must have been several school groups visiting she concluded. They had names like – Raquel, Marisol, Alexa, Max, Ian, Julia, and Mercedes. Did the people who live in the Arctic have names like this?

"Let's go look at the polar bears. – Let's go potty first. – Where are we going? – Why can't they make these things closer together? – Does anybody need to go to the bathroom? – I'll stay out here – Wash your hands when you're done."

Amanda tried to ignore the chatter as she looked around. She noticed the large water pump system next to the bathrooms of the polar bear exhibit. The incessant hum of the water pumps groaned ever louder. More kids streamed by, some in colorful strollers. She noticed a few hardy kids wearing shorts. She noticed the sign asking people to please stay on the path. A path. Were the paths in the Arctic marked?

Just when it couldn't get more unreal, two zoo employees began to walk past them.

"Anteater, coming through!"

Sure enough, they were pulling an anteater. It was a bizarre sight. There were no anteaters in the Arctic, that much Amanda was sure of.

At least she could take comfort in the natural setting. Her gaze went upward. The whole area was surrounded by tall and ubiquitous, Northwest evergreen trees. But, something didn't look right. Her thoughts went back to the documentary and photos that she had seen on her polar bear calendar. There weren't any trees, the Arctic was treeless.

This zoo was a place of constant stimulus as visitors went from one exhibit to the next. Wild nature was not a place of such different stimulus. Did the Arctic have ice cream stands with coolers and cola machines? The focus on convenience was disturbing to Amanda.

This zoo was an illusion, and a very bad one at that, but it seemed to fool the majority of people.

CHAPTER 5 – SEEDS OF DOUBT

She closed her eyes and just listened. The thought crossed her mind that there was something to be panicked about at the zoo, but that was wrong. It was just the loud and boisterous, uncontrolled school kids, making a ruckus. Amanda and Haley sat quietly, resting, trying to make the best of the situation. Haley looked out of place as she sat while the other kids, older and younger, screamed up a storm.

"Excuse me, is somebody sitting here?"

"No, not at all," Amanda answered.

An older lady sat down in a chair next to Haley. "Thank you. Crazy, isn't it?"

"I'll say," Amanda responded.

"Did you bring your child here to see the polar bears?"

Amanda hesitated for a moment. She didn't want to bother explaining all the circumstances of the recent past. A simple, yes, was all she could muster.

"The bear didn't look very happy," Haley commented.

"Is that right?" the lady responded.

Amanda hesitated again, now thinking she didn't want to make such a fuss, but she couldn't resist. It was why she was so good at marketing, she could be very chatty. "I don't think we are terribly impressed by the living conditions or the atmosphere here."

The lady sat forward. Raising a hand to the side of her mouth, she whispered loudly, "I have a secret, I don't like it either."

"Why are you here then?"

"I was waiting outside for my daughter and her kids. They're driving over from Eastern Washington. My grandchildren really want to see certain animals. She called to tell me that they were delayed by traffic and a temper tantrum or two. I want to see my grandchildren, so here I am. I've already been waiting for thirty minutes outside."

"That's too bad," Amanda replied.

"Of course, I told my daughter that I think zoos are really sad and that we should go somewhere else, but she wouldn't listen. I decided to come in and wait for them. I was a little hungry, too. Maybe I thought I could get rid of some inner angst too and pretend to like the zoo for my grandkids sake."

"Sad? What do you find sad about it?"

"The whole idea of having zoos bothers me."

"How's that?"

"Zoos give us the impression that we are separate from nature. The setting is just unreal. It's a distortion of their natural behaviors too."

"How's that?" Amanda asked, wanting to hear the lady's explanation, although, she already suspected the same. No ice, no trees, she told herself.

"Well, we're here by the polar bears. A single polar bear's natural territory can be hundreds of square miles. Polar bears have been known to swim for hundreds of miles at a time."

"Hundreds of miles?"

"A typical zoo enclosure for a polar bear can be up to *eighty million* times smaller than a wild bear's home range. It depends on the home area of the polar bear in question though."

"*Eighty* million times?" Amanda was flabbergasted. "What about other animals?"

"Many zoo animals live in an area much smaller than their minimum home range. It affects big animals more than others. Like elephants, chimps, and sea lions. Polar bears are the worst."

Amanda tensed up.

"Even the best zoos can't be much better. Of course, zoos don't make a point about highlighting these facts."

"Why is that not surprising." People, organizations, not highlighting the negative. 'Focus on the positive, not the negative.' Whatever, whatever, Amanda thought to herself.

"Some animals luck out by being in an area only a little bit smaller than normal, relatively speaking. I think it's really bad for chimpanzees and birds though too. You know, they like to swing in trees and fly around."

"Didn't you mention something about their natural behavior?"

"Maybe it is better if you see it for yourself. Are you staying much longer? I'm going to walk back toward the entrance. We can continue talking while we walk. I can take the long route. My daughter didn't sound very optimistic about getting here soon. My husband and I live near Port Townsend, that's why I am here early."

"Sure, why not." Amanda sized up the lady who appeared to be in her fifties. Amanda had learned in her life that sometimes it was the random people you met who could tell you something interesting. "Are you ready to go, Haley?"

"Ready when you are."

"I'm sorry, I didn't catch your name," Amanda asked.

"Oh sorry, my name is Ruth. Your daughter's name is Haley?"

"My name is Amanda. She's a friend's daughter."

"Pleased to meet both of you." Ruth felt a hint of tension in Amanda's voice and decided not to press further.

The three of them got up and worked their way around the zoo. They walked back toward the entrance. They passed reindeer, musk ox, some birds, then some red wolves. A black crow flew over them as they passed the kettle corn popping station. A bus roared by on the road surrounding the zoo.

Soon, they came upon the kid's zone. It was a riot of color and attention grabbing play pens. There was the seal slide, dancing water spouts, climbing bars, and swings. Kids were wildly running around. Kids were hopping up and down on the water spouts. Hop, leap, said the writing on the ground, so they did.

It all struck Amanda as very artificial as they walked by. She looked at how Haley reacted to the sight of the various contraptions, but Haley was disinterested if anything. In the end, they were more artificial creations, pandering to the whims of children, or was it just adults' perceptions of what kids needed?

They kept walking and soon reached the Asian forest exhibit, spread over several acres the literature claimed. It was home to Sumatran tigers, tapirs, otters, monkeys, and elephants.

Large tents of metal netting were the first things that captured their attention. They were enclosures designed to contain the first animals they came across in this 'sanctuary,' monkeys. At first glance, none of them could see any animals inside.

"Look, up there," Haley shouted.

The monkeys were at the very top of the steel netting, like they were trying to escape. The monkeys left alone the lifeless, bare leafed tree. None of the visitors seemed to notice. They had either bought into the fantasy or subconsciously submitted to the illusion.

They walked by some signs about conservation, but nobody had stopped to read them, nor did they. They soon arrived at the tiger exhibit. The three of them gazed out at the two tigers.

"What do you see?" Ruth asked.

Amanda saw two tigers. Their orange fur coat with white highlights and black stripes stood out in the enclosure. They were both at the edge, trying to get away from the human eyes which were now fixated on them. One of them got up and began to pace around amongst the green foliage. Amanda wasn't quite sure what she was looking for.

The sound of a faux waterfall provided a backdrop for the area set below, an artificial pond. Some other visitors were also looking at the tigers, but they were too busy gawking and taking photographs to even attempt to notice anything amiss. "They look lonely," Amanda commented.

"It's not barbed wire. – It's angled so they can't escape! – Tiger! Tiger! – Why is the water green? – You don't wave back to me, bleh! – I see a tiger up close. – It's my turn with the binoculars. – Let me see!"

Amanda refocused her attention on the tigers.

"Tigers are solitary creatures. That's not what I was thinking though," Ruth responded.

And there it was. The tiger was pacing the same path, again, and again. She pointed her finger at the tiger. She hoped that tigers didn't think it was rude to point. She moved her finger to the left and right in a steady rhythm.

"I think you've got it."

"What does it mean?"

"Animals don't behave normally when confined, Amanda."

What else were you supposed to do when you were stuck in a small space for your entire life, Amanda realized.

"I haven't been to a zoo in a long time, but I remember seeing animals lick the walls and chew the bars of their cages. It's like they were trying to escape. I've read that apes have been known to masturbate over and over again."

Amanda felt a moment of uncomfort over Ruth's casual use of the word, masturbation. "That's what happens when your stuck in the same small space your whole life?"

Ruth didn't answer.

Amanda frowned at Ruth's comments. She considered herself an animal lover at some level, but this was continuing to challenge her basic views about zoos. She realized that somehow she had connected a 'love for animals' with going to the zoo. It was time to break and unlink this connection in her mind.

It occurred to her suddenly, that she had done something similar to this confined tiger. When cooped up in her office, or even at home too long, she paced back and forth frequently. It took on a whole new meaning as she watched the tiger repeat this behavior.

"It's just so unreal. They group animals together that don't want to be together, they feed them junk."

"They can't migrate or go anywhere else when the weather changes too," Amanda answered out loud.

Once again, Amanda thought about how she spent her average work day, or work year. She would binge eat sometimes after, or even during work. Junk food, fatty fried foods, fast food. Could this be like the inappropriate diet that zoo animals were fed? She got fidgety when the seasons changed, but she was tied to her job with limited vacation, she couldn't go anywhere for a very long time. She toughed out her seasonal affect disorder in a gray and often cloudy Pacific Northwest, every year. She liked her co-workers, but sometimes they just got to be a little too much, no wonder she didn't like after hours corporate social functions.

"Are there any better zoos that you know of, Ruth?"

"I don't think so. They're all built on the same premise. People go to zoos and don't know what to look for. If you don't have animal encounters in the wild where you can see them behaving normally, how would you know?"

Amanda pondered the question and the apparent conundrum. For a fleeting moment, she wondered that if everyone she knew was cooped up in a zoo like cage, in an office, how would she know what normal behavior was? The thought terrified her, she quickly dismissed it.

"These tigers can't do what they were born to do, Amanda. Tigers like to hunt stealthily, they can't do that here."

"Is there a cheetah here?" Haley shouted.

"I don't know, Haley."

"If there was a cheetah here, it can't really run anywhere."

"Aren't cheetahs the fastest animal on earth?"

"They're up there," Ruth replied.

While animals were fine-tuned to their environment, a lot more of their behavior than we had previously thought, was learned and passed down from mother or group to infant. It explained why species re-introductions often failed or only exceeded at great expense. Thus, a wild animal was markedly different than a caged animal.

Amanda glanced over at Haley, who switched between paying attention, and watching the other children and adults walk by. The activities of the crowd and other children were more engaging than the two tigers.

She took a moment to wonder about this learned behavior idea as it applied to her own life growing up. She had always wondered what life might be like and how she might view the world if her parents never divorced. Would she still be fearful of commitment? Was she really fearful or was it something else? This was too serious of a thought while at the zoo.

Ruth's phone rang. "It's my daughter, probably." She talked for a few moments before putting her phone away. "Aie. They're still being delayed by traffic. She thinks there's been an accident or something. We can still talk, if you like."

Amanda felt a lump in her throat. "Yes, yes, of course."

The two majestic Sumatran tigers that once instilled fear and respect in men, were good for less than a few minutes of observation, by mostly noisy and unruly children no less. Even the most quiet and introspective visitors lasted only a couple more minutes. Perhaps they looked on, sensing something was wrong, but they persisted with their morbid fascination, as if the tiger's predicament looked familiar.

They left the tigers and moved on to the elephant exhibit.

"I want to ride an elephant!" Haley shouted.

"What do you see now?" Ruth asked again. It was a benign question, yet asked in the right way, terribly thought provoking.

Amanda looked again, this time she noticed the repetitive behavior right away. "I got it. I see the elephants rocking and shifting from side to side. Is that a repetitive, unnatural behavior?"

"It can be. Anything else?"

Amanda didn't notice anything particular. If her knowledge of polar bears in the wild was limited, her knowledge of elephants was even less.

"Elephants may walk from fifteen to twenty miles a day in the wild. Do they do that in this tiny enclosure?"

"No, I guess they can't." It was the same story as with the polar bear, there was no hint of what was missing.

"Would you like to hear an interesting story?" the woman proffered as they watched the elephants.

"Sure."

"One of my most life changing moments was when I went to Africa for the first time. My husband and I went on a safari. There were no fences, no signs, and little, if any, tourist facilities. No injury waivers either." She laughed. "All we did was drive on the roads past the gate. We saw giraffes, zebras, warthogs, a rhino, and monkeys crossing the road. Supposedly a lion too, hiding in the bushes. Our driver saw it."

"Where?" Haley's ears perked up at the mention of so many animals.

"Not now, Haley. Look at the elephants."

"The best moment was when we were driving down the road and had to start backing up because a large African elephant was walking toward us, a *wild* African elephant with tusks. At one point, we couldn't backup anymore because two other elephants were fighting, quarreling, and blocking the road behind us. The elephant in front was now just fifteen feet or so in front of our car, flapping its ears and making a lot of noise. We were there for a few minutes. Our driver then casually tells us that he once saw some people get killed when their car was crushed by a mad elephant. He didn't sound like he was joking."

"Whoa! Were you scared?" Amanda gasped.

Ruth hesitated for a moment as if she was vividly reliving the moment. "A little, but that was the beauty of it. This was raw nature. Once the elephant realized we weren't a threat and that we respected it, it went off to the side to eat some leaves on a tree. We then sped around it and watched as another car that was right behind us, try to make it out. This is how animals behave naturally, not confined in some playpen."

Amanda felt no fear as she gazed out at the elephants, nor was there any hint of danger at the tiger enclosure. It had all been safely sanitized.

They made their way back toward the entrance, stopping to sit for awhile and chat on a terrace as Haley munched on a light meal they picked up along the way.

They talked about how zoos might say that animals didn't need to hunt or look for food, or migrate with the seasons. How natural was a captive life for wild animals? They both agreed that there was no sense of their true lives.

Amanda, being in marketing, liked to come up with simple analogies for her clients. She shared with Ruth if this sense of one's true life was how she felt when stuck working in a cubicle or office, day after day. Wasn't technology supposed to make our lives easier? Or had heightened expectations thwarted this? Going 'public' with her feelings that had been building up inside her was a bit of a relief.

But, it was apparent to Amanda that she was making a choice, the animals weren't. Perhaps more perplexing was why she would make such a choice to spend a majority of her waking hours in a cubicle or small office, or even a corner office. Yes, the money was good, but one only needed so much money. Maybe the trick was to rein in her desires. Was there a better way? Maybe she just had to be more efficient or not work overtime. Better office design? Better job diversity and variety? More vacations?

"I'm retired now, but I used to work in a cubicle. I know what it's like. Do you ever feel like you don't have enough privacy?"

"Sometimes. I have an office now, and I still feel that way sometimes, if not confined by the four walls too."

"Many animals are solitary for most of their lives and what we might label, shy. They are creatures of the night. Yet at a zoo, they cannot spend a day away from human eyes. It would be like living with a camera around you all day that you didn't want, like some of the stuff on TV these days."

"Or the Internet," Amanda remarked.

"Yes."

"Other animals are incredibly social, more so than those who study animals ever believed, but they can't live like that either at a zoo."

"It sounds like some of the movies I've seen, or some of those 'reality' shows. I know I would never want to be on some of those reality TV shows. Every moment of my life for public view? I'm not an exhibitionist." She noticed the sign for the amphitheatre.

"At least the contestants have a possibility for a big prize before they leave, no such luck for these animals," Ruth added.

"True."

Amanda thought about the home area ratio between wild and zoo polar bears again. Up to *eighty million* times smaller for a zoo polar bear. It was mind boggling. Was keeping animals caged up just a reflection of our own insecurities and fears?

The thought of office life entered Amanda's mind again. She began to count the hours in a day. Eight hours of sleep, nine, if she needed to look particularly radiant. At least eight hours at the office, most spent in a confining cubicle or office. Then, there was the commute home where she sat in a car, sometimes in a traffic jam. How many hours of her life did she live in a small space, not really moving? She was afraid to realize the truth.

A part of Amanda still wanted to like zoos. "Zoos must be good for something. What about endangered animals? Don't zoos do good research?" Amanda hoped to justify why she decided to visit the zoo with Haley, apart from seeing a live polar bear.

"A lot of the research just relates to breeding and making more zoo animals. It's for the benefit of the zoo industry, not the animals. The research often just tells us about wild animals in zoos. It's ironic, as it wouldn't be necessary if there were no zoos. The research has little to do with wild animals in their natural habitat."

"I'll have to research that on my own, Ruth. How long have zoos been around?" Amanda wondered aloud.

"Officially, 250 years. If you count the menageries of the Roman Empire, Egyptian pharaohs, and the like, then much longer."

"The zoo has been ingrained in our consciousness for a long time it sounds like."

"I'm not against nature reserves. It's really just the places where animals are confined to small areas, strictly for the convenience of the visitors. The way I think about zoos mirrors how I think about life, more and more."

Haley interrupted, "I want to see a wild elephant."

"Maybe someday, Haley. Maybe someday." Ruth's vivid recollection of being on the plains of Africa face to face with an elephant sounded both exciting, and a little nerve wracking. "You're lucky to have experienced that trip to Africa, I wish I could afford to go to Africa."

"It's not as expensive as you think. There are lots of ways to travel for cheaper. Airfare sales in the off-season, and staying at cheaper hotels or even hostels. Look at all the fancy cars people buy, Amanda. For many people, I don't think it's really a matter of affordability, it's a matter of priority. Accumulate stuff or accumulate experience."

Amanda thought about all the things she owned. She had her new car, designer purse, nice jewelry, lots of nice things. She remembered how she was also dumbstruck when visiting some of her co-workers or friends' homes. Their garages were full of stuff. She strained to put Ruth's words out of her mind. While she understood what Ruth was saying, it contradicted part of what she believed. Stuff was good, it was very good. More is better. Bigger is better. She helped companies to sell more.

Ruth talked on, oblivious to Amanda's blank face which was frantically wondering about her own existence. "If that is still too much, maybe it is better to just leave it to television. Every part of the world has wildlife to view naturally, people just need to make an effort."

"An effort?"

"You can see orca whales in the San Juan Islands. You can whistle with marmots in the meadows of Mt. Rainier. You can go whale watching from the Oregon Coast. It's relatively inexpensive to charter a boat or do a flyover too. They're a magnificent site from the air, I've seen them myself. If you like birds, in late

December and early January, hundreds of bald eagles can be seen around the Upper Skagit river as they pick off dead salmon along the river every year. You can see them there for free. My husband and I belong to a birding club."

Amanda snapped out of her daze in time to answer. "I've never seen a bald eagle." She felt a sense of shame. So much for patriotism she thought.

"It's not as easy as going to the zoo, but I think the reward for making a small effort to see the real thing is life changing and liberating. You don't have to go far."

"Liberating?"

"It's nice to see the real thing, but you go to see 'wild' life. Not caged life. Live free or die."

Amanda wasn't comfortable with any word reminding her of death. She forced out an answer, "That sounds familiar."

"It's the state motto of New Hampshire. The question is – what is the definition of free?" She changed the subject to involve Haley. "When is the last time you came to the zoo, Haley?"

Haley hesitated for a moment. "I don't know."

"What do you remember about that trip?"

"It was a different zoo. The Seattle Zoo! We saw lots of animals. I remember the giraffes. The lions. The zebras. The wolves. The leopards."

"You have a good memory. Did you learn anything about the animals?" Ruth asked.

"I just remember the animals."

"When is the last time you went to a zoo, Amanda?"

"Good question. I don't remember. It's been a long time. Maybe when I was a young teenager? I think we're lucky, Ruth. I bet if we came during the summer, this place would be packed with screaming summer camp kids."

"Zoos seem to be a prerequisite on the summer camp itinerary. These are the same school trips to zoos that leave our children with a distorted view of wildlife."

Amanda nodded her head in solidarity. She looked at Haley.

"The main education is in viewing animals behind cages," Ruth added. "Zoos mislead us into believing that it is acceptable to keep animals for our entertainment, intentionally, or not. It doesn't matter if the animal was captive or wild born, the result is the same. Companionship is one thing, crass entertainment, quite another."

Amanda was coming to terms with these new perspectives. The zoo was a sanitized experience devoid of any danger. They were scripted, predictable routes. They preyed on our desire to collect things and a 'more is better' philosophy. A philosophy of quantity over quality.

"Where does that come from?" Amanda wondered out loud. She should know the answer, she was in marketing.

"I'm sorry, what did you say?" Ruth responded.

"Oh, nothing. I was just thinking out loud."

"Animals don't need saving, our souls do," Ruth blurted out.

Amanda stared out blankly, her mind absorbed with these new ways of looking at things. Haley was off in her own world, mumbling and singing to herself. She started to mark up a coloring book that she brought along.

It was mind candy we were being fed, not soul candy, Amanda thought to herself. It was knowledge, but not experience, not a 'real experience.'

"I have a couple more stories if you'd like to hear them."

"Go ahead, Ruth," Amanda answered in a somewhat dejected tone. "We need to get going soon."

"I'll make it quick. Thanks for listening to my inner angst. Maybe when my grandkids come I won't be so mad about being here."

"Sure."

"My husband and I once went to a game reserve near Port Elizabeth, South Africa. We and six or seven other people were being driven around in a covered safari jeep. What that means is that it is covered on top, in case of rain, but that it is open on the sides. Anyone can jump out the sides immediately if they choose to." Ruth took a deep breath.

"Continue," Amanda exclaimed.

"So, we were being driven around and seeing lots of various animals up close. I won't bore you with the kinds. At one point we drove up right next to a big, adult, male lion. It was literally about five or six feet away from me because it was on my side of the vehicle. If it wanted to, it could have leapt into the jeep and mauled one of us, it could have mauled me."

"Really?"

"I was protecting my husband because he was sitting next to me on the left."

Amanda laughed. She was speechless with her mouth wide open.

"Maybe it was recently fed, I don't know. But, this is the kind of experience and understanding of animals that one doesn't get at a zoo. It doesn't have to be a lion, it can be another kind, closer to home."

"Why didn't the lion attack? That's the impression I have of lions. They are just bloodthirsty."

"I want a pet lion," Haley shouted out as she continued coloring a drawing in her book.

"That's a question you'll have to answer, Amanda. I don't know. I just know it didn't."

"So, the only way to learn about the true nature of animals is to observe them in the wild?"

Ruth nodded. "It's impossible to respect and appreciate the full capabilities of wildlife while they are caged. Or when they are confined to less than their natural habitat. You don't have to jump very far to go from a lack of respect for animals, to a lack of respect for ourselves."

This last statement troubled Amanda. For the moment she responded by mentioning an observation she had made that people didn't seem to spend that much time looking at each exhibit. It was short attention span theater, like flicking channels on a television remote control.

Ruth noted that studies conducted at zoos found that most visitors spent less than a few minutes looking at each exhibit, and sometimes as little as ten seconds. "Children are the most impressionable. That is when most go for the first, and sometimes only time, until they are parents."

Amanda raised her hand. It was simple math Amanda realized. Many children had a short attention span, though she wondered about some adults too. If the typical zoo visit was two hours, you came out with precious little time to look at an animal when you divided the time of the visit by the number of animals in a typical zoo. Whether it was the majestic tiger, or a small group of otters, time was limited.

"Finish coloring that drawing, Haley. Then we'll go."

"Ok."

"There's an ongoing trend to make zoos more 'immersive' and 'naturalistic.' It's just a grander illusion."

"What's an immersive zoo, Ruth?"

"You can find examples online. They are zoos that try to trick us into believing that there are no barriers or cages. There are some near major cities. We visited one in Singapore. Paris, and New York City come to mind. There's one nearby, too. Though on my last visit, many years ago, it wasn't totally changed over."

"You mean. . .?"

"Yes, the Seattle Zoo."

"Oh. I remember going there a long, long, time ago." Amanda looked down on the ground in sadness.

"Some zoos are better, relatively speaking, in that they just show native animals to an area, not exotic species from far away lands. There's one nearby too if you want to see an example of that."

"But, it's still a zoo, right?"

"There's another category, a step up from most zoos, but still pretty much the same thing."

"What's that?"

"Free range parks. They are sometimes called open range zoos too. I can think of one in San Diego and one near us here. It's near Mount Rainier. Some are better than others. Beyond these, which are much smaller than native habitats usually, is just going out into wild nature."

Amanda looked at Haley and realized it was time to leave.

"Our zoos keep animals without talking about whether we should change our attitudes toward them, or nature itself, by and large. That would undermine their very existence over the long term."

Amanda wondered how many people visited zoos. Her later research would show that perhaps up to 10% of the global population visited a zoo every year. "Perhaps the zoo keepers have forgotten what it means to be wild," Amanda added stoically. "What do you think should happen to zoos?"

"I can see a future where zoos as we know them will just go out of business because nobody will want to support them anymore. Consumers will vote with their feet and pocketbooks. They will be closed and phased out while allowing expanded free range parks for native animals. Then, maybe someday, they are just enhanced nature reserves or something like that. All the people that work at zoos could work at these new parks. It would be a more fun job."

"Then watching animals being gawked at all day? Might that be a little drastic though? Closing all zoos."

"Zoos don't have to be like ball parks. The whole experience is just unnatural. We could teach our children about reserves and just take them to places where animals live naturally, like we talked about earlier."

"What do you think that would mean if all zoos, as we know them, were closed?"

Ruth was staring out into the distance. She ignored Amanda's question. She had gotten worked up and needed a break. Haley was fidgeting more now after having completed her meal. She was still marking up the coloring book they had brought along.

"What about the animals that are endangered?"

"Maybe they should go extinct. Let their extinction be a testament to how we live. Live free or die," she repeated. "To tell you the truth, Amanda, I'm not worried about saving animals at all."

"You're not?" This came as a complete surprise to Amanda. "What are you worried about?"

"It's not about animal rights or animal welfare. It doesn't matter if their self-aware or not. It's only about saving ourselves. Animals don't need our care, only respect."

Saving ourselves, Amanda repeated in her mind.

"I'll have to respectfully disagree with 'vegetarian animal lovers' too. There is nothing wrong with eating meat in moderation if it is raised humanely. These animal lovers often send the wrong message."

If Amanda thought she should know what this message was, the dots weren't connecting in her mind. "What message is that?"

"The same one that zoos give, that we need to save animals rather than respecting them. When we realize the implications of the most popular exhibit in most zoos, gorillas and chimpanzees, then we will understand."

A silence enveloped their table space as Amanda pondered this question. "And what is that?"

"The unconscious acceptance of our own imprisonment."

Ruth's mobile phone rang. "Just a second, Amanda." Ruth started talking on her phone.

As Ruth talked, Amanda thought about Ruth's answer about gorillas and chimpanzees, the closest relative to us genetically. She put it out of her mind for later. Instead, she wondered about her own separation from nature. Was there some way to live more harmoniously with our fellow creatures rather than being confrontational or trying to save them? How did we get to this point?

"It's my daughter. They are finally here. I have to go now. I have one more story that I always love to share with people. Would you like to hear it?"

"Sure, why not," Amanda answered in a somber tone of voice.

"A few years ago, my husband and I went to visit Japan. We read in our guidebook about a place called Nara. It's just outside of Kyoto. The people there co-exist with 1,200 wild deer. There's a large park set aside for them, but they can go anywhere they want to in the city."

"Over a thousand deer running around?"

"You can even buy and feed them deer biscuits. It was so fun! There's a ceremony every year to cut their antlers so that they don't hurt anyone. Traffic is kept at low speeds and many of the streets are pedestrian friendly."

"Can you imagine 1,200 deer running around Seattle, Haley?"

Haley looked up at Amanda and made a funny face while putting up her fingers next to her ears as if she was a deer.

"Cute, Haley."

Ruth smiled at Haley. "I think the way we treat and view animals reflects how we choose to live our own lives. Live free or die."

Amanda hesitated for a moment. "You wouldn't happen to know where the best place to see polar bears in the wild is, would you?"

"We've been to Churchill in the province of Manitoba, Canada."

"Where?"

"Sorry, I just assume people know about these obscure places we've traveled to. Churchill is a few hours flying north of Winnipeg. It's in the middle of Canada, by Hudson Bay."

They all got up and approached the zoo exit. "Thanks. I'll have to look on a map when I get home. Thanks for sharing your views and experiences. Haley is getting tired. I hope we can manage to get out of this circus." Another crowd of visitors was massed outside the gates.

"If you like, I can give you a business card of a woman who helps us with traveling. She knows a lot about where to go see animals in their natural homes."

"That would be great!"

Ruth rummaged through her purse and dug out a card. She paused to write some words on the back of the card before handing it over.

Wild polar bears - Churchill, Manitoba, Canada and Greenland, Ruth Williams

"One more thing. There's an alternative to Churchill with less tourists and photographers. Different landscapes and culture too. Mary can clue you in."

"Another place?"

"I wrote it down on the back of the card, we hope to go there one day. We're saving up for it. Maybe you can tell us about it, I wrote my number on the back too."

Amanda looked at the card then turned it over. "Greenland?"

"Beautiful icebergs I hear."

"Thanks for the referral."

"My pleasure. Good luck finding a wild polar bear. I'm going to go find a bathroom before I meet my grandkids! May this be the last time I ever come here." She turned around and disappeared around a corner.

"Shall we go?" Amanda asked Haley.

"I'm tired."

Amanda couldn't help but notice the large green and blue child strollers in the shape of turtles cruising over the paved walkways as they headed for the exit. It was as if more money was spent on landscaping and things for human comfort than the habitats themselves. They heard more chatter.

"Did you see the owl? – Guys come here, a caterpillar! – I want to see the sharks again. – Mom, I want to see a giraffe. – The only thing left is the ox and polar bear!"

The polar bears were just another attraction in a circus freak show, just another item to check off the list. Passing through the exit, Amanda glanced over at the entrance gate, a different set of kids were sitting and standing atop the polar bear sculpture. It was representative of man's disrespect for nature. They walked up the hill to the parking lot.

If zoos didn't exist she thought, maybe we would be more motivated to go out in the wild. At the very least, the discovery of nature must occur without large crowds she realized. Maybe it would have been better to bring Haley to the zoo right when they opened, but few people did that she suspected.

The zoo's thirty acres, around half a square mile, had made an impression on her, a decidedly negative one. They quickly walked past a stand where you could buy a t-shirt commemorating your visit. While Amanda left more depressed than when she arrived, there was a question hanging over her head. For animals born in a zoo, how would they know what a life in the wild was like if they had never experienced it before. She thought of herself and everyone she knew.

She also realized a lot of the descriptions at zoos must be wrong, it wasn't *wild*life at a zoo, it was just *zoo*life.

CHAPTER 6 – TRAVEL PLANS

"Wildlife Travel, this is Mary."

"Hi, Mary, this is Amanda. I met a client of yours at the Puget Sound Zoo recently, Ruth Williams. She gave me your business card as someone who could help me out."

"Hi, Amanda. Ruth, I know her well. She is quite a character. How can I help you?"

"Ruth told me you would be the best person to talk to if I wanted to see polar bears in the wild."

"She's right! What did Ruth tell you about it?" Mary responded in a self-assured voice.

"She told me about a place in Canada. She also mentioned Greenland of all places. I'm pretty clueless on where to go or how to get there. I don't have time nor the energy to sort through all the options on the Internet."

"It's a good thing you called me then, Amanda. I specialize in genuine animal encounters."

"Oh, good."

"It all depends on what kind of experience you are looking for. Are you able to come into my office in the next few days? It's a lot easier for me to plan the right trip for you if I get to know you. We can go over maps and possible schedules. Or I can just mail a packet of information to you."

"No, no. I can come in. Where are you located?"

"In Pioneer Square."

"I thought the address looked familiar. I've probably walked by your office."

"When is a good time for you?"

"I can come in over lunch this Thursday at 11:30 a.m."

"That would be perfect. Do you have my address?"

"Yes, I do. Ruth gave me your business card."

"Oh, right, you mentioned that. That was nice of her. Let's plan our meeting on Thursday at 11:30 a.m. then."

"Excellent."

It was Thursday in the blink of an eye to Amanda. That is how meaningless her days had become since her best friend departed this planet, even before that fateful day she was beginning to realize. One work day blended into another. Another client meeting, another presentation, and another advertising campaign for another ho-hum company in the mindless pursuit of selling more widgets to people who didn't really need them. Is this what her life had been reduced to?

Amanda walked through the pleasant and historical Pioneer Square district of Seattle and arrived at the address on the business card. She had walked by this spot before, but had never noticed anything special. Etched on the door window was the name of the business, Specialty Travel Group. She paused for a moment wondering if she was at the right place. Underneath the name were listed various specialties, Wildlife Travel among them. Amanda opened the door right on time at 11:30 a.m. A hanging bell rattled against the door window of the modest storefront.

There were several desks cluttered with office supplies, brochures, and computer screens. Hanging on the walls were small maps and colorful travel posters.

A middle aged woman looked up from staring at her computer screen. "You must be, Amanda."

"Hello."

"Did you find our place alright?"

"Yes, I did. I was confused for a moment when I didn't see the name of your business, on the door, then I read a little further down."

"Sorry, I forgot to mention that to you. I share this office space with a couple of other travel agents. We each specialize in a different aspect of travel. They're both out to lunch. Stacy specializes in volunteer travel and Margaret specializes in extreme sports. We all do corporate travel, too."

"Where were these pictures taken?" Amanda pointed toward a cluster of pictures on a wall behind one of the desks.

"Those over there are from Ecuador, Kenya, Colombia, Madagascar, and Tasmania."

While she had heard of the first three, Madagascar and Tasmania sounded foreign, almost otherworldly. She made a mental note to improve her geography.

"It's a natural combination of subjects we think. We find that people who travel are more likely to appreciate the world they live in, they often want to do something about it. You know, save the world kind of stuff. Let's not get ahead of ourselves though, let's go back to the conference room to talk. We have a lot of atlases and maps in there. Can I get you something to drink?"

"A cup of tea would be good."

"With sugar?"

"Yes, please."

"Milk?"

"Oh no! Who puts milk in tea?"

"It is normal in England, India, Sri Lanka, and Egypt, but not in China, Japan, Russia, Turkey, or here, of course."

"Shows you how much I know about the world," Amanda replied somewhat dejectedly. "It sounds like you've had that question before."

"Maybe this adventure to see polar bears will be just the first of many travels for you."

"Maybe."

"I'm sure it will be."

Amanda looked up at the walls as Mary left to get some tea. On one wall hung a large world map, but it was the other wall that attracted Amanda's attention. The wall was split into three columns, one for each agent's specialty. In the Extreme Sports column were people ice climbing, scuba diving, paragliding, parachuting, bungee jumping, hot air ballooning, kayaking, and hang gliding.

In stark contrast to all these sports was the column for Volunteer Travel. There were photos of people in various locations around the world. Some were with natives, some with animals, and the others were of people doing various activities in natural areas. Amanda couldn't identify the places. Some looked like they were taken in America, others looked foreign.

Would she ever have enough conviction and passion about something to volunteer in a faraway place? Or even some place local? Volunteering wasn't really in her blood, at the moment. What was her passion now? Was life just school, work, marriage, kids, and then retirement?

At the moment, she realized she'd been lied to about zoos. Or maybe, lie, was the wrong word, maybe she had just been blind to other possibilities for whatever reason. Or maybe it was just a lie she told herself at some point in life. Zoos were now a reality that she didn't want to be a part of.

Maybe she would one day end up volunteering for some nature or animal rights organization. But, it didn't feel right. She had to learn more.

The column for Wildlife Travel had photos of animals in various landscapes and poses. Bald eagles, colorful fish, sharks, grizzly bears, macaws, lions, elephants, zebras, butterflies, hump-back whales, killer whales, and of course, a polar bear.

Mary returned to the conference room with two cups of tea. "Here you go."

"This is quite a room here, lots of inspiration."

"We try. I put together a few different options for you. Before we talk about these options, maybe you can tell me a little bit about why you want to see a polar bear. I find I'm better able to recommend an experience when I know a little bit more about why people want to do certain things."

This was clearly not your typical travel agent, Amanda realized. Instead of sharing with Mary the whole story about how she ended up in this office, she decided on a few select moments.

Mary interrupted, sensing Amanda's hesitation. "It's okay if you would rather me just explain the options to you."

"I'm sorry, it's just that a lot of things have happened over the last few months."

"No, please don't be. How about I just show you some of the plans, and then you can tell me which option sounds better to you?"

"That sounds good."

"As you know, polar bears only live where it is very cold. They only live in the Arctic zone, generally speaking, near the North Pole. The first thing to know is that it is not inexpensive to visit them, relatively speaking, due to the remoteness and harsh conditions of the Arctic. Secondly, there are a few places where polar bears are found in higher concentrations."

"Not inexpensive?"

"Anywhere from a few thousand dollars for a shorter trip to six or seven thousand dollars for a longer trip. It can go higher if you want a luxury lodge. Is this ok?"

"Sounds pricey, but go ahead."

Mary began pointing at each place on a map that was laying out on the table. "The best places to find wild polar bears are in Northern Canada, Greenland, Svalbard - a group of islands north of Norway, some remote parts of Russia, and one particular place in Alaska. I am going to set aside Russia."

"What is wrong with Russia?"

"Russia is not really setup for Arctic tourism. The polar bear areas there aren't in the most accessible places."

"Ok, that leaves us with Canada, Greenland, Alaska, and what do you call it again?"

"S-v-a-l-b-a-r-d, Svalbard."

"Svalbard," Amanda repeated.

"Let's start with Alaska first, since it is relatively close to us."

"Ok."

"Polar bears are only found in the extreme far north of Alaska. The sea ice extent is receding further every year due to our warming planet, which impacts the polar bears there."

Amanda sensed bitterness in Mary's voice.

"If you think Alaska is more well known for grizzly bears, it is. There are a lot more grizzlies than polar bears. Ten times more."

"What a difference."

"There is only one reliable place in Alaska to view wild polar bears that is set-up for tourism of any kind, that I know of. It's in a place called Kaktovik, on Barter Island. You would fly through Anchorage or Fairbanks, and then to Deadhorse."

Mary pulled out a larger Alaska map and traced her hand across the cities to emphasize the remoteness.

"From there, a small plane would take you to this island that is located on the Northern coast of Alaska. September and October are the best times of year to go there. There are whale carcasses, remains, that wash up onshore or that are left there by native hunters. Polar bears will then congregate at the sight of the dead whale." She shared a photograph.

"Of course, chow time!" Amanda joked. "Deadhorse, what a name. That looks interesting, all these bears just eating."

"It's pretty much flat terrain there with mountains, the Brooks Range, in the distance. Very few tourists go there. Those that do, are for the polar bears. There are no economies of scale. A trip to Barter Island with two days of viewing time, by boat and car, and a night or two in Fairbanks or Anchorage, will be a little over three thousand dollars. There are only two places to stay there. The town has less than three hundred people. They are simple places to stay, not luxurious by any stretch of the imagination. I might even call one of them a little eccentric."

"Eccentric? That's ok, I think. It sounds and looks interesting, but very expensive for just a few days. What's the next place, Mary?"

"Let me next tell you about Northern Canada. This is the most famous place to see polar bears in the world. It is easy to get to as well. There are direct flights and a train option. It, along with Alaska, are the best choices if you don't have as much time to take off." Mary pulled out a map of Canada and focused Amanda's gaze on Northern Canada.

Making plans to see a polar bear in the wild was starting to get exciting.

"The most famous place is called Churchill, in the province of Manitoba. It lies just off the coast of West Hudson Bay. Every year, about 1,000 polar bears gather off the shores to wait for the ice to form again on Hudson Bay. After the bay starts to ice over, they venture out to hunt for seals."

Amanda's eyes lit up. "Did you say 1,000 polar bears?"

"Yes, not all at once though! It takes place over the course of a few months. The area encompassing the 1,000 bears is quite large too, you would only be visiting a small area. It's an annual migration and the Churchill area is the best place to see it. The prime time to go is from mid–October to mid-November."

"I never imagined there could be so many in one place, I thought they were more solitary."

"They usually are, but they are more social in the right circumstances. Many animals are like that."

"Can it get better than that?" Amanda asked sarcastically.

"That depends on what you are looking for."

"What do you mean?" Amanda asked, surprised at the answer.

"Do you just want to see a polar bear or do you want a profound, deep, perhaps, life changing experience?"

She thought about her recent trip to the Puget Sound Zoo. She was so excited to go see a few bears, but bitterly disappointed when she got there. "I remember when I heard about the polar bears at the zoo. I was looking forward to seeing them, but was so disappointed. The living conditions were terrible, kids were screaming everywhere, and people were gawking at them like lab specimens. Is there something you haven't told me yet about Churchill?"

"You won't get screaming kids and the bears are wild, not penned up, like at a zoo. Churchill is the most famous place for polar bears. They like to call themselves the World Polar Bear Capital. With popularity means people."

"How many people?" Amanda asked sternly.

"I've read that close to ten thousand people visit Churchill every year, mostly for the wildlife. A large percentage of that will be during the prime season to see polar bears. So, during the October and November months, in total, there will be thousands of tourists visiting."

"Is that a lot? Didn't you say there are around 1,000 bears though?"

"Yes, but in reality as a tourist, you will only have access to certain areas. There is a special area where the bears are most common and that only a couple of licensed companies go to."

"How many bears might I see in a day?"

"Anywhere from zero to twenty-five or so bears."

"Zero to twenty-five? That's a lot less than 1,000!"

"Timing is crucial, too. These are wild animals we're talking about. They aren't arranged conveniently for you to look at, like a zoo."

"Of course."

"A safer bet is the last week and a half of October and the first couple of weeks in November. Too early and you might not see any bears. I've never had any clients come back who say they haven't seen any. But they told me they heard stories about those who went too early and saw none."

"That would be disappointing to spend a bunch of money and see none."

"As you may know, weather conditions are changing. So definitely, do not expect to see near twenty-five bears. Safer expectations would be less than ten."

"Ok. A several week window though?"

"Yes. "

"Just like marketing campaigns and holiday seasons, I suppose. Precise timing." Amanda studied the map.

Mary continued, "You might appreciate the company and new friends you make. It all depends on what you are looking for. Don't be put off by the tourist numbers I told you about earlier. For the most part, the other tourists you will be around are those that are in the large all terrain vehicles with you. That will be anywhere from fifteen to thirty or so. You'll encounter other tourists at gift shops or at restaurants, but it's not a lot, by any stretch of the imagination. You'll see tourists in other vehicles, but they will be pretty far away usually."

Amanda looked at the map and wondered how seeing a polar bear up close would make her feel.

"I get a feeling you might want something more unique, more individualized. Some clients I have are like that, they want to be away from everyone else in near exclusion, literally."

"What you said sounds a lot better than the ratio at the zoo," Amanda interjected.

"It's not like your zoo experience."

Mary brought out several brochures. "Let me show you some pictures. The way most people see polar bears in Churchill is via these large all terrain vehicles. You can even sleep in some of them that are linked together like a hotel on wheels."

"They look big."

"They are very big." Mary turned the pages. "You share a vehicle with about fifteen to thirty people all day. You look like a young, energetic woman."

"That's why I'm in marketing."

"You need to ask yourself if you want to be aboard such a vehicle with other people, snapping pictures. The age range is going to skew older rather than younger."

Amanda took notice of a framed quote mounted on the wall beneath the large window separating the conference room from the desks. It read: It's not just the journey, stupid!

"What does that quote mean?"

"Oh that? The three of us got so sick of people saying it's not the destination, but the journey that is important. Hogwash, place matters too. Where you go and when you go is important, that's where the three of us come in."

Amanda gave more thought about these tundra all terrain vehicles. "All day in a truck like that with twenty people or whatever? It looks both claustrophobic and cool at the same time. Kind of intimidating. Do the bears really get that close? That would be awesome!"

"It is a fun experience, especially if the bears get up close to your vehicle, but they may not, which disappoints some. You might only see them really well from a farther distance with good binoculars or your camera zoom lens. There may not be snow. It is also a passive experience, not active. You might want something more physically engaging. Some clients like the 'thrill of the hunt' or want to be in more dramatic surroundings. I do often recommend Churchill for many of our clients, with the right expectations. I do have a different feeling about you."

"Most agents wouldn't bother to point this out."

"We try to be impartial here and just present things as they are. We want to find a solution that works for you. The company we use has comfy vehicles."

"Thank you for your honesty. You're very clear, Mary. I appreciate that. You're giving me the pros and cons and not just marketing spin."

Mary smiled. "There is 'safety' in numbers, if that is a concern of yours. There is also the excitement of seeing the bears with other like minded people. It is *the* place to go if you want to see a lot of bears, guaranteed, or as guaranteed as one can get with wild polar bears."

Amanda looked closely at the brochures.

"I should add that you are also looking down on the bears and are not on an 'eye to eye' level. Though you may certainly have an eye level encounter anywhere in town, at anytime of day. Again, it just depends on what you are looking for. We can also rent a car for you and you can explore on your own. But, you can't drive in certain areas where the tundra all terrain vehicles go."

"I want to be alone, but I don't think I want to drive around by myself. That sounds a little scary. I prefer a guided tour." Amanda frowned. "To tell you the truth, I don't really want to be with any other tourists at this moment, or at most a few."

"There are also small luxury lodges along the shores of Hudson Bay. They are geared more toward couples and families though. They aren't necessarily ideal for single travelers, in my opinion, but take a look for yourself. You will have eye level encounters at these lodges. Here are the brochures for those places."

Amanda sat back in her chair and sighed. "What about Greenland? It's weird, just saying it."

"What do you know about Greenland?"

"I don't know anything about Greenland. My impression is that it is just a big piece of ice, it sounds exotic."

"You are right about that." Mary moved aside the other brochures and brought out a map of Greenland. "Unless you've been to Antarctica, or certain places in the far north of Canada, much further north than Churchill, Greenland is unlike anywhere you have ever been."

"Not me."

"This trip can be more expensive and will require more time than if you were to go to Churchill or Alaska. A trip to Churchill or Alaska can be done in less than a week. Greenland will require two to three weeks to do it properly."

"I have enough vacation time saved up, go ahead."

"Greenland is part of the Kingdom of Denmark. You will have to fly through Copenhagen or Reykjavik, Iceland to get there. There are some charter flights from Canada to Greenland, but they only operate in the summer. Seeing a polar bear in Greenland isn't quite as easy as in Churchill, where you are almost guaranteed to see them if you're there at the right time. Because it isn't quite as easy, if you choose to go to Greenland to see a polar bear, I am almost sure that you will be the only person. No tourist atmosphere there."

Flashbacks to the zoo and the comment that Ruth had made entered Amanda's mind. Specifically, that the extra effort to see wild animals was worth it. "The only person?"

"Of course, you will have a guide. I work with an English speaking Danish man. He's a wildlife biologist too, so he knows his stuff. He doesn't charge too much, relatively speaking, for this trip, because he just enjoys it up there. If he can cover his costs, he's happy. Instead of sitting in a nice tundra all terrain vehicle in Churchill, relaxing at a luxury lodge, or viewing bears devouring a whale carcass, you will have to really search hard for your polar bear."

"You mean, I might have to actually make an effort instead of it being handed on a silver platter to me?"

"Exactly. Polar bears roam across a wide range so it won't be easy. He works with the native Inuit if necessary. They know where to go, that should increase the odds. You would travel by dog sled and small boat perhaps, to find a bear. You will be traveling much further north than if you were to go to Churchill or Alaska."

"By dog sled? That sounds fun and adventurous. How far north?"

"Polar bears in Greenland live on both coasts. Northeast Greenland is not very accessible. I'm working on a Southeast Greenland trip, but I only have the West Greenland trip ready. In the West, you have to go to the northwest of Greenland, near a place called Melville Bay." Mary showed Amanda on another map she pulled out from a small pile.

"That looks remote, do people really live up there?"

"The further north you go, the less people there are. No one lives in the interior of Greenland, just occasional visiting scientists during the summers. Most people live in Southwest Greenland where it is warmer. Very few live in the places you would go. I'm talking about in the hundreds, more or less. In some cases, mere dozens."

"Mere dozens?"

"So you see, Churchill, or near Churchill in the lodges off Hudson Bay, is the choice for many of my clients. Some have gone to Alaska and some to Norway."

"Mere dozens. That's incredible. How would I even get to Greenland? Is it safe?"

"You fly into a town called Kangerlussuaq, an old US military base. From there you will fly to Ilulissat, a major tourist town in Greenland, relatively speaking. From there you will fly to Qaanaaq. You would fly a modern Airbus to get to Greenland from Denmark, then smaller prop planes within Greenland. All flights are with Greenland Airways. You can also consider flying to Greenland through Iceland versus Denmark. Do you have a preference?"

"Whoa!" Amanda took a deep breath. "Greenland Airways, it just sounds funny saying that."

"Yeah, I've heard that before. Do you have a preference for Iceland or Denmark as your gateway city?"

"Ummm. . ., Denmark sounds more interesting to me than Iceland."

"Ok, noted. Another highlight if you choose to go to Greenland, is a stop in Ilulissat, the premier spot in the Arctic to see beautifully sculpted towering icebergs."

"Icebergs?"

"They come from the ice sheet that sits on Greenland. The glacier in that area is the most productive in that region I think. It calves icebergs that sit out of the water a couple of hundred of feet tall, it is quite a sight from the pictures." She showed Amanda a photograph of a ship with an iceberg as a background.

"Cool," Amanda answered, while immediately realizing the irony of her words.

"This trip isn't for the weak or non-adventurous with a capital A. You will have to survive outside in winter time temperatures approaching -10° Fahrenheit, colder with wind chill. All while dog sledging for around one week straight. You will have supplies, but will also live off the land. You need to be prepared to give up some of the creature comforts you are used to." She paused. "Most of them."

"Dog sledging? What is that?"

"It is similar to dog sledding, but they use a different term there. The dogs don't run in two single files, but in a fan shape."

"How many dogs are there?"

"About ten to fifteen."

"Do you have any pictures?"

Mary rummaged through the file folder on the desk and pulled out a picture and trip plan.

"Interesting. Did you say, one week of dog sledging? Are you crazy?"

They both laughed.

"You will camp out on the ice. It is quite warm sleeping in the tents he provides from what I understand. You will carry food and supplies with you. It is about as extreme as an adventure that you will ever find."

"So, there is the easy way and the not so easy way."

"I also want to make clear that I can't guarantee a polar bear sighting in Greenland. But, as they say, half the fun is getting there."

"No guarantees?"

"Think of it this way, it will just make it that much sweeter when you do find one. The probability is high, but again, not guaranteed. If for some reason you don't see a polar bear, you could still go to Churchill, where the probability is higher for less effort. Either way, I don't think you will ever look at anything the same way again if you go."

"Have you done this before?"

"Huh?"

"Have you sent anyone else on this trip before?"

"A middle aged man went a couple of years ago, he was looking for something special. That is how I made the contacts there to offer you this. Haven't had any takers since."

"What did he have to say about the trip?"

"When he returned, he quit his job, traveled for awhile, and then made a career change when he came back."

"What does he do now?"

"He was a computer guy, but now he runs a small B&B with his family."

"That's quite a change!"

"Indeed."

Amanda took a deep breath and opened up further. "Last year, my best friend from childhood was killed in a car accident, it really affected me. We shared the same birthday. I haven't been the same, work seems so meaningless. Everyday since then has just seemed like a blur, it's all been blending into each other. I'm not sure where my life is going. My favorite stuffed animal as a child was a large polar bear, it helped me through my parents' divorce. To make a long story short, for some reason I felt as if I needed to see a live polar bear in person. When I went to the Puget Sound Zoo, I was very disappointed. Now, I'm here talking to you." Amanda's eyes watered up.

"Thanks for sharing that, Amanda. I'm sorry to hear about your loss. Another factor is, when do you want to go?"

"As soon as possible."

"For Churchill or Alaska, you'll have to wait until September, October, or November. Although, you can potentially see polar bears in the summer near Churchill, too. No snow or cold temperatures though."

"That seems too far away, Mary. I need to go somewhere now."

"You can probably guess which trip I would recommend to take then. The best time for Greenland is March, early April, at the latest."

"What about that other place? Svalbard?"

"Svalbard has what many would call, incredible and spectacular mountain scenery, like Greenland, maybe nicer. There are several options there that I can offer. By ship, snowmobile, or dog sled. Here are some photographs. Here is the map of Svalbard."

"Tell me more, it looks very beautiful."

"One option is to be on a cruise ship for a good portion of the time. A polar bear sighting isn't guaranteed either, but some clients don't mind because they enjoy being on cruise ships with land excursions and spectacular scenery. These cruise ships sail only in the summer, June, July, or August. Some routes offer a higher probability than others of spotting a polar bear. If you see a bear, it could be far away and you will be looking down on it from the ship. Again, good binoculars and a good zoom camera are important. The ships do land excursions. You might get a better encounter that way."

Amanda smiled as best as she could. "What about the snowmobile tour?"

"A snowmobile tour would be a single or multi-day adventure leaving from Longyearbyen, probably heading east where it is colder with more ice. Instead of dog power, you cover a lot of ground by snowmobile. Due to the rules and regulations there, you may not get as close to a polar bear as you may like. I've had only good reports from the clients I have sent there though. These snowmobile tours are available from February to early May."

Amanda thought for a moment. "I think I like the idea of dog sledding or dog sledging better than a loud snowmobile. Maybe I could do this snowmobile tour another time though, it sounds interesting." Amanda looked around the room, wondering what to do. A cruise sounded nice too, just not something she wanted to do alone. "Dog sledding in Svalbard, what about that?"

"Yes, that is possible. There are multi-day adventures available. They are not as 'rough' as the trip in Greenland would be. I haven't had any clients do this yet, so I don't have any first hand reports. From what I've read, I recommend it. You wouldn't be living off the land as you would in Greenland. It is also less of a cultural experience, as sledding is not native to Svalbard. There is a longer history of human settlement in Greenland versus Svalbard. Thousands of years, compared to hundreds of years."

"I'd like to learn more about another culture. Score a point for Greenland."

"Would you like me to summarize all the options now, Amanda?"

"Yes, please. I need to get back to work."

"To summarize, you can see a wild polar bear by various means. I can only 'almost guarantee' a sighting at Churchill. Alaska has a high probability too. All options except Greenland involve being with other travelers that may or may not be very agreeable to you, from what you are telling me. At least for this moment in your life." Mary paused to drink some tea.

Amanda let out another deep breath.

"The scenery is nicer in Svalbard and Greenland than it is in Alaska or Canada. Churchill is mostly flat. Alaska is flat with mountains in the distance. If you want to do it alone, it sounds like Greenland is the right place for you, but you have to be prepared to do what many might consider extreme, to just see a polar bear. If you factor in the immediacy with which you want to see a real polar bear, Greenland and Svalbard are your best options."

"I don't think I can wait. Is there anything else I should know?"

"There are some additional details in this folder that you can have, but I will summarize a few of the details. First, the kinds of bears you may see in each area will be different too."

"What do you mean, kinds of bears?"

"In Churchill, the bears are what I would call, lazy bears. They are waiting to go hunting. They haven't eaten much at all, if anything, in awhile, so they are rather lethargic. They are resting up. But because there are more of them in a relatively small area, sometimes they brawl."

"Like when they're on their hind legs sparring? I have a photo of two bears doing that on my calendar."

"Yes, like that."

"That would be cool to see."

"In Svalbard and Greenland, the bears will be hunting there. So, they are more active and independent."

"Active is good."

"Another difference between places is the ratio of males to females, and whether there are cubs."

"Cubs are good."

"In Churchill, you are more likely to see male bears. Pregnant females are in the nearby Wapusk National Park to the east, and in an area about forty miles south of Churchill. For the most part, they are inaccessible. Besides, the mommies to be are in their dens from October to January. They come out in February. So, don't expect to see a mother with her newly born cubs if you go to Churchill in the prime tourist season."

"Interesting."

"The last difference between each place is whether it is an active or a passive search. An active or a passive vacation."

"You mentioned that earlier. Oh, no, you were talking about the bears being more or less active. Now, you are talking about the trip itself?"

"Yes, Amanda. In Alaska or Churchill you are being driven around to where the bears are, it's a passive activity. If you take a cruise ship in Svalbard, you are just one passenger of many. If you rent a car in Churchill, go sledging in Greenland, or take a snowmobile or dog sled tour in Svalbard, you are more engaged. In Greenland, you will have to live off the land."

"So, I need to choose between an active or passive experience?"

"Yes."

"Sometimes I feel I am searching for something, but I just don't know what."

"Doing something different and solitude can help. Some of my clients want to go to a place with almost zero tourism, if not zero. They want to get away from it all. You'd think it would be difficult in this day and age, but it really isn't."

"I will think about what you have said, Mary."

"Don't forget to lower your expectations from what you see in books or documentaries. The photographers have often spent a lot of time just getting a few prime photos. Or a short documentary may have taken months, maybe years, of being on-site and following a few polar bears around. They may have access to places that regular tourists don't have."

"Yeah, I understand."

"Here is the information and pricing on the options we just discussed. Take it home, think about it, and get back to me. If you decide to go to Greenland, you'll have to make a decision soon, as the best time to go for what I described is in a month. Svalbard, you have a little more time. If you decide on Churchill, you can wait a little longer as the season of migration is during October and November. Churchill is very popular and you should tell me as soon as possible so I can reserve a spot for you. Some hotels and time slots there are getting close to being sold out."

Amanda looked at the Greenland itinerary.

Day 1 and 2:
– Seattle to Copenhagen, Denmark flight, arrival next day, overnight in Copenhagen

Day 3:
– Copenhagen to Kangerlussuaq, Greenland flight
– Kangerlussuaq to Ilulissat flight
– Afternoon free to explore Ilulissat, see icebergs
– Overnight hotel

Day 4:
– Ilulissat to Qaanaaq via Upernavik flight
– Overnight hotel

Day 5:
– Helicopter one-way – Qaanaaq to Savissivik

Day 5-12:
– Dog sledge & small boat ride to search for polar bears near Melville Bay. Wilderness tent camping, hunter's hut, and homestay in Savissivik.

Day 13:
– Helicopter one-way – Savissivik to Qaanaaq
– Overnight hotel

Day 14:
– Qaanaaq to Ilulissat via Upernavik flight
– Overnight hotel

Day 15:
– Ilulissat to Kangerlussuaq flight
– Kangerlussuaq to Copenhagen flight
– Copenhagen to Seattle flight

"A helicopter ride?"

"I forgot to mention that, a little bonus excitement. The rides are subsidized by the government there, it doesn't cost much to include them."

"I've never been on a helicopter before. It doesn't sound exciting enough," Amanda replied sarcastically.

"I've never been," Mary replied. It looks fun.

Amanda looked at a summary sheet of all the places. She thought out loud. "Greenland costs more, but it's a better value per day. Alaska and Churchill are shorter trips, but I feel that a longer trip would be better if I want a real deep change to occur. I could stay closer to home, but something about going farther away has its appeal. I don't want to be on an overly organized tour. Svalbard sounds and looks like it could be the place, but I don't want to do a cruise or a snowmobile. I guess I could dog sled in Svalbard, but Greenland just sounds more different and exotic. Whatever I choose, I am going to have to spend at least several thousand dollars or more?"

"Depending on the place, most meals are included too. The flight costs add up fast anytime you fly this far north, there just aren't the same economies of scale and competition. Getting to Svalbard is relatively cheap, but Norway is just expensive compared to almost every other country. Everything costs more in the Arctic. The Greenland trip is the best value per day. The Greenland trip is a better value because you would be traveling off-season. Most tourists go to Greenland in the summer. If you have any air miles, we can make the trip cheaper."

"I doubt I have enough air miles, I haven't been very good at collecting them. I know you mentioned it earlier, but I didn't think it would be so expensive."

"If you had air miles, some of these trips could be significantly cheaper. One of the benefits of using me as your travel agent, is that I can show you how to earn and maximize miles in the future. We can also help your company. We do corporate travel, too."

"I think I will mention you to someone in our office, Mary. You are very thorough."

"Traveling doesn't have to be expensive, but the Arctic is, comparatively speaking. I believe there are times and places where if you spend too much, you will miss the whole essence of the travel experience. But if you spend too little in other places, you might miss the bigger picture or finer details. All three of us make a living with our expertise in matching people like you, to the method and place. Did you have an original budget in mind?"

"No, but I guess I just wasn't thinking of spending so much money."

"Too bad your favorite stuffed animal wasn't an elephant, lion, or tiger. They would be much cheaper to see in the wild."

Amanda giggled.

"Price is a valid concern, Amanda. Maybe a better way to think about this is to ask yourself - how much would I spend to change my life in a deep way? People spend extra money on car options or home additions. I had a client come in one time and state that they just took out a home equity loan for twenty thousand dollars to remodel their kitchen and ten thousand dollars to re-landscape their backyard. And yet, they decided that they couldn't go on a very nice exotic trip I had planned for them because it was two thousand dollars more than what they wanted to spend. It was a very good price for what they wanted to do. Yet, they also drove a late model SUV with all the trimmings. How long does the thrill or benefit of the things we purchase last? Sorry, I'm getting too philosophy minded on you."

Amanda thought about her new car. She knew countless co-workers who got a new car every few years. "No, carry on."

"Ok. Are they just convenience upgrades? Vanity? Ego? How much would you spend to change your heart? Your mind? I think it is a question of priorities. Even though a vacation or experience occurs in a more finite time period and isn't a 'material object' to own or show off, how much are defining experiences worth? It is subjective to be sure, even the material things we buy are too. Why do people spend so much extra money for a little horse and polo player on a shirt, or certain brand names on a purse, when the equivalent is many multiples less?"

"You're good, Mary."

Mary smiled. "Of course, you don't have to spend a lot of money, Amanda, or even anything, to have a life changing experience. . . but you want to see a wild polar bear."

When her parents' divorced, times were tighter financially for Amanda and her mother, despite the fact that her father usually made alimony payments on time. Her mother never got married again. She had worked hard in school to succeed financially and materially. She was proud of where she was today. But, these weren't the only measures on Amanda's mind today, nor for even the past few months, and perhaps even before Stephanie's untimely passing.

"Go home and give it some thought. Let me know as soon as possible," Mary replied, without a hint of worry over Amanda's inner turmoil.

"I'll think about it. Thank you, Mary, you have been so helpful."

"One more thing, do you have a passport?"

"No."

"You'll need one for all these places except Alaska, of course." Mary rummaged through a nearby cabinet and pulled out a piece of paper. "Here are instructions on getting one. They have a rush service too."

Amanda glanced at the application and wondered why she never had a passport before.

"How can I reach you?"

Amanda handed over her business card, it was her very identity. A feeling was getting stronger though, that she wasn't being loyal to someone much more important – herself.

"Pleased to have met, Ms. Foster. What is Northwest Marketing Associates?"

"We convince people to convince themselves that they need things that they don't really need."

"Excuse me?"

Amanda covered her mouth in embarrassment, wondering what secrets she had just spilled out. "I'm just an advertising account manager. Please forget whatever I said."

With that, Amanda left and walked back toward her car, all the while thinking of Mary's words and her own Freudian slip. But perhaps the better question was, why did she do what she did? Was what she did tantamount to trickery? Acceptable lying? What was lying anyway? Why did we think one thing and do another? Why did we say one thing and do another? Wasn't that a recipe for unhappiness?

She passed by the shop front of a clothing store, the mannequins were dressed up in the latest season's fashions. Rather than look through the glass and imagine herself wearing those clothes as if superimposed on her reflection, she touched her own image. She didn't recognize the woman in the mirror. Who was she?

Looking up at the second floor of the building, the bright lights of a health club beckoned. People were walking and running on treadmills, like lab rats. Walking more briskly back to her car, she passed by a self-improvement nutrition center and a stock ticker glowing through the window of a brokerage office.

They all reminded her of things she had been neglecting, due to pressure from work and the grief she was still suffering from. She was feeling out of shape from lack of exercise, she wasn't eating well, and she wasn't managing her finances. She needed a spark.

A small city church came into view as she rounded a corner. A co-worker who knew about the grief she was going through invited Amanda to her congregation. Perhaps she should take her up on that offer, maybe that's what she needed. Maybe she needed to get closer to God, whoever that was.

The few times she had gone as a child to church with her mother, weren't particularly positive. Maybe if she had gone to church to begin with – all would be right in her life and none of this would have happened. She would love her job, Stephanie would be alive, and she would be well on her way to marriage. Or maybe she would already be married to the 'love of her life.'

Then she began to wonder about something more basic. Could she get the time off on such short notice? Business was picking up again after the holiday lull and plans were afoot for the next series of marketing campaigns. New campaigns and new clients.

Maybe she would get fired if she demanded time off for a vacation now, maybe that would be a blessing. After all, she was getting tired of the drama kings, drama queens, and self-anointed wonder children running around at work some days. How did brand names become so ingrained in our psyche?

She weighed the pros and cons. Would she miss out on a larger bonus? A future promotion? Career first was her mantra, though she did not remember when this became so. Maybe she should just stop questioning things and just accept these ups and downs of life. She could fool herself again, but she felt a sense of mortality that she had never felt before.

As she approached her set of wheels, she noticed the car parked in front of her new car and felt a sense of pride. It was an older car, almost identical to the car she drove before she 'made it' and could afford a nicer sedan. Her modern day chariot was not just an entry level one though, it was at the mid-level. What was this obsession we had with status? Shouldn't she know? That was her job, after all. How much did she really know about her own field? About how it affected her.

She wondered if a trip like this was just a waste of money. Perhaps time did heal all wounds as the saying went. Instead of wasting money on this trip, she could go on a shopping spree, buy some perfume and a new designer purse. And she could also work even harder, win more business, and get an even bigger mid year bonus. She could pay down her mortgage sooner. Yeah, then she would be happy, no mortgage. You could buy happiness with stuff and material possessions. Maybe she should stop being choosy in her love life. She could try harder to snag the right man.

She knew it wasn't true.

If she wasn't happy now, she wouldn't be later. Time only healed wounds if you changed your life within that time. And money could buy happiness, but only if you used it wisely. And there was a point of diminishing returns. And if you weren't happy in your own skin by yourself, a relationship wouldn't help. Maybe temporarily, but not over the long term.

Maybe a trip to Greenland was what she needed, a spiritual quest for her soul. The other options sounded easy, too easy. Sometimes the 'dirt' road was the one to take. Getting back into her car, she pulled out her small journal and began to write.

How much is a life changing experience worth? I know I need to make a change in my life soon. I need to put myself in a new direction. I've worked so many hours, got pay raises, and for what?

All the money is no good if you don't like what you do anymore or if you're not content, at peace, deep down inside. It is like a devil's bargain, some fancy toys and creature comforts in exchange for your soul. How many times did I put off going out with Stephanie because I was too busy? How many times have I ignored my deep desires? Have I been too busy making money or impressing the big bosses, or have I been too busy trying to impress myself? I hope I make the right decision.

Amanda closed her journal, she was going to put her year end bonus to good use. It was time to follow her instincts for this decision. She wasn't fifteen minutes out of the Wildlife Travel office and she had already made up her mind.

CHAPTER 7 – GREENLAND BOUND

Spring in Seattle, the time when long days of gray only skies are beginning to end. Amanda wasn't waiting around to enjoy the spring, nor for summer to arrive, she was getting ready to go to Greenland.

It was only a few days earlier that she had received her passport. Amanda felt like she was joining a special club, though she did not like her 'mug-shot' at all. Because it was her first time applying for a passport, she had to do it in person. She had to wait in line that day. Another woman in the line told her that until recently, due to the requirement of a passport for travel to Canada and Mexico, only a little more than 20% of American citizens had a passport, which were good for ten years. The woman wondered why more Americans didn't want to see the world for themselves, considering that so much of what we bought, ate, and used, was produced and made somewhere else. Nevermind all the beautiful sights and cultures to explore.

Whatever the answer, Amanda was about to find out first hand what this world looked like, with her own eyes, not the filter of a television reporter, travel writer, newspaper columnist, documentary editor, or a book author. What good was freedom for if you didn't leave the boundaries of your own country or cozy area? Amanda wondered why she hadn't done this sooner.

Amanda's remarks on having been to Canada made other people in line laugh, as she added that it didn't count as another country when you lived so close to the border in a northern state. If you lived in the southern part of the USA and visited Canada, ok, it was another country.

Greenland, being one of the least understood and touristed places in the world, would give Amanda a lot to boast about in the international travel club. Amanda knew she had always been open to new ideas, it just didn't occur for her to look beyond the US borders and know it first hand. Maybe she had been a little fearful too, but now the door of real world experience was opening.

The telephone looked more prominent as she ran around her home taking care of final details. She could pick it up and pretend she was sick. Then do a last minute cancellation and get most of her money back from the travel insurance.

"Shut up, Amanda," she blurted out to herself.

The days on her bear calendar were littered with checkmarks as she had counted down the days left before her trip.

Greenland wasn't the first place that came to mind when she told her friends and co-workers about her plans to take a vacation. Ever since that fateful day at the zoo, Amanda decided that she must see a polar bear in the wild, and now, to see it without feeling like she was gawking at it or while taking gratuitous photos of the bears all the time. She gave herself two weeks to see one. It was like going to an important meeting or meeting someone on a first date. Hopefully, he or she, a male or female polar bear, would show up.

She checked her backpack, no extra shoes on this trip. She was only bringing one pair, the waterproof boots on her two feet. The rest of her twenty-something odd pairs would be left at home. For a moment she recalled the research from a marketing magazine that said she fell smack dab in the American woman average of owning fifteen to twenty-five pairs of shoes. Men owned an average of six to ten pairs, and twice as much money was spent on children's shoes than school books.

While she had traveled for work, this was going to be her longest trip. Pack light was Mary's advice. She squeezed her bag tight and looked around her home and wondered just how much of the stuff that she had accumulated was really necessary in life.

As she finished packing her bags, it occurred to her that she hadn't yet bought a travel guidebook for either Denmark or Greenland. All she had were a few pages from Mary on general travel tips. In her rush to hastily finish up and hand off projects at work, she had forgotten. The phone rang and she put it out of her mind.

"Hi, Amanda, it's Jack."

"You just caught me before I was about to head off to the airport."

"I'm glad I caught you in time, Haley wants to talk to you."

"Put her on."

"Amanda!" Haley announced excitedly.

"Hi, Haley!"

"Are you going to Greenland today?"

"Yes."

"Will you see polar bears there?"

"I sure hope so."

"My dad says it's really cold there."

"I'm packing all my warmest clothes. Brrrr."

"Who are you going with?"

"I'm going by myself."

"Take me! Take me!" Haley's voice erupted in a whirlwind of enthusiasm. "You can't go alone."

"What? You're silly."

"No, you can't go alone. Take me!"

"Maybe next time, Haley, I have to go on this trip alone."

"You can't go alone. Take your Polar Bear."

Amanda wasn't quite sure how to respond to this.

"He might want to see some of his friends."

Haley had a vivid imagination, it reminded Amanda of when she was younger. She paused, unsure of how to answer still.

"Did you ask him if he wants to go? My tiger and panda tell me that they get lonely sometimes as they are far away from home. You can't go alone."

"How am I going to. . ."

"You can't go alone," she shrieked.

She gave in. "Ok, ok, ok, I'll bring him." She stopped, wondering what she had just agreed to.

"I'm sure you'll both have a fun and happy time. My dad says maybe I can go with one of my stuffed animals sometime to China."

"Yea, when you get older."

"Don't forget to take lots of pictures. I want to see pictures of you and Polar Bear together."

"Right." Now, she really had to take him. A lying god-mother she was not going to be. There had already been enough lying, to herself, and other people to her, or themselves. If this trip was a journey of self-discovery, she didn't want it to start on a lie.

At the very least, her stuffed bear was low maintenance. Perhaps he would be a worthy traveling companion who never talked back. He was a familiar comforting face, that was for sure. As for how to carry him around, that was another matter entirely.

"My dad wants to talk to you. Bye."

"Thanks, Haley."

Jack came on the line.

"Kids are always coming up with crazy ideas."

Amanda half-chuckled, realizing that Jack didn't think she would actually take Haley seriously.

"Amanda, can you spare a few moments?"

"What's wrong?"

His demeanor changed and he started weeping.

"What's wrong?"

"I did something very wrong, Amanda." His voice cracked. "She'll never, she'll never be here to forgive me. Will you forgive me?"

"Jack, what's wrong? Forgive you for what?"

"I'm sorry. So sorry. Please forgive me."

Amanda felt a lump in her throat.

"I had an affair, Amanda. I had an affair with another woman, Amanda, a co-worker. I ended it shortly before the accident. I was so ashamed, I couldn't tell her." He wailed even louder.

She thought back to her last lunch with Stephanie and the conversation about the seven year itch.

"I miss her so much," he wailed. "I think she knew somehow. Maybe it distracted her. . ."

"Don't be so hard on yourself." His voice was starting to sound very annoying.

"As her best friend and Haley's godmother, will you forgive me?"

"Don't be so hard on yourself," she repeated. She felt a feeling of rage surge inside her. She was going on a vacation, she didn't need this. She controlled her urge to be angry. "Give it some time, Jack, it will all work out. We can talk more when I get back."

Jack regained his composure, though his crying was still evident. His voice changed. "I'll let you get going. Good luck and be safe."

What was Haley thinking? Amanda hung up the phone. She turned on the stereo loudly. Jack's frail and weak voice was echoing in her mind, it needed to be purged. She needed an upper now, not a downer. For all the drama, she was no longer going alone to Greenland.

While she now had a furry companion, she realized again that she had never given a second thought to asking her estranged boyfriend, Chip, to go with her. Some things had to be done alone. He accepted her explanation.

Estranged boyfriend, even that description might be a little strong. He was still interested, but they hadn't gone out in quite a while except for a cup of coffee and a movie. He was a good man and he was patient with what Amanda was going through, but he lacked a sense of excitement. While he had ambition, it didn't go beyond his own work arena. He was right for someone, just not her. She needed something more or maybe just someone different. It wasn't clear what kind of man that might be or where she might ever find him.

Rather than dwell on relationships, an old college classmate came to mind. A girl that came to mind now and again. They were never more than semi-good college classmates, but the life of this other girl intrigued her for a time. After high school this girl had taken a year off to go traveling around the world before starting college. To Australia, Thailand, Turkey, Egypt, South Africa, France, Spain and who knows where else. It sounded utterly irresponsible and 'delicious' at the same time. It was common in some English countries she recalled now. It was called a 'gap year,' if she wasn't mistaken.

This girl even took off to go travel during college summers. Internships, not for this girl. This girl had been bitten by the travel bug and she was always sharing stories with Amanda during the school year. She worked part-time jobs and saved up for her trips. She knew how to travel cheaply. Amanda wondered if they would be friends now if they met today.

It was time to go. Under a litany of books and paperwork on her kitchen table were buried two vital documents, her airline tickets and passport. They were covered up by paper from her last few late night work cram sessions. She clutched the documents like missing lottery tickets in excitement.

As she made a final check of her home, she gazed for a moment at the mobile phone and her notebook computer on the kitchen table. These were electronic tools that had become a part of her everyday existence. It seemed as if she had been tethered to them for nearly everyday of her life. She took a deep breath, left them behind, and headed out the door.

They were time savers, but like many things in life, too much of a good thing was a bad thing she realized. Like alcohol, coffee, fast food, soda, or prescription drugs, it was 'all good' unless you overdosed or became addicted. Or became dependent on them.

From humble assistants, they had become electronic leashes, digital leashes for the rat race. The race to nowhere in both work and personal arenas. The maintenance of them had in some places become a full time endeavor themselves. If these gadgets were supposed to make our lives easier, why did she seem to be more rushed in life?

Every day there seemed to be another computer virus, more email then humanly possible to read, and another upgrade to learn about and install. There were more intrusive phone calls from co-workers and more text messages. She was tired of chasing her own tail. At least for this trip, she would be free of these personalized digital leashes.

At the airport parking garage, she couldn't help but notice the car she was parked next to, a shiny new SUV. Her reflection gleamed in the tinted glass. She wondered again if she was making a mistake, spending all this money on a two week vacation. She turned away, reminding herself of the decision she had already made. She would save money in other ways later.

Airport terminals largely appeared to Amanda as an evil maze that required navigation while traveling to visit clients, the feeling was distinctly different this time. She was going on an adventure, not an ordinary vacation. This adventure had a mission and a game plan.

The all too familiar Seattle airport was beginning to look not like an evil maze, but as a transitory marker in time. A point from which she shed her old skin and acquired a new one. The old skin was left behind at the airport, like a snake, as a new set of experiences would create a fresh one.

Before she could acquire a new skin though, she would have to get over feeling a little foolish for carrying around a large stuffed polar bear. She was no child, but a grown woman. A kid at heart, she reminded herself. She dismissed the smiles and chuckles of other travelers and airport employees who had been gazing at her stuffed polar bear, with her own smile. She spotted her airline counter and walked up to an open spot.

A woman came out from the backroom. "How can I help you?"

"I would like to check in for my flight to Copenhagen, here is my itinerary. I'm going to Greenland."

"May I see your passport?"

Amanda handed over her passport, it was devoid of any stamps. It was like announcing to the world you were a virgin, a travel virgin.

"Would you prefer a window or an aisle seat?"

"Aisle seat, please. How full is the flight?"

"There is plenty of room."

"Can you make sure there is no one sitting next to me? I would prefer not to put my stuffed bear in the overhead compartment." Amanda picked up her stuffed animal that was hiding under the counter. She realized he probably wouldn't even fit.

The agent smiled. "Nice bear. Yes, of course. That's one big bear. Shouldn't be a problem. I'll make sure you have an open seat and row. You are going to make a kid somewhere very happy." The agent winked at Amanda.

Caught off guard for a moment, Amanda stood speechless. "Yes, yes, of course," she stammered.

"Do you have any bags to check?"

"Just one."

The agent tagged it. "You will need to pickup your bag in Copenhagen due to the overnight layover. Your nonstop flight from Seattle to Copenhagen departs at 7:00 p.m., arriving at

1:30 p.m. Boarding time is at 6:15 p.m. at gate C5. I've heard Greenland is beautiful. I'm sure you'll love it."

"How long and far is the flight to Copenhagen?"

The agent worked her computer. "Nine hours and thirty minutes to Copenhagen. Flight distance of Seattle to Copenhagen is 4,868 miles."

"I've never flown this far from home before."

A colorful brochure inside stood out as Amanda went to put her passport to adventure and ticket to an icy paradise in her backpack. It was the tri-fold brochure of the zoo, it was adorned with colorful attention grabbing colors. Any product and service could be made to look 'super wonderful' with enough gloss and 'creative attention' as she liked to call it in the industry.

The exhibits on trying to educate people painted a veneer of legitimacy to the whole idea she realized. The exhibits that nobody seemed to be reading amongst the screaming of children she recalled. She crumpled up the brochure and handed it to the agent. "Can you throw this away for me?"

"Of course."

"Thanks."

'I'm sure you'll love it.' Those were the last words Amanda decided to remember as she embarked on her journey. She walked off wearing her small backpack with her arms wrapped snugly around Polar Bear. It was her first international flight and she was starting to feel a little frisky.

After causing a bit of a scene carrying a large stuffed polar bear through security, Amanda suddenly had a panic attack. She was starting to second guess this entire idea of traveling beyond her known comfort zone again, she wanted to hear a reassuring voice. Looking around, she spotted a couple of public phones.

She was surprised they even existed. She wondered who she might call. She realized there was no one she could trust with her feelings right now.

The thought that was occupying her mind was that, as she increasingly realized, all the worldly goods and comforts had not been buying her long term happiness, only momentary pleasure. It was like throwing good money after a bad idea at work, it just didn't work in the long run.

That was her comfort zone, more stuff was better. If not consciously, then subconsciously. This is what she had been brought up to believe. It was the culture she knew, and it was central to her line of work. Had she been too smart for her own good?

While she was spending good money on this trip, there was a crucial difference. It was an experience, not a physical item to possess and collect. It was expensive, but she told herself she would seek out local animals next time. She took a few deep breaths and headed for the gate. She would get over this panic attack with courage, patience, and her trusty stuffed bear, regardless of the stares and attention it garnered. Haley was right, don't go alone.

Most importantly of all, she left behind all her worries at home. Retirement plans, gyrating stock markets, work gossip, her love life, traffic, social expectations, climbing the career ladder, client meetings, and presentations. They all faded from her mind with every passing moment.

CHAPTER 8 – OVER THE ATLANTIC

The early wake up to leave work early, and arrive at the airport with enough time for her flight, had put Amanda in a sleepy mood as she settled into her seat. She awoke to realize that she had slept through the entire takeoff. The intercom system crackled to life as she opened her eyes.

> "Good evening, ladies and gentleman. Thank you for choosing to fly with us. My name is Captain Andersen and we are now cruising at thirty-six thousand feet. I have turned off the fasten seat belt light now, so feel free to move about. I still recommend you keep your belt on during the flight for safety reasons. If we encounter any turbulence I'll turn the light back on and make an announcement. You may now use your electronic devices such as CD players, laptop computers, or other portable electronics. Please sit back, relax, and enjoy the flight."

The intercom crackled as the captain went off the air and a flight attendant started to speak.

> "We will be serving refreshments and a light snack before our Danish-style meal. You may now take advantage of your in-seat personal video system. The headphones and instructions are in your seat pocket. If you should have any problems please contact the nearest crew member."

Amanda checked her watch, nine hours to go. It was a long time to be sitting still in a small seat. At least she had a bit of leg room and her seat section to herself. She noticed a young woman seated in the aisle seat across from her to the left. The woman was focused intently on reading a magazine.

Pulling out the seatback in-flight entertainment guide, Amanda turned to the Seattle – Copenhagen listing. Recent Hollywood movies were listed for most of the channels, but she wasn't in the mood for any of these. Maybe she should just get some more sleep she thought. Before she closed the guide, a picture in the lower right caught her eye, a picture of large icebergs. It was a documentary about Greenland, how fortuitous. This could kill a couple of hours she thought to herself. Amanda looked up and saw the beverage cart approaching as she put away the guide.

"You're lucky that polar bears aren't prohibited from being carried on. Is he sedated?" Amanda looked up at the practical joker. It was a tall and slender Danish flight attendant named Kirsten, her English was impeccable.

"No, he's not sedated. Just sleeping, you better be nice."

"Of course, does he have a name?"

"No, just Polar Bear."

"Would you like something to drink?"

"Yes, please. How about a hot tea."

"With milk?"

"Just sugar, please." Amanda wasn't surprised by this question now.

"Would you like some Danish biscuits with that?"

"Yes, please."

"When your friend awakens, do you think he would want anything?"

Amanda smiled. "I think he is alright, but maybe he could use a biscuit too."

They both laughed.

The attendant poured Amanda a cup of tea and placed two packages of biscuits on her tray table.

"May I get a cup of coffee with cream and sugar too?"

"Yes, of course. We'll be serving dinner shortly, you can find the menu in your seat pocket."

"Thanks."

Amanda put on her headphones and reclined her seat. The documentary was just about to start, but there was one thing left to do. She popped the tray table down in front of Polar Bear and placed a package of biscuits on the table along with her cup of tea, she would be drinking only coffee for now. She lifted the arm divider and twisted Polar Bear's body to face her video screen. Everything was perfect now.

As the video screen sprang to life, she was treated to a lesson about the geography of Greenland, the world's largest island. Greenland had often been mistaken for being larger than it was due to inaccurate map projections.

On the popular Mercator projection that had been used in schools for a long time, Greenland appeared to be as large as South America. In reality, it was only one-eighth the size of South America! It also appeared to be the same size as Africa, yet, Africa was fourteen times larger!

The Mercator map projection was made in 1569, but had remained popular until the 1980s when schools and atlases began using newer projections which more accurately portrayed the size of the continents.

Greenland had always been this spot on a world map that Amanda just glanced over, it never made an impression in her mind. Now, she was learning that there was a major distortion. This map deception was starting to sound like some of the tricks she employed as a marketer. Or tricks that she knew others in the industry used to deceive people. All the distortion and half-truths had helped to create a world in which we needed to be hyper-vigilant in, if we preferred the 'truth,' whatever that was. How stressful, Amanda reflected.

Making something out of nothing, or making nothing out of something. That's what this map distortion reminded her of. If she kept up this international travel she thought, a globe would be a good investment, and maybe even if she didn't. A globe would not suffer from this flat 2-D distortion. Sure, there were digital globes, but something about touching a physical object had its appeal.

The video noted that Greenland was about 25% larger than the US State of Alaska, three times the size of Texas, and five times the size of California. Ice covered 85% of it and it was one of the last remaining ice sheets from the previous ice age. The ice sheet was over ten thousand feet deep in the thickest sections and had depressed the land beneath it.

Despite the size exaggeration, it was still large. Amanda now had a conversation starter when anyone mentioned the word ice.

The video continued, noting that the majority of Greenland was located in the Arctic zone. This zone was defined in several ways. The most common definition was if the area lay within the Arctic circle, an imaginary line at 66 degrees and 33 minutes. This line marked the latitude at which the sun did not set on the day of the summer solstice, usually June 21st, and where the sun did not rise on the winter solstice, usually December 21st.

Another definition was the area north of the tree line. This line crossed Northern Russia, the tips of Norway and Sweden, Northern Canada, and Northern Alaska.

The third definition was the northern areas where average daily summer temperatures did not exceed about 50° Fahrenheit.

Greenland was an island where the seas around it changed dramatically depending on the season. During the winter, except for the south, it was surrounded by pack ice, known as perennial ice. It was ice that was formed by the freezing of the top layers of ocean water. In the summer, only the most northern part of Greenland remained surrounded by permanent pack ice.

Amanda continued watching as the documentary proceeded to discuss the history of Greenland habitation, starting with the arrival of the Inuit across the Bering Strait land bridge between Russia and Alaska. The bridge was now undersea due to the end of the last ice age. Greenland Inuit were related to the peoples of Alaska and Northern Canada. Human migrations had begun five thousand years ago, culminating in modern day Greenlanders. They were believed to have descended from the last culture which arrived, the Thule, which absorbed the prior dominant culture, the Dorset.

The whole idea of Greenland habitation sounded rather odd. How did people survive in such a harsh world for thousands of years? How did they do it? How could people live on a block of ice? What did the different cultures all have in common to survive? She was about to find out firsthand.

Amanda wondered what the people were really like. Was it modern there? How different was life in Greenland compared to America, the only world she knew. The brochure from Mary seemed to give a modern impression, but Amanda knew the secrets of marketers. She was, after all, one herself. Photographs could be manipulated and retouched. As could video, in real-time.

As she was thinking about the natives, she was reminded of Chief Sealth, the namesake of her hometown, Seattle. He coined the phrase – we do not inherit the earth from our parents, we borrow it from our children. The one or two times she heard it, she dismissed it in the midst of wondering about how to sell more widgets. Besides, she didn't have any children.

She changed the channel to see if anything else was on, stopping momentarily at a cartoon. Various talking animals were running around in funny situations. It reminded Amanda of all the cartoons she watched as a child, and a few of the more recent cartoon movies. But she felt a little strange watching it now, for she was going to see the top land predator of the Arctic, in the flesh. She flipped back to the documentary.

The video was now discussing the arrival of the Vikings in the tenth century. The most intriguing point to Amanda was the European naming of Greenland. It was named so as to make it sound attractive for others. It was an encouragement to get people to go there. While Greenland was warmer during this time period, commonly known as the Medieval Warm Period, it was still maybe an early example of marketing Amanda thought.

She learned that the settlements thrived for the first two hundred years with some estimates of up to five thousand people. Archaeological ruins of up to three hundred farms and twenty-two churches had been found.

A voice interrupted the video. "Excuse me."

Amanda looked up. It was Kirsten, the flight attendant. She took off her headphones.

"Would you like some dinner?"

"Yes, of course."

"Salmon steak or ham and pasta salad?"

"Ham and pasta salad, please."

"Would you like something to drink? Wine?"

"White wine, please, and some tea."

"We have Chardonnay or Sauvignon Blanc."

"Chardonnay, please."

"How is your polar bear doing? It doesn't look as if he has finished his biscuits." An unopened package of biscuits lay on the tray table. The cup of tea was empty though, Amanda had decided to drink it.

Amanda blushed and looked over at Polar Bear. "I think he's still sleeping."

"I've heard bears sleep a lot." Kirsten smiled and finished serving Amanda.

As she looked at the meal in front of her, she wondered what she would be eating in Greenland. Mary had warned her that eating could be one of the tougher cultural adjustments while traveling over the ice in Greenland. She put her headphones on again then enthusiastically opened up her set of utensils and dug into the meal. The story of Greenland Vikings was intriguing.

The Viking story continued with how they managed to survive in such a forbidding place, and their eventual demise and somewhat mysterious disappearance in the early 1400s. While the primary reason given for their demise was a changing climate, it got colder, perhaps more importantly, the stubbornness with which they clung to their mainland European values rather than adapting to the limits of the land, doomed them.

She thought about this deceptive naming of a harsh land – *Green*land. There were no photographs, videos, magazines, and probably no books back then for someone to learn about a place before they moved there. What a leap of faith. It was all word of mouth. But, how different was our modern world, really? Our world was different now because it had become a lot more complicated, with people saying all sorts of things, many of them hiding behind the magic of technology.

It all sounded kind of similar to some of the tricks Amanda had pulled in her life, both work and personal. On the personal side, it was something girlfriends and wives did all the time. Slick 'marketing lipstick' to cover up a product that was sometimes not so pretty. Lipstick on a pig, and sometimes, she was the pig. In her personal life she realized, she might be feeling terrible *inside*, but a few fresh coats of cosmetic paint and no one would be the wiser. It often worked on the men she had dated, such suckers.

Thinking about the Vikings in Greenland again, perhaps more intriguing, was the disappearance of an entire group of people to the 'rest of society.' Was something like this even possible today? It was like that saying – if a tree falls and no one saw or heard it, did it really fall? Maybe the better question was, would anyone care?

She recalled a newspaper article about species of animals disappearing due to deforestation and other man made events. Did anyone care? Were these species like the falling tree? What if the polar bear disappeared in the wild, would anyone care? Of course, some people would care, but would society at large care? Or would it just be chalked up as a casualty of our modern times? Even if enough people did 'care,' would we actually change our existence in some way to prevent it?

Did it matter if polar bears disappeared in her lifetime? The lifetime of the next generation or two? Did it matter if they still existed, but in much reduced numbers? How many polar bears were there anyway? She was afraid to accept it, but she didn't really have an answer.

She needed to learn more about the plight of the polar bear, a species that she knew now was at threat of disappearance due to warming seas. Hopefully her guide in Greenland would have some answers.

As the documentary concluded the discussion on the Inuit and Vikings, the one idea that stood out, was that the Inuit survived, and the Vikings didn't. The reason was given that the Inuit lived more in harmony with the land, while the Vikings stuck with their dairy economy. Why didn't the Vikings adapt sooner? Were they stubborn, too proud, or too stuck to European religious ways? Was there some other force at work? Were they pig-headed? Or just fooled by too much, lipstick on the pig?

Amanda's imagination went wild as she began thinking about the people of Denmark and Greenland. While the stubborn Vikings went extinct on Greenland, what had their real life ancestors turned into? After all, if they were too pig-headed to survive in Greenland, maybe they were brutish and unsophisticated? What were Scandinavians, Danish in particular, like? How many of the traits of Vikings, as shown in marketing advertisements, had been retained. Her memory came up with a credit card ad that repeated itself every so often.

Did the people still wear horned helmets? Wearing top hats and flat caps used to be common not so long ago in America. Amanda knew this from studying fashion trends. Were the Danes long haired and gruff?

Amanda realized that she didn't know anything about the people of where she was going. Everything and everyone looked normal so far on this flight, but initial appearances could be deceiving. It just might be a carefully crafted image to sucker people to go there. She chuckled to herself over her silly fears. We lived in a globalized world. Everyone was the same, more or less, weren't they? She needed to sleep.

She didn't know anyone who had returned from a visit to Denmark or Greenland, but then again, she didn't know anyone who had visited. Her heart skipped a few beats in anticipation of this meeting with a culture and people unknown to her.

The documentary continued with more trivia.

Far from being just an insignificant backwater in modern times, present day Greenland had served as a strategic location during World War II with both weather and refueling stations at fourteen locations around the island. They were named Bluie West or Bluie East. The forecasts had even proved to be a very important factor in planning D-Day. Past US president and American general, Dwight D. Eisenhower, went ahead with the Normandy landing despite strong winds in the English Channel, based on Greenland weather reports. He knew it would be calm the next day!

This bit of trivia provided some comfort to Amanda. Perhaps the people of Denmark and Greenland weren't so raw or brute. Maybe all she really needed was to get more sleep. Maybe it was her playful mind reacting to having to sit cooped up in an airline seat for so long. She needed some alcohol.

She restrained herself and made a point of watching the rest of the video. She managed to learn that while Greenland still was part of the Kingdom of Denmark, in 1979, it had been granted home rule. This meant that the government of Greenland was responsible for most aspects of society. Her eyes perked up as the video noted that in August 2004, US Secretary of State Colin Powell visited Denmark to conclude an agreement on upgrading the radar station in Thule.

She was captivated as the video revealed the population statistics for where she was going. The largest island in the world was home to about fifty-six thousand people, less than 10% of her hometown, Seattle! It was roughly split between 90% Inuit and 10% Danish. The largest town was Nuuk, with fourteen thousand people. The rest of the towns had less than six thousand people each. Of note was an apartment building in Nuuk with about 1% of the entire Greenland population living in it!

But didn't the natives live off the land, too? She was confused. This apartment block began to sound similar to a reservation for native Indians in America. Had the Danes treated the natives of another land similar to how Indians were treated in America?

What sorts of rights did they have? Would they be friendly or stand offish toward new visitors? Then she realized, she had never met a native Indian in America. Everything she knew about any Native American Indian cultures were from school books, television, and a visit to an Indian-run casino. She felt a quick sense of shame over her ignorance.

Amanda took another look at the tea and coffee on the tray tables. She needed some more alcohol. While she was by no means an alcoholic, she was conscious of drinking more since Stephanie's death. She wondered if the Inuit had alcohol issues like some of the Native American Indian tribes that she recalled hearing about. If they did, maybe she would join them.

Some of her questions were answered soon enough as the video revealed that while modernity had arrived in Greenland, the Inuit past resonated strongly in the people's practices and sense of cultural identity, most evident by the preservation of the Greenlandic Language.

In contrast, younger generations of Inuit in other regions of the Arctic such as in Canada, were losing their ability to speak and understand their native language. Younger generations of Inuit in Greenland were commonly fluent in English and Danish. Traditional ways were still practiced by Greenlandic Inuit too. They still hunted seals, whales, birds, and polar bears, often by traditional means.

Modernity, this was an encouraging word to Amanda. Perhaps all her wild visions were completely unfounded. Mary had warned her that things might get a little rough, from living off the land in the remote wilderness. How hard could it be, really? She was supposed to have an English speaking guide. Besides, the video stated many people were fluent in English. How difficult might things be?

The video continued with a look at the primary industry, fishing, before providing a window into other more interesting aspects as it related to the rest of the world today, adventure travel and science. It was a land where hardy adventurers and arctic climate scientists tread.

Adventurer, it had a nice ring to it. She repeated it. She leaned over and looked at her reflection in the airplane window, Amanda the Adventurer. This sounded like the beginning of a good movie.

The video presentation continued by talking about the work of scientists over the past several decades. There was an increasing realization on how important Greenland was in learning about global climate change, or global warming. They had drilled ice cores down to the land beneath the ice sheet in order to learn about the past. By studying the ice in Greenland, scientists had learned about past weather conditions. The ice in Greenland had distinct layers which could be dated like the rings of a tree. The ice from Greenland had been dated back to 123,000 years ago.

While Amanda was finding the documentary interesting, the urge to take a bathroom break after all the wine and coffee was just too great. Her brain needed a break too from all these Greenland facts. She got out of her seat to freshen up in the toilet.

In the small confines of the lavatory, Amanda looked at her skin in the mirror, it was drying out from the lack of moisture in the airplane. She dabbed some of the cream on from the dispenser. There was something peculiar about an aircraft bathroom she thought. There were no other distractions, just you and the mirror in a very tight place.

She took a closer look at her eyes, the dreaded crow's feet were visible, the easiest lines and wrinkles to appear on the face. They appeared as well defined lines spreading out from the corners of her eyes. Along with them came puffier and dark eyes.

She shifted her gaze down toward her mid-riff. She pinched herself. She was getting fatter. No, she was already fat. She looked at her body as she squeezed her breasts. Were they big enough? Were airplane bathroom mirrors like some department store mirrors where they made you look slimmer? She made some funny faces at herself. Clenching her teeth, she made a face of anger. Then she made a face of ambivalence. She cycled through a few more emotions of the moment. She hated thinking about herself like this sometimes. Amanda slapped herself on the cheek and returned to her seat.

Putting on her headphones again, she was just in time for the final segment on Greenland. It was a segment on tourism and fun things to do.

Topping the fun list was a visit to the town of Ilulissat. Located north of the Arctic Circle, it was home to the Kangia icefjord, the most productive glacier in the Northern Hemisphere. It calved enough ice to account for around 10% of all ice calved by Greenland's glaciers. The fjord in Ilulissat was inscribed on the United Nation's list of World Heritage sites in June 2004.

Travelers to Ilulissat were assured of seeing towering icebergs more than two hundred feet tall, either floating out in the sea, or frozen in place by surrounding pack ice during the winter. Other popular activities included kayaking, dog sledging, wildlife watching, hiking, and helicopter tours.

Fun. That was a word she hadn't understood the past few months. Now, she was free from the pressures and confines of her

work environment, and the constant reminders of the tragic accident. The feeling of friskiness she felt earlier was getting stronger.
No wonder her mind was conjuring up all these strange thoughts
about Vikings, Inuit, and her own delusions of grandeur.
Amanda the Adventurer, how corny. But it wasn't just a feeling of
playfulness, the *real* woman inside of her was waking up.

As the video faded to black, Amanda knew she wouldn't have to
wait for, someday, as the video hoped one would visit. An over-
nighter in Copenhagen, and she would be on her flight to
Kangerlussuaq, Greenland, then connecting to Ilulissat. She took
off her headphones and looked around the aircraft. Most of the
other passengers were awake watching the video screens in front
of them, their faces glued to the screen. She turned and smiled at
Polar Bear. She closed her eyes for a much deserved nap.

CHAPTER 9 – LAND HO!

It was over an hour before she awoke.

"You have a handsome seat mate," a voice rang out.

Amanda turned around, it was the young woman across the aisle. "Oh, yes, very well behaved too."

The young woman chuckled. "Are you going to Copenhagen?"

"It's just a stopover, my final stop is Greenland."

"Greenland?"

"Crazy, isn't it?"

"That sounds adventurous. I've never met anyone who has been to Greenland."

"I guess I'm the first. Where are you going?"

"I just finished my junior year at university. I'm going to stay with some relatives in Denmark, then go backpacking around Europe for a little while, then go to France on a summer exchange program."

"That sounds really fun. What are you studying?"

"Urban planning."

"What's that all about?"

"Urban planning is the study of our man-made environment. The cities we live in and how we interact with them."

"Interesting. Isn't it a little early for classes to get out?"

"I've been taking extra classes the last few quarters so I could take the spring quarter off. I really need the break. I'm so excited!"

"Sounds like you deserve it."

"I do, I do, I do."

"I'm Amanda by the way."

"Nice to meet you, I'm Kayla."

"Are you staying in Copenhagen?"

"I was planning to spend a few hours in town then take a train over to my relative's home in Odense."

"Where's that?"

"It's a short train ride to the west of Copenhagen. I think it's the third largest city."

"You've been to Denmark before then?"

"A few years ago over summer with my parents. I came as a small child too, but I don't remember too much from then. Odense is famous as the home of Hans Christian Andersen."

"That name sounds familiar."

"He's a famous author. He wrote the *Ugly Duckling*, *The Emperor's New Clothes*, and *Little Mermaid*, among other fairy tales."

"You mean, like *Little Mermaid*, the movie?"

"Yea, that's the one. I've never seen the movie though."

"I didn't know it was an old fairy tale."

"I didn't even know about the *Little Mermaid* until I visited my relatives and read a book they had in their home."

Amanda paused for a moment. "How old are you?"

"Twenty."

"I guess it came out before you were born."

"Must of."

Amanda pondered the idea of how just a few years could mean knowing about something versus not.

"Are you going into town?" Kayla asked.

"I was thinking about it. I'm going to spend the night in the transit hotel at the airport as my flight leaves pretty early. Anything you recommend for me to see?"

"Copenhagen is a happening city. What are you interested in?"

"Anything, really. It would be interesting to learn something about Danish culture while I'm there. I guess there is a lot of history too. I don't want to go to any museums though, not on this trip. Just a basic tour of the city is what I had in mind."

"I know just the thing. The first thing you gotta know is that the best way to see Copenhagen is by riding a bicycle."

"Riding a bicycle? I haven't ridden a bicycle in a long time! Not since college. Isn't Copenhagen a big city?"

"Yes, but it is very smartly designed and managed. The Danes learned early on that oil and car dependency isn't a good thing. It is quite normal to bike in Denmark. Practically everyone bicycles in Copenhagen."

"Really?"

"Bicycling is huge in Denmark, the Netherlands too. I think the last time I checked, 20% of all trips in Denmark were by bicycle. In Copenhagen, over 70% of families don't even own a car, and Copenhagen has more than 500,000 people in the city limits."

"They don't own a car? Can they not afford one?"

"No, they just don't need it. They either bicycle, walk, or use public transport. Denmark is one of the richest countries in the world. I think it's like, more than half of all people who live in Copenhagen use their bike, everyday, for work, school, shopping, whatever!"

"I can't imagine living without a car."

"In Odense, where I will be going, bicycles are even more popular. They even call Odense, Denmark's National Cycle City. It's a whole different way of living."

"How big is Odense?"

"About 200,000 people."

"This sounds unbelievable."

"I know. I didn't believe it before I went there and experienced it for myself. I still remember my parents telling me about the different world they grew up in. Now that I'm in urban planning, I understand it more. Our thinking in America is so dominated by the car and a bigger is better mentality. There is a city of about 175,000 people in the Netherlands called Groningen. More than 50% of all trips there are made by bicycle. I want to go see it for myself. Sorry, if I sound like a stat-head."

"No, it's ok, really. I get like that sometimes. Won't it be cold this time of year?"

"Maybe a little. Although, I don't think it will be too cold. The Danes don't care anyway. Short of outright, very heavy snow or heavy rain, they bicycle year round."

"That's impressive."

"They learn early on from biking to school. I remember the first time I saw a heavily pregnant woman biking somewhere, even when it was rainy. That was the proverbial light bulb."

"I've gotta see that to believe it."

"It's easy to bicycle too. Copenhagen has a city bike program. Sorry, if I sound like a talking ad. I just really enjoy it there."

"No, this is interesting."

"There are about two thousand bikes at over one hundred spots in the city. You pick up at one place then drop it off at another."

"You're getting me excited about this. Maybe I could burn some fat. Where do you recommend I go?"

"Let me think. . . a good plan might be to bicycle up to Amalienborg Slot, it is the home of the royal family. After you've seen that, you could drop off your bike and walk around Nyhavn."

"Nyhavn?"

"It's a canal area by the water. There are a lot of pretty colorful homes there now, many trendy cafes too."

"Maybe I should get a bite to eat there."

"Then you could walk down to the Kongens Nytorv, which is a city square. Then down the Strøget and back to the train station. It's the longest pedestrian only street in the world."

"Pedestrian only?"

"There are no cars, it's great. It's very lively. It's a network of five long streets in the heart of the city."

"Interesting."

"There is a good viewpoint at the Rundetårn too, it's right in the middle of the Strøget. It's a round tower, you can't miss it."

"I'll remember that. You sound like you know the city pretty well."

"I spent a few days exploring all the nooks and crannies before. You'll have fun, I'm sure of it."

As quickly as their conversation had begun, they paused as both of them struggled with their next words.

Kayla broke the silence. "If you don't mind me asking, what is the stuffed bear for?"

"It's for a friend." Amanda clenched her teeth as she instinctively lied out of embarrassment.

"You have a friend in Greenland?"

"A friend of another friend actually. It's really, all a little bit complicated." A little twist to her lie wouldn't hurt anyone.

"Oh, I'm sure they will love it. He's so cute!"

Before Amanda could respond, a crew member pushed a cart in between them. "Duty free, duty free." The cart rolled by.

"Hey, thanks for the advice."

"Sure, no problem."

Just as spontaneously as their conversation had started, it stopped just as suddenly with the crew member interruption. Amanda picked up the in-flight magazine and paged through the articles. There was a map of Copenhagen in the back. She studied it and tried to remember the names of the places where Kayla had told her to go as she traced her hand over the map. She drifted off to sleep as the hum of the engines droned on.

Amanda awoke as the intercom crackled to life. It was the, put up your tray table, we are beginning our descent message.

Kayla caught Amanda's attention. "If you like, I can show you around town for a few hours. I'm not taking the train over to Odense until later."

Amanda thought about it for a moment then decided to take Kayla up on her offer. "That would be great, are you sure? Might you miss your train?"

"No, not at all. There are trains running all the time. It's no big deal. Odense is only about one and half hours by train."

"It's always nice to have someone to show you around in an unfamiliar place. Are you sure it's all right?"

"Of course, it will be good to see the city with someone who has never been there before. It will be interesting to see what you notice. Everyone sees things differently."

The intercom crackled to life again, it was the captain.

"For those of you seated on the right side of the aircraft, if you look out, you will see the Middelgrunden wind farm in the Oresund strait. The wind farm supplies the equivalent of about 3% of Denmark's electrical need. It supplies enough electricity to power the equivalent of twenty thousand Danish homes. This is one of several wind farms in Denmark that currently supply about 40% of Denmark's electrical needs. The target is to have 50% of all electricity generation by wind farms in 2020, and 80% in 2035. Enjoy your stay."

Amanda leaned over and peered out the window as the plane continued to descend. A curved row of twenty large white towers rose up from the sea just offshore from a group of smoke stacks, their large blades turning in unison. Amanda leaned back from the window. "That's totally cool. I've never seen a wind farm out in the ocean."

"It's pretty cool looking," Kayla replied.

"Yeah."

"Denmark is pretty advanced. They're trying hard to combat climate change. It's not just that, it's a quality of life choice, too."

The intercom came on again.

"Flight attendants, prepare for landing."

The plane touched down smoothly. A flight attendant's voice came over the intercom for the last time.

> "Ladies and gentlemen, welcome to Copenhagen International Airport. Local time is 1:25 p.m. We will have you at the gate shortly."

Amanda and Kayla streamed out of the plane and passed immigration. They retrieved their luggage and walked into the arrival hall.

"You can store your luggage and your stuffed animal here at the airport. I'll store my bag at Central Station. There is an ATM next to the luggage storage."

"Sounds like a plan."

They headed toward the luggage storage.

"Just a minute." Amanda looked at Polar Bear and worried about leaving him with a stranger. She opened up her backpack and wrapped him up in a large plastic bag. "Ok, let's go."

"Gotta keep him clean, eh?"

"Wouldn't want to give a dirty present." Pushing any fears out of her mind as irrational, she left her stuff with the attendant.

As they headed for the city, a small piece of paper flew around in the air, it had escaped from the plastic bag. It was the wisdom inside a fortune cookie from a meal eaten at a Chinese restaurant. Somehow this slip of paper had ended up in this bag, most likely from Amanda's collection of plastic bags under her sink. The fortune read – *You will learn to see the world with new eyes.*

CHAPTER 10 – DANISH DELIGHT

"We're here! This is Central Station."

"That was fast." Amanda looked up and around the large train station as they emerged from the carriage. She had never seen a train station like this before.

Arched beams crisscrossed the roof in giant arcs as they supported the cavernous ceiling. There were tracks terminating here for numerous trains. Shops surrounded the entire station. A train was coming to a stop on one of the lines. Passengers were waiting, boarding, and exiting trains.

The hive of activity awakened Amanda. She gazed in awe at her new surroundings, then realized that she had never taken a real train before. "I had no idea people built such buildings."

"I love Denmark, it's so well planned. It's great, we don't need to find a taxi or get in a car. Just hop on the train from the airport. Fifteen minutes later and boom, we're in the heart of the city."

"This is great!"

"Let me go put my luggage in storage and then we can go see if any of those city bikes are available."

"Sounds good."

Amanda was greeted by another sight that she thought of as most unusual as they left the station – hundreds and hundreds of parked bicycles. Bikes of all varieties were lined up in neat rows, some were even parked on double deck parking racks. "Wow."

"Impressive, isn't it?"

"I would have never imagined."

"If you can believe it, Copenhagen was overrun by cars in the early 1960s before the people decided to transform the city. They made streets pedestrian only and made things very bike friendly."

"I find that hard to believe."

The pair walked around to look for an available bicycle. They quickly found the bike stand.

"How many did you say are around in the city?"

"Last I heard was about two thousand, there might be more now. They are quite popular from what I've read. Copenhagen was largely the inspiration for getting many bike sharing systems installed around the world."

"I've never heard of them," Amanda answered.

"I've read about them being setup or installed in lots of other places, I can't remember."

"News to me." Once again, Amanda felt a pang of ignorance. Her preconceptions about the world and what was 'normal,' were being shattered.

They swiped their credit cards, removed the bicycles from the stand, and set off to explore the town on two wheels.

They rode past Tivoli, the city amusement park and gardens. And Radhusplasden, the main square where city hall was located. They passed Rosenborg Slot, the former Dutch Renaissance style palace of King Christian IV, and now a museum, home of the crown jewels. The Botanisk Have, botanical gardens, provided a welcome sight of greenery.

Each pedal of the bicycle brought more life to Amanda as she breathed in the fresh air. She could feel her heart pumping blood throughout her body. Vivid memories of her youth came to life, memories of freedom. It reminded her of the first time she drove a car too, except somehow that drug wore off.

They passed by colorful flower shops. There was a certain order, but it was loose, not too rigid. There was a well defined building height to street width proportion. Not too tall, just right in most places. As they cycled by some little brick streets, she gazed down the twisted alleys. What mystery lay just behind their corners?

It was all rather serendipitous. The view reminded her somewhat of Leavenworth, a small German themed town of two thousand people in Central Washington that she enjoyed visiting. It attracted upwards of 1.5 million visitors per year. Leavenworth was beginning to look like a 'not quite complete copy' of traditional European classical town architecture. But it was close to home.

She would later learn that these theme towns were scattered all over America. Some of them were authentic, populated by immigrants from their respective countries who were bringing a bit of their past with them. Others were converted into tourist attractions to look like something they never were. The reason for the attraction of these towns was the same though. They catered to a need for a sense of place, a sense that had been lost in many parts of America.

Amanda realized that life here in Copenhagen was nothing like suburban and urban America with its large tract homes, strip malls, asphalt parking lots, skyscrapers, parking garages, and feature less corporate office parks.

The Danish theme town in Solvang, California would become a future place for Amanda to visit. Other European theme towns in America included the Dutch in Lynden, Washington, and Orange City or Pella, Iowa. The latter town also had eighty thousand tulips.

The German and Bavarian themes were represented in Frankenmuth, Michigan and Helen, Georgia. New Braunfels, Texas, and the Missouri wine country around Hermann, Missouri were other such places.

The French theme was represented in none other than the French Quarter of New Orleans.

Of course, theme town atmospheres were also a reason for the success of Las Vegas.

The wind blowing in her face as she bicycled was like a wake up call to live. No wonder dogs liked to stick their head out the window she thought. It was like driving a convertible with two major differences, your blood flowed from pedaling, and you could smile and greet fellow humans without a metal shell in the way.

No longer would she weep for not having bought the convertible that caught her eye before, a car that she had thought about, but decided against for practical reasons in Seattle.

They kept riding and came upon the Statens Museum for Kunst, the National Fine Arts Museum, with a large collection of paintings from Matisse. As they rounded back toward the central part of the city they passed a windmill by the Kastellet, the old Citadel, now the northeastern most park in the city.

Along their entire route they had a dedicated bicycle lane to themselves, complete with bicycle traffic lights. Amanda was amazed at the sheer number of people bicycling. Young, old, men in suits, and women in skirts. It appeared that the enthusiasm for bicycling was not limited by income brackets nor ethnicity.

With her confidence rising, she let go of her handlebars and felt she was almost flying, like a bird.

They stopped in a city square and took in their surroundings. They walked their bicycles around looking for a place to park them.

"That was exhilarating!"

"Fun, wasn't it?"

"Very," Amanda replied.

"Did you see the pregnant woman?"

"Yes, several! I still can't believe it."

"The Danes don't think of cycling as a toy which is grown out of. It's a practical way to get around."

Amanda had a flashback to a rather different definition of bicyclists in her mind. There was a fellow at her office who bicycled to work. She had always thought of him as a little odd, perhaps a freak of nature, a weird-o.

The normal thing to do was to drive to work. Now, she was beginning to understand the benefits of bicycling, a very different way to live. Although the cyclist outfit and spandex he wore were still silly in Amanda's mind, there weren't many people wearing those outfits here. Riding a bike looked so normal, and trim.

"It's good exercise too. Everyone here looks so fit," Amanda commented.

Diet fads were like fashion at home in America to Amanda. There was a popular book promoting a different way she recalled hearing about, *French Women Don't Get Fat*. The book proposed a lifestyle change, not just a diet per se. Maybe there should be one called *Danish Women Don't Get Fat*, she thought. Diet or no diet, little did she know that the Danish were among the least overweight and obese of all European nations in recent surveys, on par with the French, and sometimes even less.

"I'm thinking that people don't need to go to the gym as often, exercise is built into their routine," Kayla noted.

"It feels so safe with the lanes, I don't see anyone wearing helmets either. It feels so normal." Amanda felt no hint of the fear that sometimes paralyzed her, such as the fear she felt walking in parking garages late at night, alone.

They discussed the stark contrast with America's transportation plan. Kayla explained that the Danes were very conscious of their environment and how it affected their health. She noted how bicycles were good exercise, didn't pollute, and also good for global warming. They also didn't separate people from one another behind fast moving chunks of steel.

"This is such a beautiful city," Amanda wondered aloud as she gazed at the historical buildings.

"We've built so many of our neighborhoods around the automobile. It creates a lot of dead zones that nobody cares about, and asphalt parking lots."

"I've only been here a couple of hours and I can see your point. Though the city isn't quite what I expected."

"How's that?"

"I thought there would be more high rises for such a large city."

"I studied that in one of my classes. The tallest building in a place says a lot about a city. It used to be in a lot of towns that no buildings could be taller than the church spires. Not many people go to church here, but they still prohibit tall buildings in the center. I think it's a desire to keep things at a human scale."

They passed by a window with a poster of an aerial skyline shot of the city. Amanda could count the number of tall buildings with the fingers of her hands.

"Let's go park our bikes over there." Kayla pointed to a small, single story, square shaped building, near the green copper domed marble church that came into view.

"Where?"

"Over there."

"I don't see a bike rack over there."

"Follow me."

They walked their bikes over there. Kayla inserted a coin and a door opened, she wheeled her bike inside.

"Whoa. This is crazy."

"Pretty cool, eh?"

It was an electronic, automatic underground bicycle parking machine.

They crossed the street and walked on to the royal grounds of Amalienborg Slot, the Royal Palace. They walked into the middle of a square surrounded by four modest royal palaces with an equestrian statue set in the center. Royal guards manned their posts at various entryways.

"The Danish royal family is an interesting bunch," Kayla remarked.

"Why is that?"

"There is a long custom for members of the royalty to marry foreigners. The Queen is married to a Frenchman. The younger Prince Joachim married Princess Alexandra, who was born in Hong Kong. She was the first Asian to marry into a European royal family."

"Interesting. That sounds like a good trivia question."

"She is part Chinese, English, and Austrian. They're divorced now though."

"Divorced?"

"Marital problems everywhere, I guess. I hear the Crown Prince's marriage is still going strong though. Prince Frederik married an Australian commoner named Mary Donaldson. They met at a pub in Sydney during the 2000 Summer Olympics."

"At a pub?"

"Sounds like a fairy tale, doesn't it?"

"It sure does."

They wandered around the palace grounds and the adjoining park, Amaliehaven.

A short walk along the water and they were looking at Den Lille Havfrue, the life sized bronze statue of the Little Mermaid. It was sitting on a large boulder. The statue appeared small at four feet tall, but it wasn't the size of it that Amanda thought to be a little strange. Rather, a strange sense of reality. She couldn't put her finger on it.

"Hans Christian Andersen, he's my hero," Kayla remarked.

"Why's that?"

"He lived by the maxim – to travel is to live."

Amanda looked on at the statue and nodded in agreement with Kayla.

"What a great story. It's sad, but so poignant when she turns into sea foam then ascends into the clouds."

"Huh?" Amanda cried out.

"You know, when the mermaid turns into sea foam because the prince married another princess."

"Huh?" Amanda's voice groaned louder. "Are we talking about the same story?"

Kayla gave Amanda a perplexed look.

"I don't know what you're talking about. The *Little Mermaid* I know, is the one where the mermaid gives up her life at sea, and her voice, to try and win the love of a prince within three days before she becomes a lost soul."

Kayla flashed another confused look toward Amanda.

"A love that her father, the sea king, forbids. They are about to fall in love when the sea witch, whom she made a bargain with to get human legs for three days, tries to deceive the prince into marrying her instead, by using a magical disguise."

"This doesn't sound like the story I know," Kayla answered.

"That's when the mermaid's animal friends, the talking lobster, fish, dolphins, birds, and later the prince too, help her foil the evil sea witch. The Little Mermaid and the prince get married and live happily ever after. Her father realizes his mistake in forbidding the love too!" Amanda's eyes glazed over in a trance as she recalled this movie that she must have seen many times as a younger child. Surprising herself, she remembered the story clearly.

"Talking lobsters and dolphins? Happily ever after? They don't get married in the book, and the mermaid turns to sea foam and then ascends up to the clouds."

"What?" Amanda knocked herself on the head. "Weird."

"Wow, the movie must be some strange, twisted translation of the book. Are you sure you aren't still jet-lagged?"

They both stood puzzled for a moment as they gazed at the statue along with a few other tourists who had come by to admire it.

"Are you hungry?" Kayla asked.

"Yes."

"Let's get going back to Nyhavn. We can find a restaurant there."

They returned to retrieve their bikes at the electronic parking machine, the high tech factor of the machine continuing to amaze Amanda. Bicycles were tools, not toys, or just for fitness.

"How long have these machines been around?"

"Quite a while now, there are a few in Odense too. I think they use them when there are too many bikes or when the visual appearance of an area is a concern. I think this one is pretty new. We still need to return our bikes to a regular rack."

"It's very ingenious."

"Let's go return our bikes. There should be a bike rack over near Nyhavn, the canal area. We can get a bite and take a casual walk back to the train station."

They spotted a bike rack and walked their bikes over. Amanda knelt down to properly park the bike in the middle between a couple of others. She stepped backward between the bikes, her gaze fixated on the bike she rode on and the simplicity it represented.

"Undskyld," a voice cried out.

In her moment of wonder she had backed right into a man waiting for a bike. "Oh, excuse me." She turned around, and was confronted by the presence of a graceful and dashing looking gentleman dressed in a full suit and tie.

"No, excuse me," the gentleman replied in perfect English.

Amanda blushed. This man was no Viking. Their eyes met for a brief moment. As she gazed into his eyes, there was something peculiar about them, something alive, but she couldn't figure out the meaning of this subtle observation, not that she cared why at this particular moment.

"I'm sorry, I'm late for a meeting and I am anxious to get on a bike to get there. My bicycle broke down and I didn't have time to fix it. I should have given you a little more space."

"It's ok. Please, please, take it," Amanda replied as she moved to get out of the way.

They headed over to the popular dock area of Nyhavn, it was a riot of colorful architecture. Even in the cool late March temperatures, many people were milling about enjoying the sunshine. They walked into a cafe and got their meals.

"Was that guy cute or what, Amanda?" Kayla remarked.

"He was very charming. It's cute how men in full suits and ties ride bikes."

"Maybe he was someone important."

"What do you mean?"

"It's common here for high ranking officials such as ministers or even corporate CEOs to commute by bicycle. I saw a photo once of a minister going to visit the Queen by bicycle. I saw a statistic once too that said the majority of the members of the Danish Parliament actually ride their bicycles to work."

"You mean, they aren't all chauffeured around or drive expensive German luxury cars all the time?"

"Scandinavian culture for you." Kayla swallowed some herring.

"You sound like you've dreamed of being swept off your feet the way you talk about it," Amanda noted.

"I admit it, I have. How can you not?"

Amanda smiled.

"Is there someone special in your life?" Kayla asked.

"Kind of, sort of. Not really. It's kind of a confusing part of my life. Let's not talk about it."

"Ok, we won't! It's so magical here," Kayla exasperated.

Amanda munched on her cold cuts from the buffet. "Why else do you like Denmark?"

"The drinking age is sixteen."

"It is! No way! Get outta here!" Amanda gagged on her cold cuts.

Kayla flashed a big smile. "Do we need to look it up on the Internet?" Kayla replied.

"No, I believe you. That's a good enough reason to like a place."

"Not sure why our laws still say no drinking until twenty-one. People desire what they cannot have. We can join the military and kill people at eighteen, but not drink. Go figure."

"True."

"The Danes understand tolerance. Despite a sometimes cold exterior, I always get the feeling that they are quite relaxed and casual about things."

"Is there anything in particular that makes you feel this way?"

"Lots of things my parents talk about. One thing that comes to mind is – right or wrong – the Danes were the first to legalize gay marriage, in 1989."

"1989?!"

"To be precise, it was called same-sex union or something like that, but it was equivalent to marriage. That's what I read anyway."

"How long has it been a 'political football' in our country?" Amanda wondered out loud.

"I read that the number of gay couples seeking marriage per year has gone down in Denmark."

"Maybe that's good evidence, Kayla, that the more you keep something from someone, the more they want it. Why do you think the Danes are different, Kayla?"

"Maybe just being an older country they have built up more wisdom about such things. Or maybe it is as simple as their government system. I don't know."

"There's plenty of 'old' countries in turmoil, Kayla. I don't think age, by itself, has anything to do with wisdom. There must be something else."

"You're right, Amanda."

"What kind of government do they have here?"

"In America, we have the Democrats and Republicans with an occasional independent. In Denmark and most Scandinavian countries, they have at least five to ten political parties. There is room for a lot more voices and compromise as parties have to group together to form ruling coalitions."

"Five to ten? Sounds like it could get really complicated."

"I agree, but it is either that or everything is black and white. It is a better system of checks and balances me thinks."

"Absolute power corrupts," Amanda replied in resignation. She changed the subject. "It's very cozy here."

"Yup," Kayla replied as she stuffed her mouth with some more food.

Amanda smiled.

"The Danes call it Hygge."

"How do you say that again?"

"Hoo-gah," Kayla repeated.

"Hygge? What does that mean?"

"It means to have a cozy and intimate mood."

"I get that feeling. Everything is smaller around here, almost miniature, compared to America."

"I guess they have figured out that bigger isn't always better."

"I didn't realize there were so many different ethnicities here, I figured it would be pretty homogenous."

"I thought I read somewhere that foreigners make up more than 10% of the population, at least in Copenhagen. There is a sizable Turkish and Pakistani community. I've also read about smaller Somalian and Ethiopian communities. It's not a melting pot like the USA though."

"I guess you don't know until you see it for yourself."

"That's why I like traveling!"

"Do they all get along?"

"I've read about some stories of friction, most are about newcomers having trouble integrating. My mom said it was like drinking alcohol. In moderation it is ok, but if you drink too much at once, you'll get drunk and will have trouble seeing and walking. You have to build up your tolerance, and even then, there are limits to how much you can drink."

"Ain't that the truth." Amanda paused. "Interesting metaphor, Kayla. Maybe 'oil & water' don't mix sometimes. Are all Scandinavian cities like this?"

"Like what?"

"Do they all have a similar feel?"

". . .and charming gentleman that you bump into while returning a bike?"

"Whatever. I'm unlucky in love." Amanda was surprised at how intelligent Kayla was for her age. Perhaps foreign travel had a way of expanding the mind. She could feel her mind expanding at the seams.

"The summer I was here, we went through Northern Germany to Amsterdam. I've been across the Øresund bridge to Malmo, Sweden. Malmo is very walkable and bicycle friendly too. You should check out the nice architecture in Malmo. If you like that sort of thing, of course. There's a tall building built in a twisting shape. It's pretty cool looking. The Scandinavian countries are very good at creating homey communities, and less economically extreme societies which foster co-operation."

"I noticed something interesting as we were bicycling and walking, the physical distance is less between everyone. I think I'm beginning to realize how cars and all the maddening technology we use shields us from each other."

"You don't say hello to your neighbor, or anyone else for that fact, when all you do is get in a hunk of steel in your garage and drive off to work. People need places to gather too. On our way back, we'll be walking through several public squares, I've studied all this kind of stuff in school. I hope I'm not boring you."

"No, not at all, you've studied well. I enjoy learning about these different ways of living. I'm going through a little bit of culture shock."

"I hope to go on a bicycle tour of the entire country someday."

"That sounds fun. Is that easy to do?"

"Oh yeah. The bicycle network runs across the entire country. There are lots of adorable villages along the way."

"Adorable villages," Amanda repeated quietly.

"It takes a village to create a healthy society."

"That sounds familiar."

"Yeah, it does, but I don't remember where I heard it."

"Should we get going?" Amanda wondered as she checked her watch.

Kayla agreed. They made their move to the door.

They walked back along the Strøget and stopped to explore a few shops. While it was chilly, the streets were alive with people going places. The occasional musician and clown performed for the amusement of others. Amanda dropped a few coins in a jar, she was in a joyous and giving mood.

A curiosity shop attracted their attention, they went in. Kayla stopped to look at some jewelry in the front of the store while Amanda headed toward the back. A full length mirror lay against the back wall. Amanda decided to take a look at how she was holding up with the jet lag. An odd sensation ran down her back as she first looked in the mirror. She quickly turned away. She squeezed, then rubbed her eyes and sighed. Perhaps that would snap her out of her visual funk.

She looked again at her reflection, it was different. It was her, and yet, it wasn't her. She raised her right arm to adjust her hair then snapped back in shock. Her left arm was moving in the mirror, not her right! She gasped.

She shook her head back and forth, it must be the jet lag. She raised her right arm again and the same thing happened. Then she raised her left arm and the mirror showed her right arm. This was some optical illusion she thought. Finally, she raised her hand toward the mirror and touched it, but it was her other arm moving up. The mirror was reflecting back the actual arm she raised, but from the perspective of what someone looking at you would see!

Who was this strange person in the mirror? Was it really her? Then she noticed the mirror was different.

A stack of brochures resting on a small shelf mounted to the right hand of the mirror caught her eye as she stepped back, she picked one up.

> You are looking at a full length non–reversing mirror. It shows how you appear to others, not to yourself, as all 'normal' mirrors do. This effect is achieved by placing two frameless mirrors together at a 90° right angle, then looking at the corner where the mirrors meet. This non-reversing feature is also evident when you hold up writing to the mirror. It is readable and looks 'normal,' not backwards, as with other mirrors.

> You can see yourself unreversed in a photograph or video, of course, but it is *not* the same. There is something about seeing yourself as others see you, in a mirror, live, and in real-time. Flip this card over and read the quote in the mirror. In a normal mirror it will be backwards, but not this one.

She flipped the brochure over and held it up in the mirror. A quote was printed across the card.

> *Travel not just to new places to do new things, but to have new eyes.* – Anonymous

"Hey, Amanda, quit looking at yourself! Come look at this amber jewelry I found, it's a Danish specialty," Kayla shouted from the front of the store.

Amanda turned around, "Oh! Coming." She didn't mention what she saw to Kayla, she was too disturbed by it. She forgot about it as they stepped back outside on the busy street.

A gust of wind blew through Amanda's hair as they continued walking. Amanda looked up, but saw only gargoyles looking down at her from some of the buildings. She felt as if they were keeping a watch over her, monitoring her every movement as if something was about to happen. Whether it was good or bad, she could not determine. She kept walking.

They made a steady pace back to the train station. The commotion of people formed what seemed like a very amiable community in this cosmopolitan city. While Amanda's sense of time continued to change and slow down from the sense of urgency back home, she realized that the last time she had felt a similar feeling of 'magic' was at an amusement park.

The big difference was that it had been commercialized across the Atlantic Ocean. Here, maybe they strived to live a "little more magically," everyday.

They arrived back at Central Station.

"I really enjoyed today," Amanda mused.

"Me, too."

"Let's keep in touch."

"Do you have an email?" Kayla asked.

Amanda opened up her small backpack and jotted down her personal email on a business card for Kayla.

"I hope your trip to Greenland goes well. What's Northwest Marketing Associates?"

"Let's not talk about that. I'd rather forget about work. Good luck with your summer classes in France."

They hugged.

"Shall we do as the Danes do?"

"What's that?" Amanda asked.

She realized as soon as Kayla initiated an exchange of two cheek kisses.

"I remember that from French class. I always thought we should do that back home more."

"Two kisses in Denmark is normal, make sure you get it right."

Kayla explained how the custom differed among the various countries of Europe. It was two in Spain, right cheek always first. It was two in Austria and Hungary. It was three in the Netherlands, right side first she thought. In Switzerland, it was also three. In France, it varied. One to five depending on the region. In Belgium, it was one to three depending on the age of the other person.

Yet, for all these kisses in Europe, it was rare in Germany and the UK, except for close family and friends. In Italy, it was more cheek touching then kissing, depending on who you asked.

Then there were the differences on what was normal between men, men and women, and just between women. And the rules behind who you kissed and when were mysterious. Who was a stranger and who was a closer friend?

As Amanda would later learn, maybe cheek kissing wasn't so normal in Denmark. But hey, maybe some Danish guy who wanted to kiss Kayla on an earlier trip, convinced her of it!

With this warm sense of friendship, they went their separate ways. Amanda's exciting adventure of discovery was not only intimate, but had only just begun.

CHAPTER 11 – ICE CORING

From her backpack, Amanda pulled out the pass to the airline lounge that Mary had given her. It was one of the benefits that some travel agents were still able to offer in this day of Internet travel. She had a few hours to spend in the lounge while she waited until she could check into the transit hotel. She checked her ticket, the Greenland flight wouldn't depart until 9:15 a.m., the next day. A few more hours of waiting, sleep, then she would be on the next leg of her adventure. It felt like quite an adventure already with her exposure to Danish society, a land of bicycles.

"I couldn't help but notice your friend over there," beamed the tall, well built, bearded man, seated on the couch next to Amanda's resting place.

"He's a tough one to take care of."

Amanda hoped he wouldn't ask why she was carrying around a big stuffed polar bear. Besides that, was he hitting on her?

"Where are you headed?" the man asked politely.

It was such a benign question, yet she had conflicting thoughts about men she didn't know talking to her. It must have been the advertising campaigns she had been exposed to as a child – don't talk to strangers. The message had been drilled into her subconscious. It was as if the advertising had conditioned her to be on guard and confrontational, even as an adult. She was used to men hitting on her sometimes, but something in the back of her mind always seemed to flash – danger!

Yet, there was something about this travel adventure that lowered her guard. Maybe it was just the physical act of leaving the 'security' of one's known world. Making friends seemed easier too, like Kayla. Maybe it was both the sense of safety in Denmark and the sense of confidence from riding a bicycle again too, she didn't know. She didn't have her face glued to a smartphone either as she saw other people around her. "Greenland, if you can believe it," she blurted out.

"Lots of polar bears there."

"I'm looking forward to seeing one."

"That is where I am going too. Let me guess, you just flew in and have to wait for the connecting flight tomorrow morning."

"I flew in from Seattle, you too?" She didn't bother to reveal that she had spent the last half day touring Copenhagen.

"New York. Not many people go to Greenland this time of year. Where are you going there?"

She felt a sense of relief as she noticed what appeared to be a wedding ring. "I'm going to Ilulissat to see the icebergs." While she was starting to let her guard down, Amanda wasn't in the most sociable mood given her lack of proper sleep and the day's earlier adventures in Copenhagen, she needed to stay awake though, perhaps this conversation would help.

"The icebergs are quite beautiful."

"How about yourself?" Amanda countered, trying to change focus away from herself.

"I'm a research scientist from a university in New York. I'm part of a team who studies ice cores."

Amanda lowered her social defenses further as the man sounded more legitimate. A true scientist? Harmless. "Ice cores? What's. . . oh wait, I think I heard something about that on the documentary I saw on Greenland during the flight over."

"I've seen that one too."

"I missed that part of the video. What are ice cores again?"

"Time machines."

"Time machines?"

"Ice cores allow us to study past climate conditions."

"How's that?"

"Well, when the weather was warm enough during the summers we used a big drill to extract sections of the ice. The drill went down almost two miles. Each section then got brought up, analyzed, and stored. Deeper sections reflect the climate further back in time, I'll explain that in a second. The Greenland ice is great because it shows the climate year by year, as far back as about 120,000 years ago."

"120,000 years ago, year by year?"

"Yeah. It's great, they are very detailed. We can even go as far back as 800,000 years ago in Antarctica, but the ice there is not as detailed."

"How do you analyze ice?"

"Snowfall is compressed into ice because the sun, when it did shine, was not strong enough to melt the snow. Then, due to the polar night, twenty-four hours of darkness, and midnight sun, twenty-four hours of sunshine, the composition of the snow changed by season. It's like the difference between cooked or raw meat, except it was cooked or raw snow."

Amanda chuckled.

"Each season of snowfall can be analyzed by counting the layers. Winter or polar night snow froze as a dark layer, summer snow froze lighter."

It sounded like layers of a cake to Amanda, a big cake. Or maybe it was like the layers of her life story. A good year, then a bad year, except the bad years, emotionally, seemed to standout more than the good ones when she thought about it sometimes.

"Dark and light, dark and light?" she uttered.

"Do you mind if I just cut to the chase?" the man replied.

"Huh?"

"I'm sorry. I'm just tired of explaining all the science behind what I do sometimes. Can I just tell you about what we found?"

"Sure," Amanda replied. She was interested, but half falling asleep.

"We call our current period of time an interglacial, which means our global climate is relatively stable. What we've learned from all these ice cores and other research is that the Earth has had many ice ages and interglacial periods, coming and going in predictable cycles. Recent ice cores show our current interglacial period will last a total of 28,000 years, so any excuse that climate change is good in that it prevents a new ice age is folly. Our current orbit matches an interglacial period 400,000 years ago. It will still be another 10,000 to 15,000 years before the next ice age."

"This tell us what?" Amanda was a little confused now. The succession of big numbers didn't make any sense in her mind.

"That climate change is happening."

"You mean, global warming?"

"Thank you."

"What?"

"For calling it by its real name. I've gotten so used to calling it climate change. It's bullshit. It's such a BS general term."

Amanda looked at her watch and let out a yawn. "Oh, sorry, I'm tired. It sounds like you do some interesting work."

"I hear you," he answered sympathetically.

"I have a couple of hours to kill before I go to the transit hotel, I need some caffeine, do you want anything?" Amanda asked.

"Just a soda, please."

"You're from the East, nobody says soda where I live."

They both laughed.

"I'm sorry, I don't think I caught your name."

"I'm Nathan, you?"

"Amanda."

"Pleased to meet you, Amanda."

Amanda walked over to the mini bar and grabbed a cup of coffee and a glass of cola along with a few snacks. She returned and handed him the drink and set the snacks down on the table.

"Thanks. You know, there is a really interesting little story about this cola you just brought me. For a long time, Denmark had a ban on all canned drinks, a can ban."

"A can ban?"

"The idea was to reduce aluminum waste. All drinks were sold in glass bottles. I think I read that each bottle was reused an average of about thirty-five times before being melted down."

"That sounds pretty smart. Different. What happened to the ban?"

"Denmark had to revoke that mandate due to European Union law in 2002, I think. They instituted a large deposit price on cans and added cans into their recycling program. Take a very careful look at a glass bottle sometime, they might be easier to find than the cans."

"Interesting, I'll keep an eye out next time." She swirled her cup of coffee as she wondered where the conversation would go next. Her mind was in a bit of a haze. "I've been wondering about global warming in the back of my mind more. What's your take on it?"

CHAPTER 12 – IT DOESN'T MATTER

"You must get asked about global warming a lot since you're literally on the front line of investigation. It seems so abstract to me sometimes."

"There's a lot of jargon and hype, like many things nowadays. Denial and fear mongering from all sides. I have a different perspective on the subject though. If you want, I can explain the basics first, then tell you why I think global warming doesn't really matter at all, even though I know all about it."

"It doesn't matter? Am I hearing you right? You study global warming, drill ice cores, and you just said – it doesn't matter?"

"Yes."

She straightened up in her chair, eager to hear how this man who studied the climate up close could say such a thing.

"The biggest evidence of man-made global warming to me is the unprecedented level of carbon dioxide build up in our atmosphere. It's greater than at any point found in all ice cores going back 800,000 years ago."

"That's a long time, Nathan. 800,000 years. Talk about traveling back in time. It definitely gives one perspective."

"We know temperature changes occur due to carbon dioxide levels in our atmosphere because of correlations with our industrial age and volcanic weather events."

"I just remember hearing about how the twenty hottest years on record have all occurred recently. Something like that."

"Yes. Since 1980, Amanda. It's an, alarming coincidence."

"Ok, what else can you tell me?"

"It comes down to two things, Amanda. Trapped gases, trapping heat. In recent times we've cleared so much land for agriculture, intensive agriculture. Combined with our increases in pollution from industry, and automobile growth, we get a set of converging factors."

"I'm always amazed when I look down from an airplane and I sometimes see nothing but rectangular farm plots."

"Yeah, that's a factor. Man's gotta eat."

"Well, maybe not so much as we've trained and conditioned ourselves to eat." Amanda wanted to pinch her fat, but she resisted the urge to do so. Why did we overeat so much anyway?

Nathan nodded his head. "You know, one of the cores from Antarctica has shown us that a carbon dioxide concentration increase which took nature ten thousand years, has now occurred in less than fifty years."

"That sounds pretty damning."

"This increase has corresponded between the last ice age maximum and pre-industrial times. Some warming is ok, but too much, too fast, is going to be trouble, for some."

"For some," Amanda muttered out loud.

"There are many factors at play, and we certainly don't know everything. Localized effects might come and go, like hurricanes in the Atlantic Ocean. They don't seem to be in the news very much these days, even though many of the most active hurricane seasons have just occurred."

"Short attention span theater, Nathan." Her marketing profession came to mind again. Thirty second commercials and quick sound bites. People couldn't even sit still anymore, they were so glued to their phones and electronics. Somehow, she hadn't become quite so obsessed.

"A short pause of a few years or a year in which no major damage has occurred seems to convince many that there is no such thing as global warming."

Amanda nodded her head.

"A few years is nothing in Earth years, Amanda. But it might mean that it's an issue that isn't worth doing anything about."

"Until the next big event comes along, and it gets personal," Amanda replied. "What do you think about the drought affecting parts of our country?"

"That's been an ongoing event. People are just waking up to the effects of that."

"Out of sight, out of mind," Amanda mused.

"Of course, there is the visual evidence of the ongoing melting of glaciers around the world."

"I just don't think a lot of people really care about all this stuff, Nathan. People are too busy with other things. I think people's sense of time has changed too. It affects the way people perceive events around them. I've been doing some reading related to that as it relates to marketing. People are becoming more short term focused. Something like that."

"I can't speak to that, Amanda. But, I will say another event which has been going on that doesn't get discussed much is the potential shutdown of our annual heat pump, the Atlantic

Gulf Stream. If it does shut down, it will result in much colder winters for Europe and the end of mild Mediterranean winters."

"The Gulf Stream?"

"Maybe a better way to think of the Gulf Stream is to consider that Buffalo, New York, which is notorious for cold winters, is at the same latitude as Southern France. That part of France isn't particularly known for being cold. It's a Mediterranean climate."

"Yes, of course," Amanda answered. By geography she could agree, but since she had never been to France, it didn't really resonate with her. She did realize the Mediterranean was a nice place though, in her imagination. Perhaps that would be her next trip, to a nice sunny climate. "You're saying it will get colder in Europe even though it may get warmer in other places, and warmer overall?"

"Yes."

"That explains some of the confusion."

"It may have already started. I've read reports that there has been a slowdown of up to 30% in the global water circulation which powers the stream."

Amanda bit her lip.

"So, there's a lot of cause and effect going on. Our planet is like a giant organism. There will be a lot of changes related to polar bears too."

"Polar bears?" Amanda sat up in her chair.

Nathan looked over at Amanda's stuffed polar bear. "I see you have an affinity for polar bears."

"It's a gift for a friend of a friend." She effortlessly lied again, not even blushing this time.

"Oh, you know someone in Greenland?"

"It's a favor for a friend of my travel agent. It's a long story." Her imaginary story expanded.

Nathan sat back in his chair taking a more relaxed posture. He looked at Amanda's stuffed animal and was mesmerized for a moment by its beady eyes.

"While most of us will never see a polar bear in the wild, does it matter if they become extinct?"

"It matters."

"Does it?"

"It does matter."

"Why does it matter?"

She didn't really have an answer for Nathan. "How might it happen?" Amanda pressed on with a sense of urgency in her voice.

"Most plants and animals have developed over time and don't have the same ability to adapt as fast as we can. It's like if you move to a different climate and your skin and body adjusts over time. We survive by relying on heaters, air conditioning, buildings, or changes in clothing. As we slowly adapt, we need less of those."

Amanda was only half-listening now as she imagined walking next to a large polar bear. It was a daydream. They were looking for something to eat. With the poles of the Earth acting like sponges for heat, ice was melting all around them. The impact of global warming was magnified in the Arctic. Their hunting range had decreased due to a thinner and reduced ice extent. They had trouble finding their main meal, seals. They were already thin and losing weight fast.

The polar bear could walk no more, he fell limp to the ground. She tried to wake him up, but she was so weak herself.

The bear groaned and she screamed as loud as she could, but no one cared, as the people were too busy talking about themselves. Every moment of every day, they were talking on their phones, TV, and the radio. They couldn't stop listening to the sound of their own voices. If they weren't talking out loud, they were typing and texting. Restless human minds and broken hearts that needed mending. Minds that couldn't stop paying attention to the sound bite of the moment on 24-hour news. Amanda and polar bear were left to die on the ice.

Nathan had stopped talking now, sensing Amanda's apparent disinterest.

She looked around the lounge and wondered what sort of conversations everyone else was having. Were they serious like this one? Gossiping? Were they talking about business? Or were they going on an adventure like herself?

She noticed a smartly dressed woman. She didn't look like she was going on an adventure, she was all work and no play. What was her work-life balance like? She gazed at how this woman carried herself, a glance at her purse revealed no familiar logos. Her eyes shifted to another woman leaving the lounge while wearing a fur coat. She looked at Nathan again.

"I'm sorry, my mind was wandering with the things you were saying. You know, traveling to a different country is exciting and disruptive at the same time."

"It sure is. I have the travel bug virus. It's an expensive but exciting addiction."

"This is my first time out of the country."

"You've picked quite a first place."

"I'll say."

"I like traveling to different places, it makes me look at the world and myself differently. We grow up with all these expectations about what is right and wrong, and then after traveling, at least for me, I realized many of my assumptions were just silly. There is a feeling of connectedness I feel with the world at large too. It's strange, but we are all just one big family. I don't think I would have ever felt it if I just stayed at home."

"Maybe. Some people travel and it just hardens their opinions, Nathan. That's my impression from the news sometimes. And of some people I have met. Some people seem too opinionated after traveling. Traveling is fun, but I think there's a downside. I can't put my finger on it."

He paused. "I'll have to give that more thought."

"What were you saying about global warming before my mind wandered off?"

"I was saying that it isn't just the polar bears, but the traditional ways of living for the Inuit too. While people in large parts of the world debate the effects of global warming and wonder how much impact it will have or not have, the effects on the people who live in the Arctic, are ever so real. The Arctic is like a canary in a coal mine, though in reality, the signals about our warming climate are all around us."

"Signals?"

"Advance warning signals."

"What sort of signals?"

"Did you say earlier that you are from Seattle, right?"

"Yes."

"The Pacific Northwest's rain patterns will change."

"Change? What do you mean?"

"When you get it, you should get heavier rain storms and wind. I don't know if the annual amount will change."

The idea had only crossed her mind in small fleeting bursts. She had never pieced it all together, but the picture was coming into focus with far more clarity than she would have wanted to believe. Could the heavy rains that contributed to Stephanie's car accident been a result of global warming? She thought about the conversation back home about needing an umbrella in Seattle now. Could there be a connection? She didn't want to believe it.

"The rain is a substitute for what would normally be snow. It gets wetter in the winter, but then the summers are drier."

"It gets both drier and wetter at the same time?"

"Where you live, yes. More extremes."

"More extremes," she repeated. It was like how some places got hotter and some places got colder, even though overall it was getting warmer, Amanda realized.

The bad ski seasons, the record days with rainfall, the longer summers, and record warm temperatures in the heart of winter. Could Stephanie's accident really be connected to global warming?

"Some places won't get more rain, such as in the Southwest US. As we were talking, drought conditions have been going on there for many years. The Colorado River has been well below historical levels for a long time now. It's like a whole chain reaction."

"I think I need another coffee." She needed to take the edge off, she didn't want to know any more.

"I could use another drink, too. I'll get them."

Amanda checked her watch. Another thirty minutes before hotel check in. She was starting to feel the jet lag. Wasn't it better to avoid caffeine? She didn't remember. This was a habit she would have to break someday.

Nathan got up, retrieved the drinks, and then placed them on the table. "Danes are among the top beer and coffee drinkers in the world."

"Really?"

"Maybe that's one reason why they are often ranked the happiest country in the world, it ain't watered down beer either!"

They both laughed.

"They are the happiest? I didn't know there were such rankings about happiness."

"They've been going on for over twenty-five years now."

"How does America score?"

"Somewhere around twentieth place or so."

"That far down?"

"Our ranking isn't so readily applied to everyone though, since we have such a large country and a growing income gap. In other words, it depends on who you ask. The funny thing is, that how much money one makes or has only matters up to a certain point, and it is well below what people think is necessary, then it doesn't matter."

"That's surprising," though Amanda wasn't quite so surprised about the wealth part.

"Danes can still be unhappy, I know that from experience. They are human. They'll admit that to you when you get to know them as I have. But, just observing their behavior or reading the news, one could figure that out too. Some problems are universal it seems."

"So, just because they are the happiest country doesn't mean they aren't sad or one can't be happier, right? It must be an individual thing too, of course."

"Yes, of course."

Amanda was lost in her thoughts for a few moments as she reflected on her life.

"Though in general, they complain about less issues than Americans or people in many countries I think. Less excitable too, in a good way. Less things troubling them."

"Of course, of course. Tell me more about this happiness ranking."

"There are lots of studies on happiness. It's kind of confusing. Some factor in our environmental impact, some are more economic minded, and some countries may move up higher temporarily due to temporary economic conditions. But, the one consistent thing I have found, is that Denmark is either at the top, or near the top for the ones that focus on being happy in a more profound, personal way, as much as any study could possibly reflect that. And, Denmark has been on top for decades."

"Fascinating." Amanda hesitated as she took a moment to absorb Nathan's explanation. "What do you mean, temporary economic conditions?"

"I mean that sometimes I think a country is highly ranked in some survey because the economy or material life conditions might be improving in a particular place from a very low level. It's easy to be satisfied and happy then. When the 'boom time' ends or when some plateau is reached, happiness stagnates or regresses. As I say this, I think of Panama, Puerto Rico, or Colombia for some reason, Nigeria too."

"Are you trying to say that even when economic times are bad, Denmark is still the happiest?"

"Yes," Nathan replied.

"What other countries are ranked at the top?" Amanda wondered aloud.

"If it isn't Denmark, it usually is one of the other Scandinavian countries like Norway, or Sweden. Switzerland, Singapore, the Dutch, and New Zealand are often at or near the top too. They are all smaller countries, so maybe that has something to do with it. I even once read an article that said happiness was in the genes too. The closer one was related to Denmark, the happier one would be, though I wasn't quite sure what to make of that story."

"Super interesting. I want to be happier, that's one reason I'm on this trip to Greenland."

"I thought I read somewhere that of all the countries that were already at a high level of development, the only country that had gotten notably happier since the early 1970s was Denmark, and maybe the Netherlands."

"Really? So when people say 'it used to better,' maybe they aren't just imagining it? Only Denmark?"

"I don't remember, but it was something like that. The measurement is often called life satisfaction, or well-being by the way, not happiness."

"Life satisfaction or well-being?"

"Like I said, Denmark isn't always number one. But, they have consistently been at the top for the longest period of time in more studies, in good and bad economic times. I think that latter point is really important. Because it is in the darker times when one's true character emerges."

Amanda reflected for a moment on her own happiness. She was happy and excited to be on this trip, but deep down she knew she had conflicted feelings about things in life. She abruptly changed the subject back to global warming. Something which didn't have to do with thinking about her feelings at the moment. "Didn't you say global warming doesn't matter?"

Nathan paused for a moment to change gears. "Oh yeah, there is a certain irony about changing weather, it depends on how you look at it. You may get less gloomy skies and be able to get a better natural tan, but then, you can't ski as long, or at all. Maybe you don't ski, but hike more often, so your hiking season is longer."

"I haven't thought about it that way."

"It takes time for people to adjust. We get accustomed to behaving in certain ways based on simple mental cues, the name of the month for example. If the definition of that month changes, we might not change our behavior along with what is happening, we might still be stuck in the old month mindset."

"Are you saying that if it gets warmer in December and appropriate for hiking a certain area, we may not go out to hike there just because we think it will be too cold, even though it isn't?"

"Exactly."

They continued talking about how people looked at global warming. It was all a matter of perspective. Some places would be luckier than others. Other places might suffer a lot more, even if they themselves were not major contributors to global warming.

Amanda pondered his words as she looked out the window. There were planes coming and going from their respective gates.

"I think the better question is, what kind of world do we want to live in."

"What do you mean?"

"Does it matter if it gets hotter more often and people spend more of their days indoors in air conditioning?"

Amanda didn't say anything, still wondering what sort of world she wanted to live in.

"You know, I've noticed there are places with very nice climates, non-humid and warm temperatures, for being in the outdoors, and a lot of people still 'work out' in air conditioned fitness clubs. It's like the outside doesn't matter anymore."

"Maybe it's just because we're so used to cars. Maybe our cities aren't designed very smartly. Asphalt parking lots with lots of big and fast cars aren't exactly inspiring."

"That's a good point, Amanda."

Amanda paused for a moment. She realized she was starting to talk like Kayla. She thought about her earlier exploration of Copenhagen and how different it would have been if it was car dominated. Prior to this trip, she had never questioned life from this perspective. She now understood firsthand how life could be lived in a very different way.

"I've also heard it called 'creeping normalcy' and 'landscape amnesia,' Amanda."

"What's that?"

"Just another way of saying that we forget what life once was or could be. We accept crappier living conditions. 'We' silence the negatives and 'stay positive,' because that's what we're told to do."

Amanda thought about how long it had been since she had ridden a bicycle. There was the memory of a happier time with her parents married. A tricycle, then training wheels, then just two! It was so long ago that her attitudes about it had even changed for the negative, for she could drive a car. That lusty, four wheeled, mechanical beast. Her experience in Copenhagen had made her see the bicycle as she must have seen it as a child and teenager.

Nathan continued. "Another example might be when health officials give a warning to stay indoors due to smog or avoid the beach, so we do. We do something else. Rather than demand a clean up of the beach or clean it up ourselves, we go find another one or don't go at all. Pretty soon the whole idea becomes that you have to travel some place exotic."

This was beginning to make a lot of sense. At least she didn't have to run circles around that excuse to visit exotic Greenland. There were no polar bears or icebergs in Seattle.

"What kind of world do we want to live in?" Nathan asked. He repeated it again. "What kind of world do we want to live in?" His melancholic voice betrayed a sense of deep sadness.

"A better world?"

"We need to learn from the Danes," Nathan answered.

This conversation was not cheering her up. She took a swig of coffee as Nathan shared his final story on recent climate changes and their impact.

"Something interesting I've come across that not many people have heard about, is related to when the Vikings settled on Greenland. They went there during what is now known as the Medieval Warm Period. This warm period turned into the Little Ice Age and caused their eventual demise. Apart from climate records, the interesting thing, is that one can see the change in museum paintings.

Amanda's memory was being jogged of some aspects of the documentary she saw on the plane flight over.

"A historian named Neuberger studied twelve thousand paintings in forty-some art museums in the US and Europe. Apparently, he found a distinct change in the landscapes painted by artists. From clear blue skies before 1400, to more cloudy and dark skies after, for the next 500 years."

"And?"

"The kicker is that the average temperature difference between the Little Ice Age and the Medieval Warm Period was 2° Fahrenheit. A small change, but big impact."

"So, not much of a change then, can have very big effects?" Amanda clarified.

"Yeah, that's about right, Amanda."

"This small temperature difference just reminds me of when we get sick. I don't know why I'm thinking this. Maybe it's like our planet has a fever or something. We are the cells that make up the planet?"

"Huh?"

"I mean, a small change in our body temperature can make us very sick. We get a fever, and get both hot and cold at the same time. We can still get chills even when we're under a lot of blankets. So, our planet is sick in a way. But, we are part of the planet, so maybe we're sick in some way?"

"Interesting analogy, Amanda. I might use that someday when I talk to people. I think you know more than you let on."

"Or maybe it's like bacteria and viruses. We can't see them, but they can do major damage to us. I have no idea what I'm saying, Nathan. I'm really quite tired. I'm just speaking stream of consciousness."

"That's ok. I'm tired, too. Maybe it will only be when we have our backs against the wall and when enough people decide to learn a different way rather than stick to our set ways. Or when knowledge and courage triumph over hope and fear."

"Hope and fear?"

"Fear makes people hope. And I assume you know what springs eternal for better days ahead."

CHAPTER 13 – NANOQ'S LAND

A buzzer sounded, it was the alarm clock. She was having a nightmare. First night travel jitters she guessed. Amanda freshened up and made her way back out to the terminal area.

A familiar face was already waiting at the gate, it was Nathan.

"You look like you've seen a ghost."

"It was just a bad dream."

They exchanged further pleasantries as she tore into her morning pastry.

"Will I be able to see the different layers of snow?"

"If you look at a slice of snow under the right light, you may see a brilliant blue in the layers. It is quite beautiful."

"That's good to know. I was wondering, if you have already learned about our past from previous trips here and from Antarctica, why are you going there again?"

"You want the real reason or the official reason?"

"Both."

"A few years ago, a potential new location for ice coring was found. Several of my colleagues from Denmark and Greenland are waiting for me. We're part of an advance team going to our office in Kangerlussuaq. We'll collaborate there for a little while.

If we are satisfied with what we may have found, then, during the summer, we will fly to the center of Greenland to begin drilling."

"Center of Greenland, how mysterious. What do you hope to find?"

"We think this location might give us a high resolution core that goes back to 135,000 years, an improvement of 12,000 years."

"That's all?"

"That's it, but the detailed information it could provide us would be very valuable."

"My memory might be a little foggy, but didn't you say there are cores in Antarctica that go back even further?"

"Yes, but the cores in Greenland are more detailed. Greenland is also where ice coring as a science was first developed. It is good to measure change in different parts of the world to verify the global nature of any findings. There are ice coring efforts going on all over the world, not just Antarctica and Greenland. Coring happens on glaciers whether in the tropics like Kilimanjaro, which is melting fast, to the Andes, Himalayas, or Alaska."

"I didn't realize the effort was so extensive."

"Lots of people working on it. But that's just the official reason I'm going back."

A voice crackled over the intercom interrupting their conversation.

"Greenland Airways from Copenhagen to Kanger-lussuaq is ready to board. Any passengers needing special assistance or those with small children may board first."

"What's the real reason?" Amanda asked.

"As much as I love ice coring, it does get repetitive after awhile, but I have fallen in love with the land. The stark and raw beauty. I enjoy spending a few weeks there. My wife appreciates it too. She's going to Hawaii with a girlfriend and the kids while I'm gone. Besides, it's cool to say you're going to Greenland. Who thinks about it? Although, I've been there enough times, so that isn't the reason why anymore."

"That's funny! Your family is going to Hawaii and you're going to Greenland!"

"Quite an extreme difference."

"We would like to welcome passengers in rows twenty and higher."

They both checked their tickets.

"It's my turn to board," Nathan alerted.

"I'm glad we had the time so you could explain everything more in detail to me."

"My pleasure. Wish me luck if we open another time machine."

"Good luck!" Amanda announced enthusiastically.

Nathan walked through the doors and down the jet bridge.

Amanda waved. Then in a voice just a little louder than a whisper, she said to Polar Bear, "I guess in a way we're traveling back in time too." She thought about the childhood emotions connected to Polar Bear that she had been dealing with.

The intercom sounded again.

"We would like to invite all remaining passengers to now board."

Amanda walked down the jet bridge and boarded the plane. It would be a four hour and four minute flight to Kangerlussuaq, the gateway to Greenland. There were quite a few empty seats. She remembered that most tourists didn't arrive until later in the summer. She was one of the crazy, early few.

A feeling of both happiness and sadness came over her as the country of Denmark became smaller and smaller in the window. She was happy to learn about such a place, but sad to be leaving it so soon. Maybe she would have a chance to visit again on the return trip home.

With nothing to do while the plane flew over the ocean, her mind wandered. She started to write in her journal.

> *What is happiness? Maybe Nathan's clarification of wording, life satisfaction, is better. Isn't it easy to be relatively satisfied though? A morning coffee or my favorite chocolate dessert can leave me satisfied, temporarily. A full belly. Buying a new pair of shoes or outfit at the mall can do it too. If one has all the basics and then some to live, does that qualify as being satisfied? Is there a better or different word? Is it possible to be in an 'ecstatic' mood all day? Not jump around ecstatic, but. . . maybe like the feeling after incredible sex.*

> *Just 'naturally' happy, where nothing seems to bother you. I haven't felt that very often. How does that work anyway? You can have sex with someone a few times and you feel physically great afterward, and then the next time with the same person, it doesn't feel as great. It's like your*

compatible, then your not. Is there something wrong with me?

Is it possible to be 'naturally' happy without sugar, caffeine, or buying something? Those wear off eventually. There must be a better word.

She settled on the word, happiness, for now, for lack of imagination. Looking out the window, she wondered what it would be like to fly as a bird in the wind, or swim in the oceans like a dolphin, or whale. She continued writing.

Does happiness mean you are smiling all the time? No, that couldn't be it, could it? It's definitely not in the media, many of those smiles are fake or just momentary. Paid smiles. I would know, I'm in marketing.

Does it mean you have a big house? Live a life of luxury? Have a high salary? That definitely isn't it, in and of itself. A quick glance at rich and famous people in the news and those with their fifteen minutes of fame is a good enough reminder of that, never mind people I know.

Being with the love of your life? Your soul mate? Being married to 'your best friend?' What is that anyway? What is love? Does that include both mental and physical attraction, all the time, without thoughts of wanting to be with someone else? I think we use the word 'love' too much, and we don't even know what it is. If love is so great, why is there so much confusion about it? Isn't pretty much every song, ever written, about love?

What a misnomer – happily married couples. A watered down version of happiness perhaps. Maybe it is true in the beginning of relationships, but certainly not after awhile. Perhaps it is true for a very select few, but not the masses. Nobody I know personally. My co-workers and friends – "a good marriage takes work – a good marriage is a give and take - it's compromise." Do I want to compromise on my happiness? Maybe I'm just too idealistic.

Having a 'happy' family with loving kids? If Stephanie's life and people I know are any guide, this is not it either.

Not worrying about money, got that covered. Though I would worry, if I didn't have enough. That in and of itself is not happiness. Not worrying at all. Is that possible?

Being successful. Is that happiness? Plenty of people are successful, but they seem to just want more and more. I see it in myself, sometimes. If successful people are so happy, why do they keep wanting more and more? Why do some successful people look so unhappy. Their faces. Fame, money, power, material possessions, whatever. Success is not the road to deep happiness, I think.

Having parents that are proud of you? That doesn't seem like it is right either. Though it might not hurt.

Seldom to never sick? I don't get sick very often, that's not it. Being sick would certainly be a downer though.

To think positive all the time? No, that's not it. All those self-help gurus, new age or not, whatever. Being more efficient, and finding the power within, being your best, etc. . . whatever, whatever. Worthless in the long run.

Following one's passion? No, I don't think this is it either. Maybe for a certain period of time, but not over the long term, as doing the same thing over and over usually gets boring and mundane.

A good sex life. What is that? In the beginning of some relationships the sex seems to be great, but after awhile with the same person it just gets less interesting. I think it is like this for everyone with anyone. Maybe I just haven't found the right guy. I don't think it is this either.

A life free of stress? Is that even possible? To have no stress would be to have – not a care in the world. To not worry about anything. Is that even possible? No emotional baggage.

She closed her journal, looked outside again, then closed her eyes.

As the plane approached the eastern coast of Greenland, the pilot's voice crackled over the intercom. Amanda woke up out of her light slumber. The pilot finished speaking in Danish then started in English.

> "Ladies and gentlemen, we are cruising at about thirty-five thousand feet and will begin our descent in about forty minutes. I'd like to call now for your attention to look out either side of the aircraft as we are now passing directly over the east coast of Greenland."

> "Lucky for us, it is a very clear day. You should be able to see the pack ice that has formed on the water near the coast. In a few months a lot of the pack ice will melt."

> "The larger pieces are icebergs calved from glaciers. The rocky patches you will see are the tops of mountains. You only see the top due to the thickness of the ice sheet."

Amanda gazed in awe at her first glimpse with her own eyes of this mysterious and strange world. The time passed quickly.

The intercom crackled again.

> "We are now beginning our descent into the Kangerlussuaq area. You may notice some small blue colored lakes out there on the surface of the ice. These are surface ice melts where meltwater has collected. They will get larger as the spring and

summer progresses. If you look carefully, you can
see the outlines of streams also."

Amanda's eyes were hypnotized by the ice sheet of
Greenland. No videos, no photographs, the real thing.

The view outside gave a whole new definition to the saying, a winter wonderland. Blue melt pools among the glacier
ridges stood out like backyard swimming pools over a city.

The plane continued to descend. She saw the open ocean
and some pack ice along the west coast of Greenland as she
looked out toward the horizon. Soon, the ice cap ended and large
mountains appeared.

The intercom came to life again. It was the flight attendant.

"We are about to land. Please raise your seatbacks
and tray tables. Please turn off and put away all
personal electronics including any laptops. Please
fasten your seatbelts. The local time is now 10:01
a.m. Kangerlussuaq is four hours behind Copenhagen time."

A few moments later, the airplane touched down. Amanda
and Polar Bear had made it to Greenland.

Amanda walked down the jet stairs wearing her backpack while
holding Polar Bear. She took her first footsteps on Greenland.
Though it was only asphalted tarmac for the moment, it felt
good, despite the biting cold. The short trek to the terminal
looked daunting in the cold weather, but Amanda knew she
would have to get used to this. She walked with purpose toward

the terminal. Located at the base of a large hill, impressive mountains rose up behind the terminal building.

She crossed the edge of the tarmac and approached a sign welcoming visitors to Greenland. Underneath the Danish and Greenlandic, it read in English: Welcome to Greenland! Kangerlussuaq's 539 residents welcome you.

Below that was a digital readout, -15° Celsius, or a few degrees Fahrenheit, Amanda calculated later. She had arrived in Greenland toward the end of the two coldest months, February, and March. It felt that way. A closer look at the Greenland coat of arms revealed that it was a polar bear, it brought a smile to her face.

Waving on a nearby pole was the Greenland flag. The red and white colors matched the flag colors of Denmark. White in the upper half, red on the bottom. Set to the left of center was a circle with the reverse colors of each half, a red half circle on the white background. Amanda wondered what it meant.

Without further delay, she walked up the short flight of stairs that led from the landing area to the terminal, a sea of faces greeted her. They were Inuit faces, waiting for the arrival of loved ones.

Among them, a small boy standing in front. "Nanoq!" the boy blurted out while pointing his finger at Amanda.

Amanda froze in surprise.

A woman who appeared to be the boy's grandmother, smiled at Amanda and spoke gently, "Utoqqatserpunga."

Amanda smiled back, not knowing how to reply. Sensing other passengers wanting to walk past her, she gave one last glance at the boy and headed down the terminal to stretch her legs a bit.

As she headed down the terminal she spotted the entrance to what Nathan said was one of the better restaurants in the city, at the airport hotel. Nathan said Greenland was a strange place for newcomers, she could only wonder what other strange things lay ahead.

She grabbed a nearby luggage cart and placed Polar Bear and her backpack on it. She wandered around the small airport waiting for her next flight. A small photographic exhibit in the hallway caught her eye. Amanda examined the black and white pictures.

It was a short history of Kangerlussuaq as the site of one of the former military bases mentioned in the in-flight video documentary. The base was one of nine Western Greenland bases and five Eastern bases. As the Cold War continued, the base served as a re-supply point for radar stations that were part of the Distant Early Warning (DEW) system. The DEW system was designed to detect Soviet bombers flying over the North Pole. It was estimated that US and Canadian forces would have four, up to six hours, to prepare for an attack on the homeland, in addition to scrambling fighters to intercept. Installations were located on the inland ice, and at Sisimiut and Kulusuk.

The importance of the bases diminished as the threat from Intercontinental Ballistic Missiles gained importance. When the Cold War thawed, three of the four radar stations were closed. Thule, in far Northern Greenland, was left operational. The airport area came under control of the Greenland Home Rule government and took on its present name of Kangerlussuaq in 1992.

Greenland's history wasn't so untouched and pristine after all, she learned in greater detail. Amanda headed over to where her flight to Ilulissat was about to board. She sat down next to a middle aged woman.

"That is a nice polar bear you have there," the woman blurted out.

Amanda turned around and faced the woman. "Thank you."

"Going to Ilulissat?"

"Yes, I'm going to see the icebergs."

"They are very beautiful."

"I'm looking forward to it. Do you live there?"

"Yes."

A momentary silence interrupted the conversation, the kind of silence when two strangers aren't sure what to say next.

"It is good that you have a red bow on your stuffed polar bear."

"Why is that?"

"A hunter might mistake it for the real thing and shoot it!"

"Oh," Amanda replied in disbelief. She recoiled back.

The woman let out a hearty laugh. Amanda did not laugh along.

A voice came over the loudspeaker.

> "Due to a mechanical issue the flight to Ilulissat will be delayed for fifteen minutes."

Amanda let out a sigh. She looked over at the woman.

"Immaqa," the woman muttered. "Immaqa."

CHAPTER 14 – DARK AND LIGHT

One transatlantic flight, a day in Copenhagen, a night spent at an airport, and the flight to Greenland, was starting to make Amanda feel a little beaten up. She was looking forward to getting into Ilulissat to do some real on the ground exploring. It was now 11:30 a.m.

Now, settled into her window seat, Amanda thought about what the woman had said. She was on a mission to see polar bears in the wild, while those who lived on Greenland hunted them. It made her a little uncomfortable and she wasn't sure what to think. Perhaps she would understand this conundrum later. Amanda glanced outside, no jet engines on this plane. The black propeller blades began to spin as she continued to stare outside. Soon, they were just a blur.

The fifty passenger, Greenland Airways DASH-7, started down the runway with all four propellers spinning away in a loud steady hum. In a few moments the plane was aloft, flying north up the coast.

There were more mountains and pack ice as Amanda looked outside. She was amazed at how in around twenty-four hours, she had made it to a place that might as well have been on a different planet. The miracle of flight she mused. The short forty-five minute flight didn't leave very much time at cruising altitude before it began to descend into Ilulissat. Amanda looked out and was taken by the sight of giant white icebergs dotting the sea, it was a fascinating sight. Wasn't the iceberg that sank the *Titanic* from Greenland? She didn't remember where she had heard that.

The town and harbor area with several boats, mostly trawlers, frozen in place by the surrounding ice, came into view. Amanda's heart skipped a beat in anticipation.

The plane landed and Amanda braved the cold again as she entered the small terminal.

The small handheld sign with her name on it stood out like a lighthouse in complete darkness. While Amanda didn't know anyone in Greenland, it was a good feeling that at least someone knew of her.

She walked up and introduced herself. "Hi, I'm Amanda."

"Welcome to Ilulissat. Can I help you with your bag?" He had a semi-bewildered look as he glanced at Polar Bear.

"Yes, please." She let him take her large pack. She held on tight to Polar Bear and her smaller bag. "What's your name?"

"Josef." He was a middle aged Inuit man with dark uncombed hair and a moderate build.

"Nice to meet you, Josef."

"Where are you from?"

"I'm from America."

"Where in America?" the driver asked energetically as they headed toward a parked van.

"Seattle, Washington, do you know it?"

"That's where your president lives, right?"

"Oh, no!" Amanda laughed. "That is Washington D.C., I live in Washington State, all the way over in the opposite corner."

"Confusing. How long are you in town for?"

"Only for one night. I go to Qaanaaq tomorrow and then Savissivik to go sledding."

"Colder there, ma'am."

"It's quite cold here already."

"Not as cold as it used to be. Not as cold. . ."

They got in the small van and within minutes they had arrived at the hotel.

Amanda soon spotted five, silver, aluminum clad, igloo shaped structures, perched on a small hill overlooking the water. One of them would be her home for the night. She checked in and went to her room.

The igloo was furnished in contemporary Danish style with yellow bed sheets and a blue-green blanket folded up on the mattress. A blue curtain was parted to let in the sunlight. It was more modern than she thought it would be. There was a shower, toilet, color TV, radio, telephone, hair dryer, and a coffee maker.

The room could be like any other hotel room in the world, except the room was shaped like an igloo. The curved walls met at the center where a round window was placed. Any thoughts of resting were drifting away as Amanda began to relax in her hotel room, her sense of adventure was getting fired up. Amanda warmed up with a cup of hot tea and a nice hot shower. She bundled up for the walk to the front desk.

Amanda prepared to face the cold again. There was her expensive winter jacket covering several layers, her wool scarf, and hat. Her warm underpants were covered by snow-proof ski pants. Her extremities were covered with ear muffs, double layered gloves, and waterproof hiking boots. She grabbed several instant handwarmers from a package that she had brought along too. She had come prepared and left almost nothing to chance on this trip. She waved goodbye to Polar Bear and made quick work of the walk to the hotel lobby and restaurant.

"Hello!" Amanda greeted the clerk again.

"Did you like room?" The clerk asked in a fragmented English accent.

"Oh yes, it is very unique. I like it very much."

"Good. How can I help you?"

"I am only here for one day before I fly to Qaanaaq. I am hoping to hike to a better vantage point to see the icebergs. Do you have any maps?"

"Yes," the woman answered. She pulled a map out from behind the counter and handed it to Amanda. "You may have this hiking map."

"Thank you. Is there anywhere else you can recommend?" Amanda placed the map in her backpack.

"Many people like to go to local market. We call it kalaaliaraq."

"Where is that?" She didn't even try to pronounce the word.

The woman pointed toward a spot on a map underneath a plastic sheet on top of the counter.

"Is it open all day?"

"Yes, best when the fishermen and hunters return. We have shuttle bus, takes you from our hotel to center of town. Ask to stop at the harbor. I will call it for you. Please sit down."

Amanda turned and sat on the bench. She pulled out the hiking map from her small backpack. She turned it over and realized the hike had a detailed description.

Hike to Sermermiut

The trail is open all year and the route is marked with yellow stones. The trail starts from the old heliport and leads to a cliff view over icebergs and some ruins of an old Inuit settlement. The 1.5 km / way takes approximately 30 - 45 minutes each way depending on walking speed and trail conditions.

This trail is one of the best trails to view the large icefjord. Glaciers are calved from the Ilulissat Glacier (Sermeq Kujalleq) most frequently in the summer. They take 1.5 years to travel the 45 km from the mouth of the fjord. The fjord is 7 km wide. The icebergs move relatively freely through the 600 meter deep fjord before arriving at the mouth which is only 200 – 300 meters deep. A boat trip is recommended when they start in May.

Kaellingekloften (Suicide Cliff)

A short walk east from Sermermiut is a small path that leads to a narrow 35 meter tall cliff. Old women used to throw themselves off the cliff during times of extreme famine. In the pre-colonial period, committing suicide was more accepted and sometimes the only possibility of saving the rest of the settlement, including children and young people, from extinction due to insufficient resources.

Icefjord Hike

Follow the blue stone path east for approximately 1 hour from Kaellingekloften along the icefjord. You will pass Holms Bakke / Seqinniarfik. A little further along the rock face you will pass a lake, the route ends at the quarry.

Celebration of Light

You may wish to detour and climb the hill to Holms Bakke, it is just past the second Inuit grave. Every year on January 13th, at 12:45 p.m., the people of Ilulissat meet at Holms Bakke to celebrate the sun on the horizon after 6 weeks of 24 hour darkness.

This sounded interesting. Conflicting thoughts entered Amanda's mind. On one trail system was both a suicide cliff and a place of celebration, light over darkness. Why would two very different places be located right next to each other?

"Miss, the shuttle bus is here to take you to town," the clerk announced, breaking Amanda's concentration on the map.

She walked outside and boarded the mini-van.

"Hello, again."

"Hello, Josef. Can you please take me to the market?"

They pulled away from the hotel and headed toward the bridge to cross into town.

"After the market, I'm going to hike to see the icefjord. Do you know where I start the hike?"

"At the old heliport. I can wait for you at the market, then I can take you there. It is not busy this time of year."

"Excellent."

The mini-van drove toward the center with a thankful Amanda realizing how helpful a brief rest in a hotel room could be. She must have been half asleep on the ride over as she didn't notice quite as much as she did this time.

Richly colored homes and buildings painted blue, red, green, yellow, and dark turquoise, stood out against the barren land surrounding them. A church spire reached high into the sky. The visual contrasted with the auditory as the sound of dogs howling in the distance punctured the otherwise still air.

"The home colors are so beautiful here."

"Most visitors never learn the true story of why they are colored the way they are."

"Why's that?"

"The home colors were not painted for only beauty before, but money reasons. Red was the cheapest paint, then blue, yellow, and green. The most expensive and least durable color is white, it is a mark of status. Now, all the colors are standardized."

"That's interesting. The final result is beautiful. There must be a lot of dogs here too."

"Several thousand. It just depends on who you ask."

"That's a lot. Are there any good restaurants in town?"

"You could try the Chinese restaurant in the center of town." Josef pointed in the general direction as he steered the van. "The restaurant at your hotel is good too."

"Chinese?"

"Yes. Good food. Many people are surprised when I mention it."

"Surprising to me."

"Greenland can be a strange place. Expect the unexpected."

Something clicked in Amanda's brain. This was the second time she had heard someone say this. A few minutes later and the mini-van had arrived near the center of town.

"Here we are. The market is just up ahead by the docks. I'll wait here. If I'm not here, it means the hotel has called me back. You can walk around town and come back, I won't be gone for very long."

"That's great," Amanda answered as she pulled the sliding door open. She closed it with a thud and walked toward the market.

Amanda wasn't prepared for what she was about to see and smell. As she walked toward what she thought was the market, her eyes were transfixed by the huge carcass of a walrus, tusks and all else attached, lying motionless. She froze for a moment, unsure of how to react. This is why the clerk said people liked to visit the market. There was nothing like this back in Seattle. "This is not like Pike Place Market," Amanda spoke out loud to no one in particular. "They should come here."

She mustered the courage to walk around the large, brown colored, dead walrus, sensing that it might come alive and jump up at any moment. She was rewarded by a brilliant color of red covering much of the snow before her, it was blood. A man was butchering the carcass of a seal nearby.

It was a spotted ring seal, or what was left of one. Amanda watched both in horror and raw fascination. A few feet away was a boy sitting near a wooden rack where some unidentifiable meat was drying. The boy ignored Amanda. Some women were chatting by another building while others were cutting up some meat. Some animal skins were drying by a wooden rack over by the women, they looked like seal skins to Amanda.

Amanda walked around a few more minutes in a dazed and confused mood. She turned to walk back to the van and saw that the walrus was being butchered now, it looked nothing like its former self. A pool of blood was frozen on the ground next to it. Amanda hurried on. Her first encounter with the wildlife of Greenland, was dead wildlife.

Returning to the van, Josef drove her to the trailhead where she began her hike. It was getting late in the afternoon, but there was still plenty of daylight. She quickly made it to the first vantage point.

Amanda gazed upon the scene before her. Floating out in the partially frozen fjord were towering masses of ice, they were the huge icebergs she saw from the plane window. It was a sight unlike anything she could have imagined. Some were floating, others were stationary, surrounded by pack ice. They were like giant puzzle pieces in the ocean, yet these would never be put together. They were fated to drift away and melt.

Many of the icebergs stood more than two hundred feet tall out of the water. The size of the icebergs before her only hinted at their true size. The portion of an iceberg floating on the water was often only 10 to 20% of its entire size, Amanda recalled.

Amanda tried to count them, but there were just too many, she gave up. She sat down on some rocks and was mesmerized by the milky white color of the icebergs. The silence was deafening. The eerie silence was punctuated only by an occasional wind gust. Amanda could hear her own heartbeat. There were no cars, no footsteps, no birds, no voices, and not another human being in visual sight. How could so much be so quiet?

Cool air blew on her face, but it didn't feel as cold as she thought it would be. Perhaps it was the magical setting before her, refocusing attention away from herself, or maybe it was her layers of clothing.

She saw a sign that had escaped her attention earlier as she walked back on the trail.

> Sermermiut was inhabited from about 1400 BC to 1850 AD. This was the largest known settlement in 1737 AD. It was surpassed by the opening of a harbor and trade station at what is now Ilulissat. This area was a good place for settlement due to the melting glaciers giving off large amounts of oxygen. The oxygen helps to encourage high densities of fish and seals. Continuing on the trail takes you to Kaellingekloften (Suicide Cliff).

She continued hiking, there was enough daylight left. It wasn't long before she approached a small sign that said Kaellingekloften. She stopped for a moment and looked at the rocky terrain before her that ended with a sharp cliff drop. Her body became numb as she imagined old women running toward the cliff. Did they cry? Did they scream? Did they take a running jump, or just stand and fall over? Did they close their eyes? Were they scared?

A loud splash interrupted her train of thought.

It came from the cliff bottom. Amanda looked around, there was no one in sight. She thought she heard footsteps, but it was just the quickening of her heartbeat. Amanda stepped back, wondering if there were spirits in the area, she shivered.

Amanda's curiosity got the best of her, she had to investigate the splash, or was that just her imagination too? She slid her feet toward the cliff edge further, all the while looking around as if someone might come running up to her and push her over. She walked to the edge and looked over. There was nobody there, just ripples in the semi-frozen water. It must have been a rock, it must have been a rock, Amanda thought to herself.

She stepped back and felt her head spin in a momentary state of vertigo. She snapped her head to the left and right wondering if there was anyone around. "Who's there?"

No answer.

"What do you want?"

Still no answer.

She turned around. Perhaps there was somewhere else she could go and brighten her mood, this cliff was a little depressing and spooky. She decided to try for the top of the hill called Holms Bakke, or Seqinniarfik.

Amanda reached the top of the small hill and looked out, it was no less of a stunning view. She imagined a world filled with darkness. Then a world emerging from that darkness with the arrival of the Sun. It must be quite a sight, perhaps like a feeling of good over evil.

Or maybe, above all else, that hope would return. As she had that thought, she remembered Nathan's comment. Didn't hope 'spring forever?' People hoped because they were fearful.

Wasn't hope just another way of saying, 'I'm worried?' Was fear fated to spring forever?

The dark days after Stephanie was killed came to mind again. Amanda had come on this trip to make sense of where her life was going. Now, she was revisiting the topic of death, a subject that she had never felt comfortable talking about. It didn't seem to bother her very much up here. Maybe it was because there was nothing else to cloud one's thoughts out here. It was just her and the stark nature around her. It was simple, perhaps like life itself she thought. Birth and death. Darkness, then light, a natural cycle. In a more useful and practical sense, it was like sleeping she realized. Everyday you awoke from the darkness of sleep into the light of a new day.

She laughed out loud as if being violently tickled, her puffs of breath drifting with the wind. It was all beginning to make sense.

Perhaps this place and the Suicide Cliff were symbolic of her journey to Greenland. From sorrow and confusion, to joy and understanding. From death, comes life. Amanda resolved that one day she must return here to see that January day for herself.

Amanda woke up. It was still dark outside as she looked at the porthole in the top of her hotel room. She couldn't sleep anymore. Her flight to Qaanaaq did not leave until later in the morning. Thoughts were swirling around in her mind, she needed to write.

Amanda pulled out her small journal and turned on the light. She flipped through the pages wondering if she would run out of paper in her journal before the trip was over. This trip away from everyone and everything was therapeutic.

My 1st Day in Greenland

I'm finding this place to be a little confusing. I sit here in the comfort of my hip and comfortable modern hotel room. Yet, just earlier yesterday, I was witness to such a raw display of how the people here live off the land with nature.

I find it an interesting contrast that if anyone back home saw on TV the sight of 'poor, cute' seals being butchered, they would cry, bloody murder. Here, it is just a way of life. I wonder if the Inuit view any of the animals here as cute. Perhaps not.

What a different concept of nature. I wonder what they would think of our mass slaughter of cattle, chickens, pigs, sheep, and other animals. What would they think of all of our zoos? Perhaps we aren't so different after all, or maybe we are.

Amanda reflected for a few moments on the Suicide Cliff and she realized that these people were making a choice to die. She recalled her conversation with Ruth at the zoo about confined animals. Was it better to let the animals at zoos live a longer life in captivity? Or a shorter, but freer life in the wild?

She wondered about the right to die debate that was occasionally in the news back home. It was taken to its ultimate conclusion here. How did our society become so complicated that people tried to dictate their views on death over yours? To hell with all those bureaucrats and people with their silly religious views or whatever was at the root of their opinions. This was freedom. Why would people try and take this away from you?

What if Stephanie had ended up in a vegetative state? Maybe she was lucky to have died without suffering for too long. A living will was something she would have to write someday. She began writing again in her travel notebook.

It was pretty eerie being out there by Suicide Cliff. Old women killing themselves for the good of the rest? What a clash with how people behave today. Here the people sacrificed themselves for the rest of the group. How many people today would make a deliberate early exit and not be an undue hardship on the rest of their family?

Are we that afraid of death? Maybe we've watched too many movies. What does it say about us when we take so many drugs to live longer? How many people are trying way too hard to look young? How many people are trying so hard to artificially extend their existence?

The behavior of so many people seems kind of pathetic. If I ever need so much treatment to keep myself alive or to live a decent life, I would just as soon die.

Now that I think about this, I do remember reading about a man in San Diego who was diagnosed with incurable cancer. He rented a bi-plane and jumped out without a parachute to avoid burdening his family. But, sometimes doctors are wrong.

I wonder why people try so hard to live long lives? Maybe they worked too hard during their prime years, delaying gratification until some magic pre-determined age by some bureaucrats. Hmmm. . . that reminds me of someone I know all too well who has been going down that path. The age keeps moving higher due to the financial problems of social security and our growing desires. I probably won't get anything. :)

Maybe it's related to the 'bigger is better' mentality. Except, lots of people think 'longer is better.'

How many people think that retirement is some kind of paradise? Maybe because people think there is a heaven, they don't bother to live fully in this life, they think something so much better is waiting for them. What if they're really going to hell? Not that I believe in either place. I don't know what to believe. Do I need to believe in anything?

Whatever. Perhaps the people that killed themselves were honoring their own lives by being masters of their final earthly destiny instead of just starving to death.

It was one thing to write about something in the abstract, quite another to relate to it on a personal level. Even though the relationship with her parents wasn't the greatest, she still worried about them at times, as a good child would. What happened if they needed to be taken care of in a nursing home? What an unpleasant thought. A nursing home, was that like a zoo? A place where people doted on you in your final days. You would forever be remembered as someone on the decline, not the healthy, vibrant, energetic person of your youth. Just as animals at zoos were like, a shadow of their former selves.

"Live free or die," she whispered to herself. Amanda was getting a sense of how she would live the rest of her life, though she couldn't quite articulate it. She didn't want to go out ebbing away like a slow drain. She would go out in a blaze of glory, like the end of some classic Hollywood movies. It seemed like the only dignified option at this moment.

One positive thing about going out in a blaze of glory was that you didn't have to worry about accumulating so much money for health problems. When the rope was near its end, you would just go. Multi-million dollar health insurance policies? Naw, if it took that much money to keep her alive, she would just as soon be dead.

Amanda realized at this moment she was thankful to be where she was. She was about to embark on a grand adventure to find a polar bear in the wild. She was in one of the most remote spots in the world, living life, not reading about it. She had chosen experience over material goods and status this time. Perhaps Mary was right, this trip would be the start of many more adventures.

Amanda put her pen down and got ready to go back to the airport for her flight to Qaanaaq. She finished packing and stared outside the window. She watched the sky brighten outside.

CHAPTER 15 – 77.5° LATITUDE

Qaanaaq, at 77.5° latitude, was the second most northerly airport in the world with scheduled airline service. Longyearbyen in Svalbard beat Qaanaaq, but only by less than one degree. However, Qaanaaq was visited by far fewer people than the islands of Norway's Svalbard. Revealed by the fact that there was only one hotel in town, with just five small rooms available. Amanda was one of the lucky visitors.

"We finally made it," Amanda spoke aloud as she settled into her small hotel room with Polar Bear by her side. Polar Bear wore his usual expression, not flinching at any of Amanda's words nor making a sound. Her words cut through the warm air inside.

It had been an uneventful flight from Ilulissat to Qaanaaq. Qaanaaq had no tourist attractions such as the icebergs in Ilulissat. What it lacked in tourist attractions, it made up for in its resident's abilities to have survived this far north for so long.

"We haven't even begun our dog sledding adventure and I feel like this trip has been incredible already. What do you think?"

There was no answer.

Amanda looked at Polar Bear. "I'm going to get some snacks before we leave tomorrow, do you want anything?" She waited for an answer. "I didn't think so."

Amanda picked up the small map on her room table and walked outside, heading toward the center of town. The first thing she noticed was that it was colder than Ilulissat. The dryness of the air made the temperature of -3° Fahrenheit more pleasant than it sounded. Amanda walked down the gradual sloping hillside that the town was built on, toward the city center, and closer to the ocean. It was still frozen over in large part.

The homes in Qaanaaq were painted in similar colors to Ilulissat. Bright cheerful shades of blue, red, and green adorned the majority of buildings. She walked by the fire station, a shiny red truck was parked out in front. Following the map, she found what she was looking for, a reddish brown building, home of the local shopping centre. Amanda wondered what sort of things they would sell in a shopping centre all the way up here.

As she walked into the warehouse atmosphere of the building, there were more products than she would have guessed. The colors of the fruit and vegetable section caught her attention.

A tapestry of red, yellow, orange, and green from apples, oranges, lemons, and other assorted fruits and vegetables filled her field of vision. It was no different than any other supermarket. It surprised Amanda to see such products available in a place where no trees grow. Amanda bought some fruit and some snacks. She wasn't quite sure what to expect on the dog sledding trip. Fresh meat, such as the kind she saw at the market in Ilulissat crossed her mind. Mary's tip sheet had warned her about that much.

Exiting from the centre, she made her way down near to the frozen shoreline. There were several small icebergs in sight, solidly frozen in place, but nothing like she had seen in Ilulissat. In the distance was a large snow covered island sticking out from the frozen white pack ice. Herbert Island it said on her map. It was about ten miles away, but it seemed a lot closer. If she had the energy, Amanda felt like she could just stroll across the ice to the island.

This would be as close to the North Pole as she was probably going to get in her lifetime, unless she someday had the wherewithal to go to Svalbard she reasoned. Perhaps someday when she had other people to go with.

Where would her next trip be Amanda wondered. There was no point in asking that question until she had seen a polar bear in the wild.

The stillness of the air, the sea of white, few human buildings, and quietness surrounding her, interrupted only by the occasional dogs howling, cleared her mind and heart. This place had a way of simplifying every thought by cutting out all the distractions. The view went on forever with no trees or haze. The lack of trees was both haunting and peculiar.

Amanda decided to head back to the hotel and watch some TV in the shared living area. By the same time tomorrow, she would no longer be anywhere close to an electrical outlet.

The next morning arrived with bright blue skies. They portended a good start to Amanda's dog sledge adventure. The small hotel room with two single beds separated by the smallest of foot paths, filled with light. Luxurious this was not. Amanda woke early, dressed, washed up. She reveled in her last hot shower for awhile. She went out to have breakfast in the small dining room.

The table was already set in the dining room. Nothing exotic on the table. Toast, jam, and some corn soup would be her initial fuel for the day. As Amanda finished her breakfast, the hotel owner walked in.

"Your ride to the airport is here."

"Thank you."

"I will see you when you get back. Good luck. I hope you find what you are looking for here, expect the unexpected."

She stood frozen as the innkeeper's final words echoed through her head. She came to, only to find her already gone. What was it about Greenland and the unexpected?

She put the idea aside and braved the outdoors again. Emerging from the hotel, the bright light caused her to reach for her sunglasses. Just a few steps away was a small mini-van. She opened the door and a warm face greeted her, a different driver.

"Kumoorn"

Amanda looked at the man puzzled.

"It means good morning, you must be Amanda."

"Oh, yes."

"I am Jaaku, or Jakob if you like."

"Good morning, Jakob."

"Do you like Qaanaaq?" the man asked politely.

"I'm surprised how modern it seems here. I saw the large satellite dish at the top of the hill."

"Many people are surprised by that."

Amanda wondered how many people 'many' meant.

"We also have a modern power station, a heat station which supplies most of the homes in the central district, an incinerator for trash, and we have a water station too. We melt ice collected from the mountain behind the city, or we collect the meltwater from it during the summer. Qaanaaq is very modern."

"Yes, it is." She was taken aback by how proud the man seemed of the modern technology the city had. "I was surprised you had so many fresh fruits and vegetables too."

"Oh, yes, we have fresh food deliveries two times a week by air. Supply ships come every year in August and September after the pack ice has fully melted with more food, oil, fuel, and building materials from Denmark."

"So that's why the selection is so good."

Jakob nodded and began the short drive to the airport. With the small van approaching the airport, Amanda noticed a four arrowed sign that she didn't see before. Pointing in different directions it read:

Qaanaaq
Grise Fjord 367 km
Nordpolen 1393 km
Kobenhavn 5770 km
Centrum

She was a long way from civilization as she knew it, and she would only get further away.

The Qaanaaq airport terminal and control tower building stood out in bright blue against its monotone surroundings.

"We are very proud of our airport. Before it was built in September 2001, the only way to get here was to fly to the US Thule Airbase," Jakob remarked as he pulled up to the terminal.

"I didn't know that it was so new. Thank you for the ride."

"I will see you again when you return."

Amanda smiled and headed into the terminal building with Polar Bear and her two packs.

"Miss, your helicopter is waiting for you," the agent advised as she handed Amanda back her ID and ticket. "Do you have your Thule Air Base transfer permit with you as well?"

She had almost forgotten about the government letter that Mary had given her earlier. It allowed her to transit the Thule Air Base. "Yes, of course," she replied as she rummaged through her bag and showed it to the agent.

Amanda turned and looked out the windows to the tarmac and saw the bright red paint job of the helicopter waiting for her. This was the scheduled flight to Savissivik. This flight would take her near the edge of the coast and to the ice floe edge to search for a real polar bear in the wild.

She walked out toward the helicopter wearing her trusty backpack and holding on tight to Polar Bear as a gust of wind blew across the tarmac.

A pilot emerged from the helicopter and motioned Amanda into the back. She climbed into the helicopter and saw two bench seats, she was the only passenger. She tossed her packs and Polar Bear on the backseat. He shut the door and latched it tight. As the pilot climbed into the front seat, she made eye contact with him as he got comfortable. The pilot did not appear to be a native Inuit.

"My manifest says only one passenger."

Amanda gave him a befuddled look.

The pilot nodded his head in Polar Bear's direction.

Amanda caught on. "He's my good friend. He looks big, but he doesn't take up too much space, the agent said he was ok."

At this point, Amanda had thought of every excuse possible to explain away why she was carrying around a large stuffed polar bear. She decided she might as well have some fun.

"No problem. Maybe you will see the real thing out there," the pilot answered along with a hearty laugh.

"I brought him for good luck so that I will," Amanda responded as she came up with another excuse to avoid telling the whole story.

"It's a big good luck charm."

They both laughed.

"This is my first time in a helicopter, will I get sick?"

"Should be a smooth ride today. I think you will enjoy it. Please put these headphones on, it will help us talk to each other by canceling out the rotor noise."

Amanda grabbed the headphones from the pilot's outstretched arm.

The engine started and the rotor blades began to turn. In a moment, they were off the ground heading toward the coast. This was Amanda's first helicopter flight, but fifth flight on this trip. She looked out the window as the blue Qaanaaq airport terminal became smaller and faded from view.

The pilot was right, it was a very smooth ride and a wonderful sensation to be slicing through the air and skimming over land. The difference between this flight and the earlier ones to get to Qaanaaq is that she was much closer to the ground. Details that would be too small in a jet or propeller driven plane presented themselves in their full glory.

"What kind of helicopter is this?"

"It is a Bell 212," the pilot answered.

"How fast are we going?"

"Top speed on this helicopter is 185 kilometers per hour, with a range of 370 kilometers. We are now at 135 kilometers per hour and increasing. Feel free to ask me any questions about what you are looking at."

Amanda gazed at all of the controls, it looked complicated.

"We will fly to the Thule Air Base, refuel, and then fly to Savissivik."

"Do you guys have a lot of helicopters?"

"We have four of these Bell helicopters, and three Eurocopter AS 350s, and two big Sikorsky S-61s. They are all based in different cities. We have all the major areas covered."

"You fly this route a lot?"

"Most of the time I fly a regular schedule, but other times I fly in support of scientific expeditions. I have even done a few medical evacuations and rescue missions."

"Rescue missions?"

"Sometimes hunters get trapped on floating ice."

Amanda's head perked up. "Floating ice?"

"Sometimes hunters will be on the pack ice and the piece of ice they are on will separate from the other ice. Then they get pushed out into the open water. They either have to wait until it gets pushed back, and sometimes it doesn't, or pray that they will get rescued by a helicopter."

"Pray?"

"There are no mobile phones out here. Some hunters have portable high powered radios or satellite phones. I don't think Lars has one. He's too good for that or just old fashioned, depending on your perspective. I don't ever recall picking up a tourist."

"That's comforting," Amanda replied somewhat sarcastically. Her eyes bulged wide open. Amanda wondered just how many tourists made it out here, she knew it wasn't many. Even if a tourist disappeared, would anybody notice out here in this vast wilderness? What had she gotten herself into? Then all of a sudden, she wondered how the pilot would know who she is. "You know, Lars?"

"It's a small community of people up here, everyone kind of knows everyone. He mentioned that he was taking a young American woman out on a dog sledge adventure."

"Oh," it was both spooky and reassuring. She, or they, wouldn't be forgotten if they got lost or went missing, presumably.

"There's a lot of turbulence closer to the ground right now. I am going to fly higher for a smoother ride."

The pilot turned around and smiled at Amanda. She grinned back and looked out the window instead.

Looking out the window she noticed that not all of the ocean was frozen over. There was a large section of open water and what appeared to be channels of open water going off in different directions, like breaks in the ice.

"Why is the water not frozen everywhere this time of year?"

The pilot glanced to the right. "That's the North Water Polynya."

"What is that?"

"A polynya is an area of open water surrounded by pack ice. They form when warmer water is pushed up from deeper below. The warm water either melts the surface ice or prevents it from forming. The North Water is the largest here. It stays open year round, but contracts into a smaller area further north as winter arrives. It grows again during the spring and into summer. It becomes ice free before most of the strait is ice free."

"What about the channels over there?"

"Those are shore leads. They form due to wind and currents preventing pack ice from establishing themselves. Mammals like bowhead whales, and belugas, and narwhals, use the shore leads to navigate. Many of the shore leads stay open year round."

Amanda continued to look in fascination at all the forms of ice as they flew over them. While seeing the icebergs in Ilulissat was magnificent, this was a different visual stimulus. She couldn't help but think how special this moment was. How many people would ever get to experience such a different world firsthand?

She gazed down and saw snow covered mountains and glacier tongues up close. It was an alien world. It reminded her of photos from Alaska.

The Thule Air Base came into view as Amanda continued to enjoy this new experience.

"The Thule Air Base is also known as Pituffik."

"What did you call it again?"

"Pituffik, it's the name of the hunting village that used to be there. It means – where dogs are tied up."

"That's funny. Why does the US have a base up here?"

"It's a radar station. It is also part of your missile defense system, too."

"It seems like America has bases everywhere."

The pilot didn't respond to Amanda's consternation.

"After we land, just wait for me to power down the rotors, then you can go out to a small building, I'll point it out to you. They'll check your permit there. You can wait there while I get this copter refueled and then we'll be on our way to Savissivik. You can leave all your belongings in the helicopter, there is no one else coming aboard."

Amanda was officially on an American military base. She breathed a sigh of relief in the waiting room. Wow, she thought to herself, it was another story she could tell to all of her friends and family back home.

The primary part of her trip hadn't even started and she could talk about helicopters, military air bases, missile defense systems, dead walruses, an igloo hotel room, ice cores, and giant icebergs now. And this wasn't even mentioning anything she had already experienced in Denmark proper. Including that would add, seeing herself unreversed in a mirror, meeting the Little Mermaid, making a new friend, and riding a bicycle all over her first European city. It wasn't just the first European city, it was her first foreign city that she had visited, other than cities in Canada a long time ago. It was also her first time flying across the Atlantic Ocean.

She poured herself a cup of coffee and looked at some of the photographs on the wall. They were photos of the construction of the base, various aircraft, and of some of the barracks which she had spotted from the air. There were also some photos of local wildlife, a polar bear included.

As she glanced outside at the helicopter, she noticed various unidentifiable military aircraft parked near the runway. So this is where all her tax dollars were going she thought to herself. Even out here near the top of the world, there were machines and infrastructure devoted to war.

She let out a sigh and waited a little longer for the second part of her helicopter ride.

As the chopper glided toward its final destination, Amanda continued to look in awe over the ever changing view. Icebergs frozen amongst the pack ice stood out. The chopper glided over the peaks and valleys of the mountains covered with snow and

ice. Her attention on the passing scenery was suddenly interrupted.

"We are approaching Savissivik."

A tiny town, hugging a small, snow-covered mountain,
came into view. It was surrounded by the white carpet of pack ice
which covered the ocean. She counted a couple dozen small
buildings. Most of them were painted a darker shade of red with
some blues and grays, they were all snow covered.

The buildings closest to where the helicopter was about to
land came into focus. The helicopter pad appeared to be built
along the frozen shoreline. She saw movement as the helicopter
drew closer, they were sledge dogs. Amanda counted about a
dozen dogs. A figure stepped outside from one of the small buildings and looked up.

The helicopter set down and the rotors powered off. The pilot
hopped out and opened the door. Amanda grabbed her back-
packs and Polar Bear, then jumped out. She gave a thumbs up to
the pilot.

A figure emerged from the snow still swirling about.

"You must be, Amanda."

"Yes, yes. I am. You are, Lars?"

"Good to meet you, Amanda."

"You, too," Amanda answered in a partial state of shock.
While she had gotten used to the small town atmosphere of
Greenland towns, now she was in a different situation entirely.
She was in an even smaller town in the middle of nowhere. A
small town with well under one hundred inhabitants, surrounded
by nothing more than mountains and ice. Soon, she would be on
the snow and ice in the middle of nowhere. She had probably already flown over some of the areas she would be traversing.

"I need to have a few words with the pilot. Just walk over to the building. I'll introduce you to the dogs."

Lars exchanged a few words with the pilot while Amanda stood by the nearest building and observed some of the barking dogs from a distance.

Lars helped the pilot unload some supplies. As Lars headed back toward Amanda, the helicopter powered up again and zoomed away.

"Follow me, I have a lot to show you before we go." Lars picked up her large backpack, and they headed toward one of the other buildings nearby.

Amanda took a deep breath and then made one last glance at the helicopter in the distance. She thought about the possibility of getting stuck on a piece of floating ice. What had she gotten herself into? "Whatever, whatever, Amanda," she muttered to herself.

CHAPTER 16 – CAPE YORK DREAMING

A cacophony of howling dogs echoed through the air and woke Amanda up from any remaining thoughts of the events that led her to this place. These were the dogs she saw from the helicopter.

"How was your flight?" Lars asked as he turned around to face Amanda.

"Breathtaking."

She noticed Lars' eyes shifting up and down her figure, sizing her up. Was he wondering what a young, all-American girl, was doing so far from home?

"Have you ever driven a dog sledge before?" Lars asked as he glanced over at the dogs who were still barking, but less so as the excitement from Amanda's arrival started to settle in.

"No, this is my first time, first time to Greenland."

"Let's go inside and I will go over our plan and what you should expect. Then you need to tell me a little bit about yourself so I understand your limitations. The Arctic can be a very unforgiving place. There is no civilization to fall back on once we are out there. We have only our wits and imagination."

"Wits and imagination," Amanda repeated, wondering what he meant by imagination.

She took careful note of his outfit as he turned around. He was covered in a jacket made of animal fur with a bushy maned hood. It appeared to be some combination of animals, she wasn't sure. It was a sharp contrast to her modern day clothing. She had seen others in the earlier towns with similar outfits, but for some reason she noticed it more here. Her gut reaction was that it was a little off putting as she thought about it more.

Maybe it was because he was native Danish and not Inuit. He didn't fit the mold of her stereotype, which was that only native peoples could wear fur. She wondered what other stereotypes lay hidden in the back of her mind about people who wore such clothes. What media or self-created impressions had been driven deep inside her? Were they less intelligent, less wise, primitive?

Lars led Amanda into a small wooden building. It was warmer inside than outside. It was warm enough that Amanda contemplated even taking off her outer jacket. She spotted a small room heater.

Lars sat down and invited Amanda to do the same on a small bench. She set Polar Bear down on the bench. When her vision adjusted to the inside of the building, the first thing she noticed was the man himself. He looked to be younger than the mid-forties that Mary had said he was. He appeared a little gruff, but was clean shaven. He seemed to be a man who could take care of himself in any situation. He was here in this remote place by choice, not by accident.

As she unzipped her outer jacket, she thought she caught a furtive glance from Lars directed at her chest.

"You arrived when most everyone is still sleeping off the effects of a birthday party for a village elder. You can tour the town later when we return. We are going to go straight out on to the ice toward Cape York. So, you are here to find a polar bear."

"Yes," Amanda answered. His stature intimidated her.

"It looks like you have already found one," Lars noted as he nodded his head at her stuffed, red bowed, polar bear.

"Oh. Him. It's a long story, but he is a good luck charm."

"We will have plenty of time together for you to tell me that long story. I have some stories to tell for you, if you want to hear them."

Amanda grinned.

"Would you like some tea?" Lars asked, glancing over at a small thermos.

"Yes, please."

"Have you ever camped before?"

"A couple of times, but it was only out of a car."

Lars handed Amanda a cup with a tea bag and poured her some hot water.

"Today, we will sledge for about thirty kilometers before setting up camp. Most days we will try to average about fifty kilometers. We will head out onto the ice to search and then we will make our way back to Savissivik. We will meet up with some hunters here if we are unsuccessful, and even if we are. You can learn more about the traditional ways here, they will also know best where else to look if we are unsuccessful. We will sledge to Cape York, then back toward the Melville Bay Nature Reserve. A nature reserve here is what you might call, a national park. When we are back in Savissivik, you will take the regularly scheduled helicopter service back to Qaanaaq."

"How many kilometers to miles again?"

"Oh. Right. I can tell you in miles, Amanda. I'm used to converting metric to imperial and vice versa. A kilometer is about

60% of a mile. So, thirty kilometers is about eighteen miles, and fifty kilometers is about thirty miles."

"That's easy. Just use whatever you're comfortable with. I can calculate that. It sounds like a good plan." Of course, she knew more or less what to expect, but the details, nothing.

"You must know that I cannot guarantee that we will find a polar bear. Many times the hunters come back empty-handed. Polar bears have one of the widest territories of any mammal. I know where to look, but we must be lucky."

"I understand, my travel agent told me this."

"Why did you come to such a far away place to see a polar bear? You could have just gone to Canada to see their annual migration on Hudson Bay."

"Yes, I know. Somebody once told me that it was worth the extra effort to have a wildlife encounter. I don't think the atmosphere of Churchill is right for me at this time in my life. I just felt like doing something a little crazy too." She was thinking, big crazy, as she finished that sentence.

"I have been there myself. I think I understand where you are coming from."

"You have?"

Lars nodded and sat up. "Enough small talk for now, let's go outside and introduce you to the dogs."

"Ok," Amanda answered as she got up, surprised by Lars' abruptness.

Amanda could see far out toward the horizon as she stepped outside the small shack. This place exuded an even greater sense of otherworldliness than Ilulissat or Qaanaaq. The sense of isolation was both liberating and frightening at the same time. Here she would be for over a week.

"Amanda!" Lars shouted, noticing that Amanda had not followed him.

"Coming," she shouted as she broke out of her trance and walked over toward Lars, the sledge, and the barking dogs.

"The first thing you need to know is that these dogs are not pets like you might have at home, never treat them like that. They are not tame, only trained. They must be shown who is the strongest."

Amanda looked at the dogs and wondered how they could be so wild, they looked so cute.

"These dogs are originally from Siberia. You won't find these dogs in South Greenland, it is illegal to take them there. They are bred only here in order to preserve their purity. I use a whip sometimes to show them who is in control and to direct them. As a rule of thumb, I don't hit any of them, unless absolutely necessary, which is almost never."

The dogs were no longer howling as Amanda eyed each one of them, all fifteen of them. A couple of them let out a slight snarl as she eyed them. Amanda was getting the sense that she would have to be cautious around the dogs. "How heavy are they?"

"The males weigh a little over forty kilos, or ninety pounds on average. The females, up to about thirty-five kilos, or seventy-five pounds."

"They look like dogs, but they don't seem to sound like dogs. They sound more like wolves," Amanda wondered aloud.

"Greenland dogs don't bark, they howl and snarl."

"Oh."

"Over there is the sledge you'll be riding on. Today, you will ride the sledge. Use the blanket to keep warmer while you are seated. Sometimes you will have to get off and run on the side. Running alongside will help keep you warmer. Later, I will teach you how to drive the sledge, if you wish."

They walked over to the sledge. It was a simple wooden platform with a wooden seat back and plastic runners connected by wooden slats. All the pieces were lashed together with some rope and leather straps. A caribou skin lay on the platform.

"I have been told in the past that before wood became widespread, the Inuit used antler, bone, and driftwood for the sledge. The runners were made of caribou and seal skins wrapped around frozen fish. They were soaked and frozen. It really was quite ingenious," Lars commented as he saw Amanda inspecting the sledge.

"Clever. Why do you call it a sledge? I've been hearing that term, but I always thought they were just sleds."

"Sleds are smaller. A sledge like this is much larger and carries much greater loads. A sled is often used for races and short distance trips with minimal supplies. A sled is designed to go fast. A sledge moves slower, but moves a lot more weight, whether that be supplies or passengers, like yourself."

Amanda nodded in understanding.

"Another difference is that sled dogs are often attached to run in two parallel lines. That works for forested areas and narrow trails, but not here. There are no trees here, so there is more room for the dogs to spread out. They are connected to this fan hitch, it gives them more space to go over rough ice or other obstacles. It is also better for running on thin sea ice where the risk of falling in is greater. It spreads the risk out."

"I would have never thought. It's so easy to have preconceptions about a place."

Lars continued. "You will sit at the back of the sledge against the board I will put in front of our supplies. I will usually be sitting in front, but sometimes running in back while pushing. Sit with your legs on the sledge. We will be going over rough terrain sometimes. You may need to lean from one side to the other depending on the ground we are going over. Hold on to those straps, except if we are just going over flat ground," Lars advised as he pointed to the straps holding the caribou skin on the platform.

"Ok, got it."

"Whatever you do, don't hold the sides of the sledge, your fingers can get injured that way."

"No sides," she repeated for extra assurance.

"Sometimes we will go over cracks in the ice, don't be alarmed. It is easier for us to go over them if you stay seated on the sledge. Only if I say otherwise, should you get up. You will need to get up and walk behind or alongside the sledge sometimes, if we encounter steep hills or ridges. Do you have any other questions right now?"

"What sort of supplies do we have? What will we be eating? Do we have enough food with us for the entire trip?"

He pointed at some of the items. "Some cookware, a lantern, headlamps, extra rope, and a portable stove for cooking and heat. Over here, are caribou skin blankets and a floor mat, sleeping bags, our large tent to sleep under, and fuel for the stove. For food, we have tea, packaged soup, oatmeal, some butter and sugar, and a lot of biscuits."

"That doesn't sound like very much food."

"That is why we also have a rifle and ammunition. We also have an axe, saw, cutting knife, and ice chisel for fishing."

"A rifle?"

"There should be some meat stored at some way points, but we will need to kill some seals or walrus for meat. If not for us, then for the dogs. Polar bears are wild animals too, and can be dangerous."

"Oh," Amanda replied meekly. She thought about the man butchering the seal and walrus earlier in the market. It was quite natural for the Inuit to hunt. Her closest encounter to hunting in life was driving around to a different supermarket or restaurant. Eating seals and walrus was no different than eating a cow or chicken she thought. Amanda tried hard to get rid of the image of the 'cute seal' in her mind. But, she couldn't even contemplate witnessing the shooting of a polar bear. That would tear her to pieces.

Not that she expected a hug of comfort from Lars, but the way in which he casually mentioned killing seals or walrus troubled her for the moment. Mary had told her about this aspect of the adventure, but she must have just glossed over it. Theory and reality. "What kind of fish are out here?"

"Halibut, various species of catfish, polar cod."

At least these sounded familiar to Amanda.

"I will teach you some command words in Inuktun now, the local dialect. I'll teach you more as we go along. Inuktun is related to standard Greenlandic, but some words are quite a bit different. You can at least understand a little of what I am saying to the dogs. When you are ready to drive the sledge in a couple of days, you can use them. The first word you should learn is, aut-aut autuk-autuk, it means to pull to the right."

Amanda repeated the long word.

"The second word is haru-haru, that means pull to the left."

Amanda tried the next one.

"Then there is ahi, which means stop, and hackfui-hackfui, which means run, or get going."

Amanda spoke these two words.

"You are on your way to being a true polar explorer."

"It has a nice melodic sound."

"You might want to consider wearing some different outer clothing too. There are several different sizes inside of seal skin boots, caribou socks, hooded coats, pants, and mittens. You can go try them on inside right now while I finish preparing the sledge."

Amanda put on a face of befuddlement. She was ready to try different foods, but now he was asking her to wear animal furs. Everything she had been told since childhood was that furs were bad and evil. Why did she need to wear any furs? She had her expensive name brand ski jacket, down jacket, snow pants, socks, gloves, scarf, waterproof boots, and even high-tech ear muffs.

She went inside the shack. As she looked around she noticed several piles of folded and sorted clothes that she didn't take note of earlier. Amanda picked up and tried out each fur item until she had a complete outfit. She straightened herself up and looked at a mirror on the wall. She started to cry.

She had thought of herself as an animal lover, sometimes, and here she was doing what seemed to be heretical to her belief system. Combined with the rawness of the butchering at the marketplace in Ilulissat, she could no longer contain her feelings anymore.

In her heart she knew that this is how the natives here had lived forever, but she was not ready to make the leap just yet. She changed back into her high-tech clothing and put all the furs in a little pile. Furs were primitive. Her modern outfit was the result of millions of dollars in research and development. She picked up her backpack and stuffed polar bear, dried her tears, and ran outside.

Lars looked up and noticed Amanda in her same clothes. "Decided not to wear any of the clothes?"

"They fit, but I think I'm okay with my current clothes," Amanda said with little outward emotion.

"I need to get a lantern and a few other supplies from inside. You can admire the view. We will be ready to go then."

Amanda nodded.

"You can put your stuffed animal against the back board."

Looking up and out toward the endless horizon, she walked a few steps closer, as if it were a place she could go. The emotional breakdown in the building resonated in her mind. She was traveling through a very different world and adapting was proving difficult. The cold, no problem. The lifestyle, more different than she imagined.

"You can run alongside the sledge if you get tired of sitting."

Amanda turned around. She had been preoccupied with the view and the dogs. She hadn't noticed that Lars had returned from inside. "Run? I'm not sure if I'll be able to keep up, your dogs look very fit."

"Don't worry, we won't get too far in front of you." Lars let out a hearty laugh. "Just for short stretches of time, Amanda, I will slow the dogs down."

Amanda pulled out a small blanket from her backpack and draped it around Polar Bear's body.

They were ready to go.

The dogs were howling in excitement and ready to get moving. Fifteen dogs were attached in a fan shaped orientation. The crunch of Amanda's boots against the hard ice and deep breaths were the only sound interrupting the chorus of howls as she went to go sit on the sledge.

Amanda wondered if Lars thought her to be strange for bringing along a big stuffed polar bear. Her earlier excuse that it was a gift for a friend would not work out here, but Lars asked no particular questions about why she was carrying what was certain to be a strange sight here, or anywhere. Like he said earlier, there was plenty of time for them to share stories.

Amanda sat down and made herself as comfortable as possible on the sledge. Her heart skipped another beat in anticipation.

"Hackfui! Hackfui! Hackfui!" Lars shouted out at the dogs. They were off.

CHAPTER 17 – OFF ON THE SLEDGE

Amanda settled in front of Polar Bear and watched as the sledge glided across the Baffin Bay ice. Behind her, was the mountain that hugged Savissivik. Ahead of her, miles and miles of ice. It was like a white desert. A place where you could forget your name, before you even spelled it out loud.

The sound of the sledge rails and paws of the dogs against the snow and ice became a predictable and calming sound of progress, like the hum of a car engine on a baby. The dogs panting brought a smile to Amanda. She stared at the rhythmic movement of the dogs' legs. It was interrupted every few minutes by some grunts from Lars and his occasional yelling of directional commands. Now, if she could only remember what meant right, and which word meant left. Or did they mean fast and slow?

The ride was less bumpy than she thought it would be, except for the, every now and again, bone jarring mini-hop of the sledge as the ice and snow changed elevations. The cool wind blowing against her face combined with the movement of the sled helped to prevent Amanda from napping, even if she was the least bit tired. The dogs' legs and wind kicked up occasional tufts of powdered snow.

Amanda was looking forward to stretching her legs. Her moment came none too soon as Lars called the dogs to a halt.

"This is a good place to stop."

"Oh, good. I need to stretch my legs."

"Are you hungry?"

"A little."

Lars reached into a pack and handed a few biscuits to Amanda.

She popped a biscuit into her mouth and almost gagged. "What is this!? They're so hard! Are they frozen?"

"Maybe you don't like them because these biscuits are made by a Danish dog biscuit company!"

"It's dog food?"

"No, no, no. They just happen to make dog biscuits, too."

"Boy, that makes me feel better."

Lars had a sense of humor to go along with his excellent English. It put Amanda at ease.

Lars abruptly turned serious and looked up ahead. "Do you see how it is no longer flat up ahead?"

Amanda followed his lead and looked up. Ahead of them, the flat expanses of ice that Amanda was becoming accustomed to, changed into what looked like at this distance, white walls rising up from the ice. It was a bit spooky as the flat terrain suddenly changed up ahead. "What is it?"

"That is the beginning of some pressure ridges."

"Pressure ridges? What are those?" There were so many new words to learn out here.

"It is when an area of younger ice becomes crushed and compacted by surrounding stronger ice due to converging winds. The area of ice then gets pushed up into mounds and ridges."

"So, there is older and younger ice, Lars?"

"Yes."

"And when they meet, one beats up on the other?"

"You could put it that way."

She would never look at ice cubes in a cup the same way again. "How high are those ridges?"

"Maybe one to two meters high, they can get more than two to three times as high as that."

"How many feet in a meter again, Lars?"

"About 3.3 feet in a meter. Shall I use feet?"

"No, no, I can do that conversion in my head."

"I'll do it for you."

"Ok. Can we go around them?"

"Around some of the bigger ones. It looks like these ridges continue for a long enough way that we should go over them. When we do, you will need to get off."

"I'm okay with that. How far do the ridges go out?"

"We'll know better when we are there. They don't go out very far except in unusual circumstances. It is a place where you should be extra careful. Where there are pressure ridges, there may also be leads."

"Leads?"

"Leads are like cracks in the ice. Channels opened up by divergent winds."

She remembered what she saw from the helicopter. "Like a river?"

"Sort of. The water isn't necessarily flowing like a river. It can be very calm. You can spot new ones by looking for frost smoke."

"Frost smoke?"

"Look for smoke from the water being exposed to evaporation and condensation. But, leads don't only appear where there is smoke. You need to pay extra attention or you could fall into the icy water."

Amanda's eyes bulged open wide and her ears perked up. "How do you know which ice is safe to walk over?"

"You can look at the color of the ice. If it is dark, then the seawater is not very far down and that means the ice is thin. It could also mean that the seawater is in the layers of ice and hasn't fully frozen yet. If the ice is light colored or gray, then it is usually safe to travel over. Sometimes it is necessary to use a pole with a hook to test the ice. It's the same pole used for hunting."

Amanda didn't have a pole. Her mind was full on in inquisitive mode. "If the ice is thinner, is it better that I get off the sledge so it isn't so heavy too?"

"It sounds like a good idea, but it is better to stay on the sledge as the pressure from our feet on a particular spot of ice is greater than the pressure from any single point off the sledge, or dogs."

"Interesting."

"Some of the Inuit hunters can walk on thin ice like polar bears, who distribute their weight better, but it takes a lot of skill."

"Mimicking nature?" Amanda glanced at Polar Bear and smiled.

"Yes."

"I've noticed that the ice here isn't like the ice and snow that I was hiking around in Ilulissat, or ice I've seen anywhere else. Is there something special about it?"

"Don't forget, this is frozen salty sea water we are traveling over. There is a top wet salty layer on the surface even at these temperatures. It stays a little mushy due to the excess salt." Lars motioned Amanda to get on the sledge. "Sometimes we travel over fresh snow, sometimes old. Sometimes, small patches of ice. You learn over time."

"Is there ever a danger of just mushing out into a patch of open water?"

"You can look for open water in the distance by looking at the cloud bottoms and seeing whether they are light or dark. If they are darker, that means the clouds are over open water. If lighter, then it is ice. Ice reflects more light than open water."

Amanda took another look at the sky. "What if there aren't so many clouds like today?"

"Then you can look at the color of the sky."

"The color of the sky?"

"Snow on ice reflects about 80% of light. Bare ice, about 65%. Melt ponds reflect about 35%. Open water reflects back only 7%, it absorbs 93%. The scientific term is called albedo."

"I never realized there was a difference." She took another look at the sky, then she realized how much her vision of the world had been reduced to 'black and white.' Her vision wasn't fine tuned to see the shades of blue, nor even the shades of gray, not just of the sky or ice, but of nature itself.

"Nature gives off subtle hints, we can choose whether or not to learn from it at our own peril."

"Open water only reflects back 7%?"

Lars nodded his head.

"Then the sky above the water will be a lot darker?"

"The sky will be a darker shade of blue than if it was over ice, it's as if the sea swallows the sunlight."

"I'll have to pay closer attention."

"There are many subtle cues. In time, one learns to see them by second nature, if one doesn't die in the process. Don't expect to pick it all up right away. A simpler thing to look for is frost smoke, or what you might call, fog."

Amanda was getting a serious lesson about navigating the ice from a master. She realized there was a lot more to learn than at first glance.

"I see you are concerned about the ice conditions, Amanda."

"Yes, yes."

"That is a good trait to have, it will keep you alive out here."

"Isn't that your job?"

Lars let out a hearty laugh.

Amanda sat back on the sled as they headed off toward the ridges. They reached the area of pressure ridges before she could give much more thought to Lars' advice on staying alive. The terrain became a jumble of mounds, sawtooth like ridge tops, and depressions. Amanda got off and walked ahead to the side of the dogs as Lars deftly maneuvered the dogs and sledge up and over the ridges. Smoke rose up from behind one of the ridges. Amanda wanted to investigate, but thought better of it and decided to avoid it for now.

As they traversed the last of this group of pressure ridges, Amanda felt a surge of confidence in overcoming the first challenging terrain that the Arctic sea had presented. Not spotting a polar bear yet, Lars steered the sledge back toward land and off the sea ice.

A small rocky mound appeared out of nowhere as they headed further inland. They had arrived at the first night's campsite.

"What is that pile of rocks? Is it some sort of marker?"

"That is a storehouse for frozen meat. I put some fish, seal, and walrus meat in there earlier. We can eat some of it and use the rest to feed the dogs. Let us setup our tent first though."

Amanda grinned for a moment, her moment of truth was coming up. She was going to be eating a poster animal of countless environmental organizations. She could avoid not wearing seal skin clothing, but there was no way out of this. Her stomach grumbled. The biscuits she had crunched through earlier were a mere stopgap to satisfying her stomach.

Lars took out a large tent and a set of poles then unpacked some caribou skins from the sledge. They quickly set the large tent up. Large caribou skins were layered over the tent floor. "The ice is very cold, the caribou skins are good insulators. If you need more protection from the ground, we have an insulated air mattress too."

Amanda wondered how much colder it could get as the sun went down and the temperature began to drop. She pondered the cold as Lars left to retrieve some meat. Amanda noticed the dogs perking their ears up on alert, ready for a much deserved meal.

The wind was kicking up a bit again. While the swirls of snow began to settle, Amanda pondered her existence. With time now to think of herself again, she realized, she was in the middle of nowhere. No town, no buildings, no cars, no trees, and no birds. There was only the tent they had just setup and the dogs that helped to bring them here.

The dogs were jumping up and down as Lars threw meat at them making sure each of the fifteen dogs received something to eat. The dogs were like cars Amanda thought, they needed 'gasoline' too. Amanda's stomach was grumbling as she saw the dogs eat first. Lars finished feeding the dogs and walked over to Amanda with a large bowl.

"Our turn to eat now," Lars noted as he thrust the bowl out toward Amanda with chopped up bite sized pieces of meat.

She hesitated despite her hunger pangs.

"Have you eaten seal meat before?"

Amanda swayed her head from side to side.

"You'll like it."

"You can eat it raw?"

"Yes. Try a cooked piece first, if you prefer."

Amanda picked up a blood stained piece of meat and took a bite, it tasted better than she thought. She chewed up the rest of the piece and grabbed another. Soon, her animal instincts took over and she grabbed several more pieces. Every piece brought warmth to her body, more important as the sun retreated.

While the changing of season meant that daylight was getting longer and longer, it would still be about a month until the day of the midnight sun would arrive. Once that day arrived, the sun would not begin to set until late August. The sun was fading from view in a glorious sunset on Amanda's first night outside in the cold Arctic. It soon became dark, with only the light of the moon, stars, portable stove providing heat, and a lantern inside the tent.

Amanda settled into the warm tent with her cup of tea. It was larger than she expected with more than enough room for the two of them. She realized the strange situation she had managed to put herself in. Here she was, in the middle of nowhere, in a tent with a man she had only met earlier in the day. What would her friends think?! She needed to know more about this mystery man whom she was putting so much trust in.

"How long have you been sledging?"

"I have lived part-time in Greenland for twenty years, sledging every year since I arrived from Denmark."

"How many of these sledge trips have you made?"

"Maybe over one hundred short trips from Ilulissat. Those are spring and summer trips, sometimes, just a day or two long for tourists. These long expedition style trips up here, less than twenty-five over the years. You are among a select few." Lars warmed his hands around his cup of water.

Amanda pondered his answer. One of the select few? Her initial round of adrenaline and excitement was being tested as darkness set in and the temperature dropped, even though it was warmer inside the tent.

Lars added, "I am a wildlife biologist by training, I have been to many places in the Arctic. I work for the government part-time and the rest of the time in the tourist trade."

"You must know a lot about polar bears then."

"I have learned more than most," he answered with complete modesty.

"How did you end up here in Greenland?"

"I ended up marrying a native Inuit on one of my early trips to Greenland. Living and growing up in Denmark, Greenland was always this mysterious place for me. It is a part of Denmark, and yet it isn't, because it is so different. This land captivated me right away. My wife and our son live part of the year in Greenland, and the rest in Denmark. "

"Do you live in Qaanaaq?"

"No, we live in Ilulissat. It is warmer there, but I've been a regular visitor up north here to run sledge tours and study the wildlife and ice conditions."

"What are your wife and son's names?"

"My wife's name is Makkak and our son we named Jakob."

"Those are pretty names. What is your last name again?"

"Mortensen."

"Is that common?"

"Last time I checked it was the twentieth most popular surname. Jensen, Nielsen, Hansen, Pedersen, and Andersen are some of the more popular ones. Your last name, Foster, is that common?"

"I've met a few other Fosters in my life, I don't think it is that common."

It seemed appropriate to talk about names considering all the new names she was hearing in these unfamiliar languages. At the very least, it was a conversation starter. The last time she had given any thought to surname popularity was at a water cooler discussion, which resulted in a discussion about the most common Korean surname, it had been quite a debate.

It wasn't until someone took the effort to research it on the Internet that the truth was known. She had long since forgotten that Kim at 21% was the most popular, followed by Lee at 15%, and Park at 9%, but it did kindle some interest in her on how family names might shape a nation over time in Korea, or anywhere else.

If a large percentage of the population had the same or similar last name, might they be more prone to behaving in overly similar ways, perhaps clannish behavior? How much 'power' was in a name?

"Danes didn't adopt surnames until quite recently, in the mid-1800s."

"So, you had no last names before then?"

"Yes, we did. But before that time, last names weren't inherited."

"Huh?"

"There is a naming system that was once common throughout Europe. It is called the patrynomic naming tradition. In this system, last names are not carried on."

"That's weird."

"Here in Denmark, last names were formed by adding on -sen, meaning 'son of', to the first name of the father. Other last names were created as a result of one's occupation or craft. Or farmstead, place of origin, nicknames, or even of the landlord in a serf economy."

"I've never heard of such a thing."

"When surnames were mandated and 'frozen' in Denmark, most had been using the patrynomic convention, thus the prevalence of -sen. The British and Irish adopted inheritable surnames much earlier. I think it was maybe, about five hundred years earlier."

"Wow. The things we don't even know about our own past."

"To give you an example of how the patrynomic system works, I'll use some more English sounding names: JOHN Robertson – Peter JOHNson – Micheal PETERson – Brent MICHAELson – Rick BRENTson – Alex RICKson."

"Fascinating. What about daughters?"

"The equivalent for Danish girls is the addition of –datter. Like Jensdatter, daughter of Jens, Poulsdatter, daughter of Poul, but these last names are not common in Denmark. I hear the use of this sort of naming is common in Iceland though, the ending is -dottir, not -datter though. Also, some girls are named using the matronymic system. So, same ending, but the first part of the last name is after the mother's name."

Now, Iceland was a country Amanda needed to visit. Male chauvinism she miffed. Maybe she should change her last name to Deborahdatter, after her mother's first name. After all, her father was a home wrecker. Better to have a last name as the daughter of Deborah, rather than Peterdatter, the daughter of Peter, her father. Girl power!

"Do you think there is any lasting effect of such a recent change?"

"Perhaps it helps contribute to our sense of individualism, different than your American definition. Yet, it maintained our connection with the immediate past. Since identifying by last name was never very important, we are more independent minded, while we are similar at the same time." He paused. "Not because we're told to be unique or need to think of ourselves as such, but because we are the same and unique by experience. I find it hard to explain, maybe I'm just not using the right words."

"That's ok. I think I understand what you are trying to say." She remembered a phrase from long ago at a childhood friend's house – 'That's not how a Miller would behave!' Her friend cried after that argument with her father. But, what if everyone had a different last name, a statement like that could never be used. Who mandated that everyone needed the same last name anyway?

One would no longer be tied to the legacy of the past from a name perspective, whether it be good or bad. There would be no family name pride to uphold. That's it, she would change her last name. Maybe Debdatter, Deborahdatter was too long. Then she could be free of the legacy of her parents' miserable love life and resulting divorce. She began to wonder how one would see themselves if everyone in their family, everyone in a society, had a different last name.

What about the names of the Inuit? Their real names, not just the ones they used for convenience with visitors. Were they like the names of Native Americans? Like Sitting Bull, Soaring Eagle, Sky Spirit, Crazy Horse, or Looking Glass?

Amanda wasn't quite sure how these names just popped out of her mind. Maybe she was a Native American in a past life.

Her thoughts turned further inward. What if she didn't have a name? What if she forgot her very sense of self? She could forget it out here in this vast expanse of whiteness.

She snapped out of it. "You have a fascinating life story. Is it hard coming from two very different places? I mean, the both of you coming from a different culture?"

"Oh yes, sometimes we have misunderstandings, but it isn't very often. We also travel as a family quite a bit, I've taken my family to a few countries."

"Must be exciting."

"We enjoy it, would you like a refill?"

"Yes, please."

Lars poured her a second cup from the flask and gave her some more tea leaves.

"No tea for you, Lars?"

"I only drink hot water. I've spoken too much, tell me about yourself."

"What would you like to know?" Amanda answered, unsure of what to say about herself.

"Whatever you think sounds interesting to others."

"Well, I was born in the Seattle area, I have lived there all my life. I am a marketing consultant. I study our behavior as consumers from a psychology perspective, sometimes. We have clients in different industries so I get to learn about a lot of different things. I have never been married. My life sounds boring compared to yours."

"Now, now. What else do you like to do?"

"I enjoy my time with friends. I like to go hiking and skiing. This learning about cultures through travel is beginning to be fun. I think I've seen too many movies in my life. I think I understand office politics more than I should. I would like to be more real, less materially minded. I've traveled around the US, but never outside, except Canada."

"That sounds a little more positive."

"A little," she mused.

"We all have our interesting aspects. Sometimes it just takes some prodding and a little time for them to come out and reveal themselves. Next time you can say, 'I enjoyed traveling to Greenland.' How many people can say that?"

"That's true." She wondered if Lars might want to know about her stuffed polar bear too, but he didn't ask, so she decided not to bring up the subject.

"If you are brave, you can go outside and look at the sky. It's a clear night and you might enjoy it. It could be another hobby you mention if someone asks about your experiences in life."

She gave Lars a puzzled look.

He didn't answer, instead he nodded his head toward the tent exit.

"Ok, I'm game," Amanda muttered out loud. She threw off her sleeping bag and warm caribou blanket. She put on her gloves, scarf, ear muffs, and boots. She stepped outside.

It took a moment to adjust to the darkness from the lantern lit tent. As she glanced back at the tent, she noticed the lantern was now off. Lars had turned off the light to make it darker.

She first saw the sledge dogs sleeping. A feeling of vulnerability washed over her as she found herself enveloped in the darkness. She was in complete silence by herself, with only noise from the wind and her own heartbeat to comfort herself. No traffic or street lights, no cars driving by or their headlights, no lights shining through the window of a nearby home, no tree leaves rustling, and no voices of fellow campers. No lights of a city in the distance. The sense of solitariness spooked and invigorated her. Yet, as her eyes adjusted, it seemed as if the area was not as dark as it could be. She looked up in the sky.

She was mesmerized. Dancing in the dark sky were green and yellow bands of light taking on different shapes. The lights flickered and moved around in the sky like a curtain flowing in the wind. Other bands of light arced and streaked across the sky in an electrifying show. She lay down with her back against the snow and stared at the spectacle, oblivious to the cold. This was magical. She tried to imagine the shapes the lights were creating as if she were staring at clouds, but they were dancing with too much energy.

Amanda could have fallen asleep under the lights, but the cold was getting the best of her, she climbed back in the tent.

"That was quite a show! It was beautiful. It was interesting how I could see the light glow off some icebergs in the distance too. They were like shards of colored glass."

"I knew you would enjoy it. I was beginning to wonder if you would ever come back in."

"Are those the Northern Lights?"

"Yes, also known as the Aurora Borealis."

"I never could have imagined them to be so beautiful."

"What colors did you see?"

"Green and yellow."

"Those are the most common colors. Sometimes they are blue and violet. If you are lucky, you will see a red light show, that is the least common."

"What causes it?"

"The light is caused by particles that come from the sun during solar flares and explosions. When these particles reach our Earth they are captured by our magnetic field and drawn toward our Earth's two magnetic poles. It is there that they hit our atmosphere. Good so far?"

Amanda nodded in understanding.

"The collisions between the particles and our atmospheric gases cause the energy to be emitted as a photon, or light particle. Each collision creates a flash. The aurora you see is made up of many of these particle and gas collisions. What you see with your eyes is the result of at least 100 million photons."

Amanda realized that Lars had a knack for explaining many things in precise scientific terms. He was a biologist, after all. "Wow. Are they there every night?"

"They are more common in late Autumn and early Spring. And they are more common further south. If you want to see them directly overhead more, you also have to go south. Distant view up here, relatively speaking."

Amanda said nothing as she reflected on this natural phenomenon.

"They are more common at solar maximum than solar minimum, which is just a fancy way of saying that you'll see more light when there are more solar flares and explosions during a maximum, which occurs about every eleven years. You came at an exceptionally good time. I checked the aurora forecast earlier."

"Fascinating."

"Of course, it needs to be dark too, so you won't be able to see them if you were here closer to the day of the midnight sun, even though they would still be occurring."

"Are they always so bright?"

"Sometimes the lights are as bright as the moon, sometimes they are so dim that you can see the stars right through them."

"I wish I could see the lights back home."

"There would probably be too much light pollution."

Amanda closed her eyes and envisioned the lights dancing right in front of her face.

"The Inuit believed, or believe, depending on who you ask, that the lights are the spirits of the animals they have hunted – seals, fish, caribou, beluga whales, or even polar bears."

Amanda opened her eyes. Polar bears as light she thought to herself. "What do you believe?"

"Being trained as a wildlife biologist, on an intellectual level, I am comfortable with the scientific explanation. I have spent many nights alone out here though. Sometimes, I'm not sure what to believe."

"I think if I was out here alone, I would probably have some strange thoughts."

"You hear strange things when you are by yourself. You wonder if you are going crazy or if there is something out there. Some groups have believed that the lights are the spirits of their ancestors. In times long past, people believed the lights were a sign of war or famine, or even simpler, reflections from campfires and torches. In the absence of other evidence, I'll have to be content with them being just photons."

Amanda didn't answer as she was starting to drift off to sleep.

"If you wake up in the middle of night and you hear the dogs making noise, then it could be a polar bear." With that, Lars stopped speaking and closed his eyes too.

Amanda smiled and let out a deep breath, her breath visible in the cooling air. She hoped the dogs would be her alarm clock.

CHAPTER 18 – OLD CURSES

The sun rose early on Amanda's first morning of camping in the Arctic. Warm under the caribou blanket, she didn't want to get up. She noticed Lars was already outside. She opened her eyes and thought for a moment she must be in a dream. The beautiful Aurora Borealis and stillness of the night gave her a sense that this place didn't really exist.

As she awoke, she realized something she hadn't noticed before. She was okay using a caribou blanket, but not okay with wearing the animal fur clothing that she rejected earlier. She wondered how this could be so. After a little thought, she realized it was our emotional attachment to certain words and ideas that affected our behavior. And sometimes it conflicted with our actions in seemingly random ways. She put it out of her mind.

Lars had left a packet of soup, oatmeal, and some biscuits for her by the thermos of hot water. She made quick work of them and went outside.

"Good morning," Amanda announced.

Lars turned around from sorting out the dog traces and harnesses. "Good morning. Did you see the food I left for you?"

"Yes, thank you. I needed that to warm up."

"Are you still hungry?"

Amanda was becoming acutely aware of how many calories of energy one required per day to survive out here. Already she had felt some brief moments of hunger, but she had not complained about it. Perhaps it was a throwback to a brief period of her life when she thought she might become bulimic in high school, a thought that she had hid well. Now, this 'close to the edge' existence concerned her at times, but she felt and trusted Lars' confidence in this forbidding world. "Yes," she nodded enthusiastically.

"There is some walrus meat and fish in those plastic containers over by the tent. I cooked some of it. I thought I would give all the walrus meat to the dogs this morning, but there are some leftovers."

"Walrus meat? Does it taste like the seal meat?"

"Don't ask, just try it. You'll need the energy."

Amanda walked back over to the tent and found the container. It was a darker looking meat than the seal she had eaten yesterday. She mustered up her sense of bravery and took a bite. She grunted and swallowed it down. She stuck her tongue out in disgust.

Lars was laughing as he continued to sort out the dog traces and properly securing the harnesses to the dogs.

The meat tasted like old, moldy, sharp, rich cheese. She forced herself to eat the rest, she was hungry. Hunger had a way of making anything seem edible she realized. She ate the raw and cooked fish too, it was kind of like sushi, she told herself, though not quite so.

"The meat from the walrus is perhaps the best dog food one can get."

"Oh, is that right?" Amanda beamed.

"It gets slowly digested in the dog's stomach."

"And in a human's stomach?"

Lars didn't answer the question.

"I'll stick with the seal meat and fish, the walrus meat is for the dogs!"

"Glad you enjoyed it. Are you ready?"

Amanda turned around from chewing on the last bit of fish. She wondered if she would get sick from all this raw meat. So far, so good.

"We need to take down the tent and secure everything to the sledge."

They packed and tied everything up.

"How far are we going today?"

"Maybe around fifty kilometers, thirty miles, then we are going to camp out on the pack ice tonight."

"How long will it take to cover that distance?"

"We can sledge about eight to ten kilometers per hour, so five to six hours of actual sledge time if we don't encounter too many obstacles. We will also need to do some seal hunting today. We will need more meat for the dogs and ourselves to eat. If we are lucky, we will have fresh boiled seal meat tonight."

It didn't exactly sound appetizing, but Lars made it sound better. "How many polar bears are in this area?"

"The last figures I saw were about two thousand to twenty-five hundred in the entire Baffin Bay area, this covers a large area though. In the fall, many of the bears in this area reside on Bylot and Baffin Island in Canada, then they migrate east for the winter and spring. They hunt on the pack ice near where we are right now. Most go back to Canada during the summer, but there are always a few stragglers. There are also a few hundred bears to the north of here in the Kane Basin area too."

"The chances are good then?"

"Our chances will improve as we get closer toward the Melville Bay Reserve."

"Any tips on spotting one?"

"The polar bear is well camouflaged, look for their black nose. They like to hide that with their paws when they're laying low. In the summer their coats turn yellowish, but it is too early for that. I guess the best advice is to scan the horizon with care. Polar bears tend not to move very fast, so you have to be patient."

"Good to know," she responded as she got on board the sledge.

"We should also be on the lookout for polar bear footprints."

"Hackfui, hackfui!" yelled Lars. The dogs were off and they were gliding across the snow and ice again. The panting of the dogs echoed in Amanda's ears.

They sledged for several miles until a large iceberg came into view. The iceberg was in the shape of a three dimensional flattened triangle protruding from the frozen sea. It was frozen in place, surrounded by the pack ice. When they got closer, Amanda estimated it must have stood out of the ground about 250 feet.

"I'm going to climb to the top of this iceberg to get a better view. It might be too dangerous for you to climb it though. You can walk around the base. Watch out for falling ice."

Lars fastened a pair of crampons to his boots and proceeded to walk toward the steep incline of the iceberg with a pair of binoculars around his neck.

Amanda looked up in awe as Lars made his way up. As she made her way around the iceberg, a small object caught her eye, she picked it up. Staring back at her were two bulging eyes, part of a small ivory and light brown colored figure with thin skinny legs, a pointed head, and an oversized grotesque face with a mischievous smile. She recoiled in a moment of shock, but managed to hold onto the figurine.

Amanda stared into the eyes of the small, well preserved, miniature doll-like object. It seemed like it might come alive at any moment. She stopped exploring around the iceberg and headed back to the sledge, eager to find out more about her discovery.

As Amanda reached the sledge, she looked up and saw Lars at the top of the iceberg scanning the surrounding area. She waved as he turned in her direction, he waved back. Amanda was still holding the figurine, not wanting to put it in her pocket just yet. It still looked a little too creepy, though it would qualify as a neat souvenir.

Lars walked back down the iceberg and returned to the sledge. "How was your hike around the iceberg?"

"I found this strange figure by the base of the iceberg, do you know what it is?"

"You've found a tupilak!" He picked up the figurine from Amanda's open palm and began to study it with a focused gaze.

"What's a tupilak?" Amanda asked disconcertingly in reaction to Lars' expression.

"A tupilak is a talisman, you might call it a voodoo doll. It is a form of black magic that the Inuit have historically used when they wanted to curse someone. In a secret location, they created a figure using the bones of various animals that they would tie together. Sometimes, they would use parts of dead children."

"Dead children?"

"The figure would be made into the shape of the creature which they wanted to hurt the intended victim. Such as a seal which might drag an enemy down and drown him, a polar bear which might eat the enemy, or as an invisible spirit which would frighten a victim to death or steal its soul."

"Whoa."

Lars continued to examine the tupilak in detail. "The creature was activated with a chant. Then the creator would stroke the figure against their sexual organs to give it power, then it would be thrown in the water to find its victim."

"Did it ever work?" she asked in a hopeful manner.

"Tradition says that whether the tupilak would work or not depended on the magic ability of the enemy or intended victim. If their magic power was greater, then they could reverse the tupilak to attack its creator. Stories abound, but I think that sometimes, fear itself could have been a self-fulfilling prophecy in the past, just as it is today. We react based on our beliefs which causes us to behave a certain way."

Amanda took a deep breath as Lars handed the tupilak back to her.

"I've only seem them in stores before. I have never come across one outside, in the wild, so to speak. They are only bought as souvenirs now."

"Wow, I guess I'm lucky."

"They used to be made of sperm whale teeth from the early 1930s-70s, as far as I know. Ever since whale hunting began to be regulated, tupilaks have been made from caribou horns and narwhal tusks, this one looks to be older though. It seems to be made of several different types of bone. I wonder how it ended up here and still in such good condition."

"Where do you think this one was made?"

"Hard to say, Amanda. The souvenir versions are made mostly in East Greenland as that is where this particular part of Inuit culture continues to thrive. They can be found all over Greenland though. This doesn't look like one of those souvenir versions."

"So, you think this was actually used?" Amanda asked as she held the tupilak at arm's length.

"It's possible. Maybe it got stuck in some ice and became preserved, only being released by the melting of that ice. That wouldn't be surprising. As the Arctic has warmed up, ice that has been frozen for many, many years, has revealed whole bodies in some instances. I can't see any other explanation as it should have disintegrated being such a perishable material."

"Should I keep it?"

"That depends on how superstitious you are. It would make an interesting souvenir, or maybe it is best if you leave it here." He grinned.

"I'm not too superstitious. I'm sure my friends would get a kick out of looking at it." Amanda stuck the tupilak in her coat pocket. An eerie silence followed Amanda's decision to keep it. "Did you see anything up there?" Amanda asked, changing subjects.

"I spotted some seals a little further ahead. Let's get moving while they are still there."

Any remaining thoughts about the meaning of finding the tupilak were forgotten, the hunt was on.

After a few minutes of moving forward, Lars stopped the sledge. He motioned in silence and directed Amanda's attention to a seal lying on a distant piece of ice. He pulled out a pair of binoculars and handed them to Amanda for a better look.

Amanda struggled at first to locate the seal, but then found it in the binoculars. She brought the seal into focus. It was marked with gray-white rings on its dark gray back. Its silver colored belly was lying flat on the ice. Where before Amanda would coo at the sight of such an animal, she felt a strange primal urge wash over her as she thought about the nourishment it would provide in such a forbidding place. She repressed whatever remnant feelings and thoughts of cuteness and adorability that came to mind. "What kind of seal is it?"

"It is a hair seal, or better known as a ringed seal." Lars pulled out his long rifle and sat down on the ice to steady himself.

Amanda looked on, eyes focused in the binoculars, looking at the seal which was not moving.

Lars fired a shot. The bullet hit its mark.

Amanda yanked the binoculars away from her eyes as she caught a glimpse of the seal's final moments of life and its blood spilling onto the white ice. A few tears ran down her eyes even as she was still feeling a primal urge to hunt. Amanda repressed her urge to say something.

"Would you like to help me retrieve it?"

"I'd like to stay here if that is okay."

"No problem, it didn't look that big so I should be able to bring it back myself."

Lars had not noticed that Amanda was still looking at the seal as it was shot. If he had, he said nothing about it.

Amanda watched in awe as Lars retrieved the seal carcass by dragging it back to the sledge. A trail of blood ran behind him. With methodical precision he skinned the seal with a large knife. The blood was everywhere.

When he finished, he took the skin back toward the breathing hole to wash off the blood. Amanda remained silent the entire time. When he returned, he folded it and secured it to the sledge.

"The trick is to stay downwind from the seal. It is best to shoot it while it sleeps and to aim for the brain. Even after the seal is killed, one has to react fast as there is a risk the seal could slip back into the water. Ice at the edge of breathing holes is smooth and inclined."

Lars' advice on seal hunting seemed to bounce off Amanda. She didn't want to know this much, but this was the reality of life. She couldn't hide behind the magic of consumerism out here.

A feeling of weakness came over her, maybe she should have stayed home in Seattle. She took a deep breath and remembered why she was out here, and the lessons about life she had already learned, but perhaps not accepted. She stiffened her spine against this momentary weakness.

Lars chopped up some pieces of the seal for Amanda to eat. This time was different though. The meat was fresh, and she had seen it being killed. There was also the fresh blood. She almost wanted to puke, but held back the urge.

Eating raw meat was one thing, eating a freshly killed animal was another. Eating a 'cute seal,' yet another issue she was still coming to grips with. It was easy to abstract the earlier seal meat she had been given because that had already been chopped up. It had already been 'processed.'

As she chewed the fresh meat, it occurred to her that she had never killed a live squawking chicken, a mooing cow, or a squealing pig. The meat of the latter two, beef and pork, didn't even sound like the name of the animal from which they came. Not in English anyway.

At least the meat she was eating here wasn't farmed in a factory and mistreated. She made a mental note to educate herself better on where her food came from and how it was raised and grown. There were no issues with mistreatment out here, antibiotics, or cleanliness. Perhaps someday she would become a vegetarian, or a vegan. This was certainly not that time.

The seal fat was satisfying and gave Amanda a sense of warmth as the wind kicked up. The fresh, dark, rich meat, still had a faint fishy taste. She chewed another piece and was reminded of eating liver.

It occurred to Amanda that she was eating in near silence. She wasn't reading a book or magazine, watching TV, using a computer, or talking on the phone. She wasn't listening to music or pondering some gossip or problem at work, it was just her and the food. There was something spiritual about it, though she couldn't put her finger on it.

"Tonight, we will cook some of the meat in seal fat and soup. A seal dinner is filling, and a perfect high calorie meal for this place."

"That sounds good," Amanda mumbled as she chewed away to satisfy her hunger that was forgotten about when they had found the tupilak. She wasn't worrying about minding any manners or eating etiquette out here in the wilderness. "What do you think about people who think that seals are cute and shouldn't be hunted?" Amanda asked as she licked her lips.

"Before you ask that question, I think it is better to talk about the concept of nature as people perceive it. Nature in opposition to culture is a modern phenomenon."

"Huh? What do you mean?"

"Let's leave that conversation for tonight." Before Amanda could make another comment, Lars continued. "Let's get going, we will have plenty of time to talk later."

Amanda smiled, but was eager to hear his answer. There was a time for thinking and a time for action. She wiped her hands on the ground and poured some water on her hands to clean off the blood.

He finished cutting up the rest of the seal and fed most of it to the dogs, saving a little for their next few meals. They would need to hunt again for the dogs later.

The rest of the day went by without incidence as they continued to sledge on the pack ice looking for a polar bear. They stopped to camp several miles from shore on the pack ice.

"The Inuit don't think of nature as many who live in cities might. Many urban people think that nature should be some sort of pristine environment, which isn't surprising if one spends most of their days in a concrete and steel jungle. I think the idea of national parks, and conservation groups, contribute to this belief. There is an expectation that nature should be special, but this is not always true."

"I can identify with that."

"There is an artificial classification of area in the modern world. The Inuit don't think like this. They don't look at nature as either here or there. They exist within it and it is merely a question of survival to them. Though, this is changing in the larger cities."

"A question of survival," she repeated.

"A city is an artificial environment compared to nature, Amanda. As we live in them today, they are places of excessive consumerism, totally disconnected from our land. Some of these people want to go 'extreme' on the environment now."

Amanda felt a lump in her throat. She was front and center, a part of fueling the consumer culture at both ends.

"Well, this is one reason why there is a conflict between those who want to protect seals, and the Inuit who want to continue hunting, among other differences."

Amanda thought about Lars' words as she reflected on her life. She had grown up in a world of malls and stores filled with every imaginable product. The nature she had experienced in the suburbs or the city was an illusion. There were the rows of planted trees, many imported from some other part of the world she recalled reading about. Then there were the manicured parks with their lawns mowed and trees pruned on a predictable schedule. Was it like the zoo? Had she just been a captive 'animal' for much of her life? All of her life?

Of course, man needed to control nature, didn't we? How much was too much? Had we become captive of our own desires for conquering and controlling?

Even for many who traveled she realized, we were just going from one zoo to another zoo. One city to another city. Cities that were increasingly looking the same.

The same stores with people all behaving and dressing, more or less, the same. And really, perhaps all thinking the same, in a general way. She would know, for she was in the business of convincing people to be the same, by buying or consuming certain things. By shaping people's thought patterns with the power of marketing, how did she get so good at her job anyway? That was too much to think about.

The marketing illusion was in getting people to think they were really different, unique, and super special, even though it was often just the same thing, in so many shades of gray.

She pinched herself. This line of thought frightened her. There was nothing wrong with being the same she thought further, but it depended on the definition of the word - same. "I need some music," she blurted out.

"I'm sorry, what did you say?"

"Oh, nothing." Perhaps the silence of the Arctic was getting to her. She lamented for a moment not having any device to play music to distract her mind.

Lars interrupted her swirling thoughts. "While many might see nature as a playground, the Inuit see it as home. There is no nature, only survival."

How many people still visited or lived next to a raw wilderness such as the Inuit in Savissivik or similar towns? With no, or limited access to markets. Surely there were some native peoples in Brazil, Africa, or someplace else she wondered.

"Ok, so the concept of nature is different. What do you think about people that think seals shouldn't be hunted?"

"The question isn't about whether to allow hunting, even hunting for furs, it is the scale. On one hand, the cumulative impact has increased as Inuit population has expanded from historical levels. Also, with the use of 'new' technology such as snowmobiles, guns, and faster boats, the Inuit can be more efficient. They can kill a lot more seals in the same amount of time."

"What about your other hand?"

"Do people who criticize hunting of seals for fur ever consider the impact of the clothes they wear? I think a lot of those people need to get better connected with the everyday items they consume."

"How so?"

"How much discussion is there about the petrochemicals required to make synthetic clothes like polyester? Or the leather for shoes and jackets? It comes from resource intensive cattle. Producing one half pound of beef, requires thousands of gallons of water. How about the large amounts of water required for growing cotton? The irrigated water often comes from redirected rivers using dams which affects natural water flows and river life. I know where seal skin and fur comes from, do you know how your clothes were made?"

Amanda looked at her clothes and realized she had no idea, none whatsoever. Apart from the label stating where they were made, she was completely clueless.

"Do people ever think about buying less clothes or shoes because of this?"

She shook her head sideways. "I'm sure there's a few, Lars, but probably not very many. I think it's the whole idea of - 'Buy, buy, buy, gotta keep the economy going.' Or 'buy, buy, buy, it will make you happy.' That's the message from TV, radio, the Internet, and politicians, no matter which side of the aisle they are sitting on."

"You are right, Amanda."

She thought again about what she had heard on how there were a lot more political parties in small Denmark, and how the USA had been reduced to two. So much for living in the land of the free she mused.

What was freedom anyway? America was more free in some ways she thought, but less free in others. Was there some freedom more important than others? "Our control of nature and technology has given me the freedom to be here."

"True. Maybe we can strike a better balance."

Amanda didn't answer.

"Everything we do has repercussions. Every product we own requires natural resources. On a bigger picture, do people who wouldn't wear a fur coat, think about the resources they consume that affect other wildlife? Do they live in large homes which contribute to land sprawl, which forces animals into smaller and smaller areas? Large homes which require more furniture, wood, and a whole range of consumer products."

Visions of suburbia flashed through Amanda's mind. "How about the cars and planes we drive and fly, and the energy they consume?"

"Of course. Who thinks about how all this contributes to global warming in the Arctic? It is magnified here. Who thinks about how this might affect the wildlife here?"

Amanda thought about the people she knew who might be anti-fur, with an exception here or there, they didn't qualify. "I see. The complete answer is a lot more complicated than the question."

"The Inuit lost a major source of income when seal furs were banned from importation to America and later, Europe, due to the whole anti-fur movement. Some seal skin fur gets through to Europe now due to an exception in the law, but it is not much. These laws were a loss of a major source of livelihood for the Inuit."

Amanda drank some tea.

"But we are talking too serious, Amanda. I'll tell you a funny story, but I must first go outside to relieve myself."

"Yes, of course."

Lars stepped outside.

"Maybe the people in other countries should pay more attention to burping."

"Burping?"

"Cow burping."

"Huh?" Amanda was confused at what seemed like a whimsical statement.

"Cow belching, or burping as you might call it, is a serious issue, to some."

Amanda had heard of mad cow's disease and growth hormones, but not cow burping. "Explain."

"Cows burp methane, one of the primary greenhouse gases that warm the earth. It is more than twenty times better at trapping heat. The average cow burps at least 280 liters per day, everyday. You might think of it as 140 two-liter bottles of soda filled with gas everyday."

A look of astonishment crossed Amanda's face.

"I've heard that a cow's burps per day is equivalent to driving a car three kilometers, or about two miles. That may not sound like much, until you consider how many cows are out there today." Lars let out a hearty laugh.

Amanda hesitated, then laughed with him.

"It's funny, but serious. Even simple and silly things can make a difference. I've heard the global population of cattle has doubled in the past forty years to 1.3 billion."

"1.3 billion? That's a lot of cows."

"It's not just cows, but also sheep, more than 1 billion now. In New Zealand, they are taxing farmers based off the number of livestock they keep. In New Zealand there are more than thirty million sheep, and only four million people."

"Well, I don't eat lamb, but I am wearing wool," Amanda interjected.

"Speaking of numbers, environmentalists may not realize how many seals live up here. I've heard environmentalists talk about there being many more seals before. That is probably true, but there were a lot more of many things prior to our growing and collective impact on the world."

"You aren't kidding." Were cow burps now somehow related to Stephanie's death and the change in weather patterns? "What can be done?" Amanda asked, almost as if in despair.

"It's all a bit silly, Amanda."

"Why is it silly?"

"Because we can't see the forest for the trees. We've gotten stuck looking at details. Except, there is one detail we've overlooked that affects how we view everything else."

Amanda gave Lars a funny look. A half-grin.

"I used to think like most other people and say that we need to change in this way or that way, we need to educate, we need to make a new law, etc. . . etc. . ., but I don't think that way anymore. Or at least I usually don't, sometimes I still 'slip up,' as you might say in America."

"How do you think now?"

"We *only* have to know ourselves."

"We *only* have to know ourselves?"

"Do you know that saying – *those who do not study the past are doomed to repeat it*?"

"Yes, I've heard that before," Amanda answered.

"Do you also know a saying – *sometimes, we are our own worst enemy*?"

"Yes, I've heard that one before too, although maybe it is all the time, not just sometimes."

Lars let out a laugh. "Excellent. That is what we need to do to solve all of our problems. We need to know who we are at the very core."

"Ok. That sounds very general."

"If we stop trying to create a 'new future' for awhile and understand our past instead, we might learn some startling things about where we come from."

Amanda gave Lars a befuddled look.

"Do you like word games, Amanda?"

"Sure, I play crossword puzzles and online scrabble from time to time."

"I've studied languages in my time, and sometimes I explain things by using simple analogies with the words we use everyday. Say the word - enemy."

"Enemy," Amanda repeated, unsure of what Lars was getting at.

"Say it, slower."

"En-e-my."

"Say it, again."

"En-uh-my."

"Say it, again."

"En-uh-my. Ummm, I don't get it."

"Don't think about the spelling. What do the words sound like? As if the word itself is a sentence.

"Ok." She tried again. "En-uh-my, en-uh-my, en-uh-me, en-uh-me, en-uh-me, en-a-me..."

Lars said nothing.

"En-uh-me, en-uh-me, en-uh-me, en-a-me..."

Lars sat patiently.

"I got it! I got it! IN ME! IN ME! IN ME! IN ME!"

Lars smiled.

"So, the worst enemy is IN ME?!"

"Yes. When we stop focusing on our external 'enemies,' and start focusing on the internal one, ourselves, then we take a big step in knowing who we are. We often think of our enemy, or opponent, as someone else, or something else. Another country, another group, another person, or another company. Or some idea that we've labeled. Sometimes we sue 'them' in our lawsuit happy cultures. We blame them, whoever it is, for *our* problems."

"Yes, the blame game."

"Maybe the word enemy is a little strong for some, but it is just an easy way to remember to stop blaming others, and look within for our answers."

They talked about all the different kinds of enemies in the world, even when we didn't use the word, enemy.

There were mortal enemies, as in physical war. A list of recent wars came to mind between the two of them. World War I and II. The Korean War, Vietnam War, Arab-Israeli War, Gulf War, Russia and Afghanistan, the Cold War. Now it was enemy terrorist groups such as Al Qaeda, or the USA if you were an Al Qaeda supporter. Physical war was now also economic war and virtual war, cyberwars, between countries.

There were political enemies. The Left vs Right, Conservatives vs Liberals, Labour vs Conservative, Republican vs Democrat, multi-party coalition infighting, the list was endless.

Enemies in the corporate arena took on an infinite number of identities. Taxpayer and consumer groups against big tax-evading corporations, big business, and big oil. Or some against fast food giants, and soda companies. Corporate lobbyists and lawyers. Who the enemy was really depended on who you were. It was all relative to your position. Of course, corporations fought one another.

You couldn't escape war in sports either. With words like offense, defense, victory, beat, defeat, strike, attack, hit, shoot, shot, goal, steal, and safe, the language of war was in sports. Maybe that is why it was so popular, Lars noted. Football – American or European, baseball, hockey, cricket, basketball, cycling, tennis, running, golf, swimming, the list was limited only by the number of sports.

Of course, there were religious enemies, too. All other religions other than your own were wrong. Or maybe religion itself was evil, if you believed in just evolution. Enemies even within the same religion. Different sects in Islam, Christianity, Buddhism, Hinduism, Judaism, and religions long dead. The devil, infidels, and unbelievers came to mind for them both.

Color was an enemy, too. Black versus white versus yellow versus red, orange, or any other color one could think of that defined our 'race.' Colors had been co-opted by political parties and corporations too.

Adversaries were everywhere.

Nature was an enemy to many. We needed bug spray and electric lights to keep insects away from biting or bothering us. Farmers needed pesticides and herbicides to keep insects off of food that we ate. We needed those same chemicals to maintain our home gardens. For some, larger wild animals, were the enemy that needed to be culled or controlled. The enemy that was nature also took the form of weather. Tornadoes, hurricanes, cyclones, and earthquakes, to name a few.

Some enemies were ideological enemies. Anti abortion versus pro-choice, gun control versus NRA, straight versus gay.

The enemy was inside of us sometimes. Cancer, ADD, arthritis, tumors, Alzheimer's, heartburn, impotence, skin rashes, toothaches, defective organs, and nervous system disorders. Obesity, colds, the flu, and sinus problems. Any name, of any disease, that had been labeled by modern medicine, was an enemy that needed a weapon to fight it, a drug, tool, or a complicated and expensive machine.

Perhaps if we knew why at the very root, we wouldn't need such things. We wouldn't need labels, Amanda mused.

Food was an enemy to some. Food with too much fat, or was it too many carbohydrates? Artificial colors, pesticides, herbicides, plastic residue, the list was endless and mind-numbing.

New technological enemies now invaded our lexicon. Computer viruses, trojan horses, SPAM, and identity theft.

Let us not forget about the personal past too, Amanda realized. Family and blood feuds. Brother vs sister, brother vs brother, sister vs sister, kids vs parents. Ex-wives, ex-husbands, ex-anyone. Current spouses and partners. Boyfriends, girlfriends, anyone.

It wasn't enough to have 'real and tangible' enemies, so we had invented virtual enemies. In computer games, cartoons, characters in books, TV shows, and movies. We'd invented enemies because we were so used to fighting them.

It was ingrained at the deepest core of our existence. Everyone was fighting someone else, something else. Non-stop fighting in some form or another.

"Wow, I never realized we were so adversarial, Lars. Maybe diversity, isn't so good," she blurted out. "So much for multiculturalism."

"We are so busy fighting *all* the time, that we don't see there is another way. Another way to be, Amanda."

"That's clever. Does this word 'trick' work in other languages, Lars?"

"Some. If your native language was something different, maybe I would have come up with a different word."

"Ok, I'm gonna refer someone from some obscure country in Africa or Asia to come visit you."

Lars smiled and the tent went silent.

"You know, all those things that we talked about earlier? Cow burping, seal fur trade, you can forget about all that now. Global warming isn't important either."

"If we defeat our IN ME, right?"

"You took the words right out of my mouth."

"I kind of see where you are going, Lars. What isn't clear though is, *what* is our IN ME, and how do we beat it?"

"There is only one thing that needs to be done to defeat our IN ME and really, it is the only thing that needs to be done. The rest will just work itself out over time, in ways that we can't fully imagine."

"So, what is our IN ME?" Amanda said excitedly.

"Let's leave that for tomorrow, Amanda. You should go out and enjoy the lights again."

"What!? You're going to leave me hanging?"

"We have time. You don't have to go outside. I get tired of hearing my own voice sometimes."

"Ha ha. Really, you're not going to tell me now?"

Lars smiled and motioned toward the tent exit.

Amanda was treated to another Aurora Borealis as she sat down by some of the sledge dogs. She took her thinking cap off and just soaked in the beauty of lights dancing in the sky. The undulating waves of green and yellow shimmered across the night sky while making no particular shape. She took off her glove and stroked the fur of some of the dogs. The blood in her hand started to freeze, she quickly put her glove back on.

She headed back into the tent.

"It is more beautiful than if all the best painters in the world got together to put on an exhibition. It's not like a painting, it's alive," Amanda remarked as she settled in under her covers.

"We are lucky to be out here."

"I hope we get even luckier soon to see a polar bear."

"In the Arctic, luck can change in a hurry. We are getting closer to prime polar bear territory. If we do meet a polar bear, just remember, it isn't like your stuffed animal. Oh, and if you get too close, polar bears usually strike first with their left front paw." Lars let out a hearty laugh.

Amanda thought for a moment about what Lars said. She wanted to ask him another question, but he had already closed his eyes to sleep.

Any feelings of concern about being in such a remote place with a man she didn't know well, were all but gone. Lars was a man she could trust. It was a good thing she did now too, for she didn't have any other choice.

CHAPTER 19 – ARCTIC ICE FLOE

The morning was another achievement for Amanda. The night before she had slept on land covered with snow and ice. Today was her first morning after sleeping on a solid sheet of ice and snow that covered water.

She did a 360° sweep of her surroundings as she stepped out to breathe in the crisp air. Due west was the rest of Baffin Bay. To the east was the mountainous terrain of Greenland's coastline.

Once again, Lars was already awake taking care of the dogs. He walked over toward Amanda when he saw her get out of the tent. "Would you like a piece of chocolate?"

"Chocolate?" she responded in a voice that was still waking up. Amanda's head perked up and she turned around. "I didn't see any at the store. I have some peanuts and cookies."

"This is a reward for your successful first night on the pack ice. It's a very special candy bar." A small chocolate bar lay in Lars' open palm.

"Oh my. A gift from the Gods! Yes, please!"

"Go ahead, take the whole bar."

"Are you sure?"

"Of course, take it."

Amanda grabbed the bar, unwrapped it, and took a bite. The bar's hardness resisted her first attempt to bite through before letting her take a chunk. "Ugh! It's hard!"

"Sorry. I wore it close to my body this morning to try and warm it up for you. Not warm enough it seems. It isn't smart to bring chocolate as it freezes up, but I thought you would appreciate it."

Amanda gave a good laugh. "I'll try melting it in my mouth." She savored the rich chocolate flavors oozing out. "It is amazing how one can forget the things we take for granted out here."

"Maybe that is the newness of being out here. If you are out here long enough, you will remember those cravings. I have, many times. My family comes to Greenland for part of the year, then we are ready to return to Denmark after awhile. It is a nice arrangement."

"Best of both worlds."

He finished with the dog traces and refocused his patient attention toward scanning the horizon for any sign of a polar bear. Amanda continued to savor the morning treat.

She decided to ask a question that had been on her mind. "Have you ever wondered why I have a stuffed polar bear?"

"I've been wondering about that. I was waiting for you to tell me. It looks like you have a very personal attachment to it."

Amanda smirked. "You're a patient man."

"Are you going to tell me now?" Lars flashed a subtle smile to put Amanda at ease.

"He's a childhood present from my parents when I was little. My parents divorced not long after." She paused. "That was tough on me. My stuffed polar bear was, after my best friend

Stephanie, the only constant in my childhood. He never talked back and was always there to give me a big hug."

Lars said nothing, patiently waiting for more.

"As I grew up, I threw him in a closet and forgot about him. It was only recently I needed his 'help' again. Does that sound weird when I talk about him like he is real?"

Lars hesitated for a moment then gave his answer. "No, I don't think so." He paused for a few more moments as if his reasoning was catching up with his answer. "I think I mentioned it earlier, the Inuit, of old anyway, worshiped the animals they hunted. They believed all the animals had spirits. They would often perform rituals during or after they killed an animal, some still do."

"That would be interesting to see."

"Your stuffed polar bear, while unusual, is no different than people in other cultures assigning value to things of importance. Family mementos, religious talismans, and other physical symbols. Some people assign emotions to cars, furniture, clothes, any material object can have value. I believe the Inuit would understand your emotions."

"That's good to know," Amanda remarked.

"What made you decide to come to Greenland then of all places, to see a polar bear?"

"What I haven't told you yet is that when my parents gave him to me as a present, my best friend's parents also gave her a big stuffed panda bear. She kept it all these years too, but then she gave it to her daughter." Amanda paused for a moment wanting to shed a tear, but the cold and her current sense of hardiness prevented her from expressing it. "These bears were like a bond between us when we were younger. My best friend died in a car accident, not long ago."

"And that is why you needed his help again?" Lars spoke without betraying any emotion.

Amanda expected him to say something more. "Yes, I'm afraid so, but it wasn't enough. I went to see the polar bears at the zoo thinking that seeing a real one would cheer me up, but I was so heart broken by it. I decided to see one in the wild. My travel agent convinced me that coming here would be better than going to Alaska or Canada. When I was getting ready to leave, my friend's daughter asked me if I would bring my stuffed polar bear, I couldn't refuse. And, here I am."

"I respect you for your quest."

A silence of contemplation descended upon both of them as if Lars was absorbing the revelation, and Amanda was breathing a sigh of relief over revealing it.

"While we're on the subject of quests, what kind of people have you taken on these dog sledge tours?'

"The people that come on these trips are looking for something to satisfy some very deep sense of self, or perhaps, to forget that sense of self. Sure, a few are adventurers who want to try something new. But, to go on a multi-day sledge ride like this, takes an extra sort of motivation. Whether it is coming to Greenland or going to some other similar place in the world, a journey like this can only come from within."

Amanda felt good about her decision.

"Nature provides many answers, though it often provides the answers on a different clock than that of modern society, nor does it happen with as much noise or flash."

"I never seem to have enough. . ."

Before Amanda could finish her response, Lars motioned her to stop talking. His conversational demeanor turned off as his attention shifted to their surroundings. "We should get going. The wind is picking up." In the far off distance, a few clouds began to gather.

"What does that mean?" Amanda asked with a sense of alarm.

"The likelihood of cracks in the ice opening up is greater when the wind and current is stronger. If a crack starts to develop somewhere around us it will open up like a zipper being pulled down a jacket."

"That doesn't sound so good."

"Hunters have been trapped on ice floes before."

"What happened to them?"

"How about we talk about it later and get to safer snow and ice sooner?"

Amanda shook her head with vigor up and down in agreement.

They took down the tent and tied everything down. Amanda lay her back against her stuffed polar bear, comforted by his presence in a situation unfamiliar to her. They finished and were ready to head off toward shore, the once distant clouds coming ever closer. The increase in wind speed that was so modest, that only an experienced pack ice traveler would perceive, was now blowing hard enough that Amanda could feel a little of it through her layers of clothing. It was blowing so hard that it was getting hard to talk.

The dogs were excited again to get moving.

Amanda and Lars could hear the ice groaning above the wisp of the sledge rails as they got closer to shore.

"Hackfui! Hackfui! Hackfui!" Lars shouted at the dogs, pressing them to go faster.

They approached within solid visual sight of the mountains which signaled that firmer snow and ice was near. Amidst the puffs of frost smoke rising up around them, the winds began to break up areas of the ice. It looked like a place where steam rises from hot springs, except the water here wasn't boiling hot enough to cook an egg. Lars slowed the sledge as they approached what looked like a wider lead.

Amanda saw the widening lead too. It extended down as far as the eye could see. "What do we do now?"

Lars looked to their left, then the right. In the far off distance to the left he saw more wisps of fog. The ice was beginning to separate down there even faster. Further toward the right, in much closer view, the lead was even wider than the span of water in front of them. A large chunk of pack ice was separating from the mainland, and they were on it.

"We can try and find a place where it is still attached down there." Lars reconsidered his thought. "But it looks pretty far off, we might be too late by the time we reach it. I think we are better off to try and jump it just a little further down. I think you can get off and jump across."

"You can tell from this far away?" Amanda remarked, wondering how Lars could determine the conditions that far. She had a vision of being trapped on a floating ice floe with no one to rescue them. She had become more courageous on this trip so far, but the fear in her eyes and voice could not be denied.

Lars ignored Amanda's question, hinting at the urgency of the situation. "Over there!"

"Ok," Amanda answered in a momentary state of shock at the suddenness of events.

Lars shouted at the dogs and steered the sledge toward what appeared to be the most narrow part of the lead.

"You need to jump across here. I'll throw the supplies over to you. Then I am going to let the dogs jump across on their own."

She looked at the water. It was the most menacing water she had ever looked at. She knew how cold it was. If only she had fur like a polar bear. Pack ice was being taken away by the increasing current. The lead was getting wider before their eyes.

"We have to hurry, Amanda."

They both picked up some supplies and threw them over to the other side of the lead.

"You can jump across, now."

Amanda picked up Polar Bear and threw him across. He rolled over on his side. Then she stepped back to get a running start. She started running, and jumped across. "Phew."

Lars untied the dogs from the sledge and let them go free. They started jumping across. A couple of them didn't quite make it, they splashed in the water. Amanda helped them out.

"I am going to tie this rope to the front end of the sledge. Then I am going to throw the rope over to you. While I push the sledge, you should pull. You will need to pull the front end of the sledge harder as it gets closer to your side because it will start to sag on my side as more of the sledge is closer to your side! It looks like it will just make it across."

Lars started pushing as Amanda pulled on the rope. The now empty sledge was part way over the lead of water when Amanda lifted with all her strength. She pulled as hard as she could. The back end was no longer supported by pack ice. It glided over to the other side.

"Now, I will jump across." He looked around to make sure they had everything. He sprinted back then started running.

It was the longest jump Amanda had recalled seeing in person.

"We were lucky today," Lars announced.

Amanda took a deep breath.

"Let's tie up the dogs and get moving."

They reached another pressure ridge a safe distance away. Lars commanded the dogs to stop. He and Amanda climbed to the top of one of the small ridges. Using binoculars, they looked at the ice that they were camped on just a short while earlier. It was now visibly separate from the ice they were on. The lead continued to widen.

"It is definitely too wide to jump across now," Amanda remarked, sounding like a battle scarred veteran who had survived a death match with the unpredictable ice gods.

"The warming temperatures here have created more hazardous and unpredictable conditions for us. I am going to take more time examining the ice conditions. It is worse than last year."

"Wow."

"Have you ever seen video of Antarctic ice shelves collapsing?"

"No."

"When you go home, you can look for it. You can think of an ice shelf as just as large slab of ice connected to Antarctica. Due to warming temperatures, at some point, a large slab just breaks away and disintegrates. They can happen suddenly and seemingly without warning. Our experience earlier, is kind of like a mini-version of that, at least in terms of how sudden things can change."

They headed toward their next stop as they sledged on safer ice. The ice floe they had escaped from had separated as far as several miles along the coastline until the primary lead had veered toward the sea. This lead would have sealed off their exit, the exact circumstances that Lars was concerned about. Meanwhile, a smaller lead continued along the coast as they sledged back closer toward the settlement of Savissivik, fast moving slush ice was flowing in it.

Amanda's frayed nerves from the tense wake-up were getting calmer, but her stomach was growling. She had already finished the chocolate bar long ago.

"Are you hungry?" Lars asked, as if hearing her growls.

Amanda nodded her head in the affirmative.

He handed her some biscuits and she ate some peanuts.

They went a little further before Lars stopped the sledge, he had spotted a seal. "Do you see it?"

"See what?" Amanda answered, unsure of why they had stopped.

"Over to your right."

Amanda strained to see what Lars was talking about, then she spotted it out of the corner of her eye. "The seal?"

"Yes."

"That is our lunch?"

"We're in a good position, we are downwind." He sat down and took aim with his rifle. He fired.

Even in the distance, Amanda could see that Lars was a crack marksman. The seal squirmed no more, it was dead.

"This is a lot easier than the traditional way."

"How's that?"

"Before they had rifles, an Inuit would wait in silence by a seal breathing hole. Often, the wait would be for many hours. He would have a harpoon with a line attached to it. When the seal came up to breathe he would strike it. It took a lot of skill and especially, patience."

"Did you say they would wait for several hours being still?"

"Sometimes standing, other times, sitting on a small portable chair. They would put a seal skin on the ground to act as a barrier between their boots and the ice."

"Does anyone still hunt like that?"

"I don't believe as a means of survival. There are annual events where only traditional methods of hunting are used, but that is more to preserve tradition. Let's go retrieve the seal." Lars got up. He remembered the earlier kill. "You don't have to come."

"I'd like to. I'm, I'm, more okay with it now." Or at least she thought she was.

The two of them walked over to the seal. Blood was on the ground. They each picked up one end of the seal and brought it over toward the sledge.

Amanda realized the energy would be important after the tense moments earlier today. "I'll let you butcher and skin it though."

"Thanks for helping to bring it over here."

Amanda looked on as Lars flipped the seal on its back and cut it open, exposing all of its organs. Whatever hint that a cute smile existed before was no more.

Lars started chopping up the meat, he gave some to Amanda. "How does it taste?" Lars asked.

"I'll live."

"That good, eh? When done right, aged seal meat in oil or blubber takes on a strong flavor. Some would say, delicious."

"I'll remember that." Amanda continued to dine on her second fresh seal carcass while Lars rewarded the dogs for their performance this morning.

The dogs howled in enthusiasm.

"Will we reach the settlement tonight?"

"Let's setup camp here. We'll arrive in Savissivik the day after tomorrow. It's a little further ahead. We'll stay off the floating pack ice tonight."

"That sounds good, I've had enough excitement today." She let out a deep breath.

Another day was coming to an end.

"I thought I heard from someone that Danes could be a little cold."

"Cold?"

"I mean, not very friendly. I can't imagine where they ever got that idea. You seem anything, but."

Lars took a moment to ponder Amanda's words. "Danes can seem stand-offish at times to the uninitiated. The best explanation I have ever heard is like that of a ketchup bottle. You have to hit the bottle hard a few times for the ketchup to start flowing, but once you do, it won't stop."

"Once you get a Dane talking they can't shut up?"

Lars didn't reply.

Amanda chuckled. "Are all Scandinavians similar?"

"I would say for you, the Danish are similar to the Norwegian and Swedish, but not Icelanders, due to distance, or Finnish who have a mixed background. Officially, Icelanders and Finns aren't considered Scandinavian, although sometimes people think they are. I mention them due to historical ties and geographic proximity."

"I didn't know that."

"Of course, between us, Danes, Swedes, and Norwegians, we see more differences, but to the outsider, pretty similar. I think as our trip progresses you will understand more about how we think. I am not a model example as I have a strong connection to Greenland through my wife and my own personal experiences. Also, I've changed a lot due to choices I've made about how I think about myself, ourselves."

It was like seeing shades of gray and colors of blue Amanda thought. As for how different Lars was compared to other Scandinavians, she didn't have a reference point, so that would have to wait. But anyone who spent so much time out in this snow and ice covered land, must be different, especially one who was not born into it.

Despite the day's events and sometimes hard work of surviving out on the ice, Amanda was feeling more energized. She was beginning to control her emotions and fears about things better. Or maybe she was just learning to let them go as they came out from within.

After Stephanie's death she had fallen into a state of despair and depression. It was fear of living without those you've cared about. She harkened back to the lessons of dark and light in Ilulissat. We should prize the time we have and when darkness is close at hand, fear it not. Easy to say, harder to do.

She strolled away from the tent and noticed a small, clear blue, pool of water. It was a melt pool. She gazed into it and saw a partial reflection of herself, and it surprised her to say the least.

While her nerves had been frayed by the earlier events, she realized she didn't feel as fearful as she might have been in the heat of the moment earlier. Was freedom from fear something she was learning out here?

CHAPTER 20 – UNICORNS

Amanda looked out on the horizon with the binoculars as the sun faded. She reflected on the earlier events of the day when a strange sight entered her field of view. A long straight pointed horn stuck up out of the water and then submerged again. She saw it come up again. "What's that?" she yelled in disbelief.

Lars snapped to attention and looked in her direction. He looked through the binoculars. The strange horn emerged again, this time revealing the rounded head from which the horn was attached to. "That's a narwhal."

"What's a narwhal?" Amanda asked as the horned creature submerged itself again.

"A narwhal is a whale that only lives in the Arctic. Come, there must be a small lead over there." He inspected the ice as they trotted over toward the narwhal. The wind was calm. They were not going to get stranded on an ice floe.

Another narwhal appeared higher up out of the water. It showed off its light colored underbelly and spots on its darker colored grayish topside, its horn spiraled out of the water.

"How bizarre! I've never seen such an animal!"

"A very unique looking creature."

"What do they use those horns for?"

"The horns only grow on males. I've seen two of them fight before with it, probably over another female."

"Figures."

"The horn might be for hunting too, maybe. Not for spearing, but for disrupting the bottom sediment while looking for fish like flounder in addition to its diet of cod and squid."

Amanda watched in amazement as another narwhal surfaced to breathe, there now appeared to be three narwhals swimming near them.

"They actually have two teeth, but it is rare for both to form a long horn. I've only seen one before with both, quite a sight."

"How long are those horns?"

He took a closer look. "They all look to be about two meters or a little over six feet long. I've seen, maybe, half a meter longer before. These narwhals look to be about average size, I would say five meters, sixteen feet, including the horn."

Two more narwhals broke the surface to blow. Their horns jutted up out of the water, then their spotted, dark dorsal finless back emerged.

"The narwhal and the bowhead are the only whales who live full time in the Arctic, they are quite remarkable. They can dive down to twelve hundred meters, around four thousand feet, and stay down for twenty to twenty-five minutes. It is more common for them to swim much shallower around thirty meters or one hundred feet though."

Amanda took out her camera, zoomed in, and snapped several photos. "My friends won't believe me until I show them some pictures," she added enthusiastically.

"I once saw several dozen migrating, but they usually are in small pods like this. I've read they gather in groups of hundreds, up to perhaps a thousand sometimes."

"Hundreds? A thousand? Wow." Amanda couldn't contain her excitement at seeing such a strange animal.

"It's strange to see a narwhal around here this time of year."

"Why's that?"

"It's unusual for them to be this far north at this time of year. They overwinter in the Davis Strait, then they come up north through the pack ice and are here in large numbers by May and June."

"Why would they be here so early?" Amanda wondered out loud.

"Sometimes narwhals get stuck in fast forming solid pack ice before they can go south toward Disko Island in October. The Inuit have a name for it - savssat. Narwhals that get stuck here over the winter, I am guessing, would die during the winter because of exhaustion from keeping their breathing hole open. These narwhals here don't look like they would have spent the winter here, they look too healthy and energetic."

"You can tell?"

"Immaqa."

"What does that word mean? I've heard it before."

"Immaqa?"

"Yes."

"It means, look carefully before drawing a conclusion."

With the unforgiving Arctic climate, this was a prudent way to think. Perhaps this word would be useful back home.

Two of the narwhals surfaced and fought with their horns. Their attention toward the new activity let them both forget the question of why the narwhals were this far north so early in the year.

This new activity made Amanda realize something else, that wild nature was not a museum like at a zoo. Or even like going to a national park, perhaps. It was spontaneous. It was all encompassing. The fellow creatures of the earth were acting out their lives naturally, if allowed to. It made her realize something else, why she was feeling a little agitated over the cartoon shows on the airplane flight over.

It was because having a cartoonish view of nature would not only be a sign of disrespect, it would also be anthropomorphic, and that wasn't real as she saw nature now. No more animated movies, TV shows, and cartoon books. No more talking fishes, sharks, or lions, to name but a few for her now. No more for Haley too, if she had a say in the manner. A cartoonish view of nature also made us more fearful of nature she was quickly beginning to realize. It mixed fantasy with reality and messed up our expectations.

Another aspect of how this was different from going to the zoo became apparent while watching these dueling narwhals. At the zoo, there were too many choices to look at. One ended up being confused and overwhelmed, it was simple psychology.

Perhaps with equal importance, there was the all encompassing near silence of nature to contemplate these narwhals, unlike a zoo with its crowds of screaming children and signs filled with mind numbing details. The world 'we' had created was filled with zoos and artificial windows into nature from TV, books, and movies. Why did we do this? Was it out of fear?

Amanda's marketing instincts came to the forefront despite her desire to forget anything work related. She recalled an article that she had read of efforts to ban advertising targeted at children. It was Sweden, now that she thought about it. Ever since then she had come to realize that the more cartoon characters and animals a company employed in advertising, the more they had to hide.

While the strategy worked on children, it was often carried over to adults who had grown up with this exposure, or rather, conditioning. Oil companies with talking cars and tigers, sugary cereals with toucan birds and tigers, cigarettes and camels, artificially colored snacks and cheetahs, flavored crackers in the shape of bears, or a host of other bastardized versions of animals.

Then there were the fast food chains with their colorful assortment of characters. There was a good reason that these companies used cute little toy animals to suck in children with meals in little boxes covered with fake animals - we'll be happy when you're addicted. Hook, line, and sinker. They used our love of animals to deceive us. Was that all? Why did we get addicted to certain foods more than others? Amanda knew it wasn't just advertising, though that was important. Was it some secret flavoring? Something else? Another question for the future.

It wasn't just the attribution of human characteristics to animals, but also the cartoonization of reality. One oil company, while avoiding the use of animals, had an advertising campaign with a false swim through of an underwater scene. Other advertising campaigns had created false versions of jungle and forest scenes. It was like the artificial landscaping at the zoo, it was all – lipstick on a pig.

Was anyone left living who understood what this meant? Was anyone left who had the spirit of being naturally, 'wild & free?'

Amanda stopped thinking to herself, she was a bit demoralized and agitated now. This negativity wasn't inspiring, but perhaps it was necessary to balance out the false positivity she had been subjected to in her life.

Lars brought back some biscuits and tea for Amanda to warm up. "The narwhal helped to fuel the myth of the unicorn."

"Unicorns?"

"In the Middle Ages, Vikings passed off narwhal horns as unicorn horns. These 'unicorn horns' were sold as cures for various afflictions of the heart and mind. They were popular with royalty too, as they thought it was a poison neutralizer."

"Poison?"

"Kings and queens drank from goblets made of alicorn, the name of a unicorn horn. It was custom for the French kings to have all their utensils, cups, and bowls made from alicorn. It was a tradition that continued right up through to the French Revolution. Fear of poisoning went along with political intrigue apparently."

Amanda looked at the cup of tea she was drinking out of, it was made of stainless steel. "Lars, you're not poisoning me in anyway, are you?" She was feeling cheeky.

Lars smiled. "There was a time when alicorns were very valuable. Perhaps a single alicorn was worth the equivalent of a million dollars today."

"Just a single horn, like the ones we're looking at now?"

"They were also symbols of imperial power. The scepter of Russia's czars and of Austria's Hapsburg emperors are both made of alicorn. The crown jewels."

"I would have never thought that people could think that unicorns were real. I just thought they were pretty to look at growing up."

"The kings of Denmark knew the secret of the alicorn. They kept it to themselves. They even made a throne of alicorn and gold to impress others. The throne is on display in Copenhagen at Castle Rosenborg, home of the Danish crown jewels. Other rulers of Europe were jealous of them because of this display of wealth."

Amanda made a note to visit this castle someday. "How would they turn a horn into a chair?"

"It's not the whole chair, but the supporting structure and accents."

"Oh."

"You can find a picture of it on the Internet."

"I'll have to look for that."

The narwhals continued to circle around in the lead. Amanda realized that alicorns were like many luxury items of today. People prized them just because others did. It was another example of how we distorted nature.

"The legend didn't stop at its medicinal properties or value perception. It was also used by the Christian Church throughout the Middle Ages to help teach morality."

"How's that?"

"According to the folklore, a unicorn could only be tamed by a virgin woman. This idea was widely used by the Christian Church in paintings to teach morality. People were taught that without chastity, Christians could not know Christ."

"I'm having a visualization with sexual connotations, Lars."

"The idea was to motivate commoners toward maintaining sexual purity, or perhaps pursue a life in the monastery. On the flip side, the lore was that hunters would use a virgin to attract the unicorn, then kill it for its horn."

"The Church used a made-up animal that they thought was real to teach something?"

"Yes, unless you think it could have existed before and it became extinct."

"Interesting. So, Vikings made up the idea of the unicorn?"

"No, no. The unicorn myth existed long before. They just took advantage of people's beliefs to make a handsome profit off it. Counterfeiters even went so far as to straighten out walrus and elephant tusks. I read that even limestone stalactites were sold as alicorns, if you can believe it."

"Crazy. Where did the myth come from?"

"If it wasn't real before, from people's imaginations. There is a unicorn like myth in Chinese history called a Chi-Lin, or in Japan, Kirin."

"Like the beer?"

"Yes. The myth may have come from there over time. Or it could also be from interpretations of the Bible. It is mentioned more than a few times in the King James Bible."

"Unicorns in the Bible?"

"I've read that when the Old Testament was translated from the original Hebrew into Greek, scholars used the word for a wild ox or ass, as a unicorn. Ever since then the unicorn has had a holy connection."

"I can't believe this," Amanda replied in a state of exasperation.

"There are only two animals that have a single horn. Rhinoceroses, which of course look nothing like a horse, and the narwhal. Have you ever heard of an oryx?"

"No."

"The oryx is from Africa and the Middle East. It might be like a deer in your country."

"Ok, I get the idea."

"People may have confused it to be a unicorn. If you look at an oryx from the side, it looks like it only has one horn. It was even portrayed this way in old Egyptian paintings. But, if you look at it in three dimensions, it becomes clear that it has two horns. Adding to the confusion, mutant goats are sometimes born with only one horn."

"That's quite a mix up. Sounds like people could pick and choose what the unicorn looked like."

"Like many myths, people retell them as they would want to envision it, not as to what is the actual 'truth,' although truth is in the eye of the beholder, and relative to one's understanding of the world."

Amanda bit her lip.

"Anyway, the myth became. . . embellished over time. The unicorn became fleet and fierce, with a white body, tail of a lion, a mane, and legs of a buck. It came to represent the love of purity and innocence."

"Parts from many different animals? Wouldn't anyone ever want proof of its existence?"

"People just thought that, 'it couldn't be taken alive.' It was a convenient excuse for not ever producing a live one."

"Amazing what people believed in those days. It sounds like that game, telephone."

"Amazing what people believe in today. What game are you talking about?"

"Somebody whispers something in your ear and you have to tell the person sitting next to you what they said. And that person tells the next person, and so on. Then you listen to what the last person thought was said. It's really funny!"

"I'm not familiar with that game, Amanda. But, I think I understand what you are trying to say."

They amused themselves momentarily by continuing to watch the narwhals play before Lars finished his story.

"The unicorn deception was self-fulfilling when a non-Viking European found a narwhal horn for themselves. It went to Queen Elizabeth I."

"Maybe he did know the true source of it, Lars. Maybe he just lied to everyone back home."

"That could be. That could be."

"It was only in the early 1800s that the myth, by most accounts, faded away. This didn't stop a fake horn from being sold in 1994 for nearly 450,000 English pounds at a famous auction house."

"Crazy. Are narwhals endangered, Lars?"

"Their numbers are stable, but many species of rhinos and oryx aren't so fortunate."

"Yea, I've heard about rhinos being endangered."

"If unicorns did exist before, long ago, maybe they were hunted to extinction. If we don't change, then rhinos, oryx, or any number of animals that have some useful 'human value,' could very well become mythical creatures like the unicorn, known only in stories and in books."

"Or that have no 'human value,' Lars." Amanda pursed her lips as she thought about endangered animals. The still mythical, wild polar bear, that they were looking for, was a no show.

What was the human value of a polar bear? A *wild* polar bear. Was a polar bear's value in getting people to drink your favorite soda? She thought of a commercial for a popular soft drink. The world didn't need *wild* polar bears for that, just digitally animated ones.

"Good point. The unicorn isn't the first myth to become larger than life as we know it, and it won't be the last to fade."

They watched in silence as the group of narwhals swam away.

Amanda decided to change the tone of the conversation. "I enjoyed this. Didn't you say there was another kind of whale that lived up here?

"Ah, yes. The bowhead whale."

"Do you think we will see any bowhead whales?"

Lars did not cooperate. "I doubt it. There used to be a lot of bowhead whales around here, but they were hunted to near extinction by the early 1900s for lamp oil by Europeans. They were much prized because they float when killed."

"Lars, you know you aren't cheering me up," Amanda commented.

"Sorry, I just try to tell it like it is. In order to learn from the past we must be honest about it."

"Yeah. . . how many are there now?"

"I don't recall the precise numbers, but maybe only a couple hundred. There are more in the Chukchi Sea between Russia and Alaska. Maybe several thousand there."

The depressing realization made Amanda realize something greater in Lars' words. In order to learn from one's own past, one had to be honest with themselves first.

For all this talk of horns and whales though, she hadn't asked about the creature she had come this far to see. Was the magic of the polar bear in danger of disappearing too?

CHAPTER 21 – PROSPECTS

The sun moved farther below the horizon. Amanda retreated into the tent as Lars secured and tended to the dogs a little longer. He joined her inside the tent as darkness descended upon them. They boiled some tea and dined on some leftover seal meat, fish, and biscuits. They heated the tent with the stove. It quickly warmed up inside.

Amanda had only one thought on her mind at the moment, to learn more about the fate of the polar bear. "What about the polar bear? Have people hunted it for any of its parts like the narwhal and the bowhead?"

"Polar bear skins were traded before. The written records say that the skins reached as far as Egypt. The biggest prize was catching a live polar bear though. There is even a story of an Icelander who brought a live polar bear to the Holy Roman Emperor and was then made a bishop."

"Bishop for bear," Amanda summarized. "How many polar bears in the world, again?"

"Maybe, a little over twenty thousand."

"Is that a lot? It doesn't sound like very many. How many are in this area?"

"Around here, there are maybe two thousand to twenty-five hundred."

"And we still haven't found one. . ."

"Historically, there were probably a lot more bears. It has probably varied due to the extent of ice ages and hunting by man in recent times. When the ice age was at its greatest extent and hunting was minimal, there probably would have been more."

"What's your guess? How many?"

"Hmm. . . there are about 200,000 brown bears in the world. Half of them are in Russia, and the rest are mostly in Alaska and Canada. Black bear estimates range from about 200,000 to 600,000 in North America, a decline from an estimated two million."

"So, what's your guess?"

"I don't know, Amanda. Any number I say would probably be wrong."

"Don't be shy."

"Sorry. I don't know. But, certainly more than there are today. Probably a lot more. Whether that means 30,000 or 50,000, or even more, or some other number, is anyone's guess."

Amanda imagined a world filled with bears. A world where bear and man lived harmoniously. Rather than give warnings, there would be instructions, on how to attract and befriend your local bear.

All this talk of hunting led Amanda to ask Lars a more pointed question about how he viewed these animals. "Have you ever killed a narwhal or polar bear?"

"I have killed several narwhal. It has been quite a few years since I last killed one, not good for business. Red narwhal meat is good for the dogs though. The skin and blubber can be made into a chewy delicacy called muktuk. In season, you might find some in town. I have never killed a polar bear, but I have been with some Inuit a number of times when they did."

Amanda pressed on unflinchingly. "What did you do with the bear?"

"We ate the meat and skinned it. You may have seen some of the Inuit wearing polar bear pants."

She remembered it now, but had chosen to not think about it. Now that she was out in the wilderness it didn't seem as uncomfortable to acknowledge the reality. "I was wondering about those pants I saw. What does polar bear meat taste like?"

"It tastes a little like pork, tastier than seal by most accounts. Polar bear liver is very poisonous though."

The description was blunt. It was no different that describing the taste of a morning slab of bacon or a Mexican taco with carnitas. "Are polar bears endangered?"

"No, but they are classified as lower risk to vulnerable on the IUCN Red List. Do you know what that is?"

"No."

"It is a list which tracks endangered and near endangered animals. This classification means their numbers are stable, but continued health is 'conservation' dependent. Though, I don't agree with conservation efforts in principle, anymore."

"But, they're still hunted in Greenland, no?"

"Yes. While several countries have outright bans, they are also hunted in Eastern Russia and Canada. In the case of Greenland, hunting is limited to native Inuit, and there are limits on how many they can kill legally each year. Hunting isn't allowed in the reserves. The last numbers I saw were about one thousand killed worldwide every year."

"One thousand? That sounds like a lot considering the population."

Lars said nothing, but he nodded in agreement.

"What about global warming? How is this affecting polar bears?"

"Do you remember how I mentioned that I didn't expect to see narwhal up here so early?"

"I remember."

"I think they are here due to warming temperatures."

"Polar bears?"

"Polar bears depend on sea ice to hunt for seals. The length of season and extent of sea ice has been changing at an incredible rate."

"I read or heard something about that."

"It's been reported, with some controversy, that some populations are losing weight, year over year, due to shorter hunting seasons."

A silence came over both of them.

The weight loss comment jogged Amanda's memory. "I remember now! I spoke with a scientist who drills ice cores while waiting for my flight from Copenhagen. He mentioned the weight loss too. This is insightful to hear it from you, someone closer to the situation."

"Not only is the sea ice season getting shorter and the extent declining, but the ice that is here, is thinner – dramatically thinner. It makes being on the ice more treacherous. But now, you already know that."

Amanda nodded her head in agreement.

"A few years ago I visited some friends at the Danish Polar Center in Denmark, they showed me some historical charts. When compared to present day satellite images, the charts only confirmed what we, meaning people on the ground here, already know."

Amanda waited patiently for him to finish.

"It has gotten more difficult since I first arrived. The ice is not as thick and it melts sooner. You are lucky that we are able to dog sledge so late in the season. Perhaps in a few years around this time it will not be possible to dog sledge this far south."

"It's that bad?"

"When you flew over here in the helicopter, did you see a large body of open water?"

"The North Water polynya?" Amanda vividly recalled the flight in the helicopter.

"That's the one."

"What about it?"

"In the past during this time of year, the polynya was only open further north. I remember when the polynya was just west of Dundas in May, not so anymore. The polynya is spreading further south earlier in the season, more leads are appearing too. While there has always been a lead along Melville Bay, the network is growing. Normally, the Davis Strait becomes ice free in June, it is happening sooner.

"Does this have anything to do with us almost getting stuck on a drifting piece of ice?"

"Quite possibly."

"Is all this because of global warming?"

"To tell you the truth, Amanda, I don't like that word or the related word, climate change. They are so loaded, Amanda. The environment up here is changing rapidly. It is changing in a lifetime. Perhaps you can learn some of the stories from this lonely part of the world and share them with people you know."

"I can try."

"I will say that many people don't see how things are inter-related and connected. On top of that, some of the major public faces of global warming could be studies in hypocrisy – do as I say, not as I do. There were times in history when generals lead their soldiers by example on the battlefield themselves. Until that day comes, nothing much will change I suspect."

Amanda clenched her teeth. She wasn't quite sure what to make of his military reference, but she ignored it for the time being. "What other changes have you seen first hand?"

"Birds are staying longer before flying south due to longer summer like temperatures. I've noticed some bird species that I've never seen here before. Inuit hunters here are falling through previously solid sea ice. I know we are not alone in Greenland. Canadian Inuit are seeing robins for the first time. In Scandinavia, birch trees are moving northward into previously icy areas used for reindeer herding. Scientists monitoring Svalbard have said that they have found seas free of ice further north than for 250 years at one monitoring point."

Amanda shook her head.

"We live in an age of too much information for most, Amanda. Besides, what happens here doesn't matter to most people. Many people often don't care about something unless they are personally affected by an issue, or until they see how it directly affects them."

Amanda realized the truth of his statement. "Ok, let's forget about these words, global warming and climate change, for now."

Silence pervaded the tent again, even as light from the lantern signaled a mood of talk, rather than sleep. It was as if they had known each other for a long time and were comfortable with silence. The remote outdoors had a way of bonding people faster.

"There's another threat to polar bears as a result of a warming Arctic, do you want to hear about it?"

"Of course. There are so many threats."

"Have you heard of the Northwest Passage?"

"Northwest Passage. Northwest Passage. I can't say that it rings a bell. Although, lots of things come to mind when I say the word, Northwest."

"The Northwest Passage is a sea route through the islands of Northern Canada. It is a way for ships to transit from the Atlantic to Pacific Ocean and vice versa. Until recently, it wasn't practical for this to be used with any regularity because there was always ice in the passage."

Lars drank some water.

"Only about fifty ships have made the crossing since the early 1900s when it was first transited. But, things are changing up here."

"Global, no, a warming Arctic?"

"Yes."

"It is expected that the entire passage will soon be ice free completely in the summer. In the next fifty years perhaps, ten years by some accounts. There are even Canadian and US government forecasts for when this would be possible. Right now, large sections, not the entire passage, are ice free in a small window from August to late October."

"So, what does this mean?"

"This 'new' passage would permit container ships, cruise ships, and oil tankers, to transit between Asia and Europe more quickly by not having to go through the Panama Canal. This would save ships thousands of miles and canal fees. Some ships, notably large oil tankers, might benefit even more as they are too big for the Panama Canal. These large ships usually end up going around the dangerous tip of South America."

"Good for business, bad for polar bears? A double edged sword."

Lars nodded in agreement. "It is being called the Panama Canal of the North by some. All change has winners and losers. Winners would include the companies who took advantage of this to lower their costs, or the developers of the infrastructure. Energy companies stand to gain from large deposits of natural gas. The country of Panama might be a loser. If development proceeds in the Arctic environment to support any transits, whether it be by Inuit or large corporations, polar bears could be losers too."

"The polar bear?" Amanda repeated, while thinking of her furry friend from childhood.

"Think oil spills, industrial pollution, hunters, settlements, and more human contact, among other ills."

She pursed her lips.

The simplicity of the Arctic helped to clarify Amanda's thoughts. She began to wonder about her own values of winning and losing and what they meant for the world at large, and her own existence.

What influenced what she truly desired? Out here, there were no billboards. There were no magazines to thumb through or glance at in a grocery aisle. There was no grocery store.

There was no materialistic competition to keep up with, unless you counted the simple belongings they had with them to survive. There were no fashion trends to follow, no 'must have' gadgets, no fancy cars to impress others. There was no television advertising to consume. There was no television.

There were no ringing mobile phones nor websites to surf from your laptop or smartphone. And of course there was no wi-fi or internet out here.

The noise of the modern world was trumpeted by her surroundings. She felt more alive than ever before. For a few moments, she wished she was a polar bear or narwhal. Maybe there was some happier medium between living free and wild as an animal and as a human. Maybe she would find it, and live it someday.

"Live free or die," she mumbled.

"Excuse me?"

"Oh, nothing. Go on."

"There's no free lunch, I think you say in America. If we collectively ask ourselves, what is worth giving up, and what isn't, instead of blindly accepting it, maybe that will lead more people to true happiness and joy deep down inside."

"You said you haven't killed a polar bear before, right?"

He nodded his head affirmatively.

"Yet, you've killed a narwhal. Why is that?"

"Opportunity, I guess. Or maybe there was a part of me that just didn't want to do the deed myself."

"I can't imagine eating polar bear meat, Lars. I don't think I would eat it even if I was starving. I would rather just throw myself in the cold ocean and drown."

"What I find interesting is that what is considered strange in one culture, is acceptable and normal in another. Italians eat horse meat, Koreans and Chinese eat dog, Indians don't eat cows, and people in West and Central Africa eat monkeys and other bush meat. Danes eat and sell pork, but Muslims and Jews either think it is unclean or prohibit it for other reasons."

Amanda pondered her own adventurous eating habits. While she reacted with mild surprise at these revelations, she wondered how her friends back home might look at her after eating seal and walrus meat.

"What is the strangest thing you have ever eaten before coming here?" Lars asked.

She blurted out, "and people in 'modern countries' eat horrifically treated factory farmed animals. I'm ashamed and disgusted with myself, Lars. I've seen how animals are raised on video. I want to stop sometimes, but I guess I love eating certain things too much."

"It's one of many things in our world that most would rather not confront, Amanda. It's a dark part of our collective existence. You took a big step to come out here, I applaud you for your bravery. You came here alone too."

Amanda's eyes teared up a little. "A friend once made me drink snake wine at a Japanese restaurant. I think of raw fish, sushi, as being a bit exotic. Or at least, I did. Some of my friends eat it so much, they don't think so."

"How did the snake wine taste?"

"Creepy. I think my nerves overpowered my taste buds. I mostly tasted the rice wine. I'd probably have to try it again."

"Do you have a favorite kind of sushi?"

"I like the salmon and tuna the most."

"There's an interesting story about tuna in sushi, would you like to hear it?"

She nodded her head enthusiastically. More tears ran down her eyes, but she didn't show them to Lars. He began to share the story of the bluefin tuna.

In manly fashion, he impressed her with the raw statistics of bluefin tuna and how they could grow longer than six feet and weigh up to eleven hundred pounds, with the record being fifteen hundred pounds. He noted that they could swim up to fifty miles per hour and live for up to forty years. And perhaps most interesting of all, they liked to travel.

"Travel?" Amanda questioned.

"One tagged tuna was recorded to have traveled nearly eight thousand miles in a year. Many swim several thousand miles each year at a minimum. They migrate all over the Atlantic and breed in the Gulf of Mexico and Mediterranean."

"Eight thousand miles?"

"Of the twenty thousand different fish species known about, they are among the two dozen that are warm blooded to some extent."

"What does that mean?"

"It means they have some ability to regulate their body temperature. That feature allows them to travel all over the world, like us."

Amanda felt chilly for a moment. She had tried not to think about the cold very much, instead, focusing on the scenery, daily activities, and their engaging conversations. The caribou blanket and stove kept her warm.

"What's even more astounding about bluefin tuna though, is what people pay for it."

"Pay for it?"

"Bluefin tuna have been sold for tens of thousands of US Dollars in Japan, each. Although, you might read about them being sold for hundreds of thousands of dollars, that's just a publicity stunt."

"Tens of thousands? People pay that much just for a fish?" she responded, somewhat flabbergasted.

"There is one more interesting thing about bluefin tuna. It breathes only by moving water through its gills and will die if it stops swimming."

"What's that again?"

"The bluefin tuna breathes by moving water through its gills. It will die if it stops swimming."

"It will die if it stops swimming?"

"Yes, one record battle had a bluefin fighting for its life for sixty two hours!"

Then it suddenly hit her, a revelation. Perhaps it was the only fact that Amanda wanted to remember, maybe it was just coincidence. With every passing day she had begun to feel more and more alive, more free. Now, she knew why.

She realized that whether it was at work, staring at her computer, at home watching television, or a movie at the theater, she was always sitting down. She was seldom moving, and lethargic. Even when going to different places, she didn't move much, physically move that is. When she drove her car, she may have gone somewhere, but her body wasn't in motion, it was sitting on a driver's seat.

It was all an illusion of movement. While one may mentally go somewhere – in the city, on television, or in a movie, one's body hadn't gone through the motions.

Most of her movement was walking in a parking lot, in a grocery store, at the office, or a shopping mall. It was minimal and they were all, relatively dull places mostly, repetitive.

And all of her walking was mostly – inside, not outside. Recycled air and artificial lighting. Lest she go to a health club to run on a treadmill or some other exercise, the effect was quite the opposite. She might run, but the scenery was constant, most likely a television. It was another kind of illusion and it was inside as well. Like a bluefin tuna who dies if it doesn't swim, she had been dying, physically, mentally, and spiritually. She had become used to dying a little each day.

She felt alive now because she was traveling, on the move to new places. Physically on the move with stimulus both in mind and motion. By bicycle or her own two legged power. She had walked and run alongside the sledge quite a bit the past few days. She had hiked in Ilulissat, new surroundings. Much of her modern routine in contrast, was an illusion of movement. It reminded her of the zoo.

CHAPTER 22 – EXTINCTION

Another mostly clear day with moderate wind greeted Amanda and Lars. It was another day of dog sledging, and another day with no polar bears sighted, despite some tracks. It was also the day Amanda took her turn at driving the dog team briefly, it was thrilling. But, four days of traversing Greenland by sledge and no luck yet.

However, with fresh, fried fish, for lunch and dinner after ice fishing with Lars, and another evening conversation to look forward to, Amanda was not yet feeling too down.

Besides, tonight they would stay at a strategically located hunter's hut. A simple wooden building used as a safe refuge by hunters in the area. Tonight, it was empty, just the two of them. It was warmer and there was more room to stretch out than the narrower confines of a tent.

"Live free or die," Amanda mumbled again.

The revelation about the bluefin tuna was still burning brightly in Amanda's head. Life – freedom – movement – travel. Amanda was feeling alive for the first time in a long time, and it was all because of her bold step to embark on this adventure.

As Amanda reflected on her experience in this truly wild place, she realized her definition of the word, wild, was changing. There was the definition that wild meant, out of control, a negative view. As in wild kids, or a wild dog, perhaps with rabies. Or wild, as in untamed and scary.

Her new definition of wild now meant freedom. Freedom to explore, and freedom to let go of the past holding her down. And freedom to just be in the moment, more and more. Wild could also mean, not being controlled by debilitating feelings as strongly.

There was an irony Amanda realized. It was that one had to have a more peaceful mind or one would be afraid of being more wild, and out in the wild. In the time after Stephanie's death she had cried out many tears.

Now that she thought about it, she couldn't even imagine doing a trip like this before, let alone being out in the middle of nowhere, so far away from everywhere. Perhaps this was the beginning of a long spirit quest for her. Perhaps it was akin to spirit quests as a rite of passage that the young in some cultures took.

Was this what we were truly meant to be, deep in our hearts? Had we somehow taken a few wrong turns in our development of what we called, civilization? Animals in the wilderness were just being themselves. Were we trying to be something that we weren't supposed to be, overly domestic? Was the difference in truly wild animals versus those at a zoo, or domesticated ones, a reflection of ourselves? She wanted to learn more.

"Are there any other examples you can tell me about?"

"What examples?" Lars asked, somewhat confused.

"Examples of animals like the bluefin, animals that like to travel."

"There are a lot of animals that travel long distances, Amanda. Of course, polar bears, as you already know about. There are the well known wildebeest of Kenya and Tanzania's Serengeti plains. The longest distance travelers are birds though. The Arctic tern goes between Greenland and Antarctica every year. It's a round trip of about 45,000 miles."

"Every year?"

"Yes."

"God, I wish I could fly like a bird. I might be willing to even eat some worms."

Was the fact that we were overly domestic, and getting more so, a reason for our unhappiness? To physically and mentally travel on a daily basis was a part of so many animals' lives. It was instinctual.

How did we come to live a largely sedentary life in front of computers and TV screens? How did almost everyone she know, if not everyone, come to live this way? Even pilots who traveled the world, they sat in a cockpit seat. They were traveling mentally, but not physically. Maybe if we could become more like wild animals, in some way, we would be happier. She put it out of her mind as just a thought that probably didn't have a realistic answer.

As she thought about freedom of movement, she was reminded of what she learned about the range of polar bears earlier. "Do you think the polar bear will become extinct in the wild?"

"That is a decision, people like you will have to determine."

"What do you mean?"

"To decide what is important and what is not."

Amanda was hoping for just a reassuring – yes, the polar bear will never go extinct, even if it was a lie. Why did it even matter she wondered. After all, she had lived her whole life without ever seeing a polar bear in the wild. Maybe it was just the idea that some creature, a powerful and stately one, still lived freely out in this vast Arctic. Maybe it was just because they were cute, but that would be a strictly human concern, no more, no less. Were they still cute when their fur and mouth were bloodied after killing a seal?

Come to think of it, what animals in the wild had she ever seen? She still hadn't seen a polar bear in the wild. Horses – no, those were at the race track or on a farm. Dogs and cats – no, those were all strictly domesticated versions of wolves or some kind of wild cat. Rabbits – no, that was a neighbor's pet. Turkeys – no, that was Thanksgiving dinner. Skunks and opossums – wild, but dead, did that count? Almost every other animal she could think of was from a zoo, except for a few small birds, geese, squirrels, raccoons, a lone deer or two, and some sea lions at a distance. And crows, lots of crows, black crows. Weren't black crows supposed to be a harbinger of doom?

Lars started talking. "Each animal is connected to us in ways we don't fully understand. Disturbing the balance causes other problems."

"What do you mean?"

"Nature can be unpredictable from our perspective. Nothing is certain, but less polar bears would probably lead to more seals. More seals would lead to a decrease in herring populations, a prime fishing target. Arctic fox numbers would be reduced, as they scavenge the kills of polar bears." He continued on, explaining an entire chain reaction of events playing themselves out over time. The problem being, we didn't know where and when the reaction ended. "The Inuit have a name for this unpredictability, uggianaqtuq, to behave unexpectedly."

"Uggianaqtuq," she repeated. Inuit was a language Amanda knew that she would never become fluent in.

"Perhaps some more examples would be insightful."

They continued to talk about how the decimation of top predators could have a cascade effect on an entire ecosystem. The over-hunting of wolves in Yellowstone, led to elk overgrazing, which caused a decline in aspen trees and riverside willows. The decline of the aspens led to less songbirds and colorful landscapes. The decline of the willows led to less beavers, migratory birds, and more riverbank erosion.

"So, if the polar bear disappeared, all sorts of things that we couldn't predict might happen?"

Lars just nodded his head.

It would be a much lonelier and more colorless world Amanda realized. "Uncertainty," Amanda mumbled. She thought about the chain reaction of events in the animals they talked about and how much she, we, didn't know.

She thought about all the conversations of global warming she had been having. It didn't seem such a stretch anymore to connect Stephanie's accident with it now. It wasn't the only factor, but it was a contributing cause. It made Amanda sad. It made her mad, and ashamed, at her own ignorance and at a world that increasingly seemed out of control. But, maybe it was our desire for control that was the problem?

As she thought of an out of control world, she remembered her earlier thought about being more wild, which allowed her to let go, and ironically, be happier, by being less in control.

"I could really use a hot shower, Lars."

"I'll boil some more hot water and you can wash your face with it. If you like, I'll go outside."

"No, that's ok. I can live without a hot shower for a little while longer. I have some body wipes with me."

"When we get back to Savissivik we can put hot water in a large bucket for you."

"That sounds perfect. Too bad we can't just jump in the ocean like a polar bear to wash ourselves up."

Lars smiled. "You should look up a guy called the Ice Man on the Internet."

"Who's that?"

"He can do what you speak of. He has the ability to generate heat internally just by thinking about it. There is a video of him swimming amongst icebergs and enjoying it."

"What?!"

"Check it out, when you get back. Some Buddhist monks have the ability to generate heat internally too after calming their minds with meditation. That's on the Internet too."

"I'm glad there is no Internet here, Lars, but those are a couple of videos I would like to watch right now."

"There are a lot of individuals with amazing physical and mental abilities, Amanda."

"Like what?"

"Watch those two and I'll email you some links when you get back home."

"Please do." A calm mind. Maybe that was the secret to happiness, Amanda wondered.

On that note, both of them stopped talking for the moment. They were lost in their own thoughts.

Lars broke the silence. "I just feel like making one thing clear, Amanda. All the things related to changes in the weather here, the extinction of polar bears or other animals, is just filler, Amanda. It's just filler."

"Just filler?"

"They are distractions to a more important thing I've learned about while I've been out here."

"I think I know what you're going to say, Lars. I almost forgot to ask about it."

"The only thing of primary importance which we need to learn about better, is ourselves."

"Does this have to do with my IN ME, Lars?"

"Yea."

"Let's have this conversation, now."

"First, I need to go check on the dogs."

"You are such a tease, Lars. I will wait for you to check on the dogs!"

CHAPTER 23 – OUR "IN ME"

Lars came back into the hut from checking on the dogs. "Another peaceful and quiet night, Amanda. The lights aren't so strong at the moment, maybe they will be later."

Amanda was busy eating the last scoops of oatmeal in her bowl at the small table in the hut. She had her fill of Northern Lights at the moment, there was something more intriguing to hear about at the moment.

"Filler, Lars? Are you saying everything we've talked about doesn't really matter?"

"That's exactly what I'm saying." Lars sat down on a chair and leaned back against a wall.

"Ok, now, I am totally confused."

"Whether polar bears, or any other animals, go extinct or not, doesn't matter. Global warming doesn't matter. Climate change doesn't matter."

"You need to explain this better." She took a swig from her cup of hot tea.

"Because if we don't get to the root of why global warming or any other major issue confronting us is happening, we will never solve these 'problems.' The problem has always been the same, it has just taken different forms."

Amanda looked around the hut, not sure of what to say.

"We can't put out a 'big fire,' when we haven't even put out the fire around and inside ourselves."

"I need to be my own fireman? No, firewoman! It's an interesting metaphor, Lars. And what is the root of all these problems, Lars? Our IN ME, right?"

"Yes, the one thing that causes us to be unhappy or unsatisfied on a deep level, and less peaceful deep inside. And the one thing that stop us from solving problems like global warming and many other 'big picture' problems, on a collective basis." Lars took a drink of water. "And by definition, the potential extinction, or sharp reduction, in the number of polar bears due to climate change."

"I want to be happier. I want to be more joyful and have more peace in my heart. I don't want the polar bear to disappear."

Lars said nothing for the moment.

"So, tell me about our IN ME. What exactly is it? How do I defeat it?"

"Not everyone is ready to confront our own deep inner self, our dark energy, Amanda. Strange as it may sound, many people don't want to be peaceful on the inside. Temporary happiness in the material realm is good enough for many of us. Lying to ourselves, distracting ourselves, or ignoring and suppressing our own inner thoughts as it relates to our current life situation is good enough. Are you sure you want to know about this? My wife and I, we don't share what we've learned with many people."

"I think we're past that point now, Lars. Dark energy." Amanda paused in contemplation. She thought about the word, dark. Then the words dark and light. "I want to know. Maybe it's fitting I had to come to a place covered in bright white snow and ice to defeat my IN ME, Lars. Or as we are calling it, my dark energy. Maybe I needed to come to a place so bright to help me fight my own darkness. Maybe this is the reason I came here, Lars. I don't know if I believe in fate, or destiny, but maybe this is the real reason why."

"Dark energy is just another name for our repressed feelings. Feelings that we keep hidden from other people."

"Like, emotional baggage?"

"Yes, that expression would be correct from my understanding of English."

"You're saying it is possible to get rid of our emotional baggage?"

"To get rid of all of our dark energy takes time and perseverance, Amanda. But, I will tell you the one thing that begins this process of freeing our minds and hearts. This is a journey inward. It is a refocusing of our thoughts from being externally or superficially dominated, to a more internal focus."

"So, what would I have to do?"

"It is quite simple. The trick is to not think too much."

"To not think too much?"

"About yourself, about ourselves, and about other people."

"Myself, ourselves, other people?"

"Yes."

Amanda paused for a moment. "Ok, now that you have started, I have to interrupt. I have to really go to the bathroom outside, Lars. I've been drinking too much tea. I can tell this is going to take a while. I should of went sooner."

"Be my guest."

"Damn, it's cold out there tonight."

"You're ok, now?"

"Yes, let's continue."

"This may sound weird, but we must first understand that how we think of ourselves is not correct."

"Hmmm. . ."

"We absorb energy in our lifetimes from different people. Their thoughts, preferences, mannerisms, and even reactions in certain situations, become our own, on a subconscious, and conscious level. We think of our behavior as our own, but sometimes it isn't."

"So, dark energy isn't just repressed feelings?"

"Would you agree that the more we 'hang around' with certain people or types of people, the more we become like them, or at least partly like them?"

"Oh, definitely," Amanda answered without any hesitation. "Did I just say definitely? Wait a second, did you just say that other people's thoughts, preferences, and how they act, become our own thoughts and behavior?"

"Yes."

"Hmmm . . ."

"Perhaps you know that expression - like father, like son."

"Yes, of course. Like mother, like daughter?" Amanda added.

"Yes."

"Our parents' thoughts and preferences are inside us?" She hesitated for a moment. "So, sometimes we might say, 'I already know what my father thinks,' or, 'I already know what my mother thinks?' We may be wrong, but we already have a 'gut feeling,' about their opinion. Is this what you are trying to say?"

"Yes, Amanda."

"Ok, I'm with you. So, our parents' thoughts are inside us."

"On a subconscious and conscious level."

She felt free to speak her mind. "Could it be like when I lied to my mother and father growing up about not having sex yet? Or never having tried a cigarette? I lied, because I 'just knew' what they would say."

"That's a good example."

Amanda sat deep in thought, pondering some of the lies she had told in her past. And the lies that she told in her present job as a marketing consultant. Creative interpretation. Whatever, whatever. All for the mighty dollar, and recognition at work, or something like that. Why did people lie? Why did she lie? It made her feel bad. Noise from a portable gas heater was the only other sound in the hut.

Lars continued. "We have other people's thoughts inside us, not just our parents. Sometimes, if we think about it, we are consciously aware of whose energy it is, for a moment. The deeper you dig into your subconscious, the more clear it will become if the thoughts are from you or someone else."

"Now, I think I understand what you are saying, Lars. Let's keep going. I need more examples."

"If there are new people we are 'hanging out' with, we might start talking like them, for example. We might use the same expression for a given situation. We might start liking the same foods. We might start wanting to do the same things. We might have the same reaction, same answer, to a particular question."

"Continue," Amanda replied.

"It's harder to tell with parents and siblings sometimes because we may already have too much of their energy in us for us to differentiate. It is easier to tell when the thoughts and feelings are distinctly different than our own. This is why we are using an example of people we are just getting to know."

"Continue."

"Can you identify with how parents sometimes become concerned that their children are hanging out with the 'wrong crowd?' Because those other kids will be a bad influence."

"Oh, it makes complete sense when you put it like that." As she said that, she wondered how much of her problems with men came from her father and mother. Was it just this dark energy? What about genetics? Both? She definitely wanted to get rid of the dark energy from her father and mother that was relationship related.

Lars nodded his head.

"Is it also like when I think of eating a pecan pie? I think of my grandmother."

"Yes. Not only might you think of your grandmother, in fact, it could be the energy of your grandmother expressing itself in you. It influences and controls our own behavior."

"I don't know where that came from, I must have a craving for pecan pie right now. There's not a bakery nearby is there?"

Lars smiled.

"So, if my grandmother really loved pie, and I absorbed a lot of her energy, I would find it more difficult to resist eating a pecan pie, or cookie, or whatever she really liked."

"Yes."

"That just sounds weird, Lars." She hesitated. "Is she still affecting me, even in death?"

"What do you think?"

"I think she is. I feel that she is. How can that be if she's dead? Does the energy linger inside of us? It must."

Lars just smiled. He didn't answer.

"It does make sense. If we have other people's energy inside us, how do I know when what I do is someone else's energy influencing or controlling me, or just my own energy?"

"It really depends on how aware you are of your inner thoughts, Amanda. It depends. Some people are more inner-minded enough to sense this, but many are not. Certain food and drink affects our ability to do this."

"Like what?"

"In time you may learn that later."

"Aie! You're teasing me. So many questions now. I think I can sense it for some people now that we are talking about this. Strange, I've never had a conversation like this, about this subject. Yet, it seems kind of obvious."

"Someday, you may learn how to sense it for everyone, Amanda."

"I had a funny feeling you would say something like that." Amanda gave it some more thought. "So, when we start to dress the same way and like the same things as people we are around, we may literally, not be thinking for ourselves? We are being controlled by other people's energy?"

"Yes."

She drank some tea. "That is frightening. I need to be careful who I hang around with! Yeah, that makes total sense now that I think about it. Scary." As she said that, she thought about when she moved out of home, she had more freedom to become who she wanted to be, but of course, she was still influenced by her mother and by her father, to a lesser degree.

"It can be."

"How does this work?"

"We absorb energy, preferences, and tastes from the people we hang around."

"How does that work though, just by osmosis?" Amanda answered, before catching herself and realizing she wasn't even quite sure what she meant by the word, osmosis."

"When you are ready you will learn it by experiencing it."

"You're not going to tell me?"

"Have you ever noticed how the 'vibe' as you might say in English, is different from place to place? Person to person?"

"People, yes, definitely. Places, let me think about that."

"Like the difference between being in a tense meeting at work, or at home relaxing by yourself, or in a crowded shopping mall during the holidays, or walking on a beautiful beach."

"Oh, yes, of course! So, what about this? How do we absorb or not absorb dark energy from other people?"

"Some things are better discovered on your own. As long as you understand the basic idea for now, we can continue."

Amanda made a funny face of disappointment at Lars.

Amanda paused and changed gears. "Does this explain how people from the same area, country, city, or town can be similar in certain ways?" Amanda asked, as she suddenly started thinking of marketing segmentation, the art of placing people into groups and classifying them appropriately.

"Yes."

"How do we absorb this energy?" She asked again, hoping for a more clear answer. "How do I not absorb someone's dark energy if I have to be around them?"

"You're persistent, Amanda. That will help you liberate yourself. The details are best for later, but avoidance would be one."

"Like if someone has a 'bad vibe?'"

"Yes, but bad is relative. What is bad? So, some people won't like your vibe, even though you may like theirs. Are you bad?"

"Well, maybe sometimes. Ok, I get it. Good and bad is relative."

"Your vibe affects those around you though too. Have you ever noticed a dog barking at some people and not at others?"

"I've never owned a dog. I can't say that I have noticed, but for some reason, it seems to make sense."

"That's an example of how somebody with a more nervous vibe is affecting the dog."

"I know dogs have good noses and they must be more sensitive to this kind of stuff."

"All molecules are vibrating. So, we each have our own vibe. I can email you some links about vibration and sound. Let's not get distracted by the mechanics of how this all works though."

"Ok, so I can read up about all that stuff when I am ready. Where were we?"

"I don't remember."

"Oh, I remember. Conversely, does it also explain why some people can be so different from people in a certain area or town, even though they may be from the same place?"

"If they are different. . . yes, it does. It also explains how some members of a family can be different and others more similar. It explains how people can grow closer, and how people, married couples for example, can grow apart, even though everything seemed great at the beginning."

"Give me an example of that."

"Let us take a married couple who has been together for awhile as an example, ok?"

"Ok, go."

"The husband or wife has to frequently go on business trips to another city. Over time, this person traveling absorbs energy from other people in this city. Eventually, the feelings become so strong that they would prefer living in this other place or doing the kinds of things that people in this city do as opposed to the activities at home. Let's say it is a big city vs a smaller city. Eventually, the preferences absorbed by the traveling spouse start to drive a wedge between the couple."

"That makes sense."

"Now, substitute city for another person."

"Oh, I get where you're going. So, eventually, the husband or wife might become more attracted to other people they work with?"

"Yes. Not necessarily just people they work with, but the kinds of people that live in this different city, or area. Over time this person becomes less attracted to their spouse who doesn't travel to the same place. And that is only *one way* how affairs start or unhappiness in a marriage begins."

"Wow. I think a lot of people, couples, would like to know how this works more, Lars. Divorce lawyers, maybe not. Ok, so where are we then?"

"Sometimes this energy even makes us do things we regret. But, we don't realize it until after the fact, if we ever do. I don't just mean someone having an affair, it could be anything. If you watch the news and it seems that someone seemingly does something totally illogical, stupid, or what you might think of as 'bone-headed,' it could be due to someone else's energy that they are under the influence of. It can make people do things that appear, out of character."

"Bone-headed. You know English well, Lars. This is scary, Lars. We think we're so smart, but we don't even understand this basic way that energy, feelings, work between us."

"Do you understand this basic idea then of how we have other people's energy inside us? You may not understand how we absorb it, how to get rid of it quickly, or how to avoid it, but you get the basic idea that it exists."

"This dark energy. Yes, I understand it. Oh my god. This definitely never gets taught in school. Ok, ok. So, what next, now?"

They both took a breather. Silence was easier to accept when there were no distractions for many miles around.

"Now, I am going to explain something that may be more difficult to comprehend."

"I'm not going anywhere, Lars. My watch is in my pack."

"Not only do we get dark energy from other people, we create it ourselves. It has to come from somewhere."

"I was preoccupied with you telling me about absorbing dark energy from other people, that I didn't even think about where it came from."

"I am not going to explain precisely where it comes from, because it's not important now, but I will give you an example of how we have been conditioned to hold it in over time as opposed to getting rid of it, or letting it go."

"When will I be ready?"

"After you've decided that you want to get rid of all your dark energy, deep in your heart."

She puckered her lips and gave Lars a funny face.

Lars saw her face and said nothing.

Amanda resigned herself to how Lars wanted to explain this. She was already learning enough.

"Imagine a child running around and being carefree, doing whatever he or she wants. When the child wants to cry, it cries. When the child wants to shout, they shout. When they want to run around and act out their feelings, they do."

"Ok, I got that."

"Now, the parents, babysitter, elders, or whomever, step in and tell this child to behave themselves. To be quiet. To stop crying. To control themselves. SELF-control. To stop fidgeting. To stop screaming and shouting. The grown-ups tell the kids this because their behavior bothers them. They often don't wonder why their child is doing this, they just want it to stop."

"I got it. Go on."

"Explain it to me then, Amanda."

She took a moment to gather her thoughts. "So, as children we want to get rid of our dark energy, or repressed feelings, but our parents, grandparents, whomever, they keep telling us to basically – shut up. Maybe they spank us, or shout at us, or feed us some sugary, sweet, treat, but eventually we learn." She stopped, unsure of what to say next.

Lars finished her train of thought. "We go from a state of getting rid of dark energy, repressed feelings, to one where we hold more in over time. Some people learn methods to get rid of it a little better over time or have less strict parents, but most don't. Over time then, for everyone, we keep getting more and more. This causes stress. We use willpower and food to hold in dark energy. Another word for this accumulated dark energy is, emotional baggage."

"Yuck, emotional baggage. I'd like to get rid of some."

"We are conditioned as children to behave ourselves, using self-control, and controlling our dark energy, feelings, rather than letting them go. We get rewarded for holding them in, and this reinforcement just cements the loop, unless you learn how to break it and reverse the flow."

"Good God, Lars. You better teach me how to reverse this flow. Are you saying, that if I reverse this conditioning, I will be able to let go of all my emotional baggage?"

"Yes, *all* of it. We must uncondition ourselves. We must retrain our hearts and minds. We must stop controlling ourselves."

"Is this really possible? To get rid of ALL emotional baggage? So, this is our IN ME?"

"Yes. And this dark energy causes us to think about ourselves too much. To be more, self-conscious. And by extension, more unhappy."

They both took another breather. Lars went outside again while Amanda sat alone, thinking of all the things that troubled her. There were some things that she sensed troubled her, but they were too deep for her to particularly tell what was the cause.

Lars returned. "Are we ready to start again?"

"You know, Lars, I've realized the last few months, the more one reflects inward on the past, the more one starts to remember things in the past. It's kind of weird."

"Yes, I have found that to be true too."

"I was looking at old photos with my friend, Stephanie. And I just started remembering the strangest little things. Where are we?"

"Now, I am going to explain our core being."

"Our core being?"

"Each one of us has an innate core being that is free from feelings such as anger, hate, fear, greed, doubt, sadness, loneliness, shame, worry, hopelessness, regret, and jealousy. Really, any and all negative feelings. All emotional baggage. It is a very peaceful state. In a little bit, you will give me some of your own examples when you were in this peaceful state, which you might have wanted to 'bottle up' and take home with you, but you couldn't."

"Ok, ok. So, once I get rid of all my emotional baggage, or dark energy, repressed feelings, inner demons, or whatever I want to call it, I will know my core being and I will be at peace?"

"Yes. What word do you prefer we use?"

"I like the word, dark energy, or bad energy."

"Which one?"

"I like both."

"Ok, dark or bad energy it is, Amanda."

"So again, our core being is surrounded, or rather, contaminated by this dark energy. From different people and that which we have created ourselves. Some of the dark energy is new, some of it is old, like that which you absorbed from your parents, grandparents, cousins, your parents' co-workers, anyone they were in contact with."

"Wow, this is deep. So, fascinating."

"This bad energy obscures who *we* are, it obscures our core being."

Amanda needed another moment to digest this. She was lost in thought. She drank some tea and breathed in the cool and clean Arctic air that permeated the hut.

"Let me repeat what we've been talking about again, Lars. This dark energy that is contaminating my core being carries with it every single icky feeling I can think of, and other ones you didn't mention?"

"Exactly."

"Excuse me if I'm repeating myself. Our IN ME then is all this 'dark energy' surrounding my core being and it affects how I react and live on a day to day basis? It makes me eat unhealthy food like too much pecan pie and cookies or whatever junk I've been conditioned to eat. Or food that people I know have been conditioned to eat, but that I really don't want to. Fattening pizza, fast food, cinnamon rolls, cake, whatever."

"Yes. Repressed feelings, our dark energy, also affects our taste buds. If you feel bitter inside, or bad about yourself, you may be conditioned to eat something sweet. Perhaps you have heard of the concept of emotional eating, Amanda."

"Yes, I have. Though I've never given it much thought."

"If you need comfort food, you might ask yourself, or maybe you already know, what am I uncomfortable about?"

"Oh God, I'm definitely guilty of this. Other women at work, too." Maybe this was the key to losing weight she thought to herself. Instead of counting calories, fat, sugar, carbohydrates, or any other ingredient, if we focused on getting rid of our negative feelings, we would stop overeating. We would stop emotional eating.

Lars continued. "Now you see, this dark energy, you yourself have created, and the energy you have absorbed your whole life from friends, family, classmates, co-workers, acquaintances, and people you are near, and people they have known, affects everything."

"If I get rid of all this 'bad, dark energy' I will be free of debilitating feelings like hate, fear, anger, sadness, despair, worry, loneliness, etc. . ." She paused. "And I'll not have to worry about my weight or following any diets because I'll stop eating things my body doesn't need, instinctually?"

"Not only that, but you will be healthier because you will release built-up stress in your muscles and mind."

"Bonus!"

"Most people just think these feelings are 'normal,' Amanda. They are normal, because *everyone* has them. Everyone has this 'dark energy.' What I am saying is that these are learned feelings and behaviors that have been passed on from generation to generation. They get created or learned everyday because we don't understand our own feelings." He paused. "I can tell you this because I've removed enough of my dark energy to understand it."

"How in God's name would one get rid of this bad, dark energy? Aren't these feelings just a part of our human experience?" Amanda's questioning side was beginning to express some doubt even though she agreed in principle with what Lars was saying.

Lars sensed her hesitation.

"Let's see if I can help you think of your own example."

"That will help."

"Take as long as you need, to try and think of a time where something happened and everyone around you was panicking or what you might say in America, 'freaking out.' While everyone was 'freaking out,' you just looked at all of them and said, 'What is the big deal?' Because for you, the thing they were panicking about was a non-issue to you."

Amanda closed her eyes for a minute and thought about this. "I've got one."

"Go ahead."

"I remember one time when I was younger our class went on an overnight trip to some campground with cabins. A group of girls, that I normally didn't hang out with, and I, went to the bathroom. While we were in there a large frog appeared from under the counter."

She took a deep breath as Lars was listening intently.

"All the other girls started screaming and some of them ran out. I was thinking to myself, what was the big deal when I came out of the bathroom stall. When I came out, I saw a couple of the girls frozen in fear. They were pointing at the large, green frog. When I saw it, and looked at their faces, I started laughing. Here were these popular girls that a lot of people wanted to be like, and they were mortified, by a small green frog." She drank some tea. "If you heard them explain it, it was a *huge* frog."

Lars started laughing uncontrollably. "What happened next?"

"I walked over to the frog and tried to catch it, but it leaped a few times. One of the girls that was frozen in fear screamed and cowered up against a wall. The other girl jumped over the frog and ran out the door. It was the funniest thing."

Lars finally stopped laughing.

"I kept trying to capture the frog, but it kept jumping away. It jumped into a corner in the bathroom. I then helped the other girl out of the bathroom. I brushed my teeth and brought out all their toiletry bags after I was done."

"So, what happened to the frog?"

"I think it just stayed in the bathroom. I don't think any of those girls ever went in there again!"

Lars smiled. "Was there another bathroom for them to use?"

"Yeah, but it was quite a walk. I had the bathroom to my-self as word got around to other cabins in our area."

"That's a perfect example, Amanda. It shows how a feeling of fear can be in some people and not in others. In this case, these girls, who all knew each other well, had the same fear, but you, as an outsider, did not."

"Yeah, that is interesting. This is super interesting."

"Fear is a learned emotion, Amanda. This means it can be unlearned. All negative feelings which we think of as normal can be unlearned. Anger, hate, jealousy, worry, doubt, fear about any-thing and everything, and any other feeling you can think of. But, 'science' doesn't understand well, or at all, how we acquire feelings and how we lose them, so we never get taught this. This is something my wife and I have learned in our lives."

Amanda paused for a few moments. "What you just said and the way you said it sounds so obvious, Lars. About any feel-ing that is learned, can be unlearned, as it relates to fear and other emotions. I'm surprised no one hasn't already figured out how to unlearn them all. What kind of world would we live in?"

Lars said nothing as Amanda kept talking.

"Now that I think of it, there are books and speakers that talk about overcoming fear, but none of them talk about unlearn-ing them. I think the ones that talk about overcoming our fears, they just cover it up. It still exists in some form, but if you have a way of getting rid of them all, you will have people beating down a path to your door, if they could find you!"

"The reason probably no one, other than my wife and a couple of very close friends, or at least no one else I have ever met or read about, has talked about unlearning them, is because it in-volves defeating and knowing our IN ME at the deepest levels in our heart and mind. It also goes against the grain of what society at large believes. There are many feelings I used to have that I no longer do, or I have them in a very diminished state."

"Amazing, Lars."

"My wife and I are also busy still getting rid of our own dark energy. We haven't been motivated to tell many. But, now we are here together."

"You are going to tell me how to do this, right, Lars?"

"Let us share a few more examples first to make sure you understand. Is that ok?"

"Of course. I'm not going anywhere, anytime soon."

The light in the electric lantern started to go dim. Lars replaced the battery. He added more fuel to the gas heater. It was more relaxing in the hut to have this deep conversation rather than in the confines of a tent.

"Do you remember how you felt while admiring a beautiful sunset or a view of a landscape that took your breath away?"

Amanda nodded.

"How about while listening to extraordinarily beautiful music for the first time? Or when you were near someone who just gave you a really good vibe?"

She nodded again.

"Or when you gazed into the eyes of a romantic interest, or at a particularly beautiful painting? How did you feel, or is there no feeling to describe these moments?"

She closed her eyes and thought of various moments in her life. She realized there were feelings for some of them, but for many of them, no words or even a distinct feeling, that she could recall at this moment in time. They were just 'happy, peaceful' moments, but really, beyond any description with words. Maybe she would describe them as zen moments or moments when she was mesmerized, like when she saw the Northern Lights for the first time.

"Have you thought of some examples in your life? Keep them to yourself, for if you try to verbalize them, you just might 'ruin' them a little. In these moments you were closer to your core being."

"I've thought of some."

"What if you could be in that state all the time, or at least more of the time? You could be as you were in the bathroom, in any situation. Never panicking, or getting scared, or worrying."

"To never be a deer frozen in headlights, you mean, Lars?"

"I'm not familiar with that saying."

"Forget it." Amanda laughed and smiled. A zen moment would become a zen existence. She would be in a state of constant peace? This sounded too good to be true.

"It is because we think about ourselves too much and that we are, to varying degrees, self-conscious. Because of this we are not able to get into these moments very often, or as often. Too many things distract us. Some people use drugs to achieve this state, but it never lasts. It eventually stops working. Plus there are side effects from drugs."

Amanda said nothing. Her mind wandered for a moment in the silence. An example of using legal drugs to become less self-conscious came to mind to her. It was at a bar when some men would drink alcohol, liquid courage, to gather up the nerve to talk to her or some other girls. But, if one wasn't self-conscious and worrying about rejection, they wouldn't need any alcohol. She snapped her mind back to the present moment.

"To achieve inner peace on the inside means we have to live more by instinct, Lars?"

Lars nodded.

"Not our overly logical conscious mind? Thinking too much and using logic gets in the way of true joy in life? I can believe that," she added.

"Thinking takes more energy than instinct, which is nearly effortless. The more we forget about ourselves, the happier we will be. I once read a quote that said the mark of an advanced society was one which required the least amount of effort to be joyful."

"Least amount of effort?"

Lars bit into a biscuit.

"Being happy is just a momentary feeling that too often goes away quickly I think, Lars. People define happiness differently too, it's just a word."

"I think of joy as a state of being, Amanda. If we have to think about being joyful, then we aren't in a state of joy."

"So, there is no word."

"Our word definitions may vary. When was the last time you forgot about yourself? Without the use of any drugs or alcohol."

"I can think of moments on this trip. The icebergs in Ilulissat took my breath away. This frozen landscape." She paused. "Laughing with friends, finishing a project, incredible sex, can I say that?" She covered her mouth in embarrassment.

"You just said it," Lars replied without betraying any emotion.

She paused. "You are right, there are no words for those moments. I could describe them, of course, but it wouldn't be accurate. At times on our sledge trip I have seemingly forgotten about myself, though it has been an adjustment."

Lars didn't say anything.

"When I saw the Northern Lights for the first time, I was speechless."

"I recall you had a few things to say about them."

Amanda laughed. "Yes, but those initial moments of wonder."

"The irony of this is that we must think hard about our own existence in order to improve it, to reach another level, but there are some shortcuts."

A few minutes of silence pervaded inside the hut.

Amanda broke the silence. "So, we forget how to just be, this core being you speak of, because we think about ourselves too much, right? Due to all this dark energy, repressed feelings."

"Yes, and it is pride in ourselves that causes us to think too much about ourselves. Pride causes us to be self-conscious more often. Pride is holding in our dark energy."

"Our pride?"

"Our parents, or whomever else raised us, they praised us, telling us over and over how good we were. How special, important, and so smart we were. And how much they loved us, every time we controlled our behaviors more. Every time we pleased them."

"Hmm. . .that could make sense. Like, when I was a baby or young child."

"Also, if you consider that we have other people's energy in us, pride in ourselves, doesn't even exist. We wouldn't be who we are, 'worts and all,' without the energy we have absorbed."

"I need to get rid of my pride then to stop being self-conscious and thinking of myself?"

"Yes."

"People who say we need more pride, should maybe think twice about that?"

"Maybe they should think more than just twice." Lars took out a piece of paper and wrote some words on it. He gave it to Amanda.

self-conscious
self-doubt
self-confidence
self-expectations
self-esteem
self-destructive
self-serving
self-motivation
self-discipline
self-control
selfless
selfish
self-critical
self-pity
self-image
self-respect
self-worth
self-righteous
self-absorbed
self-centered
self-defense
self-preservation (panic / fear)
self-aware

"Do you know anyone who has struggled with any one of these?"

She scanned the list. "Of course, some of them I have struggled with myself, some look positive, some negative."

"The more we don't think about our *self*, the more these words begin to disappear. You would no longer need self-confidence or self-worth, you would just BE. You would no longer doubt yourself, you would just make decisions based on past experience and current circumstances. You wouldn't have any stress about maintaining some idealized image of yourself, you could just BE. Am I making any sense?"

"I could draw a line through all the 'self' words and these words would start to disappear as they applied to me?"

"Yes, and many other words, that we will 'forget' about."

"I definitely need to think about this more. If I didn't have the stress of self-control, I could just BE?"

"Yes. It takes time."

Amanda stepped out from the hut and looked in the sky. There were no Northern Lights at the moment even though the moon was young. What she did see though, astounded her.

"Oh my god. How did I not notice all these stars?" She was looking at our Milky Way Galaxy and an endless number of stars.

She hadn't really paid attention to them before, for she was too mesmerized by the Aurora Borealis show on earlier nights. As she gazed in wonder at all the stars in the sky, she realized that she had never seen so many stars in her life. She had never seen the Milky Way with her own eyes, either. Perhaps she had seen a photo before.

How deprived we were in our cities she thought. Due to light pollution, we could see almost nothing. It didn't help that there were many cloudy nights in Seattle as well. "Maybe we have so many lights because we've been afraid of the dark, our own darkness," she wondered out loud in the blackness of the night.

It was a fitting metaphor to what she was now learning about herself. Everyday we lived with our dark energy, our repressed feelings, but because we were so self-absorbed and prideful, or never taught, we didn't see, or even imagine, another way to exist.

Her thoughts turned sexual for a moment. Wasn't sex less fun when we were self-conscious and thinking about ourselves? Wasn't everything less fun?

It was just like the stars and Milky Way that she was now seeing with her naked eyes. They were there all the time, but she needed a change of scenery to see them. What else had we forgotten about in the world we lived in she wondered. We spent so much time on creating comforts for our *self*, that we had forgotten our wild side. A wild side of us that wanted to be much freer than how we lived.

She marveled at the heavens until she decided firmly that she didn't want to live with her dark energy anymore. She didn't want to live with emotional baggage or inner demons. It was time to chart a new course.

She spoke out loud again, to no one particular, perhaps the sleeping dogs. "I guess it doesn't matter if I haven't been proud of everything I have done in my life, for if I take this message to heart, I don't need any pride at all."

"I have no idea how to get rid of my dark energy, or if it is even possible, but maybe I could learn. Maybe everything that has happened, has happened for a reason. To bring me to this faraway place. I've never met anyone who talks like Lars. Maybe he's learned something after spending so much time out here in this white desert. He talks about feelings so casually, in such a relaxed manner. Most men I've known, try to avoid the subject, they are afraid of their feelings. They busy themselves with doing things, fixing things, winning games and contests, or material stuff."

"Are you listening, God? Are you even there? Do you even exist?" She looked up at the stars and Milky Way. Was heaven up there? Did the stars represent something more than what we were told? Or were we just products of evolution? She sensed there was something more, but she didn't know. It didn't even matter she realized, there were more pressing things to think about.

She recalled a movie she once saw on television, wasn't pride the *worst* sin? She would need to investigate this further when she got home, or maybe she would just ask Lars.

Amanda had talked to herself out loud on some occasions before at home, but she felt freer to do so now. She thought herself weird before for doing it, but it was therapeutic. She would have to continue this habit of talking out her feelings, to herself. She was already losing self-control.

She went back in the hut to learn more about pride, and how to get rid of it. But, she had more questions now, too.

"Those words you wrote down reminded me of something in psychology, Lars."

"Sorry, I am not sure what you are talking about."

"Self-actualization," Amanda blurted out.

"Self-actualization? Give me a moment, Amanda, I must think in my native language."

"I'm thinking of psychology class."

"Maslow?"

"That's it, Lars. Maslow's hierarchy. You're not just a wild-life biologist!"

Lars smiled. "What about it?"

"All this talk about the self reminds me of something I learned in some psychology class."

"Yes, I am familiar with it, but I don't like to think or talk about organized psychology very much. It has led us astray."

"I think I kind of have the same feeling."

"Modern medicine and psychology are about labeling and prescribing drugs. That is not my way. Often, it has been a rush to judgment and then confrontation, with drugs or some other treatment, before understanding at the root level."

"It's good for immediate pain though, Lars. Or traumatic injuries. Or until we understand things better."

"Good point, Amanda. Sometimes I just get too negative. I'm working on that aspect of myself."

"Confrontation," Amanda muttered. "Enemies."

Lars continued. "I may be wrong, but this Maslow theory, presupposes that development of the 'self' is what one should do. That self-realization is the highest objective. This is not the way to peace in our hearts from what I've learned. Unless it means the self realizes that the self is the problem, so to speak. As I mentioned earlier, if you consider that we are made up of the energy from many different people, the idea of a singular self, doesn't even exist. But, don't worry about this for right now."

"Interesting."

"I don't really have any other opinion on any other psychology theory. A lot of it to me is what you might say, mumbo-jumbo. You will have to investigate that further on your own, if you wish."

"Maybe on my own time then. I have another question though."

"Yes."

"If we have feelings from multiple people inside us, does that explain why we might have conflicting thoughts about a particular person, event, or situation?"

Lars thought for a few moments. "Yes, not only that, but it also explains how we might say one thing, but do another."

"Also known as, hypocrisy," Amanda responded.

"The more conflicting energy we have, the more hypocritical and indecisive we are likely to be."

"I hate when I'm hypocritical."

"It's not necessarily negative, Amanda. When we have conflicting energy, it may spur some to wonder why they are acting hypocritically, and ask deeper questions."

"Hmm. . . I didn't think about it like that. How did you learn about all this? What made you even think about this?"

"One step at a time, Amanda. One step at a time. Lots of questions and seeking out of answers. Lots of mistakes and overturning of ingrained falsehoods. Conversations with my wife. Falsehoods, and mistruths, from my perspective. As for why, that is a story for another day. But, it has been in my heart for a long time, to know myself, ourselves, better."

"Do you have any sort of religion, Lars? Do you believe in God?"

"Why do you ask?"

"I was thinking about pride outside and I thought I remember from watching something, that pride was, or rather is, one of the worst sins, if not the worst. What do you think?"

"What I believe doesn't matter, Amanda. Simply put though, I have no religion, Amanda. Once we give ourselves any label, we put an invisible wall around our thoughts and actions. It is self-limiting. Despite this, I've learned some things in religion are true. If you want to call 'these beliefs,' a religion, that is for you to do. There are many people in the world who go about trying to convince people of one thing or another. They have their logic, and it makes total sense to them. Who am I to argue? Maybe I'm the blind one. There are also many people who say one thing, but do another, hypocrisy."

"That's the truth, Lars. That's one reason I've shied away from religion. All the hypocrisy and inconsistencies, today, and in the past. Yet, thinking that we just evolved from lower, no, I mean other, life forms, doesn't seem to explain everything. Gosh! I don't want to think of other animals as lower life forms. We are conceited. They are just different forms. That's pride, isn't it? We think we are the ultimate 'creation' of evolution, or God."

"I agree with you on religion, Amanda. I must admit, I never thought of how you explained it that way, Amanda."

"Explained what?"

"How you explained we are just other life forms. Not higher. After all, we are dependent on them. You're fast."

Amanda smiled. "We call out for forgiveness due to our hypocrisy, then we do certain rituals, and think we are forgiven. But, what if that really isn't the point? We just want to *feel* better," Amanda let out.

"Yes, without actually *being* better, deep down on the inside," Lars replied.

"You mean, those who want to feel forgiven, still have their dark energy in them?"

Lars said nothing for the moment.

Amanda leaned back against the wall and drank some more tea.

"Getting back to pride, Amanda, I will say this. Pride separates us from God. The question is, who is God?"

"People have been asking that question, like forever. Wait. You just said you believe in God?"

"No, I said, who is God? Most people in the world believe in some sort of god or gods. Some, with very different interpretations. So, who is it? Or, who are they?"

"I'm not sure what to believe. Maybe God is unknowable."

"Is God unknowable? Are the Gods unknowable? Or is that just lazy thinking? Maybe there is more than one God? Yet, on the other hand, lots of people claim to know who God is. Do they really? They can't all be right, or maybe they are. Some major religions, past and present, have many Gods. Is God just a reflection of our inner selves? Do people make God in their own image?"

"I don't really know, Lars. Can more than one definition of God be correct?"

"These are questions you have to answer, Amanda. From my perspective, the more dark energy we get rid of, the more we will know who God is."

"What if I don't believe in God?"

"Most people do, Amanda."

"Maybe all this dark energy confuses us?"

Lars didn't answer.

"Didn't you say this dark energy, our repressed feelings, gets passed on down from generation to generation? It makes sense to me."

"Yes, Amanda."

"So, if this dark energy has been with us for a long, long, time, maybe it is confusing us, Lars. How far back does this dark energy go? Do I have repressed feelings from my great grandparents, and their parents, inside me? And the people they knew, and the people they knew, and so on? How far back might I have energy from?"

"There is no limit to how far back in time the energy inside you is from. You could even have energy from famous dead people in you."

"Really? Is there any way I could figure out who, if anyone I've met, knew or knows someone famous?"

"Probably not. You could guess at it perhaps. Go visit your library or a physical bookstore. In the biography section, look at all the titles. Don't bother going online. The sight of someone's name or picture may trigger something in you. You won't be able to think of it first. You just have to see what catches your eye. The people who may seem more interesting than others, may be an indicator. This in and of itself does not mean you have energy from that person in you, but it is a starting point."

"I will have to try that someday. I haven't been to a library in awhile. I'm not even sure where my library card is."

"Lots of people think that everything that is worth discovering on Earth, has already been discovered, Amanda. This couldn't be further from the truth. The greatest adventure is in our own hearts and minds. It is for you to discover."

Amanda looked down and touched her heart. She sat quietly and listened to her own heartbeat. What mystery lay inside, that biological science could not explain.

"I can only help you if you want to get rid of your pride and let go of all your dark and bad energy, repressed feelings. Really, if you want to understand yourself. If you don't want to be a prisoner of your pride, repressed feelings, and inner demons, then I will show you how to get rid of them."

"Isn't pride good sometimes though, Lars?"

"It just leads us to being more self-conscious. Pride demands recognition, and when we or others don't get this recognition we crave, we are prone to getting angry, irritated, or jealous. It's a trap."

Amanda pouted her lips, unsure of what to think.

"For us to be proud of something, we often have spent a lot of time and energy just focusing on it. Thus, we may gain in one part our life, but we lose in other aspects. We attach too much importance to what we are proud of and we miss a larger picture."

Amanda reflected for a couple of minutes. There was no sense of urgency to talk from Lars.

"Hmm. . . could it be like when we earn a lot of money or gain fame and power, but we are unhappy about our personal or emotional life?"

Lars bit his lip and nodded his head, as if he was recalling some frustrating thought.

As she said that she realized there were people who were externally successful, but because they became more self-conscious along the way, they had less success and happiness on the inside. Perhaps both sexually and intimately too, fractured personal lives. This knowledge came courtesy of the water cooler gossip fountain. Did her co-workers tell her this, or did she just learn it by osmosis? All of a sudden, she wasn't quite sure. She knew it was true for people in the media, though she couldn't identify any particular celebrity at the moment.

Or maybe their success came at the price of neglecting their kids or a marriage, or even their own physical health. This came from news articles and co-workers she seemed to think. Or the price came at neglecting the environment or community, or some other factor that pride had blinded the proud to.

For those who became too self-conscious sexually, some of them started wanting drugs to boost their sexual lives, or at least a certain percentage of older men did. This was clear to her, it was gossip from her co-workers.

"We can't get something for nothing," Amanda spoke out loud. This was becoming crystal clear.

"We can still do 'good' work without pride. It's just learning by experience. I think improvement and learning takes place even faster, because we are able to admit our faults much faster, and we ask more questions. We are not afraid to ask questions and learn by mistake. We don't have to worry about maintaining our pride."

"Some people at my workplace could eat some of their own pride. I think we lost some accounts because of pride."

"Pride causes a hardening of the mind and heart, which leads to stubbornness and inflexibility to change. This reflects an overall inability to admit we are wrong, or that we could do better."

"If pride affects our heart, maybe the stress causes heart attacks and other diseases. Yeah. You can't teach an old dog new tricks."

"I'm sorry?"

"Oh, it just a saying, Lars."

"I'm not familiar with that."

"Nevermind."

"Pride stops our natural curiosity, because we think we know it all, because pride makes us feel smart. Even if we only think we are smart in a few areas, that same 'feeling of smartness' may more easily attach to new activities that we try."

"Arrogance and ignorance," Amanda responded.

"Pride makes us more demanding and needy. We fall into addictive behaviors easier. We are also more susceptible to being manipulated. It makes us angry easier and it makes us more paranoid and fearful." Lars reached for another biscuit.

"Because we fear falling off the pedestal we've put ourselves on," Amanda answered. She knew it was true. "Does pride also affect our ability to forgive others? We might say we forgive someone in our mind, but it isn't with our heart?" She felt a lump in her throat.

"Yes, of course, Amanda."

She knew it was true. If we still even thought negatively about someone over some event, we hadn't forgave them. It was the thought, or rather lack of thought, that counted. Thus, with more pride, we would know our peaceful core being, less and less.

Both of them went quiet as if their minds and hearts needed a rest. Lars pulled out a map and began studying various routes. As he looked at the map he spoke again. "Pride is an illusion. Pride is a fool's game, Amanda."

"Ok, I see the benefit of getting rid of my pride, all this bad, dark energy, that I've created and from other people. I can definitely see the benefit of not thinking about myself so much. I don't want to be fearful. I don't want to feel lonely. I don't want to feel insecure. I want to stop emotional eating, too. I'm sick of going up and down like a roller coaster with my weight. Can I still eat chocolate though?"

Lars laughed.

"How on earth do we go about defeating our IN ME, our pride?"

Suddenly, the dogs began to bark.

CHAPTER 24 – MIND / NO MIND

They settled back inside from scouting outside with their flashlights, it was a false alarm. If there was a polar bear, it had disappeared in the darkness. The excitement gave a shot of adrenaline to Amanda. Now, she was also feeling a bit flustered and frustrated.

"You look like you are sad."

"How can you tell?"

"Your face betrays your feelings."

"It's that obvious?"

"A famous Danish philosopher once said there are two kinds of despair – one of no possibilities, and the other of infinite possibilities."

"I'll believe that. At the beginning I thought we would have plenty of time to see a bear, now, time is ticking. I'm still glad to be here, but I must admit, I would be a little disappointed if we didn't get a good sighting and encounter."

"Have I failed you?"

"No, you've been wonderful. You don't tell polar bears where to go."

"A spotting at night wouldn't be that good anyway. We will have to trust another."

"The Inuit hunters?"

"Yes, tomorrow we will head to Savissivik. They live here year round and know the terrain and current conditions much better than I."

"You are very well qualified, you saved us from getting stranded on the ice!"

Lars blinked his eyes in gratitude, but remained silent otherwise to her praise.

"Now, how do I get rid of my dark energy?" Amanda interjected, eager to learn more.

"As we were talking about, we must lose our pride. The more we lose, the more we and others around us benefit. Because as we change, people around us will notice and sense it. They will react to us differently. It's like when we are around people who are relaxed, we feel more relaxed, no?"

"Yes, of course."

"When people around us are more tense, we feel more tense, and maybe we want to get away from them because of their 'bad vibe,' no? They make us *feel* uncomfortable. Just as certain places may make us feel uncomfortable too."

"Of course. So, you are saying losing my pride will change my 'vibe,' Lars?"

"Yes."

"How?" Amanda asked a little impatiently.

"By getting rid of pride, we get rid of our dark energy and internal stress, which changes our 'vibe.' To start down the road to losing our pride there are a few statements we must train our mind to accept without thinking."

"A few statements?"

"Before I share them with you, I have to tell you about a way of thought that dominates Scandinavian thinking. These statements that I am going to have you read out loud come from Denmark, but you will find them followed and talked about in Norway and Sweden. And to a lesser degree in Finland and Iceland. The wording differs slightly between each country, but they have the same end result. They may seem counterintuitive, but then they are meant to get rid of our pride, and most of our world is pro-pride."

"Interesting, I'm ready to read them."

"Lastly, I will mention that my country, Denmark, the origin of these statements, often scores as the happiest country in the world. Many Danes would probably not mention it out of modesty, shame, or fear, but from my perspective, they don't understand just how very relevant these statements are in today's world."

"I remember hearing about that earlier."

"What?"

"That Denmark scores as the happiest country in the world. I didn't have too much time to think about it when a man told me about it at the airport. I'm ready for the statements."

Lars rummaged through his bag and brought out a laminated card with ten sentences on it. "These statements form the foundation of Danish thinking, a Scandinavian approach to life. They were originally codified by a Danish-Norwegian author, Aksel Sandemose, in a book from the 1930s called, *A Fugitive Crosses His Tracks*. There are variations on how the statements are translated, but they all have the same meaning. READ THEM OUT LOUD now."

Amanda clutched the card, wondering how a few sentences could affect a society. She sat up and read the statements out loud.

Janteloven / Law of Jante (Yan-tay)

1) You shall not think that you are special.

2) You shall not think that you are as good as us.

3) You shall not think that you are smarter than us.

4) You shall not think of yourself as being better than us.

5) You shall not think that you know more than us.

6) You shall not think that you are more important than us.

7) You shall not think that you are good at anything.

8) You shall not laugh at us.

9) You shall not think that anyone cares about you.

10) You shall not think that you can teach us anything.

"Whoa. Those don't *sound* right, just as you had warned me about. Weird."

"READ THEM AGAIN, OUT LOUD."

Amanda read them again, somewhat hesitantly.

"Many people may find them a bit contrary to how they have been raised. Some, very contrary. And with more cultures mixing via travel or the Internet, some, perhaps many native Scandinavians also view them as a negative. Dark energy is increasing and spreading."

"I can certainly see why!"

"If you read them enough times, they will begin to eliminate your sense of pride, your sense of self."

"Just by reading these sentences?"

"Changing ourselves is partially what we do and experience, another part is how we think about ourselves. You being here in Greenland is the experience part. Later, if you take these statements to heart, you can change your body too, but that is another story. These sentences can help you change how you think about yourself. It's a long process, but it's a starting point."

"So, these can help me get to know my core being?"

"Yes. Your core being, with uncontaminated instincts."

"Uncontaminated?"

"Uncontaminated by all the undesirable dark energy and thoughts inside you that have altered your natural instincts. Our instincts can be programmed like an athlete."

"Ok, so I need to re-read. . ."

Lars interrupted, "Don't read those."

"What?! Why not?" Now, Amanda was quite confused.

"Because I made them, the sentences, more powerful, simpler, and less confusing. I got rid of a few that I didn't think were needed, or appropriate. The Law of Jante is something I have thought long and hard about out here, but I realized the statements could be improved and streamlined."

"Huh?"

"Turn the card over. READ THEM OUT LOUD."

She hesitated before turning the card over. As if the dark energy inside herself was resisting her attempts to challenge it. Looking around the hut, she suddenly felt a chill up her spine. She imagined her heart with black spots and scars on it. She turned the card over.

Mind / No Mind

I-Version

1) I shall never feel special

2) I shall never feel important

3) I shall never feel smart

4) I shall never feel anyone cares about me

5) I shall never feel I can teach anything

6) I shall never feel shame

"Whoa. That was a little hard, Lars."

"READ THEM AGAIN, OUT LOUD, LOUDER!"

She did so, grudgingly with a couple of them.

"You have to want to do this, Amanda. You have to overcome the thought processes, what we are calling dark energy, that are telling you that you are something that you don't want to be. They are inside you, us, telling us just the opposite of these phrases."

Amanda sat speechless after reading them aloud. She took in a deep breath, unsure of what to think of these statements as she drew in another breath of cool air. She looked at Polar Bear. She looked around at the simplicity of the hut.

"Some of them are more relevant to you than others. Which means that some are more difficult than others."

"Yes, I agree with that."

"I've met people who have been unable to speak them aloud. Just hearing them aloud is difficult for some. Which ones are harder for you?"

"They all are difficult to one degree or another. I think a few months ago it would have been harder. Let me just think about all of them for a little while."

"Think of how many times you've been made to feel special or had your ego boosted. People told you these things, the sound of their thoughts is still inside you. How many times have you been told to be ashamed of yourself, or had it implied? Repetition is important with these phrases. Understand why to say them, and keep repeating them until there is no resistance to accepting them. In the future, you may need to say them again from time to time. Some will have an easier time, some more difficult than others. Many have spent their whole life building up their pride."

"The bigger they are, the harder they fall?" She read Mind / No Mind again to herself several times. Her face contorted. "How do I know this is going to make me more happy?"

"Because Jante Law is at the very core of what has made the Danish and Scandinavians, the happiest people in the world. Look it up online. Many people who study happiness look at *how* the Scandinavians live, but this is superficial. Jante Law is the why. Other regions of the world who score high on happiness, *consistently*, also accept some of these, even though they don't have a formal list of statements that I'm aware of."

Amanda was both convinced and unconvinced at the same time. She knew many things on TV, newspapers, books, and photographs were illusions of happiness. Marketing spin, and a desperate public. Now that she thought of it, it was easy to build up our pride in ourselves, because that is what we wanted and thought was right. Another feel good statement that masked deeper feelings of inadequacy or whatever other emotion that troubled us.

"Do any of them stand out as harder to accept than the others?" Lars asked.

"There's only six. Explain, please."

"I think a little history is in order, first. How I came about to changing Jante Law."

"Go right ahead."

"I grew up with Jante Law since I was a child. I just accepted them, not liking them, and sometimes disliking them. But, something happened to me out here to actually make me like Jante Law, and strive to understand it better. Traveling to different parts of the world, living in Greenland, and my wife, changed me. I'm Danish, and yet I am not. We would not be having this conversation if it wasn't for my wife and a few close friends. The cultural labels that we grow up with or that we apply to ourselves, they limit our freedom."

"Limit our freedom?"

"You call yourself American, no?"

"Yes."

"Well, automatically, you have created invisible mental boundaries about who you are. If not to yourself, than the way others perceive you. You may or may not be a 'stereotypical' American, but you classify yourself a certain way rather than thinking more freely."

"Might it be like, if I was a stay-at-home mom, and I labeled myself as such, over and over. . . then it might prevent me from say, pursuing any career opportunities or doing something else that was very different?"

"Exactly."

"Yeah, ok. So, I'm not American and you're not Danish!"

"Heh heh."

"So, the sentences, they look quite different." She flipped the card over and back several times and compared the two sets of sentences.

"Ah, yes. As we were talking earlier about pride, I started to think about why we treat our planet, our home, the way we do. I mean, environmentally. I also thought about why there have been conflicts and war, throughout history. One thing led to another and soon I started to think about why we get angry, jealous, fearful. Why we are hypocritical. Why we say one thing, but do another."

Lars ate a biscuit as Amanda patiently listened.

"I thought about both world and personal problems. In a world sense, more global warming than anything else. I wondered why it was such a contentious issue. Did I use and say that word correctly, contentious?"

"Yes, it sounds perfect."

"I haven't used that word in awhile."

"I haven't heard that word in awhile, Lars."

"In the end, I realized the problem isn't global warming or climate change at all, or any issue in particular. Global warming hasn't just happened, Amanda. It's a result of the way we think about our ourselves and our place in nature over hundreds, no, thousands of years."

"That's an interesting perspective. Like how we see ourselves as separate from nature?"

"Yes. Yes. In addition to that, opposing sides of an issue, think they are always right. Sometimes, even if they know, on some level, they are wrong. They don't want to admit it, out of pride. That's when I realized that *pride* was the problem. Pride is the problem at the root of all others. Pride is just the name for all the primary feelings noted in Mind / No Mind."

"Pretty deep, Lars."

"An ounce of prevention is worth a pound of cure. That's a saying in English, is it not?"

"Yes, it is."

"For every ounce of pride we get rid of, we will get a pound of cure for our problems. Something like that."

Amanda chuckled.

"I started to stop blaming other people and look inside our own minds and hearts for the answer on why this is, starting with my own. My own pride. To make a long story short, this led me back to Jante Law. Eventually, I learned to modify it, and make it more powerful, and remove the jealousy component." Lars let out a sigh.

"Pride locks us into thinking a certain way, because we become afraid of change, doesn't it?"

Lars nodded his head. "If everyone thinks and feels their way is better, then we will never agree. Yet, how could I expect others to change, to lower their pride, if I couldn't?"

"This Mind / No Mind is what you came up with then?"

"I've had to get rid of my own negative, or dark energy. I've had to exorcise my inner demons. It has not been easy, but in a way, it hasn't been hard. My wife has also been challenged. It is a good thing we were quite compatible to begin with. Maybe we were meant to meet. We've had many deep discussions. I didn't do this alone."

She took a moment to compare the Mind / No Mind sentences with the original Jante Law. There were five sentences derived from the original Law of Jante. She noticed that statement six had no relation to the original ten though.

"Where did this idea of not feeling shame come about?" Amanda was feeling quite analytical about these statements.

"That came about because we found it was at the root of the other statements. There is a seventh statement, too."

"What!" she exclaimed.

"That you will discover on your own, if you are serious about these. This is the fastest route to getting rid of one's pride and not being self-conscious. Time has revealed to us that there is more to dark energy and who we are than just this, but some things you just have to experience for yourself."

"Tell me."

"All I will say is that it relates to what we eat and drink."

"Emotional eating?"

"Yes."

"The challenge is in breaking the emotional eating circle. When you get back home, every time you eat, write down whether you think you are eating because you are hungry, or due to something you are trying to repress."

"Oh, I'll be happy with that. No more diets or going to the gym, or skin breakouts. Expect an email from me someday. Can you explain the logic behind how you changed this Law of Jante to Mind / No Mind."

"That, I can do. The original Law of Jante uses the word 'think' or 'believe.' I realized that on the inside, before we think or believe we are proud, we feel it. We feel that we are special or smart. Do you agree with that?"

Amanda pondered it for a moment. "Yes, I can think you are correct. We may think we are this or that, but the feeling comes first. I'll have to think more about this later."

"It should also be noted there is a difference between FEELing and BEing. We can BE special, important, or smart to someone else, but that is their choice to think or feel that. If we desire the feeling, and don't get it, then we will become angry or disappointed."

"Go on."

"We can BE a teacher to someone else, or help others by sharing something with others, but we don't need to FEEL it. As a teacher may always learn from a student, in essence, everyone is a teacher and everyone is a student. It is only when we 'elevate' ourselves over others does it lead to problems in the future. Teaching, or rather, helping others, just comes out of our core being from our heart. Over time, I have found, my behavior has changed. I interfere less or comment less on other's actions, unless I'm asked for my perspectives. Or if there is some emergency."

"Interesting."

"I'm still getting over my pride, Amanda. It has been a long process to know who I am, who WE are, very deeply, and to flush out all the dark energy in me. Anger, jealousy, resentment, fears."

Amanda was pensive, unsure of what to say. A feeling of humility washed over her as she listened to a grown man talking about getting rid of his pride. Didn't men take pride in their manhood?

"I feel like on some level I might be lecturing to you, Amanda. I hope it doesn't come across that way."

"No, no, I don't think so, Lars. It's a deep subject. We should have classes on this in school. Maybe someday we will. My gut feeling says that at least some of this makes sense, but I need to think about this more. Where did this shame statement come from?"

"We realized that when we hold shame, it makes us hide, or rather suppress, certain feelings, thoughts, and negative actions and experiences. We then feel the other feelings to compensate for this negativity. So, if we have a very negative experience, we will try to boost ourselves by making ourselves feel special or important in some other way, rather than deal with that deep darkness. Thus, shame is a deeper, or a stronger feeling than the others."

Amanda immediately thought about Chip's confession about cheating on Stephanie right before she left for Denmark. He must have enjoyed the affair on one level, but feelings were two-faced, love-hate.

"If you embark on this anti-pride path, so to speak, at some point you will feel a physical change on your forehead. Our forehead is one of the primary places related to how we think of ourselves. Think of it as a relaxing of pressure in our mind. If you ever learn the art of face reading, you will see how people's inner thoughts about themselves and others is reflected on their face."

"Reflected on their face?"

"If we want to be angry, or unhappy, or any other feeling, but we use self-control to suppress it and not show it, or we 'smile or grin' instead, imagine what that does to the muscles in our face. Our heart wants to express one thing, but we force it to do another."

Amanda thought about this for a moment. "Very interesting." Two-faced people she thought to herself. Wasn't there some cartoon character with that name? She couldn't remember the cartoon at the moment. What about bipolar behavior and people who were passive / aggressive, she wondered to herself.

"There is even a name for it, which has origins in Asia, but it is everywhere. Perhaps you've heard it as – saving face."

"Yes, I have. Though, I'm not sure where."

"Saving face, literally makes our face age in certain ways. Most people would find these ways, undesirable."

"Yie! So, I am distorting my own face over time by using too much self-control?"

"Yes. And since everything is connected in our body, it will also cause tension in our neck and shoulders, as well as other health issues."

"But what about when I need to 'act' a certain way?"

"That is your choice. Learn to release all your repressed feelings, sorry, dark energy, and you won't have to 'act' anyway at all, you can just BE."

"You said I should feel a physical change just from reading these short sentences over and over again?"

"Yes. Look in a mirror, Amanda. Make feelings of anger and sadness. Certain muscles contract. Now, if you willfully stop this, what do you think happens to those muscles? You can also look at babies crying, they have dark energy in them that they are trying to get out."

It was new and yet not new to Amanda. As she thought about these insights, it was painfully obvious. She had never realized this, nor anyone she knew, because we were too busy focusing on our enemies, not our IN ME. Was this a secret to staying young looking?

As she would realize later, many people who rose to the top in social circles, business, and certain professions, were masters at controlling the expressions on their faces, and in controlling what words did or did not come out of their mouths. But, they ultimately paid the price in other ways. Be careful what you wish for, because you might just get it, was an expression that would echo in her mind later.

"Can you just tell me one thing, what was it about Greenland that changed you?"

"I have seen it many times out here, and experienced it myself. People come here with a bigger sense of themselves, then they are humbled by this place. I thought about this change in people's behavior, myself, before and after. I think you might call it, pride before the fall. A good fall."

"Fall?"

"To become something different, we must *smash* the image of what we are today and were before. Our pride is an image that we project inward and outward."

"Smash," Amanda muttered to herself. Amanda 2.0, or was it Amanda 0.0, she wondered to herself.

"Don't try too hard to accept Mind / No Mind immediately. Just think about them for a little while, but maybe you are different, Amanda."

"Well, I do study behavior and consumer psychology, so that gives me a leg up."

"Someday when you leave this place, perhaps you will understand. Or maybe you will understand some of them sooner. We have been conditioned and rewarded over time that self-control and self-discipline is a 'good thing.' It cannot be unlearned 'overnight,' as you might say, but rather, only over time."

They still sounded like belittling statements to Amanda, if not odd. They seemed contrary to the very ideas she had grown up with, that she was unique, she was an individualist, she was special, she was going places. But, maybe she quickly thought, she could BE special, without FEELing special. "That's it?"

"Yes. One more thing, Mind / No Mind will eventually protect you from acquiring negative dark energy and thoughts. For you will learn how we acquire, emotional baggage, over time."

"That would good to know. That would be really good to know."

She excused herself and ventured outside to admire the Northern Lights again. She activated a pair of hand warmers. She needed to think, but she couldn't do it if she was being distracted by the cold. As she breathed in the cool air and made funny faces at the resting dogs, she thought more about why she would want to believe in such statements. She brought out the card with the statements and focused on the first statement.

She READ the first statement OUT LOUD several times.

- I shall never feel special
- I shall never feel special
- I shall never feel special

As she watched the dancing light spectacle, she had an epiphany. If she thought she was special growing up, or made to feel that way by parents, teachers, or friends, then that would explain why she felt unhappy when she didn't get the attention she had become accustomed to. Her ego had been inflated. If a boyfriend, her company, or whomever, didn't make her feel special or give her the recognition she felt she deserved, consciously or subconsciously, she would get irritated, and perhaps a little angry, or resentful.

Then there were those people, some men, who would try to manipulate you and make you feel special and important to get you in bed. Then they would ditch you and leave you vulnerable. Pigs.

The same kind of people were at school and work, anywhere. Back stabbers. Bitches, assholes, and pigs.

These sentences were powerful she realized. By needing, or wanting to feel special, Amanda realized she would also be jealous of others who were made to feel more special than she was at a particular given moment. It could be a boyfriend looking at another girl, somebody else getting more recognition in spite of her efforts at work, or something about the lives of people in the news that she had heard or read about. Jealousy was something she wanted to let go of.

Perhaps she always assumed that her parents and friends were supposed to love and care about her because she was special. This led her to demand that she be treated a certain way, even if the other person was incapable of that, for whatever reason. No wonder she didn't always get along with her father or mother.

By constantly needing to feel more special she reasoned, our self-expectations constantly went up too, wasn't that a recipe for disappointment and unhappiness?

She scanned down the list and reread one of the other Mind / No Mind statements OUT LOUD.

– I shall never feel anyone cares about me
– I shall never feel anyone cares about me
– I shall never feel anyone cares about me

The sledge dogs were all soundly sleeping as the Northern Lights continued their dance in the sky, creating undulating waves of green and yellow against the night sky. Stars twinkled as Amanda gave this statement more thought.

Maybe an assumption to believe, or rather feel, that anyone cared about you, setup false expectations she wondered silently to herself. Is this why she had problems in dating? Would we take relationships for granted too, if we automatically felt that those around us, cared about us? Perhaps this statement could protect herself from those who made empty verbal promises and gestures rather than real substantive actions. "Back the smack," she muttered to herself.

Did having this feeling make her more needy? She didn't want to feel needy, she wanted to be more independent, without feeling lonely.

This statement seemed to be similar to the 'I shall never feel special' sentence, but perhaps it looked at the same thing from another angle. This would require more thought.

Had she been too proud to ever forgive her parents because she never got her idealized childhood? Did anyone get an ideal childhood? What was an ideal childhood? Was that just a marketing invention?

At work, the sense that other people should care about how she felt only set the stage for more combativeness or false friendliness later as people were afraid to get their ideas shot down. Maybe this sentence would help end political correctness.

Did feeling that anyone cared about us, make us too touchy-feely because we were afraid to get our feelings hurt?

She picked out another sentence to analyze. She READ it OUT LOUD.

- I shall never feel smart
- I shall never feel smart
- I shall never feel smart

This one seemed to be easy to understand, especially in Greenland. If one became overconfident of their abilities up here, they probably wouldn't last long. A white desert, while serene and beautiful, could be a very unforgiving place for the ill-prepared.

She thought about how it affected her back home. Maybe feeling too smart made her less open to some other people's ideas at work. Maybe she was too smart for her own and the company's good at times. If not her, other teams and groups. Companies that missed shifts in technology came to mind. Companies that underestimated new competitors was another she realized. Weren't there battles in the past where one underestimated their enemy?

Outside of work, if she was so smart, why had she been unhappy? What about people who got cancer or had other health problems. Many people would offer sympathy, but wasn't a lot of this stuff preventable? Didn't stress cause a lot of health problems? People were smart about one thing, but dumb about other things in their life. Our pride, and this was only one aspect, blinded us. She reread the sentences, this one was a keeper as well.

She picked one more statement to understand from the list.

- I shall never feel shame
- I shall never feel shame
- I shall never feel shame

"What an unpleasant feeling," Amanda muttered to herself. She paced around the hut. She spoke out loud again, to herself. "People feel shame because they feel guilty about something. Yes? They feel like they violated some sense of right or wrong, or good and bad. But, what if there is no good or bad? There's just cause and effect? Maybe there are a set of core rules in our core being? But, if dark energy is corrupting it, we wouldn't really know what those rules are, would we?"

She stopped talking to herself out loud. Corrupt politicians, corrupt and overzealous businessmen and women, hypocritical religious figures and followers, rightfully convicted criminals, lying and cheating spouses and partners, didn't they all carry shame? Didn't many of them only realize the errors of their ways, after they were exposed?

If that was true Amanda reasoned, then it was only once their shame was exposed did their repressed feelings, reasons for lying, and other dark energy start to come out. Lars was right, shame hid our dark emotions. But, if nobody felt shame, then nobody would be holding these feelings back to begin with. They would get rid of them healthily, and the 'dirty deeds' and deception would never have occurred.

Maybe it was only when we were able to overcome our shame did we change. Shame as a component of pride, held in dark energy, just like Lars said.

There was another kind of shame Amanda realized. One that didn't hold in deception and lies so much, as it hid dark energy related to feeling inadequate. Women who thought of themselves as overweight or women who felt they didn't fit some ideal of beauty. False, manipulated beauty in fashion magazines and on the Internet thanks to photo retouching, manipulation, and creative attention. Of course, men were victims of this too, they compensated in other ways.

It wasn't just beauty, but any perceived measurement that we were beholden to. Income, intelligence, or physical ability in sports, in bed, or anywhere else.

And feeling inadequate or bad about ourselves led us to turn to both legal and illegal drugs, or some other addictive idea or behavior, probably unhealthy. Maybe just the feeling itself was responsible for the physical inadequacy that she had encountered with some men in bed.

Shame was insidious indeed she realized, and we were so busy shaming each other that we didn't even realize how destructive it was. Amanda didn't want to feel shame, this statement was a keeper too.

She was seeing how all the sentences connected to each other. She wasn't ready to accept the other two statements just yet. "I feel important at work. I feel like I can teach people something," she announced to no one in particular.

She'd always hated cold weather, but the cool air cleared her mind and spirit. On this evening, the cold weather was good. She retreated back into the warm hut.

As she readjusted her vision, she noticed that Lars, for a moment, looked different. Were the sentences already working their magic? Or was it just her imagination?

"How was the show?"

"I barely noticed it, Lars. I was too busy thinking about the statements."

"And what conclusion did you come to?"

"I am beginning to see why one should accept them, but I need more time to think about them. I also realized why they seem so negative."

"And why is that?"

"Because we are constantly exposed to *positive* messages and *positive* spin. You know, I am a marketing consultant, so I'd like to think I know a few things about this. Is that pride?"

Lars said nothing.

Amanda started again. "Well, commercials never talk about the down side of products, or almost never. Companies are always trying to minimize any negative aspects of what they sell or represent. Often, it isn't what they say, it's what they don't say. This way of thinking has infected large parts of the world I feel. Now we see it in people's social networking profiles. Well, I haven't traveled much, but I have read stories and statistics from many parts of the world. I think I'm part of the problem."

"That's a good point, Amanda. I hadn't really thought of that."

Amanda couldn't stop herself. "It isn't just commercials, it's product packaging. We buy food and they highlight *real* ingredients. Made with 100% *real* honey, whatever. They never say, made with 100% *fake* honey! They never mention all the preservatives and other fake things in tiny print. We buy frozen dinners, which is already pretty pathetic. We know that all the photographs are fucking fake. The food almost never looks like that when it comes out of the microwave. Have you seen how food stylists and professional food photographers operate? Trickery everywhere. Pathetic."

She took a breather.

"Then there are the commercials glorifying some new whiz-bang gadget, or new technology, but they never say, our technology is used to trick other people by making fake images of how we look. Our technology is used to commit crimes. Or if you use our technology, you might get a brain tumor or other form of illness from all the energy it puts out. We keep only hearing about the positive aspects. It's like the zoo, they don't tell you the whole story. It's a positive-bias world."

She gurgled some tea and threw it down her throat.

"Some advertising says, made with humanely treated animals. But, they never say, inhumanely treated animals are for breakfast, lunch, and dinner today! Made with added hormones and antibiotics. You have to learn all that shit for yourself. Low fat, low sodium. The package never says full of fat and sodium. Full of preservatives! Full of teeth eroding sugar. Traces of insecticides included. They never say, eat this and your gums and teeth will decay. Or made by unfairly treated workers."

"You have a lot on your mind, Amanda."

"I'm sick of the fashion magazines. Airbrushing, digital editing. The right angles and lighting. We women are guilty of it. All the makeup we slather on. All the chemicals in makeup. I'm fucking sick of it, Lars. I'm fucking sick of it, and that's all I have to say."

Lars could only smile. He was a little taken aback by Amanda's outburst.

Amanda continued. "I'm fucking sick of fake social networking profiles. Fake 'happy marriages.' I can't take it anymore!!" Amanda got up and walked around the hut. She had gotten herself worked up and needed a break. She opened the door and went outside.

Then she screamed into the darkness at the top of her lungs. "I'm fucking sick of it! I'm sick of controlling myself!" The dogs howled to attention, but she ignored them. She headed back inside.

"I've heard scream therapy is good sometimes."

Lars looked on unflinchingly. "Are you trying to scare all the dogs?"

Amanda let out a mischievous smile.

"Perhaps it might help to hear the other version of them."

"The other version?"

"They affirm your own state of being and help you deal with other people's feelings. They defend your sense of being that you are trying to re-establish." He handed Amanda another laminated card. "You can keep these cards. I carry one around, in Danish, of course, to remind myself every now and then. We have more at home."

What started out as just a search for a wild polar bear was turning out to be something else entirely. Something of a more profound and deep nature. It suited a, thinker of life, such as Amanda.

She READ THEM OUT LOUD.

Mind / No Mind

You-Version

1) You shall never feel special

2) You shall never feel important

3) You shall never feel smart

4) You shall never feel anyone cares about you

5) You shall never feel you can teach anything

6) You shall never feel shame

She again felt resistance to accepting these statements. Focusing inward she tried to find the source of the resistance, but she wasn't sure where it was coming from. She persisted and read them out loud again. "They're basically the same phrases, but directed at someone else?"

"They protect your mind from manipulation by others. They also give control of your sense of being, back to you and not others."

It seemed to make sense to her as she thought about it. The first two sentences seemed like they would be useful to protect one's mind and heart from those who chose to 'elevate' and raise themselves above others and appear to be better than they actually were.

"We forget that everything is relative, Amanda. Because we think too much about ourselves. By thinking and feeling that others are smart or smarter, we unwittingly make ourselves feel dumber. It happens little by little. By basking in the glory of others' pride, we weaken ourselves."

"Can we inherit feelings of thinking we are dumber? Could it be dark energy inherited from our past?"

"Yes."

"Everyone knows something different, don't they? Just like at my company. We are knowledgeable about different things. I was once talking to a new hire and they had some really interesting things to say about business and life in general. I remember it now. It was something like. . . at any moment in time, our unique skill set and knowledge could be useful. And that it might be the most important knowledge to the entire company, or world, if we are talking about a bigger picture."

"That sounds like good reasoning to me."

"We've been deceived into thinking only certain kinds of people are smart and important. People who dress well, people who make a certain amount of money, or people who appear to have a certain material status, or title."

Lars nodded his head in agreement.

Amanda shared more of her perspective. "Yea, at school we're conditioned, implicitly or explicitly, that people who score well on exams, quizzes, and tests, and get good grades are smart. Everyone else just doesn't measure up. The world needs all kinds of knowledge."

Lars added, "Or people who have high IQ scores. As you say, Amanda, we need all kinds of knowledge. There are other kinds of smart. Such as EQ, emotional intelligence. The people who have high IQ scores often ignore this though, because they know next to nothing about it! Either that, or they are afraid of their own feelings!"

Amanda gladly muttered the first three sentences, even though she personally still felt important. She would speak these you-forms out loud later, again.

"Some teachers implicitly put themselves in a superior position above us. They may know something, we do not, but all students could teach their professors about certain things, because we all have unique experiences."

"Yeah, I think that's how a good teacher should be." As she said that, Amanda still felt like she could teach clients and her co-workers about her psychological insights. Perhaps by elevating herself subconsciously she was closing off her mind to learning something useful.

"If we don't want to feel unworthy or inferior, we need to repeat the you-version of Mind / No Mind while we think of the people who we feel put themselves in a superior position. Sometimes, maybe they aren't, we just imagine it. Think of people in your past and present, Amanda. Elementary, middle, and high school. University, church, work, social groups, extended family, and your immediate family. Anyone you suspect with any aspects of pride, think of them and direct the statement at them. Scream it at them, they don't have to be anywhere near you."

"Or even our kids," Amanda added. "I hate it when people talk down at me, really." Amanda thought of girls in school who thought they were better than her. She thought of classmates and teachers who felt they were better than her. Her parents came to mind. Boyfriends came to mind. Co-workers and people whom she had met on social occasions. People in the news. People she had looked up to or respected in some way.

"These sentences protect us because they give us back the power we have given away at some point in our life journey," Lars added. The 'you' statements equalize you, when comparing yourself to others on an emotional level. No man or woman is better than you. Do you want to feel inferior to others? Do you want to feel weak?"

"Umm. . . no."

"You shall never feel anyone cares about you, and you shall never feel shame, protect us from feeling bad about other people's situations, that they created. It protects us from two insidious feelings – misery and pity."

Amanda was beginning to see the power of such simple sentences. Victims of cyber bullying and name calling at school would probably want to learn Mind / No Mind. People with low self-esteem and people who were just tired of other people's behavior. People with inferiority complexes. Abused spouses and children.

Perhaps women in certain cultures and countries should be screaming these statements out at others. More often than not it was probably the women who were weaker, but sometimes it was the men. Were a few sentences mightier than a sword, a gun, an army, an established system of repression?

Here, in a simple form, was medicine for the mind and body Amanda realized, but it wasn't a pill, it was just a thought, or rather, a set of thoughts. Maybe people contemplating suicide would benefit from these simple statements. Maybe people who turned to illegal and legal drugs, alcohol, smoking, or overeating, because of emotional difficulties, could find power in these simple statements.

"Does it matter if one tries to internalize the You-version instead of the I-version, first?"

"No, it does not. Pride comes in different forms. There is one more version still."

"What? Another one?" She turned the second card over.

"READ THEM OUT LOUD."

Mind / No Mind

We-Version

1) We shall never feel special

2) We shall never feel important

3) We shall never feel smart

4) We shall never feel anyone cares about us

5) We shall never feel we can teach anything

6) We shall never feel shame

"Why are there three sets of statements?"

"There are three sets of statements because sometimes we think of ourselves individually, sometimes as part of a group, and lastly, sometimes apart from others as an outsider. The I-version helps to get rid of our individual pride, the We-version our group pride, and the You-version protects us from the pride of others. Repeat these enough, and eventually, they become second nature. Then you don't think about them unless you're sharing them with someone else."

As Lars explained it, the I and We-versions were used for ourselves and the You-set was directed at other people – friends, parents, or even people on TV or in newspapers. They could help someone maintain their sense of being and identity amongst a sea of conflicting messages.

"Why is it called Mind / No Mind?"

"The idea is just – to be. To exist and learn by experience without interference from debilitating repressed feelings."

"To be? Like the core being state you mentioned earlier."

"Being out here in the wilderness alone gave me a lot of time to think, read, and reflect. Talking to my wife, too. I've met a lot of people and I ended up just listening to a lot of stories. It is easy to get rushed in our life and not ponder such things."

"How many times do I have to recite these, Lars?"

"Until you feel none of these feelings anymore."

"How long will that take?"

"I don't know, Amanda. Everyone has pride in differing amounts. This is something you either want to do, or don't. The less you think about yourself, the more you will know the beauty of your own heart, and who you are. Oh, I almost forgot to tell you one thing."

"What's that?"

"If you have no shame, then you have no secrets. If you've lied to anyone, in any meaningful way, then confessing the lie to them, not a priest or anyone else, is something that should be no problem. Not to be confused with making honest and sincere mistakes, or saying something and then the situation changed at some point, of course."

Amanda didn't answer, but realized the truth of Lars' statement. "I wish I had more time," Amanda reflected. Overjoyed by this sharing of ideas and stories, she was distraught at the inevitable return to her existing life which was starting to creep into her mind again as the days ticked away, but perhaps these sentences would help her, 'be better' over time. They would help her find her core being, her true heart she surmised.

Lars scratched his head. "I have traveled several times to California, Florida, and Texas, for research, conferences, and just vacation. There is something I never understood about America while I was there. When I was there, we biologists, would talk about differences between our cultures. I was surprised when other researchers told me about the average vacation allowance and workweek in America. I think they said it was about ten days vacation plus holidays every year, maybe twenty days total, and even that wasn't guaranteed."

"How many do you get in Denmark?"

"We get at a minimum, twenty-five days, but many get thirty days."

"Thirty days? You mean vacation plus holidays total?"

"No, I mean thirty days, plus holidays. Forty days total."

"That's six weeks off plus two weeks holiday! Two months off! Are you joking? How long do you have to work in the same place?"

"We earn holiday at that rate in the first year."

"You don't have to wait six months or anything like that?"

"No. Our average workweek is probably around thirty-five hours per week. Many of my friends in America work significantly longer. Happy workers make for more efficient workers."

Amanda was in disbelief. She had been led to believe that her land was the promised land. Where did she get that idea anyway? "I don't think I would earn thirty days per year, forty days total, even if I worked in the same place for the rest of my life. I think we're getting the short end of the stick."

Lars let out a big yawn and Amanda followed shortly after. They fell fast asleep.

CHAPTER 25 – METEORITE LAND

It was early afternoon as Amanda and Lars sighted Savissivik. In front of them, the tiny village stood out against the vast expanse of white that covered the mountain behind the settlement and beyond.

The now familiar home shades of red, yellow, blue, and gray, came into view. The contrast was even more stark than in Ilulissat or Qaanaaq. Amanda felt a sense of relief upon arriving in town. The last several days they had been sledging, they had seen no other people or man made structures, apart from the hut. It redefined the word, remote, in her vocabulary. Despite her sense of relief, she still had a strange feeling, as if they and the people in this town were the only people left on Earth.

Lars commanded the dogs to stop as they neared the center of town. "Welcome to Savissivik, again. This place is also known as meteorite land. In 1968, a nine hundred kilogram meteor was found here, almost two thousand pounds. It is the world's sixth largest meteorite ever found. Meteorites have a high iron content, and the iron found in this area was used in Inuit tools. Savik means iron knife."

"Is the meteor still here?"

"No, it's at the Denmark Geological Museum in Copenhagen now. However, you can see part of a smaller meteor at the Thule Museum in Qaanaaq."

"Oh, I missed that. Maybe on my way back."

Not only was this town remote, it also had a cosmic connection. At least there was some truth in the name of the town she thought. It was a simple thing that could be manipulated she learned in marketing. The best one of all was creating a myth of nature by using catchy names for a subdivision or street name. Names like Oak Creek, Chestnut Grove, Riverside, or Woodside. Never mind that these natural features had often been destroyed or marginalized, if they ever existed at all.

Then there were the places, apartment complexes usually, named after some 'exotic' locale faraway, like the name of a European city. Or simply names that described a place in a 'soothing' manner, whether or not it was actually true. The power of a name.

There was a list of top ten place names she recalled reading once, but she only remembered the first and last ones. The 287 places named Fairview and the 140 places named Pleasant Hill.

Amanda counted the number of buildings that they had passed and those that were in front of her, she counted about twenty-five small buildings. "How many people live here?"

"About eighty."

Several villagers approached and greeted Lars. He talked to them in a way that only long time friends could. Amanda waved to the villagers as Lars introduced her while speaking Inuktun. She muttered a few of the words that Lars had taught her over the last couple of days, but mostly just smiled. She was feeling a little self-conscious. That was something she needed to work on.

Then, dashing around one of the buildings, a stout man bounded toward Lars and gave him a big hug. He looked to be in his early thirties. It was the man who Amanda would later come to know as Kampe, the man who would try to satisfy one of the reasons Amanda came to Greenland for. At the moment, he did not introduce himself to Amanda, instead he approached the dogs near Amanda and began to comment about the dogs that had carried Lars and Amanda over here.

"What is he saying?"

"He said that he saw us approaching from up the hill. He said our dogs are very tough and work well together as a team."

Kampe continued to circle around the dogs, making comments as he visually got excited.

Amanda gave Lars a questioning look.

"He said he saw the dogs become more excited and run faster as they approached the village. They were happy to see him and the rest of his friends here in the town."

"He saw all that?"

"Dogs can become bored running across the long distances of flat snow and ice. They are no different than you or I. When they see something different, they can get excited."

Kampe continued to comment about the dog team.

"He said that it is clear that our dog team has grown up together. He made a particular comment about the ones in the middle, as those are the strongest."

"What do you mean, grown up together?"

"Greenlandic sledge dogs have a strong pack and territorial instinct. There is a fixed hierarchy with few fights, the alpha dog keeps order. If an adult dog is introduced into a pack, it will rarely survive. Newcomers are not accepted unless they integrate as puppies. The puppies need to be submissive or they could get killed by an adult in the pack."

Amanda looked on, amazed by the observations and unerring eye of Kampe. He turned and smiled at Amanda as he seemed to compliment her.

"What did he say?"

"He said your dogs are good and pure. None of them have blue eyes."

"What does that mean?"

"It means that there has been no cross-breeding with other non-Greenlandic dogs. Pure breeds have eyes that are dark brown to amber in color."

Amanda smiled back.

Kampe responded by asking Amanda a question.

"He asked if you have found what you are looking for?"

"How does he know I am looking for something?"

Kampe answered again in Inuktun.

"He said no one comes this far without looking for something."

Kampe was wiser than he might appear Amanda realized. "I'm looking for a polar bear."

Kampe responded excitedly before Lars could translate Amanda's statement. "Nanoq! Nanoq!" He pointed at his legs.

Amanda noticed the polar bear skin pants he was wearing. Somehow they had just blended into the rest of her new surroundings. She was reminded of the boy yelling at the airport. It wasn't exactly what she had in mind for the fate of the polar bear she hoped to find. She wasn't sure how to clarify that she wasn't here to hunt a polar bear, only to see one. Amanda couldn't think of what to say. She was caught off guard by Kampe's energy, and in a momentary state of shock.

Lars interrupted and spoke in Inuktun to his friend.

Amanda awoke from her moment of shock. "What did you tell him?" she asked firmly.

"I told him we were looking for a polar bear on the pack ice, but that we had no luck. I told him you weren't here to hunt and kill one, only to see one."

"What did he say then?"

"He didn't. . ." Lars was interrupted as Kampe all of a sudden noticed Amanda's stuffed polar bear sticking out from behind the blanket that had covered him up to his neck. Kampe ran over to the sledge and looked at the stuffed animal as if he had never seen a polar bear in his life. He circled the sledge, then he pressed his face closer to the stuffed bear, sniffed it, then backed off. He pulled back the blanket and touched it. He started laughing, uncontrollably laughing.

Now, he was attracting the attention of several other villagers who also approached Amanda's stuffed polar bear. Some of them were wearing polar bear fur pants too.

Several of the kids shouted "Nanoq! Nanoq! Nanoq!"

Kampe motioned the others to quiet down. He finally introduced himself to Amanda, in broken English, as he pointed to himself. "Kampe. Kampe. Hunter. I find you polar bear."

Amanda wasn't sure what to be more surprised by, his broken English, or if in a strange sort of way, maybe he understood Amanda's quest. She stared at him for what seemed like an eternity then pointed at herself. "A-man-da. A-man-da." She then pointed at her eyes as she pointed out in the distance. "Nanoq. Nanoq," she repeated.

They both smiled as they seemed to arrive at some common understanding.

With introductions out of the way, Kampe helped Lars to tie up the dogs and unload some supplies from the sledge while Amanda decided to tour the town. A half dozen Arctic rabbits were hanging from a line next to one house. It was an unexpected sight, but certainly not out of place. She was becoming better adjusted and ready for the unexpected.

Amanda looked around some more and noticed a four posted platform raised about six feet off the ground with an upper railing. She had seen a similar structure in Qaanaaq. A seal skin was hanging to dry from the upper railing. Perhaps they would be drying the seal skins that Lars brought from their hunting earlier. She noticed a polar bear skin being dried as she continued to make her way around the town, it was very surreal.

The raw existence that these people lived, impressed Amanda despite her feelings about polar bear pants. Every time she saw another animal skin being dried or worn, she got a strange feeling as if the skin could come alive at any moment.

If worn, man and animal would merge and become one she thought. Maybe all the animals had spirits after all. Maybe this place was driving her mad. Much to her surprise, she hadn't shed any tears about the polar bear skins, yet. There was no denying the integral relationship between the polar bear and life here. She thought about the attitudes and impressions from her visit to the zoo at home, and the beliefs of her friends. Her world was indeed, a separation from nature.

She returned to where the sledge was and found Lars feeding the dogs. She looked at the dogs differently this time and noticed how the dogs took turns eating, but not in a strict hierarchy, but more like a sense of co-operation. Interpretation of reality was in the eye of the beholder.

Amanda followed Kampe and Lars into Kampe's small home as they had finished with the dogs. His wife was warming up a teapot. She invited Amanda and Lars to take a seat at the small table.

"Do they have any kids?"

"Two children, they are over at the local school," Lars answered.

Using Lars as the interpreter, Amanda managed a simple conversation with Kampe and his wife, Suusaat, going over the basics of what life was like. They talked about the different foods they ate, what they thought of the modern world, what kinds of things the children learned in school, and their hopes for the future. Amanda felt like she was interviewing them for a television documentary special.

Suusaat excused herself to go outside and pick up the children. As if on cue, Kampe rummaged under a table and brought out a small radio.

"Radiu!" he announced. He turned it on. Static. He fumbled with the dial until a familiar melody blared out of the tiny box, it was an American country music song.

"Huh?" Amanda thought there must be some sort of trickery going on.

Kampe closed his eyes, stood up, and started to shuffle dance to the music. The sight was surreal.

"Where is that music coming from?" Amanda asked trying to be heard over the blare.

Lars answered, "It's from the Thule Air Base."

"Oh."

"Yes. Sometimes they play American pop music, it is very funny. They have a pretty powerful transmitter. Not much interference up here."

"Surely," the bizarreness of the scene still resonating in her ears.

While Amanda was surprised by the music, it did have a certain calming effect on her. In a world of so much unfamiliarity, even a little piece of home seemed to calm her nerves a little. She thought of home, work, her friends, all the creature comforts, and all the complexities. These were things which she was forgetting about more and more as the days went by. Life seemed so much simpler out here without all the noise of the modern world. Yet, here they were inviting it in, at least one of them.

"What does he think about America?"

Kampe's enthusiasm for the country music went on unabated. Lars didn't even try to interrupt his enjoyment and answered Amanda's question directly.

"I can't speak for Kampe, but I know many of the older Greenlanders like Americans. The Americans helped to open up Greenland during World War II from my country's trade monopoly which lasted from the late 1700s to the end of World War II. In the 1960s, my government decided to change forever the way the Greenlanders live. Instead of letting the Inuit rely on traditional ways of hunting and living off the land, my government changed the Greenlanders into commercial fishermen by closing roughly half the towns along the coast."

Amanda glanced at Kampe. He was still dancing around to the music with his eyes closed.

"The Danish government built housing blocks in Nuuk, Sisimiut, and Maniitsoq, among others. Many Greenlanders were moved into these four story, gray, charmless, very sharp-edged rectangular buildings. Many of them are simply named Block A, Block B, Block C, Block D."

"Sounds like government housing projects in the US."

"Perhaps. They know it is a positive and negative relationship, Amanda. Many Greenlanders are embracing the modern world, I know many of them have computers. Yet, they are trying to hold on to past traditions, the very source of their identity. They know that my country subsidizes their entry into the modern world. A lot of krone, hundreds of millions of dollars per year, is spent by the Danish government and people. That is a lot for a small country like Denmark."

She listened without speaking.

"It is important to make a distinction between those who continue to live more like their ancestors, such as the Inuit here in Savissivik, and those who live in larger towns. Kampe may very well not have too strong of an opinion about America or Denmark, we'll have to ask him."

Their whole conversation went on oblivious to Kampe, who entered into an almost trance like state listening to the American country music. Lars raised his voice and snapped Kampe out of his trance.

"What? You not dance?" Kampe said in broken English. It was barely comprehensible over the radio blare.

Amanda disguised her chuckle at the sight of Kampe speaking English.

Lars explained his conversation with Amanda then asked him the question that she had asked initially. What did he think about America?

Kampe sat down at the table and lowered the volume on the radio. "I like music," he answered in broken English.

Lars responded in Inuktun then translated for Amanda. "I told him he can say anything he wants and that you are very open-minded."

Kampe turned off the radio and took on a serious look. He began to speak in Inuktun to Amanda. He suddenly came across far different than the goofy demeanor that he presented to Amanda since they met. She waited patiently for him to finish so that Lars could translate. He finished by looking at Lars squarely in the face.

"He said that first of all, you are the most peculiar and charming American he has ever met."

Her face turned red. She knew it was because she was traveling with a stuffed polar bear. How many Americans had he met anyway?

Kampe chuckled.

"He also said that your government disrespected his people when they, along with the Danish government, all but forcibly moved his fellow Inuit from their ancestral home in Thule, in 1953. He says you should see the toxic dumpsites, thousands of empty fuel barrels, and scrap metal that now contaminate his homeland."

Amanda said nothing, she didn't know what to say.

"He also says blaming a government is pointless. It is the culture and people behind the government. He also says we would be wasting our time blaming anyone. It is just better to realize our situation and improve."

"It sounds like some of the conversations we've had, Lars."

Lars said nothing as Kampe continued to talk.

Lars translated. "He says maybe our souls have been put in a particular position in life for a reason. Maybe in his next life he will be born in America, but he would prefer to be born an animal. Life would be simpler!"

Amanda didn't know what to say. "Anything is possible, I suppose. I don't know. I need to learn more."

"The families took their case of returning to their original lands to our supreme court, they lost," Lars added.

Amanda pursed her lips in a show of disgust. "How big is the base?"

"There are about one hundred each of American military personnel and Inuit civilians, and there are about five hundred Danish civilians."

"Sounds very small."

"Even if it is small, the impact can be much larger. In 1968, a B-52 bomber carrying nuclear weapons crashed and triggered some conventional explosives it was carrying. This spread its nuclear cargo of four weapons over the ice, about twelve miles from Thule base. The upper layer of snow was removed with the help of the Inuit. In 1995, about 50,000 Danish kroner was paid to each of seventeen hundred Danish and Inuit workers for radiation exposure. Hunters and fisherman avoid the area to this day."

"How much is that?"

"I think it was the equivalent of about nine thousand US dollars."

"When was the crash, again?"

"1968."

"After thirty years, less than ten thousand dollars each?"

Lars said nothing.

"Whatever. It all seems so pristine though, or whatever I might have saw from the air."

"Looks can be deceiving. Sediment was measured in the area of the crash in the early 1990s and radiation levels were found to be one thousand times higher then before in shellfish. Currents can spread the effects over a much wider area, just like Chernobyl. I've heard rumors of mutations and strange behavior in some animals, though I have never witnessed it myself. Who knows how these toxic materials affect the food chain. I have even heard of polar bears acting strangely."

Amanda shook her head. "War and weapons."

"Official Danish public policy had been that no nuclear weapons would be stored on Greenland. In the mid-1990s it was leaked that nuclear weapons were stored on Greenland in the 1960s contrary to public policy. It was called Thulegate."

"It sounds like the arrogance of government."

"The base has been in the news relatively recently too. Some years ago, your then secretary of state, Colin Powell, came to sign an agreement to upgrade the radar station. People feared that this would be the first step before the installation of interceptor missiles there."

"Are there any missiles there now?"

"To tell you the truth, Amanda, I don't really follow such news anymore, so I don't know the latest. I've been more focused on my IN ME."

Amanda puckered her lips.

"On the positive side, there were agreements, non-binding, that involved increased trade and economic ties, along with environmental and technical cooperation. Your country has also agreed to upgraded environmental protection standards in the Thule area, as well as including Greenland in various economic and research projects."

"To clean up those barrels?"

"Yes, to clean up fifty years of chemical and general waste. I only wonder how effective that will be. There were also some provisions for guaranteed fish exports to the US and university admission to Greenland students. When you transit again, maybe you will see the Greenland flag flying alongside the Danish and American flags on the base. I think it is a tentative first step in the right direction, all things considered. But, like we've talked about, IN ME."

She heard Lars, but couldn't stop. "Aren't there other places that a base could be located for missile defense?"

"I don't know, Amanda."

"I guess it all kind of takes me by surprise. It is as if there is no place left in the world that hasn't been touched by war or some sort of capacity to make it." IN ME, she thought again to herself as she pinched her arm.

Lars was about to respond when Kampe interrupted in Inuktun, though he did not understand their entire conversation.

"He says enough talk about the US base, he will help you find your polar bear. He says there aren't as many polar bears as there have been in the past and some have been getting smaller. He knows where to go."

"Ask him why they are getting smaller."

Lars continued to interpret both ways.

"He says he isn't sure why, but that maybe it is because the ice is melting sooner so that the bears do not have as much time to hunt seals on the pack ice before returning to Canada. He said he was traveling on the pack ice recently and saw a polar bear hunting beluga whales. He said he normally would not hesitate to kill it, but for some strange reason, he decided to respect it as a fellow warrior and left it to hunt."

"It sounds like the bears are getting smaller here for the same reasons we talked about before. Can you clarify to him that I am not here to hunt again?"

Lars restated Amanda's purpose in coming to Greenland.

"He said he understands, but hopes you don't look badly upon him for wearing polar bear pants."

She thought that to be an interesting observation. "Tell him I think no such thing. Tell him that they should be proud that they live in such close connection with their surroundings. Tell him I like his waterproof seal skin boots. Tell him I feel the spirit of the polar bears all around the village." Amanda wasn't sure just what got into her, but this place was definitely changing her outlook. As she said that, she realized she had used the p-word. She also said something a part of her didn't believe in, was it someone else's energy coming out?

Kampe responded.

"He said he is happy that you are beginning to understand their ancient ways. Maybe you will learn more about the spirit of the polar bear, you will learn to respect it as both foe and friend. He says he isn't sure of your religion, but he believes all things have spirits. Only when we respect and let these spirits inside our very core can we truly understand what they represent, the spirit of freedom itself."

Suusaat arrived back with the children. She prepared dinner while Amanda amused the children until going to rest in a small guesthouse nearby. She fell asleep with her most intense dream about meeting a polar bear yet, and wondering if she would fully understand the spirit of a polar bear's freedom too.

CHAPTER 26 – ON THE WATER

It was a clear morning in Savissivik. Amanda could see forever. There was no visible pollution or haze here. The surrounding treeless mountains looked close enough to touch, almost as close as the few lone icebergs out in Baffin Bay. Some looked to be frozen in place, others drifting. She knew they were much further away. It was a distorted perspective tricking the mind and eyes. In the Arctic it was easy to underestimate distances and heights.

What crazy sequence of events had brought her to this point in life? Greenland, a place she had never imagined nor had any desire to visit before. It was just a boring block of ice before on a map. Now, the battle for survival by a few hardy souls and the lessons this part of the world had on her, touched her deeply.

"We are ready," Lars shouted to her.

She smiled at Lars without saying a word.

"All three of us will dog sledge together until we get closer to where Kampe thinks we should go. He said it would be best to take an umiak as a wide shore lead has probably opened up."

"What's an umiak?"

Lars turned around and pointed toward the frozen shoreline.

"We're going to take that on the sledge?"

"No, no, there's a boat closer to the lead. The Inuit often leave a boat for the community to share and use out closer to the hunting area."

"We won't have to worry about getting stranded on a piece of ice then, right?"

Before Lars could say a word, another sledge and pack of dogs appeared. It was Kampe, but he looked more like an alien. He was wearing Inuit snow goggles. They were made out of solid bone with a small slit to see through.

"Interesting sunglasses."

"You can tell he's old school, as you Americans might say."

"Old school?"

Kampe took off his snow goggles.

"He was just trying to get a reaction out of you, Amanda."

Amanda all of a sudden realized that she had never seen Lars wear sunglasses. Didn't he mention something about natural sunlight? Now was not the time for that question. "Where did you learn to speak slang like that?"

"When I visited California!"

"Of course."

"Let's go." The familiar Inuktun words of hackfui, hackfui, were heard again as both Kampe and Lars let the dogs run.

Amanda's heart raced with anticipation that this could be the day when she would finally see a polar bear in the wild. Despite everything she had seen and experienced, the trip would somehow not be complete without a good sighting.

The horizon seemed to stretch forever as the three of them began their journey along the coast. A little further and what appeared to Amanda as a small rock outcropping, came into view.

The rock came closer and Amanda realized it wasn't a rock at all, but an overturned boat. It was the umiak.

Amanda could only wonder how Kampe had been able to lead them out to this spot with little visual reference, it blended in as if well camouflaged. Kampe and Lars called the dogs to a halt.

Kampe and Lars turned over the snow dusted umiak, the boat was in good condition. How they were going to use it remained a mystery to her for there was no open water nearby.

"Kampe says that the ice has broken up just over there," Lars proclaimed as he pointed off in the distance. "He left this boat here a few days ago. He says we need to take the boat to go near where he spotted a polar bear a few days ago."

"What next?" Amanda wondered aloud.

"It looks like the umiak is ok. We need to bring it to the floe edge."

"How are we doing that?"

"We'll hook it up behind a sledge and drag it."

"That won't damage the boat?"

"This umiak is made in the traditional way with driftwood and whalebone. It is covered with bearded walrus skin. We don't have to go very far. Walrus skin is more durable than wood out here. It's tough, but very flexible."

They hooked the umiak on and headed toward the edge.

She looked up at the sky and with her recent experience, she could tell the floe edge was not far away. They soon reached the edge. She was getting better at this Arctic survival business.

"I will stay behind to watch the dogs and sledges while Kampe and you will go out on the umiak."

"You're not coming?" Amanda's words pierced the cold wind.

"Somebody has to watch the dogs."

"Right."

Amanda watched as Kampe and Lars untied the umiak and placed it near the edge of the water. Kampe grabbed some supplies and put them in the boat.

"No guns," Amanda said firmly and instinctively. Kampe was about to throw his rifle into the umiak.

Kampe turned around, unsure of the meaning of Amanda's sudden concern.

Lars conversed with him.

"Kampe says one must always carry a gun, polar bears are unpredictable."

Amanda's contorted face of disagreement did not change.

All three stood still not knowing what to do next, both sides unsure of who would back down first.

"He said he will make an exception for you," Lars blurted out.

"He did?"

"Yes."

"I didn't hear him say anything."

"We know each other well enough."

"Thank you."

Kampe handed Lars the rifle then shouted out in the air as if giving up his position.

"What did he say?"

"He said, never argue with a woman."

Amanda laughed heartily. "Wise, very wise."

Lars grimaced.

"I'm bringing my stuffed polar bear. Is that a problem?"

Lars spoke to Kampe. "He doesn't see a problem with it."

She went back to the sledge and grabbed Polar Bear and the blanket she covered him with and put him in the umiak on the blanket. She snapped a photo for Haley.

They pushed the umiak off the floe edge onto the water. Kampe spoke a few words in Inuktun to Lars, then climbed into the boat.

"You will probably be out for several hours. Get in the boat now."

Amanda stepped into the umiak and seated herself. Kampe sat in back and Amanda sat in front. Polar Bear was in the middle. The cold water glittered in Amanda's eyes. She had come to trust her ability on the ice, now she would have to learn to trust herself on the water.

Kampe held the umiak at a distance.

She put her hand over the edge of the umiak and touched the water. Her fingertips created small radiating circles, she went no further. "That's cold." She already knew it was cold, she had washed her hands of seal blood earlier. This time, she would be surrounded by it.

"Kampe is now going to rock the boat a little bit side to side so you get used to the motion. Have you ever paddled a canoe before?"

"I think so, it was a long time ago when I was a child."

"Good enough."

Lars made sure Amanda was comfortable in the umiak and with rowing. "Good luck out there." Lars gave them a big push as they paddled out.

Kampe and Amanda paddled out to sea and down the coast. Soon, more pieces of ice appeared. A short while later and they were paddling in what seemed like a different world from the Arctic that she had become familiar with. It was as if the ice had different personalities. Sometimes it arranged itself like giant icebergs in Ilulissat, and here, sheets of ice shaped like pancakes sprawled out.

Navigating the waterways here did not look to be so easy. The pack ice was still plentiful although the warming temperatures of the approaching spring were creating navigable pathways. Her life was in the hands of Kampe, the best hunter in Savissivik.

They soon arrived at the entrance to a large shore lead. He spoke in Inuktun trying to explain something, but it fell on unintelligible ears. Even if Amanda could understand, she might have ignored it. Now, she was rowing a small boat in complete and utter silence, passing by an occasional modest sized iceberg. But more often they were pieces of pack ice, or bergy bits, smaller chunks of ice, six to twenty feet in diameter.

They spotted a seal. She took some photos. They moved on.

Once again, Amanda found herself in awe at the tranquility of the moment. No howling dogs this time. Just the sound of their paddles hitting the water. Kampe steered them down the lead. After twenty minutes of rowing, Kampe cleared his throat loudly.

Amanda turned around and saw Kampe making a sweeping motion while pointing to the left of the umiak. A large bergy bit on the right hand side was monopolizing Amanda's attention. To the left was pack ice closer to shore. Amanda looked back at him with a look of aloofness as to what he was making a fuss about.

Kampe started turning the umiak toward where he had pointed. Amanda knew there must be a reason for Kampe getting excited, she took off her sunglasses.

Then she saw it, two black eyes looking straight ahead. It was a polar bear, about forty-five feet away. It was laying low on a piece of pack ice. Its paws were covering its nose. It was very well camouflaged. Amanda was surprised she hadn't seen it sooner. Her eyes were not trained.

This was why she had come all this way. She turned and looked at stuffed Polar Bear and smiled. While stuffed Polar Bear sat motionless as always, this whole trip now took on an even greater meaning.

Her gaze was fixed on the real polar bear as if a magical spell had been cast on her. Nothing could take her laser like focus away from staring at the bear. Time slowed down.

She imagined the freedom that this powerful polar bear had as it lived out its life on these vast seas, true freedom. The freedom to go wherever it wanted, whenever it wanted.

The bear loomed ever closer in more detail as the umiak drifted closer. A splash. Had the bear been stalking a seal? Had the seal sensed their presence? Had they just ruined a potential meal?

The polar bear in the distance rose up on its four legs, then on its two hind legs. It must have been six feet tall by Amanda's guess. It stood up as if surveying its territory and wondering what strange and crazy human visitors would enter its remote domain and disrupt its quest for a meal.

It was a majestic sight. Amanda picked up her camera and snapped a few photos. She had almost forgotten about it in the glory of their meeting. As she raised the camera again, she saw her reflection in the black LCD screen which she had left off to save battery life.

She suddenly realized that magical moments like these were rare indeed, and that by picking up a camera to take a picture, she would remove herself from the moment. It would no longer be personally magical, it would be robbing the present to pay for the future. She put the camera away, and put to rest any fleeting thoughts of satisfying her ego-driven desire to snap a photo of herself with the polar bear in the background. She realized that this would be silly and she would only make a fool of herself.

She remembered that polar bears had a very good sense of smell. It had probably been eyeing them ever since they entered the area. Maybe it wasn't hunting a seal, maybe it was hunting them.

Kampe held the boat steady while Amanda wondered how such a large creature could support its own weight on the ice. How did it know which ice was safer to travel over? Did it learn from a parent, as Amanda had learned from Lars? Amanda motioned to paddle closer, the bear was now thirty feet away.

The polar bear crouched onto its four paws again. It moved closer to the boat and then leaped forward over a break in the ice. It moved to the edge of the ice it was now on.

The bear was now about twenty to twenty-five feet away and Amanda's heart was filling with pure magic. The magic of the moment was making her oblivious to all else. While Kampe had seen many polar bears, he seemed to be captivated by this bear and the magical aura that seemed to envelop Amanda. His search for a polar bear would often be in a hunt, this bear would be spared.

Kampe came to his senses and realized how close they were to the bear though. One more leap across another break in the ice and a few steps on the last piece of pack ice and the polar bear would be in leaping distance and a short swim. He signaled to Amanda his concerns, she understood. They began to steady and reverse their forward progress, but neither of them noticed the small bubbles floating to the surface of the water around them.

Unseen to Amanda and Kampe, a chunk of ice was about to break off from the underwater section of the iceberg now behind them. Tiny air bubbles rushed to the surface as it began to separate. Neither Amanda nor Kampe noticed it as their paddling and the presence of the polar bear distracted their attention.

CRACK, CRACK, more bubbles started rising. The chunk broke off completely and started rising from the depths. KOOSH!

The chunk of ice hit the bottom of the umiak. The umiak launched into the air. Amanda flew to the left and into the chilling Arctic water. Kampe flew off to the right and splashed into the water too. The umiak landed upside down. Stuffed Polar Bear, with his lighter weight, was hurled off into the water, but further past Amanda. Her stuffed bear began sinking into the depths of the cold Arctic waters.

Amanda hit the water hard. The cold frigid water rushed under her clothes and covered her skin. She swallowed some seawater. She knew she had to start moving and get to the surface, but the cold water, and concussive force from hitting the water, dazed her. She was frozen like a block of ice. Except she wasn't floating to the surface, but starting to sink to the bottom.

As her natural instincts to survive kicked in, she tried to move her arms, but they would not move. It was as if she had slept on both of them in bed and they had both fallen asleep. They felt like unwanted appendages from the body. She was in shock, her heart rate and blood pressure increased while her world was getting darker and darker. The blurred light from opening her eyes underwater was fading to black.

Were these her final moments? She was still struggling to mentally and physically gain control, time was running out. Before she could ponder any more thoughts of her fate, she felt herself gently being lifted up by something below. Suddenly she was being levitated across the icy water. Was this her soul being picked up and transported to heaven? Was this the work of an angel? Was she already dead?

Amanda re-entered the world above convulsing and coughing as the water in her lungs was forced out. She struggled to cough out all the water. She was barely conscious. She blacked out from the sudden change in temperature and blood rushing to her head.

Meanwhile, Kampe had been able to climb back into the now upright umiak. He had retrieved one of the floating oars and started paddling toward Amanda. Everything had happened so fast.

She lay on a piece of ice as Kampe paddled up to the ice she was on. She was cold and wet. He put his hand to her mouth, she was breathing. He dragged her body into the umiak.

They started the paddle journey back to the sledges. Unbeknownst to both of them, there were now more than just one pair of polar bears' eyes watching them leave.

CHAPTER 27 – RECOVERY

A warm sensation moved across her arms and legs. She felt it across her stomach and then chest. They were like hands on a body, her naked body.

She opened her eyes.

Two faces looked at her, their hands on different parts of her body. She saw their mouths moving but couldn't hear them. She couldn't speak either.

She closed her eyes and drifted back to sleep.

Amanda woke up to the glow of the stove warming up the igloo. She was no longer in her original clothes, but covered in the furs she had tried out earlier. Around her, the reflection of shadows from the flames reflected off the white walls. Was this heaven? She heard distant voices. Could these people be debating on whether she was worthy enough to enter heaven?

She looked at her clothes, they were not the clothes she thought she was wearing last. The clothes on her body now looked familiar, yet, they seemed strange at the same time. Not repugnant, just different. They seemed to represent some aspect of her that she had denied before. It was a feeling of the union between the 'animal world' and her very self. The fur she had so vilified before, now felt comfortable, though it still felt like only a dream.

"Where am I?" She spoke aloud to no one in particular.

"You're safe," a muffled voice answered.

"What time is it?"

"Time doesn't matter right now," the muffled voice answered again.

"What happened?"

"You're in an igloo." It was Lars emerging from the under snow line entrance.

This wasn't heaven!

She lifted her head and looked around. "Oh my, I thought I was somewhere else entirely. What, what happened?" she asked again.

"Are you alright?"

"A little cold," she replied in a raspy voice.

"We were warming you up with our hands earlier, your core body temperature was low from being in the water. You didn't hear us earlier, did you?"

"Thank you. I don't know. It seems like a dream. I must have passed out again."

"It must be the concussion. Kampe thinks a piece of ice hit the umiak from below. Both of you were thrown into the water. Kampe managed to get back in the umiak again, then he saw that you had somehow made it on to a piece of pack ice. When he got to you, he saw that you were unconscious. He said he couldn't see what happened because of ice blocking his view and his own struggle to survive. He made it back here with you and we decided to build an igloo to warm you up instead of risking a cold sledge ride back to the village."

"All I remember is looking at a polar bear, then being very cold and wet. Then everything started to get dark."

"You are safe now. Have some tea and save your strength. We will rest here tonight and go back tomorrow to Savissivik."

Kampe entered the large igloo as Amanda drank tea and ate boiled seal meat and fish that Lars insisted she eat to warm up. While she fought to get back to a sense of normalcy, Lars and Kampe spoke in Inuktun as if trying to solve a riddle. She sat quietly, trying to warm up.

"We were trying to figure out what happened out there. Kampe says that has never happened to him before."

"What has never happened?"

"A piece of ice breaking off from the underside of an iceberg right under the umiak. In the distance, yes. Icebergs do roll over, but they usually make noise before that happens. My best guess is that there was a warmer current in the area and it was focused on that area where the iceberg was. Perhaps the iceberg was just floating around in that same area, which gave this warm current time to melt that area. I really don't know."

"What happened to the boat?"

"You were lucky, it only suffered minor damage. It was still seaworthy though. The walrus skin must have flexed when hit."

"What happened isn't common?"

"No, not in my experience. The underside of an iceberg breaking off like that, is something I haven't seen often. I guess there was a warm current of water and it was focused on that iceberg. Things are changing around here."

"Figures, just my luck."

"I looked at the umiak. You were lucky, the umiak was probably hit by a blunt area of the ice. If it was a jagged or a pointy piece, you would have been in more trouble."

"That's encouraging to know."

"There may be another reason."

"What's that?"

"Do you still have the tupilak?"

Amanda thought hard for a moment. "It was in my coat pocket. Why?"

Lars grabbed her drying jacket and rummaged through the pockets. "Nothing here."

"It must have fallen out during the accident."

"All the better I suppose."

"Why? What about the tupilak?"

"I mentioned to Kampe the tupilak we found earlier. He thinks that maybe that is why you had bad luck out there."

"Huh?"

"He confided to me something he has never told me before in all the years I have known him."

"What is that?" she asked anxiously.

"He said his grandfather told him in his final days that he murdered another man over a woman. It was once common in traditional Inuit life. Nobody could ever prove it, but some people suspected Kampe's grandfather. Most convinced of it was a relative of the murdered man. Kampe thinks that maybe the tupilak we found was created by this relative to haunt Kampe's family."

Amanda pondered the revelation while staring into the flames of the stove. She wasn't a believer in such things, but in her current state of mind, she was open to hearing about anything which might account for their recent turn of events. Greenland was indeed turning out to be a strange place.

"On the positive side, he says that because both of you survived, it means that your combined magic power was stronger today. If there was a curse, it has been broken. He will have the village perform a celebratory drum dance tomorrow."

"Wow. I'll look forward to that," she quipped.

Kampe asked Amanda a question, then let out a small chuckle.

Lars laughed too, then interpreted. "He asks if you are happy that I brought a spare set of caribou & seal skin clothing?"

Amanda took notice of the clothes she was wearing again. She stroked the fur, only now fully realizing she was wearing none of her original clothes. She was wearing some spare undergarments under the fur. "Yes, I am glad you brought them." She smiled appreciatively.

"He jokes that you brought all this high tech clothing, but the 'low tech' skins protect much better." Kampe pointed at her drying clothes.

Amanda shared their laughter and wondered how arrogant it was of her to not accept the clothing offered to her earlier. Newer is not always better she thought to herself. Brand names are just that, logos stitched on fabric. They have their place, but she shouldn't have been attached to them.

She kept it to herself, but it also occurred to her that they had stripped her naked in order to put on her new set of clothes. She was unconscious and naked with two men who barely knew her.

Amanda's mind didn't dwell on the subject too long as her thoughts turned toward another matter. "What happened to Polar Bear, my stuffed animal?"

Kampe and Lars stopped joking. Kampe sat up from his crouched position and explained. He wildly moved his hands around to simulate the events earlier in the day.

"Kampe says he is sorry. He did not remember to look for it because he was busy rescuing you. He said it probably sunk to the bottom of the sea."

Her stone faced look, betrayed a great sense of loss. "Did I lose my camera too?" She took a deep breath. Her desperation to try and grab on to anything material and familiar in the face of so much loss was readily apparent. Now, not only did she not have her stuffed companion anymore, she no longer had any photographs of her entire trip.

"I'm afraid so. Even if we had found it, it would probably be ruined. I am sorry, too. Kampe also says he hopes that while your loss is great, and the circumstances less than ideal, that you will remember those moments when you were staring in awe at a real polar bear up close."

"Yes, I'll try. I guess I should be thankful to be alive. What happened to the real polar bear?"

"He thinks it ran off. He thinks it was scared off by the commotion."

The igloo fell silent with only the sound of the stove making noise.

Amanda broke the silence. "Lars, does your family ever worry about you when you are out here?"

"There is risk in everything we do, Amanda. There is a risk in living itself. I've been in situations, both here and elsewhere, where my life has been in danger. I've had close calls. I've seen friends and family die. If there is one thing I've learned, it is that when we strip away all the ideologies and beliefs about how we should live, or ideas about past or future life, life is simple. Very simple."

"How is life simple?"

"We live, then die. We are either here or not here. While we're here, we're going to be free. Free of the controlling fears and expectations that hold us back as much as we can. Whether they be physical or mental. And the more we've lived, the more, my wife and I, have learned that it is the mental and heart parts which haven't gotten nearly enough attention from either of us, or society as a whole. The Mind / No Mind we talked about, those statements can help liberate you."

"Free. . ." she muttered as she cleared her throat.

"Don't get me wrong, I am a careful man, but to live life controlled by our fear of death or anything else, is to not live at all. Some people may say they don't fear it, but look at their actions, not words."

"What if something really does happen?"

"My wife and I have agreed before, that whoever dies first, we will cremate the other and spread their ashes over Greenland, if there is a body. No sense in being stuck in the ground of a cemetery, though realistically, this does not matter to either of us. If either of us is severely injured, we will make sure the other one doesn't suffer."

"I wonder what I would do, cremation or burial? What do you think about heaven, Lars?"

"As a child, I was influenced by stories from my ancestors, the Vikings. I always remembered one aspect of Viking views on death. There is a mythical place called Valhalla, you might think of it as heaven. Except, Valhalla was reserved only for valiant warriors, men of valor. If you died in your sleep or just of old age, there were other lower, less desirable after lives awaiting you."

"Like Hell?"

"Not exactly, just less desirable."

"You try to live a life of valor?"

"Valhalla proper isn't something I believe in, Amanda. I'm just saying it influenced me. Valhalla was for warriors, but not all battles are fought with swords. As for a more general sense of heaven, if there is one, don't you think it would be peaceful? Do you think souls with dark energy would be let in? That's just my definition, though."

Amanda didn't answer.

"It sounds like the wind is picking up tonight. Good night, Amanda."

"Good night, Lars. Good night, Kampe."

With that, Lars and Kampe got up and went outside to take care of the dogs and the camp site.

As she lay in her sleeping bag covered by caribou skins, she wondered about the afterlife. Was Stephanie in heaven? What was that, really? Was everyone who ever died in heaven? Wouldn't that be crowded? People died at different ages too. That just didn't make sense. Yet, the few times she went to church, it seemed like everyone *thought* they were going to heaven. Pride. Positive bias. How often were our beliefs wrong? Was there really a hell? What was that like? Eternal fire and damnation?

Was Stephanie reborn again into another body and person somewhere on this Earth? Did we all have past lives? Didn't some places on Earth, look like hell on TV and in magazines, and some places like heaven? Somebody had mentioned at Stephanie's funeral that reincarnation was the only way to explain child prodigies. Was it also the only way to explain young children's dreams and early interests? Interests unrelated to their parents.

Or was it just evolution? You lived, then died. We came from apes on a big evolutionary tree. If that was the case, why would anything matter? Survival of the fittest during a few moments in time.

Maybe it was some combination of evolution and religion. Or was there some other explanation she hadn't read or heard about? Or was there an explanation that she wasn't open to because of her pride?

For a moment she thought of asking Lars for his opinion, but then realized, he would probably give her the same answer as he did about God. Learn for yourself. He would probably just say it didn't matter until we quenched our inner fire, to use a metaphor that he had used earlier. Get rid of your pride and dark energy. If pride was the worst sin and separated us from God, and everyone had dark energy, inner demons, and repressed feelings, then how would anyone know? Lots of people pointed to their holy books, but who wrote those holy books? They had dark energy, too. Didn't they?

She recalled some articles she read shortly after Stephanie had died. There were over a billion followers in each of Christianity, Islam, and Hinduism. There were hundreds of millions of Buddhists, and millions of followers of various other religions. But, all these religions started with a single individual. Wasn't it just like how new companies and technologies started? The ideas from one or several people spreading across society.

Were they all right and wrong in some way? It sounded much too complicated for Amanda. Before worrying about the afterlife or anyone else's thoughts, she realized, she should just clean up the mess on her inside.

If she asked all her co-workers to describe accurately the stars and Milky Way galaxy up above in Seattle, or anywhere near it, all of them would give her a blank stare. Because nobody in the city could see them. We could all be blind, and totally wrong, or partially wrong, but pride made many of us talk and think about the afterlife, as if we knew it.

But the afterlife could wait, for she was still alive. And while alive, she didn't want to be a prisoner of her dark energy.

"Live free or die, live free or die," she whispered to herself. Tears streamed down her eyes. She had accomplished what she had come to Greenland for, but at the price of losing her lifelong stuffed friend. To others it may have only been a lifeless stuffed animal, but it meant something to her. It was a price she hadn't yet come to terms with.

CHAPTER 28 – TOUCH

Sunlight seeped through the entrance of the igloo, it awakened Amanda. Kampe and Lars were already outside. How did they wake up so early, Amanda wondered.

"How are you?" Lars greeted Amanda as she emerged from the igloo.

"Feeling better and warmer."

"Are you still sad about losing your stuffed animal?"

"Yes," Amanda answered unequivocally. "I know it must seem silly."

"I know nothing can make up for your loss. At least you got to see a real polar bear in the wild. You can live with that memory."

Amanda nodded in agreement without verbally confirming.

"In my travels, I have had good and bad moments. Sometimes they occurred very close to each other on the same trip. It may be hard now, but the bad moments fade away and the better memories shine brighter. I hope this trip will one day be like that."

She didn't respond.

"Can you help me pack the sledge for our return trip back to Savissivik?"

"Of course," Amanda agreed quickly, thinking that anything she could do to take her mind off her loss would be good. She spotted Kampe walking back with his rifle. "Where did he go?"

"He was out hunting for seals, it doesn't look like he was successful."

Several of the dogs started to howl as Kampe approached the igloo, Kampe and Lars immediately looked around with a sense of alarm.

"What's wrong?" Amanda inquired.

"I'm not sure," Lars responded.

Kampe shouted and pointed off in the distance by a ridge covered with snow. An Arctic fox trotted across the ridge top.

Amanda looked up and didn't notice anything. "What is it?"

"It's an Arctic fox."

Amanda looked more carefully. She spotted it.

"Where there is a fox, there may be a polar bear," Lars explained.

The three of them gazed intently at the ridge top. Suddenly, slowly emerging over the ridge was the unmistakable face of a polar bear. Amanda, without thinking, sprinted a few steps forward to get a better look. "Don't scare it off!" Amanda exclaimed while waving her hands.

Kampe took heed of Amanda's words and went over to calm and quiet the restless dogs down. Kampe moved each sledge and dogs farther away from the camp site and the approaching polar bear, who seemed unfazed by the howling dogs.

"It might be hungry looking for food," Lars warned as he went to grab his rifle. "I wouldn't get too close."

Amanda stared at the bear, her second sighting in as many days. Was it the same bear? The bear began to crawl closer toward them, it moved down the ridge. As it moved forward slowly, Amanda thought she saw a flash of red around its neck. She blinked and rubbed her eyes. Was she hallucinating? She saw it again.

Had the red bow of stuffed Polar Bear, presumably at the bottom of the sea, somehow manage to get stuck on the other, real, polar bear? No, that seemed too implausible. Had her stuffed animal somehow become real? This made no sense at all. How could she even have such a thought? Her bear was a stuffed animal, not real in any shape or form, despite the emotions, imagined conversations, and personality she had given it all her life.

She tried to remember the day before. She closed her eyes for a few seconds and thought about the accident earlier. She thought about how she ended up on the ice after being thrown off the boat. She knew she didn't crawl up on the ice, or at least she didn't remember that. Maybe she did?

Then it struck her. Could it possibly be that the feeling she felt of being carried over water was from a polar bear? Her stuffed Polar Bear? Everyone had been telling her to expect the unexpected. Maybe it had something to do with the lost nuclear cargo.

Preposterous she thought to herself. Was she losing touch with reality to think that somehow her stuffed animal became real and saved her? There was just no other explanation at the moment. How else could this polar bear be wearing a red bow around its neck. Did the real polar bear save her while somehow getting the red bow tied around its neck? How would that happen? Why would the polar bear save her?

Lars emerged from the igloo with his rifle. Kampe came running back from quieting and moving the dogs away, he was carrying his rifle too.

"If it gets much closer, I am going to fire a shot into the air, Amanda."

She turned around to see if Kampe and Lars had noticed anything unusual about this bear. She wasn't that far in front of them, but perhaps she had a better angle. She looked again at the bear, she could see no red. Perhaps her imagination was getting the best of her. Perhaps she was imagining only what she wanted to.

The bear raised its head higher as if sniffing the air. Amanda clearly saw the red bow this time, it was unmistakable. Perhaps a magic of a different sort was working. "Put your guns down!" Amanda shouted back. "I saw a red bow on the bear."

Kampe and Lars looked confusingly at each other, but walked forward to take a closer look. They joined Amanda. The bear's head was down. Lars had his rifle ready.

"We shouldn't get any closer, the bear could charge us and we might have to shoot it. What did you say?"

The bear approached slowly and lifted its head up again.

"Do you see it? Do you see it? Do you see the red bow?"

Neither of them could find the words to respond, unsure of what she meant.

She turned toward Lars, stared him down, and grabbed the top part of his rifle. She pushed it back toward his body and shook her head from side to side. She then pushed the rifle butt to the ground.

Kampe's eyes widened, but he got the same unspoken command from Amanda. In this moment, she was more powerful than either of them. He offered little resistance as she did the same with Kampe and his rifle too.

Lars was about to speak, but before he could say anything, Amanda sprinted closer toward the bear. Any fears she had about approaching this potentially deadly animal had disappeared. She had a connection to this bear, it knew her. She felt a sense of calmness and confidence as she approached closer.

"Amanda!" Lars shouted. He started to chase after Amanda, but Kampe grabbed the back of his coat and held him back, muttering a few words in Inuktun.

Amanda moved ever closer to the bear.

The bear grunted.

Amanda got on her hands and knees. She was going to slowly crawl the rest of the way, she didn't want to scare it. It wasn't courage, it was her instinct. Now, she was fifteen feet from the bear.

The bear crawled forward to meet her.

Lars snapped out of his prior frame of mind, got a better angle, and raised his rifle, ready to shoot the polar bear.

She was confident that somehow she was doing the right thing. For the moment, she was fearless. She could hear the bear's every breath. "Polar Bear, Polar Bear," she cried out in a more childlike voice. "What happened?"

There was no response, only grunting from the bear as it cautiously moved forward in a non-threatening manner. Now, it was ten feet away. It moved its head around again.

"What?" Amanda thought. The red bow wasn't there!

Amanda was still on her hands and knees, but it was too late. If she moved, she might startle the bear and it might attack, or so she thought for a moment. She wasn't thinking at all. She decided to just wait.

The bear let out a puffing sound, it was waiting for Amanda.

Amanda's face reflected a state of confusion, unsure of whether to back away slowly or lie still.

The bear puffed again as it moved forward, it was only several feet away. The bear's breath drifted up toward the sky, then it abruptly sat on its butt. Still looking forward, it then put its nose into the air. It was as if it was doing some form of polar bear yoga.

It appeared to be anything but threatening to Amanda, as much as a large bear could.

Amanda lay motionless.

Then the bear did a belly flop and rolled around on the ground and settled in a low crouched position. The bear put its paw forward toward Amanda, the paw was only a couple of feet away.

Amanda looked around and had a strange thought as she glanced at some of the snow drifts. They appeared to take the form of the shapes she had seen in the Aurora Borealis. Spirals, undulating waves, snakes, and even a genie coming out of a bottle. It was magic uncorked.

She refocused and moved her arm toward the bear's paw. They touched. She could see the bear's black claws. She could feel it as her hand glided over the bear's fur. She brushed the fur some more. The bear puffed.

It slowly dragged its paw away and sat up on all four of its legs. Amanda was alarmed as the bear towered over her crouched body which was flush with the snow.

The bear turned as if it was about to run away and go back over the ridge, when it turned to face Amanda again. She could feel every breath it took in slow motion. The polar bear gingerly stepped forward and craned its neck out toward Amanda. Its eyes were closed. The bear stood motionless, patient.

Amanda realized the bear was waiting for something, she was confused as to what it was. Calmly, she sat up on her knees, undeterred that she was face to face with a real polar bear, the largest predator in the Arctic. The bear leaned forward a little more. It perked its ears.

She could see the bear's true black skin on its face, covered with a healthy amount of fur, colored white as it shone in the sun. She could see its muscles quivering. They both stood motionless until Amanda finally realized what the bear was waiting for, or at least so she thought. She put her trust in her instincts by crawling closer. Then, leaning forward and closing her eyes, she rubbed her nose against the bear's big black wet nose. They exchanged rubs several more times. The motion felt familiar, the setting, unworldly.

The bear backed away.

They exchanged another firm glance, then the bear turned around and ran up the snow bank. It turned around one final time and sniffed the air. As it kept its head raised, another polar bear face appeared from behind the ridge. There were now at least two polar bears.

Amanda waved at both of them.

The bears gazed intently for a few more moments then ran off.

Lars lowered his rifle.

She closed her eyes wondering if this was all a dream. She heard footsteps running up behind her.

"What just happened?!" Lars exclaimed in disbelief. "It took all my training to not fire."

She turned around until she was looking at Lars squarely in the face, still in an almost dream like state. "Things aren't always what they seem."

CHAPTER 29 – HARMONY

Amanda's spirits did a complete turnaround from the earlier accident. Rather than seeing the accident in a negative light, she saw it as part of a positive transformation. The moments of her encounter were running circles in her mind. She paused long enough to remember what the woman at the zoo told her before. She remembered Ruth's dislike for zoos and how it led to confrontation. She remembered the comments about her eye opening experience with wild elephants, lions in Africa, and deer in Japan. Now, Amanda had one of her own. Would anyone believe it? Did it even matter?

Nothing had changed in the village of Savissivik as they returned by sledge, but the three people who had left the day before, were much changed.

The inhabitants of the village came out to greet the three of them and learn of their success or failure. As Kampe replayed the events of the last couple days, looks of astonishment and disbelief appeared on many faces. The one thing they all agreed on was that a dance was to be performed.

Without much delay, the dance began. Everyone formed a large circle. Several of the villagers walked into the middle of the large circle carrying musical instruments.

"What is that?" Amanda asked Lars quietly.

"It's called a shallow. It is like a tambourine. It's an Inuit version of the drum."

The dancers used their drum sticks to hit the edge of the wooden hoops which were covered with animal skin and held by a small handle.

"I'm still wondering what happened out there," Lars whispered to Amanda as the dancers continued their performance.

"Don't think, isn't that what you said?"

Lars scratched his head.

The performance ended with several dancers in ceremonial masks appearing. As quickly as the villagers had assembled, they began to disperse.

Lars scratched his head again amidst the commotion. "Maybe what you experienced can be explained by a story I read about in a book about a certain polar bear in Churchill, Canada."

"What story is that?"

"It's about a dog that became friends with a polar bear. Sled dogs are often chained up to poles in Churchill. As I read it, on one particular day, all the dogs in one group, except for one, were barking and jerking their chains as a polar bear arrived. For good reason though, as polar bears had killed dogs that were chained up to poles before, but not this time."

Amanda listened attentively.

"There was one dog that didn't bark and stood its ground. I guess it wasn't afraid. It wasn't long before this dog and bear were playmates! They frolicked around, wrestling, rubbing fur, and even cuddled I think. I even read that the bear gave hugs to the dog and that they rubbed noses."

Amanda smiled.

Lars continued. "I don't know what happened between those two, but it was as if a magical spell had been cast on both the polar bear and the dog, from the pictures I saw. They played around for something like ten days in a row before the bear left Churchill and went out on the ice. You can find photos of it on the Internet. Apparently, there are recurring stories of this happening with more dogs and bears."

Amanda could only smile at the cute story. She hadn't even told Lars about the touching of noses.

"There's another explanation I was thinking about on how you survived such a close encounter with a polar bear."

"What's that?" Amanda's face glowed.

"Have you heard of the Galapagos Islands? They're off the coast of Ecuador in South America."

"It sounds familiar, but I've never been there, of course."

"The animals there are different, despite being wild. Some of the birds are so tame that they might land on your shoulder. A tourist I met told me that story. At the very least, they stay on or near the walking paths and don't run or fly away as quickly, if at all. Sea lions and fish may swim and play with you if you are scuba diving. I went scuba diving there and a puffer fish even followed us around. The sea lions touched me with their nose. They were very fast."

"Interesting."

"They have little to no fear of man. Perhaps this polar bear had no fear of man either."

"You mean woman!" Amanda clarified.

Lars let out a laugh. "The native wild animals were hunted initially, but now, they're all protected and allowed to 'live in peace.' What's interesting is that the introduced animals such as sheep, which are from domesticated stock, are now 'wild.' Yet, they've learned to fear man in a generation or two."

"That is interesting."

"These 'wild' domesticated sheep, live on the most remote and least accessible parts of islands. It is as if they quickly could remember how they had been treated at the hands of man. It is as if animals have a collective conscious and memory. They are scared of us because we over hunted or abused them."

"Maybe domesticated animals have dark energy in them, Lars. Just like we were talking about earlier, except with people."

"Yes, that could be. I haven't thought of it like that, Amanda. I don't know, I'd have to think about that more."

"So, if domesticated breeds, animals, have more dark energy, and truly wild animals have less, or none. . . or at least animals that have been wild for more generations, then we should stop trying to be so domestic? We should be more wild, so to speak, if we don't want to be fearful."

Lars hesitated, unsure of what to say next.

"Maybe it's just like you were saying, Lars."

"What's that?"

"We have to stop thinking about ourselves, being self-conscious. We should stop controlling ourselves. We need to let go and be wild."

"You're quick, Amanda. You got my head spinning. Maybe we were meant to meet in some cosmic way, except I was supposed to learn from you."

"Maybe we were supposed to learn from each other!"

"Yes, maybe. Perhaps the spirit of this bear recognized your gentle intent."

"I think so," she imagined as she closed her eyes.

"The animals in Antarctica are quite tame too due to lack of human contact, I know that first hand as well. I once saw a documentary on crows too and how they could recognize human faces."

"It sounds like we still have a lot to learn."

Perhaps it wasn't magic at all, Amanda thought to herself. But just a logical outcome of knowing ourselves better. Knowledge that would bring harmony among man, woman, and fellow animals. We were all kindred spirits.

"You must be strong in mind and spirit."

"Why is that?"

"For only the strong in mind, body, and spirit would have the courage to do what you did earlier."

Amanda could hardly contain the glow of her smile. "It wasn't courage, Lars. I was just acting out of instinct."

"Yes, yes. If you want to be mean, stay weak I like to say," Lars added.

She wondered if she told anyone the true details of her experience with the polar bear, would anyone believe her?

Lars interrupted her train of thought. "Despite this, next time, get your eyesight checked before coming. I'm going to get mine checked too, Kampe better too." He let out a hearty laugh.

"Yes and no, Lars. My eyesight was confused for a moment, but it's okay now. Really, we just need to get rid of all our fears, our dark energy, our pride."

Kampe wandered over to the two of them. Looking Amanda straight in the eye he grabbed her hand and placed a small object in it. He closed her hand in a tight fist around the object before she could see what it was. He offered a few final words.

"He said he is glad you found what you are looking for, not very many people do. He says he hopes you will always remember this place. He says he will share your story with others here. He asks you to share what you learned and felt here in the Arctic with others too."

"Of course."

Kampe then shared another insight.

Lars translated. "He said he thought of an explanation for what happened earlier in the water and on land. He thinks that maybe the real polar bear saw that you were friends with another polar bear, your stuffed animal. So, when the real polar bear saw that you were in trouble, it saved you."

"I like that explanation," Amanda mused.

Kampe had a few more words which Lars translated. "They will continue to honor the spirit of the polar bear. He said they must continue to honor all life even as their ability to hunt them changes. He said they have quotas, but perhaps, just maybe, if they become as friendly with polar bears as you have, they will hunt it no more. He also said you will have to someday return here to teach them your magic power."

She opened her fist. It was a small, hand carved, polar bear figurine. She smiled for a few moments then looked up at Kampe and embraced him.

"Qujanaq."

"Yoo welcome," he replied.

As Amanda woke up from one of her final nights in Northern Greenland, she looked at a mirror inside her small, simple, guest house.

Facing right back at her was the face she knew well, except it looked different. Her face was more radiant, her wrinkles had softened, and her complexion looked better. It was a reflection of her spirit beginning to be more free, and more rest from the daily grind.

She couldn't wait to go home and buy or construct a similar mirror to the one she saw in Copenhagen, the one that showed herself unreversed, the way everyone else saw her. Perhaps she would get one final chance to look at the unreversing mirror in Copenhagen again.

As she looked at the mirror, she made faces of anger, rage, and jealousy. She could feel these feelings coursing through her body. This dark energy was inside her, she wanted to get it out. She needed to draw it out, but these dark feelings wanted to stay hidden. She repeated Mind / No Mind at herself as she looked in the mirror.

She still had another day to reflect on her recent polar bear encounter. She strolled around the village, burning all the shapes and colors into her mind. She held on to the polar bear figurine as she walked around Savissivik.

After an evening meal with Kampe's family, she retreated to the cozy confines of her small guest house. She breathed in the cool evening air from an open window and felt the growing sense of freedom inside her. She knew she was ready to stop imagining the possibilities of life, she was ready to live them. Now, she had the courage to be freer, from the inside out. It was a choice.

This trip into the Arctic had helped her to forget about the troubles, hopes, fears, and daily emotional struggles that followed her around. It was a place where you easily forgot your own name. The power and legacy of your name, and the expectations of your name. The name you saw written on your business card, mortgage payments, utility bills, emails, school report cards, credit cards, on your diplomas, in the company newsletter, and on your social networking profiles, or even the name implicitly attached to a photograph online.

It was a complete forgetting of your sense of self, a forgetting of your ego. It was a step in learning to *just be*. Modern technology for many was only increasing our sense of self. There were some things Amanda would have to re-evaluate.

A strange sense of here and now pervaded her feelings at the moment. She wasn't excessively focusing on the past or the future. Too much of either made one hold on to old grudges and unhealthy ways of doing things, they would only limit her ability to live a better life. Both past and future had their place, the trick was to find the right balance. It was a balance that Amanda felt was realigning itself inside of her.

We held on to grudges because we thought about ourselves in relation to others too much. We got angry because we didn't let our feelings out earlier. We let others control us because our sense of being was too weak.

This choice to free her inner spirit was one where she would stop lying to herself and see the truth about her own life, and the world we had created. She was going to follow her instincts more. She was going to follow her heart more.

Pride in her career success and her perception of rising up the imaginary ladders of life had blinded her to many other possibilities of life. Climbing the ladders had also made her fearful. After all, it was scarier up high, than on the ground. She was learning 'to ground' herself. There was more than one way to play and interpret the game of life.

She didn't want to be like Stephanie either, letting a marriage suppress her heart either. There would be a better balance for Amanda, she just had to find it.

In fact, she didn't want to be like anyone else, she just wanted *to be*. There was no need for any role models.

Now that she was feeling good about herself, she better understood the Mind / No Mind phrases. In fact, they seemed to make obvious and perfect sense. If she was overly self-conscious during her bear encounter, she would have panicked. The earlier accident had helped to put her in a different state of mind. Was there a way to make it last, without having to be in an accident?

She READ OUT LOUD the I-version again.

Mind / No Mind

I-Version

1) I shall never feel special

2) I shall never feel important

3) I shall never feel smart

4) I shall never feel anyone cares about me

5) I shall never feel I can teach anything

6) I shall never feel shame

Out here, she wasn't special or important. She thought she knew better with all her high tech clothes, but that clearly turned out to be wrong. She had a lot to learn. Now, she wondered why she ever felt smart at all. There was so much about the world that she had no first hand experience with. She was 'dumber,' and not feeling threatened by it. For the moment we felt too smart, we stopped learning. It was becoming more clear that we could learn from anyone at anytime. Anyone, included animals. This would help her at work, in relationships, and everywhere else in life.

As for the last few phrases, they seemed to make more sense now too. For too long now she had been crippled in her relationships by her parents' divorce and her mother's lack of attention afterward.

If people accepted that nobody needed to care about them, they would avoid being dependent on them for their own happiness. Children wouldn't be smothered and spoiled with their parents' love, nor would children have too many expectations that their parents, and family, be perfect and normal, whatever that meant. There was no such thing as normal.

Perhaps parents wouldn't use their kids as distractions for their own inner lives. Of course people would still care about each other, but it wouldn't become a requirement, nor taken for granted. Her experience out here had shown that people instinctively helped each other.

There were more lessons, but she didn't want to think too much now.

As for not feeling like one could teach anything, Amanda realized that Lars never looked 'down on her' for her lack of Arctic knowledge. He was just sharing his experience and stories.

As for shame, she had always been self-conscious of her own body, perhaps unhealthily so. It seemed so normal, as all the women she knew behaved the same way. All the women she knew wore makeup, in part because they were ashamed of their real faces. Later, she would learn how dark energy and repressed feelings and stress aged our faces faster, much faster.

Shame was also because they had all grown up the same way more or less. They all saw and heard the same messages from television, magazines, Internet, and each other's actions. It was a cult of shame over our own bodies. It was like her memory of the frog in the camp bathroom. She didn't need to be in this group any longer.

She could think of the times of being naked before in front of others, she had always felt a little uncomfortable and embarrassed. Now, she felt this much less after having been changed out of her wet clothes by two men she barely knew. There was no shame in being naked, and there was no shame in the naked human body. There was no shame in accidentally being seen going to the bathroom out here. She knew she still had shame, but she looked at it differently now. More mind work was necessary. More *heart* work was necessary.

There was no shame in failure, there was no shame in not meeting the expectations of other people or society, or ourselves. There was no shame in being wrong, or doing wrong. It was just cause and effect. There were other forms of shame, she would have to write about them later in her journal.

Here she stood now in this vast expanse, happier than at anytime before. It wasn't a superficial happiness, it was a deep contentment. It was a deeper comfort with her being.

She headed outside and took a look at all of the twinkling lights again in the sky. The stars of our Milky Way galaxy contrasted with the light from the few homes of Savissivik. She would clearly miss this part of her trip when back in Seattle.

For the first time, she could connect the twinkles and see constellations. They were something that she had never been able to see before with her own eyes.

We had traded the beauty of lights in heaven for artificial lights that spread throughout our cities. Maybe we had so many artificial lights because we were afraid of the dark, our dark energy. We were afraid of confronting our own deep feelings.

Amanda would later learn of people who could see better in the dark, better night vision. Much better. Maybe we all had this ability if we got to know ourselves, our core being better. These people had better eyesight than what was considered normal or good. Eyesight that could identify objects in the night sky that those with what was considered good vision, 20 / 20 or even better, could only see with a telescope.

Perhaps one day when more people got to know their core being, the light of heaven would replace the artificial light of those who had feared their own dark energy.

She noticed a familiar show as her gaze scanned the sky, it was the Aurora Borealis. This time, it took the form of a coronal aurora. Parallel lines of light seemed to go out into space and touch infinity.

She did a triple take and rubbed her eyes to make sure she wasn't seeing things again. Not this time. She was reminded of Polar Bear's red bow. For the most striking feature of this light show, was that it was filled with fire red streaks of light, the most rare color of them all.

CHAPTER 30 – NOTES AND LETTERS

The peaceful atmosphere of the airline lounge was a welcome sight after looking at mostly ice for the better part of two weeks. Amanda found herself here again after a late arrival. As she went to find a seat, she walked by a mirror and noticed that she had lost a few of those extra pounds she'd been piling on over the last year. Adventure could be good for you. She flashed the mirror a cautious smile and took a seat.

It would be nice to hear some familiar voices she thought. She searched out the nearest phone and rang up Jack and Haley. Their familiar voices were comforting to her travel weary mindset. A few pleasantries aside, the toughest questions were from Haley, who wondered whether Polar Bear enjoyed the trip. To her surprise, Amanda informed her that he wasn't coming back. She would explain the whole story later.

As Haley asked about the pictures she took, Amanda answered that while her camera was lost, a picture *only* told a thousand words. She would have to try and show Haley how she felt.

Now that she was back in civilization, Amanda thought about what really happened out there again as she hung up the phone. It was something magical.

Perhaps it had something to do with the sunken nuclear weapons affecting animal behavior, probably not. Maybe there was some truth to that Inuit curse and magic. Or perhaps it was just a friendly and unafraid bear that saved her life. Maybe it was unafraid because she wasn't afraid in that moment.

Maybe it was Kampe's explanation that she was seen to be friends with another polar bear, her stuffed bear on the umiak. Or maybe, it was because in her heart she was always fond of polar bears and somehow the other bear knew it. Perhaps the bear sought her out once it picked up her scent from far away. Maybe it was all meant to be, some larger force at work.

A trite and romantic explanation was that there were two bears. The stuffed bear of her childhood who listened to her troubles while far away from home, and now the free bear – who helped teach Amanda her most important lesson in life. Maybe her stuffed bear was trying to tell her something all this time when she imagined him to be real.

Perhaps things would have turned out differently in her life if she had 'listened' sooner. What about all the other stuffed animals out there? What if everyone started 'listening' to their stuffed animals more? Maybe all the stuffed animals wanted to return to the wild to join their brothers and sisters? What if we just learned more about how to live and be free from our wild counterparts, rather than looking down on them? Rather than imprisoning and gawking at them.

With that, Amanda wondered just what she could possibly show Haley that would convey any semblance of the photographs in her heart, not in her head. A sense of dread over going back to the concrete jungle entered her mind.

Almost as quickly as she thought of the words concrete jungle, she realized there was something wrong about it. A jungle, a wilderness, was a place of timelessness. Not crime, confinement, or fear, apart from basic survival. It was largely free of greed, anger, hate, jealousy, despair, brand names, machines, and bloated egos. Maybe it wasn't a jungle she was returning to, it was a concrete and steel zoo. But if more and more people got closer to their core being, maybe it would become something, completely different.

She went over to the counter and grabbed a few pastries, then decided to drink a beer. She looked at the beer differently. The Danish treated beer casually and drank it frequently. It wasn't evil, it was just a drink. It was like how the Danish looked at bicycles, not as a toy, but just as a mode of transportation.

This wasn't a drink of guilt, it was just a drink to relax. Though she started to wonder just what was causing her to be 'unrelaxed' and more tense and wanting to drink a beer. Why did she need a beer? On that note, why did people think of tea and coffee as calming? Didn't that mean we weren't calm and peaceful on the inside? Didn't Lars mention that caffeine was a pain-reliever? What pain was she relieving? Did he really tell her that? Or had she absorbed these thoughts by osmosis? This investigation would have to be for another day.

It was time to get back in touch with what was going on at work in her other life. As she looked around for a computer, she noticed an open newspaper lying on a desk. It was a popular British tabloid newspaper, with three million daily readers it proclaimed.

She leaned down and glanced at the story that someone had been reading. The heading said: *Denmark is Tops in Happiest*

Surveys and Least Corrupt. She leaned over and read the first few paragraphs. It said the same things she had learned earlier about Denmark consistently being the happiest country in the world, but then it mentioned something else she had not learned before.

It said, once again, Denmark was at the top of Transparency International's list of least corrupt nations in the world. It was a ranking of nearly every country in the world based on the perception of corruption.

Wasn't that another way of just saying, which countries had the most honest people? She looked at the abbreviated list of countries which were in a small table. Behind Denmark at the top were the other Scandinavian countries and those near it - Norway, Sweden, and Finland. New Zealand, Switzerland, and Singapore were other notables near the top. The USA was in twentieth place. Amanda immediately noticed the correlation between countries that were the happiest and the countries that were the least corrupt, or as she saw it, the most honest.

What was more interesting to Amanda was the Transparency International score shown to the right of each country. Denmark's score was approximately an A-. After Denmark, there were the other top countries with the equivalent of B grades. America's score was the equivalent of a C. The USA's neighbor to the north, Canada, received a B-. Mexico, to the south, received a grade below an F. Now, she understood why Mexico was always in the news over drug and crime problems. But, a better question was, why were the people there so dishonest?

Why were some countries more honest or less? Was it culture? Weather? People with too much pride? A culture with too much pride? Why did some cultures have a lot more pride than others? She didn't know the answer to that, but perhaps someday she would learn the answer. Maybe she had to get rid of her pride to learn the answer.

When it came to honesty, apparently, no nation, as a group, got a perfect score of 100%. There were no A+ countries. There were no countries with a straight A score either. There were no brainiacs who got everything right when it came to honesty, like there was in the many college and high school classes she had taken.

But weren't some travel articles always glowing about how great the culture was in various countries? At least the travel articles she had happened to read in the newspapers or on the Internet over the years and remember at the moment. From Amanda's perspective, it seemed that culture played a large role, not the only one though, in determining how honest people were.

These corruption statistics did not get advertised in the tourism brochures or mentioned in travel articles, Amanda thought to herself. Of course, it was just marketing, her forte. Eliminate the negative, emphasize the positive. Or maybe it wasn't marketing, it was just a positive bias that blinded us to something darker. We saw only what we wanted to see.

Funny, how she had never seen this statistic in the news before. Was eliminating the negative, by not talking about it, and emphasizing the positive, a recipe for personal happiness? Collective happiness? Positive and negative were all relative to one's own experience and level of observation though, and now Amanda had a new perspective.

Maybe there was something in all of our cultures that caused us to be dishonest. She knew what it was.

If Jante Law was at the foundation of Danish and Scandinavian thinking, then pride made you lie. Yet, people the world over were always trying to be more proud. Because we had convinced ourselves that it was better for us. Perhaps on the outside sometimes, but not on the inside. We had become suckers for pomp and circumstance, and our self-image.

She let out a yawn, she was tired. She sat back in the chair and closed her eyes for a few minutes, wondering about this new revelation about Denmark. She drifted off to sleep.

Amanda woke up and panicked for a moment, until she realized she was still in the lounge. Her belongings were still with her, and after checking the clock, she realized only ten minutes had passed. She had been cat napping.

The paper she was reading was still on the desk in front of her. She looked at the article again, then it hit her right then and there, the complete secret to happiness, joy, and peace in mind and heart.

We couldn't be *completely* happy unless we were honest with ourselves, and all of our feelings, thoughts, and actions, *all* of them. The more honest we were with ourselves and others, the less we had to worry about keeping track of lies, even little ones, and more importantly, less worry about maintaining our self-image. Wasn't that how hypocrisy started? We said one thing and did another, or vice versa. And as she had that thought, she realized again, the power of Mind / No Mind.

Along with the other benefits she had thought about earlier while still with Lars, she realized the statements did away with self-image, so there was no image to worry about. It wasn't immediate, but she sensed it would happen over time.

Women, like herself, were good with that, it was almost automatic. Putting on makeup, covering up blemishes, hair spray, looking as perfect as possible, and having the right accessories and jewelry on.

Then there were the push up bras and shapewear to deceive others about one's figure. Screw perfect. She hadn't touched her makeup while in Greenland and she was wearing what was comfortable, not anything specific to accentuate or exaggerate some part of her body. These were just related to the *physical* self-image she realized. Maybe if she got rid of her dark energy, somehow her physical body would heal and improve. After all, didn't getting rid of stress make you not just *feel* younger, but *be* younger?

Then there was the *personal* self-image. There was saying the right things in a diplomatic manner and all sorts of unwritten rules about how to say what and when. People wrote books and newspaper columns about this. Social graces and manners, it was enough to make your head spin. Next time she got a Christmas fruitcake from some distant relative, would probably be the last.

People she knew at work did the same thing in regards to self-image, but they were self-conscious of their *professional* image. Some were more self-conscious of their *social* self-image, marriage included. Some people worked harder to keep up appearances more than others. But, in every case it was people being self-conscious. We were thinking about ourselves. Wasn't that stressful and by definition, unhappy? Why did 'we' do it then?

It was because we had been dishonest with ourselves for so long, over so many generations, we didn't even know the definition anymore of what it meant to be truthful to ourselves or others. 100% truthful. Dark energy was in everyone.

The truth was relative Amanda knew, but wasn't this all about being truthful to one's self at the very core? Or rather, one's core being, as our 'self,' was an illusion. The layers on top and around our core being had to be stripped away. Tears would have to come out like peeling an onion.

We kept covering up our inner feelings, until for some, the urge was too strong and it couldn't be covered up. We covered it up by doing things that distracted us from our inner thoughts and in some cases, life situation. Whether that was by shopping, some form of entertainment, or work. We covered it up by eating certain things. Chocolate immediately came to mind for Amanda. She knew alcohol did the same too, it just delayed the inevitable. What else?

People usually didn't think of themselves as liars, but it was true when you included the little lies, and sometimes big, lies of the heart Amanda realized. These bigger lies included those in relationships and marriage from one or both sides, and lies between friends, for whatever reason. Those lies were sometimes at the very deepest part of hearts. When we told someone else we didn't want to be with anyone else, even though we secretly did. Sometimes we told ourselves that we loved our job, when in fact we didn't. Or people lied to other people in order to get ahead. Maybe some called it exaggeration, stretching the truth, or selective fact telling.

Then there were the lies to protect our image in certain professions which came as part of the territory. Politicians running for office, lawyers, and executives came to mind.

Amanda decided then and there she didn't want to be like this. If others did, that was their choice. She wouldn't make the same mistakes as her parents, Stephanie, or people in the news, or anyone else she suspected of living a lie in some form. Any lie to others and to ourselves slowly ate away at our soul. She knew she couldn't change overnight, but she could change.

Then she suddenly remembered something she had read once in a book. It said that the more you lied to other people, the more you lied to yourself. Did that make one happy in the long run?

Lie was the wrong word, really, she thought to herself. For what was the truth and what was a lie was in the eyes of the beholder. They were just individual choices based on our experience and knowledge base. She would have to continue to improve both of these, by learning from others, more questions, and traveling when appropriate to gain more varied life experiences.

It was tricky these days. People you thought were 'happy,' you realized were not *that* happy or free as portrayed, when you found out the *whole* truth, or rather, whole story, about these people's lives. Happiness was relative.

She focused again on the article. It went on to note how the Danes lived and other details of their lives, but it didn't mention the real deep reason. The really deep reasons that she had learned from Lars and from just thinking about it, as it applied to her. The why behind how to be happy, behind the more superficial reasons given in the article about how the Danes lived, which Amanda realized, weren't particularly important for now.

It was simple, the Danes, and people of other countries that were consistently at the top of *both* happiness and honesty lists, as opposed to the temporary happier countries, just didn't think about themselves as much. It wasn't all about me-me–me and I-I-I. Social networking profiles came to mind.

The happier people were those who forgot about themselves more and had less to worry about. And now she had an exact recipe on how to forget about herSELF more. There was more as Lars alluded to, but she would learn that when she was ready.

She would learn what she needed to, when she needed it. Whether it was from Lars, or someone else, or some other experience.

She pulled out the laminated cards and read the statements again and again. Tears streamed down her eyes. She sensed she was fighting the energy of other people, but couldn't yet tell whose they were. It didn't matter, she wanted to let go of all her dark energy. She didn't want her emotional baggage.

No more emotional demons. No more feelings of awkwardness and shyness in any situation. No more feeling bad over other people's problems. No more legacy feelings from her parents or whomever that would limit who she could be.

No more fear in any situation, just cause and effect. No more worrying about things she didn't have control over, nor the things she did have control of. No more superficial act to maintain appearances.

No more moments of depression. No more feeling foolish or ashamed about anything. No more feeling fat, ugly, or worse. It wouldn't all go away at once, but the tide was turning.

I-Version

1) I shall never feel special

2) I shall never feel important

3) I shall never feel smart

4) I shall never feel anyone cares about me

5) I shall never feel I can teach anything

6) I shall never feel shame

As she repeated the statements, she realized maybe we didn't need to feel anything, we could just BE, with natural emotions, that didn't include all the icky ones. We wouldn't be heartless, but just the opposite. Heartless people were those who suppressed our true 'heart,' and relied on too much logic, logic that could be twisted.

She started to think about everyone she knew and started directing the next sets of Mind / No Mind statements at them.

You-Version

1) You shall never feel special

2) You shall never feel important

3) You shall never feel smart

4) You shall never feel anyone cares about you

5) You shall never feel you can teach anything

6) You shall never feel shame

We-Version

1) We shall never feel special

2) We shall never feel important

3) We shall never feel smart

4) We shall never feel anyone cares about us

5) We shall never feel we can teach anything

6) We shall never feel shame

As she read aloud the last statement, as loud as she could in an airport lounge, she felt a strange sensation across her forehead. It was as if her mind was relaxing. She remembered learning about that. There was a seventh statement too, she would discover it later when she was ready.

She stood up and glanced around the lounge and noticed an open computer terminal. As she looked into the computer screen, nearly unconsciously, she saw her complexion was blurry, yet, she was feeling rejuvenated and full with a new sense of freedom.

She had been incommunicado with the whole world that she had ever known for more than two weeks. It was one of the best decisions she had ever made. It was time to return though. Changes would be in store, but she didn't know what they were yet. She logged on and checked her email, there was a message from Kayla.

Hi Amanda,

I hope everything is going well over there in Greenland. I'm having a great time traveling in Europe. You are never going to believe what happened after you left on the train back to the airport. You know the guy you bumped into at the bicycle stand? The tall charming one. He started bicycling to an important meeting, then realized he had to meet you. So he went back looking for us. He ran around looking for us.

After you left on the train, he saw me at the train station. What luck! Of course, he asked all about you and where you were going. He really wants to meet you. Maybe it was meant to be.

I met him for lunch on another day to see if he was legitimate before I bothered you. We talked about you like we were old friends. Forgive me for any embellishment and excess flattery. I even got to meet the people he put off to find you later.

Who is he? Did I tell you that high ranking officials still bicycle in Denmark? Well, he turns out to be a businessman in the city who had some civic issues to discuss with people of note. He was impressed with my knowledge of city planning and ideas for improvement.

He said the people he was going to meet were not
terribly happy, but understood his predicament
when he told them. Danish tolerance! Danes aren't
normally like this, so you must have really put a
spell on him in those brief moments.

By the way, his meeting was with the Queen of
Denmark.

– Kayla

Amanda chuckled. She turned away from the computer
screen and noticed the mobile phones and laptops. They brought
back memories of her boss and Billy. She scanned the other
emails waiting in her inbox and realized that she had forgotten to
send an important presentation file to Billy. A potential multi-
million dollar account was dependent on that file.

"Damn it," she whispered to herself.

The email continued that it was urgent that she return for
the meeting, the client was ready to make a decision. She com-
mitted the meeting to her mental to-do checklist.

She always did the right thing, it was nothing to worry
about. Perhaps they were just exaggerating in the email anyway,
drama kings and queens. There was a difference this time though.
She quickly directed a 'You shall never feel special' thought to-
wards Billy. Maybe it would somehow reach him.

Maybe we were all connected in some unknown way.
Maybe it was akin to how some mothers 'knew' what you were
thinking, before you even told them. Or when you answered the
phone sometimes and it was someone you were just thinking of.

Or when you had a gut feeling about something and it turned out to be true, beyond any rational explanation. Or when someone whom you knew was feeling bad, made you feel bad, even though there was no particular reason in your life that you should be feeling bad. Perhaps it was a question she would ask Lars someday if she saw him again.

If it were true, wouldn't our thoughts and actions affect people whom we shared energy with? Both with people whom we knew and people we didn't know personally. If we had violent and angry thoughts, it would affect someone else. That someone else, could be an important person. If this were true, then to make the world a better place, we could flush out our dark energy and it would make other people happier, over time, just like having a better 'vibe' around other people. Double bonus she thought to herself.

She sensed it could be true, but it wasn't until she learned about a physics principle, quantum entanglement, that she began to realize it really could be. As for how and why we might all be connected, that was another mystery for the future.

As she directed that thought to Billy, she thought about Chip again and his affair that he hid from Stephanie. Maybe they weren't right for each other, even if Stephanie was still alive. She directed a 'You shall never feel shame' at Chip. Maybe she would tell him in person someday. Maybe she would share Mind / No Mind with him. After all, Chip was connected to her, just as she was connected with Haley.

The world didn't need any more feelings of guilt, which led to shame, which led to people holding secrets, which led to holding in feelings, which led to stress, and worse, once it became too much tension to hold in. There was dark energy in his past, that he didn't understand, that caused him to lie.

She got up from the computer and headed over to the restroom. As she walked past the sinks she saw herself in the mirror
again. It was different this time when she looked.

Just as the special 90° angled double mirror in Copenhagen
had shown her, 99.9999% of mirrors out there did not present
an accurate image of who we truly were. As she turned away, she
also realized why she had never given Polar Bear a real human
name. And why Polar Bear had been her most reliable and un-
judgmental friend, even if he was just a stuffed animal.

She left the restroom and sought out a desk. The clean de-
signs of the Danish furniture which surrounded her helped to
clarify her thoughts. She started a letter on a notepad she found
nearby.

Dear Haley,

*Happy birthday! The world around you is a magical
place. Don't believe for a moment that it exists only in
some artificial kingdom. It exists all around us in nature,
wild nature. As you get older, forces will conspire
against you to try and crush your soul, which wants to be
wild and free. Trust your instincts more, not completely,
but more. Over time they will become more accurate, until maybe someday you won't have to 'think' at all, you
can just be.*

*Don't ever try to grow up too fast, and don't ever lose your
ability to see the world as a child. Adults are stubborn
and get set in their ways. As you know your instincts better, and I'll show you how if you want, someday, when*

you least expect it, spontaneous, unexpected magic, will find you. It's the best kind of magic there is.

Enclosed, please find your birthday present. Here is a coupon for a round trip ticket anywhere in the world to begin an adventure. A search for a wild animal of your choice. Maybe a tiger or a panda bear in India or China. Or maybe whales in Mexico.

She folded up the letter to give to Haley when she was older. In the meantime, maybe there were some wild animals close to Seattle that Amanda would take Haley to visit.

Ripping out an empty page, Amanda started writing a short note. It said that the joy of living freer was when we learned to live closer to our uncontaminated instincts, and that the way to better our instincts more and more was to let go of our pride and just learn *to be.* She wrote down the Mind / No Mind phrases by combining all three versions into one statement.

She felt another relief in pressure on her forehead again. Maybe she needed to learn about face reading someday she reminded herself. Did people with foreheads that bulged out have more pride and stress to maintain that pride? This was another question for the future.

Amanda grabbed her bags and walked up to the agent at the lounge counter. "Excuse me, can you confirm when the flight to Seattle is scheduled to leave?"

"It is on-time and scheduled to depart at 8:00 p.m., arriving Seattle at 8:55 p.m."

She checked her watch, it had stopped working. It must have been when she fell into the frigid water. It was supposed to be waterproof. Perhaps it wasn't Arctic cold waterproof though.

There was an irony to this. While during her adventure she felt a sense of timelessness, now that it was over, she could remember every day, night, and story, distinctly. The days had not blurred together, like they did in the rat race. "What is the fastest way to the seashore?"

"You can either hail a taxi and go to Dragør, about five kilometers away, or Kastrup. You can also go back into Copenhagen and bike, walk, or hail a taxi there. There is a map at the information counter outside."

Thanking the agent, she ran out of the lounge.

Throwing caution and fear to the wind, she put her large backpack in storage once again and ran to the train station as quickly as she could.

There was one stop to make before the sea, she needed to see her unreversed self again. Returning to the small shop, she gazed into the mirror made from two frameless mirrors at a 90° angle. Looking into the corner, she saw herself unreversed again. There was no need to turn away now, she was not as dismayed by her image. A part of her still felt uncomfortable, but that would go away she knew. Pride was still masking who she really wanted to be, but it had been weakened.

She spotted a souvenir message in a bottle and quickly purchased it. As she was waiting for her change from the attendant, she wanted to know more about the mirror. "Can you tell me anything more about how this mirror works?"

"What would you like to know?"

"I don't know, I mean, I understand how it works physically, but in terms of how we perceive ourselves?"

"I've seen many people look at themselves in that mirror. Some people, more or less, think they look the same, or as they expected. But, there are many people who look at it and hate it. They don't like the way they look at all. They think they are ugly, sometimes, really ugly."

"Really?"

"And then, there are some people who look at it and they realize they are a lot more beautiful than they thought they were."

"Interesting."

"It has something to do with how we are wired inside, right and left brain. And how vain or ashamed of how we are on the inside. How we think about ourselves. Looking at a photo or video of ourseleves is not the same."

"Thanks for the explanation!"

"Enjoy your souvenir bottle."

Amanda left the store. The beach beckoned. She hailed a taxi. A feeling of satisfaction swept over her.

True freedom wasn't loud and boisterous like fireworks on Independence Day. This quiet freedom of the heart & spirit didn't come from being powerful, having expensive status symbols, having fame, notoriety, or even needing recognition, even on a small scale. It was a quieting of our restless minds and hearts she would come to realize more and more.

She got out of the taxi and ran to the shoreline. She opened her backpack. Grabbing the note she wrote earlier, she stuffed it in the souvenir bottle and capped it with the cork.

She *shouted* out whichever phrase in each form that she could say out loud, at the top of her lungs.

Mind / No Mind combined

I/You/We shall never feel special!

I/You/We shall never feel important!

I/You/We shall never feel smart!

I/You/We shall never feel anyone cares about me/you/us!

I/You/We shall never feel I/you/we can teach anything!

I/You/We shall never feel shame!

She visualized people she knew.

"Live free or die!!" she yelled out as she threw the bottle as hard as she could out into the sea. It was a phrase first spoken by an American revolutionary war general, though Amanda didn't know this. The current picked up her bottle and floated it out to sea.

Amanda wanted a heart *free* from debilitating feelings. More feelings were locked up inside her, she knew that, but now she knew there was another way, at least for her, a better way.

It was a message of another way to exist, not a curse. This was her 'good' tupilak to someone out there. Amanda breathed a sigh of relief. She now knew how those old women felt when they decided to jump off the cliff in Ilulissat. They weren't afraid at all, they were just following their instincts. Except the only cliff Amanda was going to jump off was a metaphorical one. She found another taxi and headed for the city.

Maybe this mystery man would turn out to be her knight in shining armor in a fairy tale romance, but maybe he wouldn't, that was ok. Did she even really want such a thing? She'd been conditioned to want it by countless stories and movies. How well did that work out for many people?

Happiness wasn't in encouraging ideas that gave her a sense of self, rather, it was in losing herself as much as possible. Wasn't there some saying about happiness being carefree? To be without a care in the world? Was it possible to care about others and not care about them at the same time?

The goal she was beginning to realize was to use our minds and hearts to create more effortless and instinctive lives. Satisfying our egos was a never ending proposition and only created a more complex and demanding world. Pride was a fool's game in the end. It would take courage and humility to look in a mirror to see one's own true nature, and she had begun to do it.

Pride made us feel guilty or inadequate when we didn't live up to it. Sometimes it was the pride of others, sometimes it was the pride of our own self-expectations. She was beginning to see and realize that pride wasn't necessary to improve or be better, those came naturally at our core. It was part of our core being, but it didn't have to be called self-improvement, it was just improving and getting better. Pride could be a moving target too, which led to never being satisfied, and never being truly happy and peaceful on the inside. Amanda didn't want to feel guilty or inadequate about anything, anymore.

Every country was like a different experiment in how self-conscious people were and what its effect on us was. Why not emulate the happiest ones? Not by copying their actions, but by knowing the thought processes.

Amanda knew now too a secret about animals in the wild. Animals like polar bears were just being. They had adapted over time to live a certain kind of existence. It was a balance over time. We had assigned human emotions to animals in books, movies, and television, which confused what they were truly like. In general, wild animals didn't have the stress of trying to be something they weren't meant to be, they just reacted based off experience.

We, or at least people like herself, were seemingly always trying to be someone else, never satisfied with just our current state of mind. One marketing message on top of another, getting us to buy this or do that to become whatever state of mind they wanted us to be in order to support their company.

Mind / No Mind could help erase all those messages and get her back to a 'default' state, her core being. What was that final state, she couldn't answer that right now. She sensed the statements working more and more in her mind and heart.

There was only one enemy, the IN ME within. She made a conscious decision to stop blaming others or external events and look within for peace and happiness. Amanda wanted peace in her heart, down to her very most inner thoughts and feelings. No conflicts, no hypocrisy.

She 'turned off her brain,' followed her instincts, and found herself back in the city of Copenhagen. The return flight to Seattle could wait.

EPILOGUE

Post-Trip Entry #1 – The Real Me

I bought two frameless mirrors the other day from a local mirror shop. They are both about the size of a piece of paper. It was only like, $25 for both of them. Holding them at a 90° angle on a table and looking at them once in a while is helping me to accept who I am. I don't want to feel bad about myself nor do I want inflated feelings of grandeur running around in my body. I'm going to have some handyman, carpenter-type, build me a custom little wooden holder for them.

#2 – Thorsten, The Danish Bicycle Guy

The memory of meeting Thorsten for coffee is still fresh in my mind. It was a nice way to end the trip. Maybe it could turn into something, but distance is a killer at the moment. A long distance friendship it will have to be, as we get to know each other better.

#3 – Thorsten, Part 2

I've been more cognizant of my inner feelings than ever before. The strangest thing happened to me when I was talking on the phone with Thorsten the other day. He started mentioning some things he was doing with other women, nothing serious, and I started to get jealous, just a little.

How could I be jealous of women I don't know? Who are just hanging out with a guy I have only met once, who is thousands of miles away. On that note, why are some people more jealous than others? Why are some young children more jealous than others?

#4 – OMG! Number Seven!

I can't believe it. I've finally found the seventh statement that Lars mentioned! He confirmed it by email. I found it after thinking about why we get jealous. Jealousy that can turn to rage and all other sorts of ugly emotions I've realized. In this case, it was jealousy re: Thorsten, people at work, and people in the news. I've never been a strongly jealous type, but I knew it was always there in some form. I've been diligently repeating the other six statements, now and again. Somehow repeating the other six made accepting the seventh one easier. Every now and then I have felt changes in my mind and heart as my pride has receded. I feel more relaxed!

I shall never feel love
You shall never feel love
We shall never feel love

That's it! Love is at the root of jealousy. I need to sit down and write about love more in my next post-trip entry.

#5 – Being Blind

If love is blind, as the saying goes, then why do we keep seeking it out? Why do we want to blind ourselves? Maybe we are just afraid of the alternative. Maybe if we knew what the alternative was, we wouldn't be so timid. I have a few answers I can articulate now.

First of all, generally speaking, there are two kinds of love. 1) The kind which needs a word, and 2) The kind which doesn't. The one that needs a word can be many things. The kind which doesn't, is the one that is in our core being. We all experience it, but it often gets mixed up with the kind that we use a word for. The kind of love which doesn't have a word is the kind we really desire. Maybe we could call it <u>un-self-ish love</u>, but it's better not to have any word.

My old college psych book says there are many kinds of love. Why so complicated? It didn't really say what it was, from my perspective. The definition in the dictionary isn't that helpful either. We use the word in place of other words we really want to say, which is one reason why things get so confusing.

We throw around the word – love – so cheaply. We are told, or conditioned by advertising, for example, to love certain fast food. That comes to mind right away for me. Lots of snack foods and drinks, too. Of course, none of that is particularly healthy for us. But, hey, that is just my perspective. We are told to love _____. Really, it could be any product, service, company, TV personality, experience, sport, whatever. Whether by paid endorsers, actors, or whomever. Sometimes we believe them, if not consciously, then subconsciously. Nevermind it could be unhealthy, not a good deal, hurting someone else, or just really, not that interesting once we strip away the hype.

Aren't most songs about someone crooning about love or having trouble with it? Some genres more than others. Aren't musicians seemingly always having problems with 'love?' If love makes us so happy, why all the heartache? Selfish love, I think. Why all the confusion? May I never listen to sappy love songs again, but I'm sure I will. It's interesting when we step back and listen to what music we enjoyed when we were younger and what we enjoy as we're older. But, I'm being too analytical. Shut up, Amanda.

There are many marriages that end in divorce and many unhappy marriages once the 'honeymoon' phase is over. Or a watered down version of happiness that we condition ourselves to accept. Yet, each side must have told each other, hundreds, or thousands of times, 'I love you.' In some cultures anyway, not all. Some might say love needs to be renewed constantly, but words are cheap. Actions can be contrived too. I think *more* important, is how we feel, or don't feel on the inside. So, what is love?

The definition of the word, love, has so many definitions. Here's another one. Love can be romance. When we ROMAnticize something or someone, we falsify it or them. What is being romantic? It is a fantasy which fades, and an idealization that cannot sustain itself over the long term, or even the mid-term. It isn't real. Rather than see things and people for how they are, we create a fantasy. That's what marketers like me are always doing. Why did I capitalize ROMA? Because spelled backwards, it is AMOR. And that is the word for love in French, Spanish, and Italian, among others. Maybe it has something to do with seeing things unreversed, like the mirror, I don't know. Left-brain, right-brain. That's how I realized it when a friend of mine was looking at herself in the unreversing mirror setup. We were comparing ourselves in front of a regular mirror and a two mirror setup. I'm no linguist. Not enough time to think about this now. Weird.

A lot of love is self-ish love. We expect or want something in return. Sex, money, power, security, whatever. Women are sneaky with this, but so are men. We may want our partner to change in some way, so we tell them we love them while manipulating them in some way to change more to our liking. A little bit can be fun, surely, but too much is nauseous.

Selfish love can make us jealous. Because we want what is best for us, not what is best for the other person.

Now, here is the kicker. Then we are told to love ourselves. There is even a famous song saying exactly that. I forget who sang that. But, when we tell or remind ourselves, that we love ourselves – we are thinking about ourselves! And that is being self-conscious!

It happens so automatically for many of us, that we don't even realize it. It happens to me.

I think this is what happens to actors and actresses on TV, and really self-conscious people. They fall in love with an image of themselves at a certain point in time, and then they try so hard to maintain it, rather than adapting to change. They resort to plastic surgery and chemical injections.

Ok, so now for the other kind of love – wordless love - I'll call it. It is something all of us know and do at some point in time. It's like how mothers care for their newborn babies. It's like when someone un-self-ishly helps another. It's instinctive, though as I know now, our instincts are corrupted. This, wordless love, is in our core being. It has not faded away. We just need to rediscover it, by getting rid of our dark energy. Dark energy which includes self-ish love. Then we'll all have new hearts. And we won't be blind. Phew! Glad I got all that off my chest. I wonder if it would make sense to someone reading my post-trip journals.

#6 – Line In The Sand

I told Thorsten about my feelings. It was kind of strange, but I feel much freer with my internal thoughts. I don't have to hide them. He seemed genuinely interested in Mind / No Mind as a way to find peace and happiness. It made sense to him. I also told him that before I get involved in any kind of relationship in a serious way, I want to clear out my dark energy, or at least more of it. I'm 'drawing a line in the sand.' The 'buck stops with me,' so to speak.

Not only do I not want this emotional baggage of icky feelings inside me, I don't want to pass on dark energy to my future children. Now that I know about this, it wouldn't be fair either.

The Danish and similar countries are happier on the inside because they have less repressed feelings, less dark energy.

#7 – Polar Bears

I don't think I could do what I did in Greenland right now. On one hand I feel more relaxed, I've let go of a lot of dark energy, but I still feel that I have more repressed feelings. What am I missing? I accept the seven statements. I can shout them out loud!

I was more fearless in that moment when I was face to face with the bear. My self-awareness was down temporarily at that moment due to the incident while I was on the umiak. Maybe it was meant to be. I've begun to notice that people behave differently when sick, or when their pride is down. Pride is a chemical of sorts or a collection of chemicals and electrical pulses. Just like anger, shame, or shyness is. People's faces get red when they are angry or shy. The shamed look down toward the ground more. Something biochemically is going on.

Our pride not only separates us from nature, it separates us from our more kind hearted core being. Most wild animals don't have pride. Those that do, it's a simpler form.

#8 – Other People

Everything looks different when you have less pride. Things that used to bother me, don't bother me as much. History will have to be looked at differently. Aren't the victors full of pride and dark energy? The losers, shame. History is distorted.

#9 – Learning

I can't believe how many mental blocks were in my mind that were preventing me from learning certain things. Emotional blocks. The fog of dark energy in my heart is lifting. I've started learning things that I never would have learned about before.

#10 – Mind / No Mind – Full combined version

1) I/You/We shall never feel special

2) I/You/We shall never feel important

3) I/You/We shall never feel smart

4) I/You/We shall never feel anyone cares about me/you/us

5) I/You/We shall never feel I/you/we can teach anything

6) I/You/We shall never feel shame

7) I/You/We shall never feel love

#11 – Emotional Eating

After emailing with Lars, I know why I still have repressed feelings. It makes perfect sense now. He said it was because of emotional eating and drinking. We eat not only because we are physically hungry, but because we are emotionally hungry.

That's why there are more overweight people these days. Our world is more stressful. We are trying to eat and drink our stress away, rather than deal with it. But, suppressing it just leads to other problems. To deal with it, means we need to face it. We have to acknowledge them. Lots of thin people are stressed too, I can feel it. They suppress it in other ways. Caffeine, smoking, alcohol.

So, we have feelings from childhood and throughout life that have been repressed by eating, drinking, and smoking. We need to reverse that process. We need to un-train our habit to suppress feelings with food, drink, or drugs. He said there is a very specific process and that he would show me in person. Some friends whom I've shared Mind / No Mind with, and I, are going to invite him over to explain to us how to do this.

#12 – Sharing

I have a few trusted friends. A few other girls and a couple of guys. We support each other in getting rid of our pride and self-consciousness. Lots of men, and some women, are afraid of their repressed feelings, dark energy, so they don't like to talk about them. They think feelings are for sissies. They think crying is for sissies. Really, who is more cowardly? I don't really like using labels, I'm not playing this label game.

Lars shared with me some interesting words. The word anGRY and the word reGREt. They are just different forms of crying. According to the etymology in the dictionary of the word, re-GREt, it means to cry again over something. And GRY = CRY, once we realize C and G can be the same character. Like the word for cat in spanish, gat-o. It is common for words to have extra vowels at the beginning or end. He said there were a lot more forms of crying. Like GRIpe, GRIef, agGREssive, CRIticize, CRAnky, CRIme, CRIminal. Emotional Eating! – hunGRY. He said we have to understand how sounds relate to written characters and how they've changed over time. I-Y (enemy – ennemi, French), and vowels are often interchangeable – a,e,i,o,u. This can best be done by comparing words across different languages. Since, I only speak English really, maybe one of my more multi-lingual friends can decipher it all. Maybe I'll learn more about this some other day. He said our health has a lot to do with sound.

I know sound is important as a marketer. That's why commercials are louder than the regular programs we watch on TV. They crank up the volume because we have a higher probability of remembering their commercial jingles, or whatever.

He also said that as we let go of our dark energy, we would become less fearful. It would change our vibe. At some point we would reach a point where no one could deliberately harm us physically. In other words, I wouldn't have to worry about being raped or assaulted. He said it had nothing to do with how physically strong we were, it had to do with our heart. Light conquers dark! After all, we want to be light-hearted! NOT heavy-hearted!

#13 – Good Bye Emotional Baggage, Inner Demons, Dark Energy, Repressed Feelings

I almost forgot about these post-trip journal entries! It's been so long. But, I feel like updating this little notebook. It's strange not having certain feelings anymore. So many things that used to bother me, I don't even think about. So many things I used to worry about, I don't even think about it.

I read in the newspaper about people with PTSD. Maybe somebody I've shared Mind / No Mind with will share it with them. PTSD is just repressed feelings that have been trapped. That's what I think anyway.

Well, Lars and his wife came to visit us many moons ago. She was charming. They shared with us exactly what we needed to do in order to stop emotional eating and drinking. There were so many things about nutrition and environmental health that we didn't know about. Whoa! It's a good thing we had opened up our minds by getting rid of dark energy, because it is the strangest and simplest thing ever to do. Though it does get a bit repetitive. It's hard at times, because I've had to relive certain events over again emotionally as I let them go.

They taught us about how we are attracted to food by our eyes, nose, ears, and mouth.

#14 – Other People Part Deux (Two – same sound!)

I'm feeling a little French. I've learned so many profound things about myself and who we are. So much dark energy has come out. Amazing what it has been obscuring.

Anyway, people around me have changed. They've changed because I've changed. It's like when people around you have a positive vibe, you react differently around them. People with a more negative vibe, your reaction is different. My vibe has changed as my heart has become 'lighter.' I've read some articles and they talk about getting a higher vibration. Actually, it's just the opposite. We want to slow down our vibration, and not be tense or jittery.

This whole experience I realize is contrarian thinking. It is getting happier by getting rid of sadness and deep ugly feelings. Not by seeking out more temporary happiness.

Dogs and other animals react to certain people, usually tense people. They are pretty calm around me now.

#15 – Are We All Connected?

I've released so many negative thoughts and feelings! The more I learn about myself, the more I realize we must be connected on another level with other people. I've been learning about Quantum Entanglement. It's also known as Einstein's 'spooky action at a distance.'

It is an explanation for why some old couples die at the same time, or shortly after their partner dies. It explains how mothers, and some fathers, can sense things about their children. Parental instinct. It explains how some people in relationships can sense whether the other person is hiding something from them or if they are in trouble. It explains why some people do things that seem 'out of character.'

It explains why we have opinions about things that we have no first hand experience with, nor things that we care about. Such as a person, group of people, a movie, a new song, or tabloid magazines at the supermarket checkout. It's as if someone else's opinion is inside of us. This might be easier to sense with people who are close to us, their values may be our values, for better or worse. Or at least it influences our viewpoint on life. Ok, not sure if this would make sense to anyone reading this. Maybe some might call this – synchronicity. Except, this isn't always a positive thing.

Now, I know how to improve my 'gut instinct.' Well, I don't feel like writing it all down right now. But, this is it. <u>To make our planet a better place, all we have to do is change ourselves, not other people. IN ME!</u> Lowering our pride, lowers the pride of others. Our pride is linked.

#16 – Physical

Getting rid of dark energy has led me to get rid of internal stress. My eyesight and vision have been improving of late. I have less tense shoulders. My muscles are unwinding or something. It's as if they were all wound up with dark energy. I have no desire to get a massage, because I feel A LOT less tense.

My face has become younger because I have been letting go of feelings which were tensing my facial muscles tighter over time. All those people who talk constantly about the 'power of inTEN-SION,' whatever, whatever. If we have no inTENSIONS, but just respond to situations out of knowledge and experience, we are a lot more flexible. Maybe this is hard to explain in writing.

People have asked if I am into meditation, naw. Formal meditation is like forcing yourself to be still, it's using willpower. I don't doubt it works for some, but there is another way, better for me.

I just got an eye exam. My vision has improved dramatically – 35%. My understanding is that my eyesight can improve to much better than 20 / 20 in a few years. Better than 20 / 10. Maybe even as good as an eagle at 20 / 5, from the research I've done. Woo – hoo! Who does that with or without surgery? For the rest of my life! I get compliments on how young I look for my age. People who don't already know my age, have no idea how old I am. I don't even think about my age, to tell the truth.

It's funny, 'we' are smart enough to create whiz bang technology like the Hubble Space Telescope that scans the heavens far away. When it had an optical problem, we fixed it. But, 'we' don't even know how to fix our own eyesight, without resorting to lasers or implants, or wearing glasses or contacts, which don't fix our vision over the long term, let alone the side effects. When we're born as children, most all of us have much better natural vision than we have as adults. Why does it go bad, and what about the children who are born with bad vision. Dark energy! — We have never *fully* understood why our eyesight goes bad in the first place. Pride!

Maybe it's like a metaphor. If we are nearsighted, it really means we are focusing too much on just a few things, and we don't see a bigger picture. If we are farsighted, we need to pay attention to more details. We get either condition because of pride and dark energy. This pride and dark energy causes stress to our muscles both around and in our eyes, not to mention the rest of our body. This stress, along with pressure, then compresses or pulls our eyeball out of shape. For those with astigmatism, like me, our cornea is not shaped correctly because of too much pressure in the eye that makes our cornea the incorrect shape.

Based on my research, even those of us with 'perfect 20 / 20' or 20 / 10 are nearsighted. I'll never get it, but presbyopia, fixed by bifocals or progressive lenses, is a symptom of inflexible eyes. Or rather, a less flexible mind and heart, *relatively* speaking. I can't wait for my next eye exam.

#17 – The Future

Am I going to become Amanda 2.0? Or am I going back to 0.0? When we love ourselves, we are attached to our existing self, and we prevent ourselves from evolving to something much better. Why should we love a version of ourselves that has so much crap attached to it? Better to get rid of the crap. Best not to think about this at the moment, though. I feel like a caterpillar about to become a butterfly.

What will it be like when I have zero emotional baggage? When I have no dark energy, at all. Will I make it? That day is coming. What will my relationships be like? I can't say romantic relationships, because they won't be a fantasy.

I think someday I will 'magically' meet someone who also has no emotional baggage. And that's the best kind of magic. Who will it be? Who will they be? I'm ahead of my friends, because I've been more motivated to get rid of my dark energy. They are also getting rid of their darkness, just at a slower pace. But, I sense there are others. Unexpected magic!

Perhaps someday when enough people purge their dark energy, the news headlines will be different, too. But, I don't really read news headlines anymore. Because for the most part, it's about people with dark energy, fighting enemies, not our IN ME. NEWs should be called OLDs. Because it's the same old thing, over and over with just different names, faces, places, and tools. History repeats itself until you *really* study it and find out why. The history of your - self -.

BE the light!

Take the Next Step

Have you felt a change in the pressure on your own forehead after reading this book? Reading Mind / No Mind out loud and accepting it is crucial.

Mind / No Mind as presented in this book is the beginning in learning how to defeat your IN ME and having a more peaceful mind, heart, and joyful state of being. Changing how we think about ourselves is the first step. Changing how we think about other people is another. Beyond this, knowledge about how we treat our mind & body, with what we eat, and what we expose ourselves to everyday is another step. Mind, Heart, & Body. To learn more visit: www.quietfreedom.net

Dog sledging out on to the pack ice – Credit: Mogens Trolle / Shutterstock

If you would like to get a laminated card of Mind / No Mind as in the book, visit us online!

Going Beyond

To learn more about many of the things you've read about in the book such as the aurora borealis, cycling in Denmark, Jante Law, happiness studies, zoos, global warming, and of course, polar bears, go to www.quietfreedom.net. Photos and videos are waiting for you there.

As you heal your mind and heart, you may be naturally inclined to improve your physical health as well. There is more information online about a variety of aspects related to our health and environment that you may not have given a second thought about. Amazing things can happen when we redirect our focus inward, rather than projecting it outward. Amazing things can happen when we lower our pride and open up our minds and hearts to things that other people have learned.

You may also follow my journey of vision improvement online. This is akin to seeing our world and ourselves, with new eyes, literally. At a minimum, I've determined that optimal eyesight is 20 / 6 (6 / 1.75 metric), much better than 20 / 20 (6 / 6)! By the year 2020 (ironically), I expect my vision could be this good, based on my recent and on-going improvement rate.

If you've begun to take Mind / No Mind to heart, and you need further help in finding internal peace or traveling to your "own Greenland," you can contact me online.

WC Peace

Reader's Guide

For an up to date list of questions, please visit the Quiet Freedom website at www.quietfreedom.net.

1) Amanda learns early on in her adventure how zoos distort our view of nature. How do you think your view of nature is distorted, if at all?

2) How many wild animals have you seen in person? Make a list and compare it with others. Is it similar with Amanda's list? What animal in the wild would you most like to see? Make a plan and go!

3) When is the last time you went to a zoo and/or aquarium? Do you think you will go to a zoo again?

4) Amanda gets a passport for the first time in her life so she can travel to Denmark and Greenland. Do you have a passport? How about your friends and family? If you do, compare your foreign travel experiences with your friends. How do your travels differ? How have they been similar?

5) Amanda decides to spend a significant amount of money on her trip to find a wild polar bear. Is there a place in the world or something you have wanted to do since you were young, but have not? Why not? What is holding you back? If you rearranged your priorities, could you do it?

6) When is the last time you rode a bicycle? If you visit a cycle friendly city like Amanda did in Copenhagen, will you rent a bike?

7) Amanda learns that global warming / climate change doesn't matter from both Nathan, the ice core scientist, and Lars, her guide because a) it affects places differently, and more importantly, b) until we know ourselves. Do you agree?

8) Changing weather patterns affect Amanda's life. Compared to when you grew up, has the weather where you live changed from what you remember?

9) How might people's opinions of climate change be different if they lived it first hand in the Arctic?

10) Did you feel a relaxing of your forehead after reading through the Mind / No Mind phrases? If you did, does it feel as if a burden was being lifted off you? If you didn't, do you think you will keep reading the statements until you do?

11) Are you able to say the Mind / No Mind phrases aloud? Are you able to scream them out as Amanda did at the end, at the top of your lungs?

12) Amanda learns that she doesn't need to live with pride, she can just BE. What are you proud of in your own life? How has pride helped you? How has it hurt you? Can you imagine existing without pride / self-consciousness?

13) Which of the seven Mind / No Mind statements do you find the easiest to accept? Hardest?

14) Which kind of pride is harder for you to get rid of – I, YOU, or WE?

15) Do you think there is an epidemic of pride in the world today? SELFies, SELFish, SELF-absorbed, etc…

16) Have you shared Mind / No Mind with anyone you know?

17) Have you ever owned a stuffed animal? If you did, do any of them from your childhood still have any meaning to you? Will you plan a visit to see the wild version of it?

18) Amanda learns that Denmark is often at the top of the least corrupt nations list – Transparency International. Where does your country rank on the list? Do you agree or disagree?

19) Of the many 'Happiest Country Lists' that are out there, where does your country rank? Do you agree or disagree?

20) Amanda learns that to be happy, we must be honest with ourselves and others. How honest are you with yourself? Other people? The people you are closest to – loved ones?

21) Feelings of shame about one thing or another are particularly difficult for many to talk about. What are you most ashamed about?

22) Make a list of all your dark energy / repressed feelings / inner demons / emotional baggage. How do you think you would view the world differently if you got rid of a significant part of it? All of it? How might your life be different?

23) Are you motivated to build and see yourself in your own non-reversing mirror? What do you think your reaction will be? [Visit www.quietfreedom.net to learn more about this]

24) What is an example of 'magic' happening in your real-life? Has it lasted or was it only temporary?

About the Author

W.C. Peace has traveled the world to more than 70 countries, around 150 United Nations World Heritage Sites (places of natural & cultural significance) and lived in several others in Europe, Asia, and both Central and South America.

Many wrong turns have been taken while on a lifetime quest to understand and know who we are on the inside & outside, while seeking out a deeper level of peace.

If he had known "where to go" and "what to do" ahead of time to find peace within, it would have been a lot fewer places and countries!

In addition to the many concepts presented in this book, the adventure has included studying what affects our health – physically, spiritually, and mentally. Areas of study have included nutrition, man-made chemicals, plastics in our environment and food chain, water, natural & artificial light, air, EMF (Electro-magnetic Frequencies), sound, music as it relates to health, and our emotions at a very deep level. W. C. has also had a particular interest in individuals with extraordinary physical and mental abilities.

As of 2016, his eyesight has improved up to 40% by getting rid of dark energy / stress and realigning the body's muscles. No lenses or (laser) surgery. At the current pace of relaxation, natural eyesight better than 20 / 10 (6 / 3 – metric) will be achieved in the next few years.

W.C. Peace is currently based in the American Pacific Northwest, but like a wide-ranging polar bear, prefers to call the entire planet, home.

www.ingramcontent.com/pod-product-compliance
Lightning Source LLC
Chambersburg PA
CBHW030643120726
47905CB00001B/41